Leaving the car running, he sw rounded the front of the convertible step as he tried to figure out the best way to get her out of this mess. It was one thing when he was following a script, but how the hell did one orchestrate a rescue in real life when the rescuee wouldn't cooperate and he had no time to explain the danger? It's not like he could play her the recording tucked in his pocket.

The girl backed away from his approach. He fought back rising apprehension and forced an easy smile.

"Look, I appreciate the offer, Shain, but—"

"Trent."

"Right." Her blush deepened. "I know. *Trent.* But I—"

"I need you to get in the car." As an afterthought, he added, "Please."

"Um..."

He used her glance down the road as cover for his own. Still time, yet his control slipped. "Seriously. Get in."

The sharp command widened her eyes. Suspicion darkened them to navy, and she took another step backward. Then her shoulders squared while her gaze narrowed with determination. "No."

The right taillight on his Alfa Romeo exploded. Trent ducked reflexively as bits of plastic flew in all directions. Adrenaline spiked through him, but other than a sharp reactive jerk, the girl just stood there holding her camera. Trent lunged forward, grabbed her arm and hauled her toward the car.

"Hey—let me go!" She pulled back with surprising strength.

He picked her up and shoved her head first into the passenger seat, then vaulted over her to slip behind the wheel. Heartbeat thundering in his ears, he gunned the gas with a sickening grinding of gears before the convertible shot out into traffic amidst screeching tires and blaring horns.

Praise for Stacey Joy Netzel's other work:

"**TRUST IN THE LAWE** was truly one of the best books I have read this year." ~ Val, You Gotta Read Romance Reviews

"**SHATTERED TRUST** has everything a fantastic book should have, romance, suspense, betrayal, and humor in all the right places. I sat down planning to read a couple of chapters and did not move until I finished, Stacey Joy Netzel continues to work written magic in this new book." ~ Emily, Single Title Reviews, 5 Stars **Night Owl Reviewer Top Pick

SHADOWED TRUST "The chemistry between Jordan and Lexie was undeniable...I lost track of the time because I was so engrossed in the story. I highly recommend this...along with the others in the Colorado Trust series!" ~ Diana, Night Owl Reviews, Reviewer Top Pick

"**MORE THAN A KISS** is an entertaining, steamy, at times funny story about two people who come from two different backgrounds. The chemistry and passion between the two is set at the right pace to allow for personal and emotional growth and makes the relationship more believable. This book is a keeper." ~ Adria, Breath of Life Reviews, **Night Owl Reviewer Top Pick

"Stacey Joy Netzel has written her most compelling story yet. **CHASIN' MASON** is 'must-read' phenomenal!" ~ Donna Marie Rogers, author of *Meant To Be*.

"**IF TOMBSTONES COULD TALK** is a sweet and romantic read. The plot was brilliant and well played out. I enjoyed every aspect of the story." ~ Dark Angel Reviews (5 Stars)

"I adored **DRAGONFLY DREAMS,** a tale that tugs at the heart and makes one feel the Christmas season any time of year." ~ Fallen Angel Reviews (5 Angels), **Nominated LASR Best Short Romance eBook 2007

LOST in ITALY

by
Stacey Joy Netzel

This is a work of fiction. Names, characters, places, and incidents are either the product of the author's imagination or are used fictitiously, and any resemblance to actual persons living or dead, business establishments, events, or locales, is entirely coincidental.

Lost In Italy

Copyright © 2011 by Stacey Joy Netzel

All rights reserved. No part of this book may be used or reproduced in any manner whatsoever without the written permission of the author, except in the case of brief quotations embodied in critical articles or reviews.

Cover Art by **Ravven**

ISBN-13: 978-1466410480

ISBN-10: 1466410485

ACKNOWLEDGMENTS

First, a note to my readers...

My editor returned this manuscript to me with the words, "Great job, but the brother and sister 'accidentally' leaving the heroine behind seems a bit unrealistic and contrived for the benefit of your plot."

My reply? "I'm Halli...minus the movie star and the kidnapping." (and the murder)

Yes, to me, being left behind in Italy is (and was) *very* realistic. Especially since it took my siblings ten minutes to even realize I wasn't in the car with them.

Second, I'd like to clarify that Ben and Rachel were only inspired by my siblings, and are not mirror images of my real family. My oldest sister is a red-head, and these days she could handle a vacation without her blow dryer. I think. Thankfully, though, we do share a great friendship just like Halli and Rachel. (so no holding the above comment against me!) And my brother... although he owns a motorcycle like Ben, in real life he speaks fluent Italian. I'd like to tell you he's as hot as Ben, but he's my little brother so that'd just be weird. Besides, Ben is a fictional secondary character and Trent is the real star of this book, so let's move on.

Special thanks to my son Cody for the boat idea and the many brainstorming sessions as we drove up north. To my brother Troy for his patient help with all my Italian related questions and for loving the book on the first read through even with all the emotional, romance stuff. And to both my siblings, Bridgette and Troy, for leaving me all alone beside Lake Como, Italy back in 1997. I got a whole book out of those twenty minutes.

Thanks to Donna, Jamie, and Dulcie for the writer's weekends that helped shape the plot. And last, but not least, I'd also like to thank my great editor Stacy D. Holmes, who challenged me to make this book the best it could be.

~ *Stacey*

Stacey Joy Netzel

DEDICATION

To Bridgette and Troy...for obvious reasons.

Love you guys!

Stacey Joy Netzel

Chapter 1

"For the love of God, Hal, we didn't travel over ten hours for you to film swans."

Halli Sanders ground her back molars together, ignored her sister Rachel, and zoomed her camera in on the flock of white birds across the water. Graceful and serene, they stood out in stark contrast to the dark, shaded water of the small inlet her brother had parked near. A shaky breath helped steady her hands.

"You guys wanted to stop, now I want to see if Lake Como, Italy and Lake Como, WI have more in common than their names," she informed her sister and brother.

"Who cares?" Rachel moaned. "And it was Ben's bright idea to pull over, not mine. I just want to find the hotel and shower away some of this jet lag. And, we still have to find a converter for my hair dryer."

Halli rolled her eyes and kept filming. Yes, she was being snotty about it, but they're the ones who threw away her meticulously planned itinerary so they could make impromptu stops like this. Ben specifically had insisted she lighten up, as if she'd chosen to become a control freak after their crazy, unstable years on the run with their parents.

The half dozen or so swans had floated into the sunlight, near a wooden dock in front of a stone villa. She wondered who lived there. The tabloids always talked about George Clooney's house on Lake Como in Italy and how he always had friends visiting—could this be it? If it was, any number of stars could be there *right* now.

That's it, she told herself. Focus on something other than the fact her plans had all been scrapped. She did not want her anxiety issues ruining this vacation. As long as she had Ben and Rachel, she'd be fine.

She allowed herself one last lingering look at the regal villa through the viewfinder. The weathered stonework was beautiful, but the shiny, reflective windows captured her attention. She loved large windows that let in natural light. Wished she had them in her studio apartment overlooking the lake back home.

Ben ran interference behind her. "We'll go find the hotel first, then an electronics store, then we'll find a place to eat. Sound okay?"

"Yes, thank you," Rachel agreed, her tone full of exaggerated drama. "Let's go, Hal."

"*Fine*. I'm coming." Halli took a step backward, but a movement in the windows caught her attention. She paused and steadied the camera. The front door to the villa burst open. As someone ran outside, the swans took flight, their startled cries echoing across the water.

Behind her, she heard car doors open. Then Ben's, "Oh, hurry up—there's a break in traffic."

Bam. Bam. Vrrooommm.

The slamming doors made Halli glance over her shoulder. She did a double take when the little blue car her brother had rented in Milan shot off the curb.

"*Hey*—" She spun around, took a few steps, then stopped with a disbelieving laugh. "Real funny, guys."

Surely any second now, they'd give up the joke, pull to the side, and wait for her to catch up as they laughed their hilarious frickin' heads off.

No brake lights.

No U-turn.

Nothing.

The blue car accelerated around the bend in the road and disappeared.

Her heart skipped a beat and her stomach sunk. Muttering under her breath, she looked around self-consciously, doing her best to distract herself from the fact that she was suddenly all alone in a foreign country. A dark-haired man across the street glanced her way with open curiosity. Thankfully, he kept walking. Cars cruised past; a couple kids on bikes; a woman on a moped. Though the kids stopped a short distance away, no one paid her much attention over the next few minutes.

Well, sure. Lake Como, Italy was probably used to lost

tourists, what did they care?

No, you're not lost. The adamant statement helped to steady her breathing. That's right. Ben and Rachel would be back any moment. She had nothing to worry about as long as she didn't leave this spot.

The man across the street gave her a more thorough inspection and a chill trickled down her spine. Halli averted her gaze and hugged her arms around her middle. Her heart rate continued its steady acceleration.

Oh, she was going to kill them when they got back. They'd pulled pranks in the past, but this one was cruel—especially her first time travelling overseas. Why would they do this now? Ben may live life with the motto "Rip the Band-Aid off", but not Halli. It had to be a joke, right? It was either that, or they didn't know she wasn't in the car. But how could anyone miss something like *that*?

If Ben's phone wasn't the only one equipped to make international calls, she'd call and give them a loud, extended piece of her mind.

Stop! You're going to be fine. There are plenty of people around and no one's going to do anything in broad daylight. She clutched the small travel purse hanging diagonal across her chest containing her passport. *See? If you need help, you can prove you're a US citizen.*

Not that she'd need to prove her citizenship. Any minute the blue car would come back around the bend. Any second even.

She stared down the road, counting seconds.

Seconds became minutes.

Maybe they *didn't* know she'd been left behind. What then? How long before they came back? Desperate to control the unrelenting apprehension no amount of silent talk would quell, Halli turned back to the lake as if she'd find answers somewhere across the water.

A lone swan near shore reminded her of the camera still clutched in her hand. The red light on the front reminded her she was still recording. Ironically, the camera was part of the reason she was sitting here alone, and yet she'd completely forgotten about it.

She stopped the video and swiveled to take a seat on the cool ledge of stone that held the lake water at bay. It was the perfect vantage point to keep the loitering man across the street in sight. A glance over her shoulder located where the other swans had landed a good distance from the villa's dock.

She frowned and faced the lake. Strange how that person had burst so suddenly from the villa.

The noon sun sat at a point that she had to squint and shade her eyes to see the structure's stone walls across the small inlet of water. Even then, it was too far away for the naked eye. Flipping open the viewfinder as she lifted the camera, she waited for it to focus, then tried to zoom. The low battery indicator flashed as she maxed the zoom.

She studied the picture. Something was different—one of the windows looked odd. Her attention snagged on a tall figure in the corner of the pane. Longish dark hair above a square jaw with a severe slash for a mouth. He raised a pair of binoculars to look across the bay. Her pulse jerked when he zeroed in and stared straight at her—

Tires squealed and an engine revved loud to her right. Halli jumped about a foot. *Ben and Rachel!* An uncharacteristic spurt of anger doubled her anxiety as she whirled around.

"I can't believe you guys left—"

Words disappeared with the heart-stuttering realization that the shiny blue convertible half pulled onto the cobblestone sidewalk was not her brother and sister. And the man in the driver's seat most certainly was *not* her brother.

Plain was the first word that came to mind when Trent Tomlin got a good, close-up look at the girl dressed in baggy black pants and an oversized black T-shirt. Except for her eyes. Almost the exact color of his car, they blazed with anger—if the shrill tone of her voice were any indication.

Because he couldn't afford to waste a second, he slipped into his carefree, celebrity character while pushing up his Ray Bans to flash his trade-mark, million dollar grin past the two day's worth of camouflaging scruff on his jaw.

"Hi." Usually that's all he needed. *One...two...*

Astonishment replaced anger.

...three.

"Oh my God. You're Shain West."

"Only in the movies, darlin'."

That always got 'em, too, the good-ol'-boy, southern drawl. Didn't matter he'd been born and raised in northern Oregon, he had a natural talent for mimicking any accent. After just a few words, he easily placed her in mid-west United States. American tourist. Perfect. It also explained why she'd been video taping in the wrong place at the wrong damn time. The opposite of his brother, and if he could help it, the opposite outcome.

Her cheeks flushed. "Of course. I know your real name. Sorry. It's just—I'm...ah...I'm..."

Hell, he'd better speed this up. "Can I give you a lift?"

"W-what?" She craned her head around, as if he might be speaking to someone else.

Resisting the urge to check over his shoulder, he kept his gaze trained on her. "You look lost. Hop in and I'll give you a ride."

Her throat convulsed, and though he wouldn't have thought it possible, her blush deepened to crimson. A fleeting smile revealed even, white teeth.

"Oh, no. I mean, um, thank you, but no."

She lifted a hand to tuck a strand of straight brown hair behind her ear as she searched back and forth along the road.

Trent cast his own quick glance in the rearview mirror, pressure squeezing his body like a starving boa constrictor as he searched for the men who'd spotted her and her camera across the bay. By his amateur calculations, he figured he had about three more minutes. *If* they were lucky.

Pushing up to sit on the headrest, he prepared to turn on the superstar charm that had brought him such success at the box office.

"I'm waiting for my brother and sister," she said before he could speak.

So that's who'd driven off as he watched the scene unfold from one street above and behind her. He lifted a tense shoulder in a careless gesture. "Quick spin around town, and I'll bring you right back. They'll never know you were gone, sugar."

Her eyebrows drew together above those deep blue eyes. *Damn.* He fought his own frown. Based on previous experience with star-struck women, she should've jumped in at the first invitation. Wasn't it just his luck, this one had common sense.

Leaving the car running, he swung his legs over the door and rounded the front of the convertible. His heart thumped with each step as he tried to figure out the best way to get her out of this mess. It was one thing when he was following a script, but how the hell did one orchestrate a rescue in real life when the rescuee wouldn't cooperate and he had no time to explain the danger? It's not like he could play her the recording tucked in his pocket.

The girl backed away from his approach. He fought back rising apprehension and forced an easy smile.

"Look, I appreciate the offer, Shain, but—"

"Trent."

"Right." Her blush deepened. "I know. *Trent.* But I—"

"I need you to get in the car." As an afterthought, he added, "Please."

"Um..."

He used her glance down the road as cover for his own. Still time, yet his control slipped. "Seriously. Get in."

The sharp command widened her eyes. Suspicion darkened them to navy, and she took another step backward. Then her shoulders squared while her gaze narrowed with determination. "No."

The right taillight on his Alfa Romeo exploded. Trent ducked reflexively as bits of plastic flew in all directions. Adrenaline spiked through him, but other than a sharp reactive jerk, the girl just stood there holding her camera. Trent lunged forward, grabbed her arm and hauled her toward the car.

"Hey—let me go!" She pulled back with surprising strength.

He picked her up and shoved her head first into the passenger seat, then vaulted over her to slip behind the wheel. Heartbeat thundering in his ears, he gunned the gas with a sickening grinding of gears before the convertible shot out into traffic amidst screeching tires and blaring horns. A frantic half-second glance in the rearview mirror confirmed a black vehicle weaving through the cars behind them.

Shit. Damn. Fuck!

He switched his concentration to the road in front. If he didn't lose these guys fast, they were dead.

The girl's brown head popped up in his peripheral vision. Three bullets spidered his windshield in rapid succession. The bobbing head screamed and disappeared. His hands jerked on the wheel, and he narrowly missed hitting a motor scooter head-on.

"Shit!"

Scrunching down in his seat, Trent shot a glance toward the passenger seat. "You okay?" Nothing. His heart dropped and he risked another frantic look. "I asked if you're okay!"

"No, I'm not okay!"

"Were you hit?"

"By what?"

He couldn't help an incredulous laugh as another bullet took out his right side mirror. He wrenched the wheel to the left. A loud thud was followed by a muffled "*Ow*". Trent cut in front of an oncoming van and slammed the car into third going uphill.

The girl's brown head appeared again, hair wild about her face in the wind.

"For crissakes, stay the hell down," Trent yelled.

Instead, she maneuvered her butt around until she could plunk it in the passenger seat and yank on the safety belt. Then she glared at him. He couldn't see it because his eyes were glued to the road, but, man, did he feel it.

"My God, slow down, would you?"

"You're kidding, right?"

"No, I'm not kidding," she hollered above the growl of the engine and whistling wind. "Did Rachel and Ben put you up to this?"

"Who?"

"My sister and brother. Did they arrange this?"

He risked a glance with a half-cocked grin of disbelief.

"What exactly do you think *this* is?"

"Look out!"

Trent jerked his attention back to the road in time to see a delivery truck blocking the way. "*Shit!*"

The tires screamed as he stomped on the brakes. Jamming the convertible into reverse, he turned to locate a side street behind them, his grip on the headrest of her seat white-knuckled. The moment he was clear, he spun the wheel, ground the gears and floored the gas. The poor girl's head jerked forward, back, forward with each successive switch of direction.

He really should find out her name. Poor Girl wouldn't cut it for long. And if they didn't make it through this—

"*This*—you driving like a crazy man—is *not* my idea of fun," the girl snapped. "Let me out."

Trent snorted, swerved around a slower vehicle and checked the only mirror he had left to see if they were still being pursued.

"I mean it! Stop the car this instant."

"Not a good idea, sweetheart."

"What in the world is going on, anyway? Are you filming a movie or something?"

"I wish." He took the next turn so hard her shoulder hit his as they cornered on two, squealing wheels. When she didn't respond right away, he saw her staring at the holes in his windshield as if she'd just now noticed them.

"You mean...those were *real* bullets?"

"What the hell else would they be?"

Another sharp turn assisted her back to her side of the vehicle.

"Real guns?"

A quick look at the girl's dazed expression and Trent knew exactly how she felt. If he looked anything like she did...he pulled down his Ray Bans from on top his head. He'd never done this in real life before, only in carefully choreographed scenes with numerous stuntmen.

The front end of his convertible took out a sign and side-swiped a garbage dumpster with the next turn. *Damn it*. He'd just bought this baby last week! Hadn't even had a chance to open it up and see what it could do on the auto strata. This was not the way to break in the engine—and he didn't even want to look at the body.

A few stuntmen right about now would be more than welcome. "Listen, make yourself useful and see if they're still behind us."

"Who?" She turned around in her seat.

He reached over and jerked on her shoulder. "Stay down!"

"How am I supposed to look if I—"

"Around the headrest. What the hell," he muttered. "You have enough common sense to not get in a car with me, but pop up for target practice?"

"Hey, I was right about you. You kidnapped me!"

"I *saved* your life, and I did say please. Now shut up and look for a black car."

Halli peered around the headrest. No speeding black car giving chase. No dangerous looking bad guys toting guns. *Real guns.* She felt a little lightheaded, but maybe it was the jetlag. Or the bump on the head when she'd hit the floor. Or the way the car swerved back and forth and up and down on the mountain roads, like a bad roller coaster. *Very bad.*

How had she ended up here? She'd had plans for this trip. Detailed plans that hadn't included a stop along the shore of Lake Como until tomorrow at two p.m.

Back home, Ben had laughed at her itinerary and tossed it in the garbage. Then he said he understood her need for structure and stability, but it was time for her to stop letting the choices their parents had made rule her life. That had really struck home and the week prior to their trip, he'd worn her down, and she'd actually convinced herself touring Italy whichever way the wind blew them could be fun. And bonus—maybe she'd even get a little control over her anxiety.

She'd even managed to keep her cool when Ben had swerved onto the side of the road out of the blue before they'd found their hotel and Rachel's stupid hair dryer converter. He'd promised to go easy on her, so she'd figured a stop by the lake wasn't too bad.

Of course, she still had an extra copy of that itinerary tucked in with her passport, but—

"Well?" Trent Tomlin demanded.

Trent Tomlin! America's dark-haired, sexy playboy god. She hadn't even recognized him until he smiled, and now she understood why. He'd taken the scruff look to the extreme with a dark five-o'clock shadow, windblown hair, and tightly compressed, uncompromising lips. He darted a glance to the one remaining mirror and she gave her head a quick shake. *Black car. Bad guys.* She squinted at the narrow ribbon of road behind them.

"I think you lost them."

"You're sure?"

"I don't see any black cars." Wherever they were, there was substantially less traffic, so she was pretty confident in her assessment.

He slowed the convertible a hair, enough so the next turn didn't throw her body against his; just close enough for her accelerated breathing to catch another heady dose of his scent. Citrus and spice, with a subtle musky base. Almost earthy. She inhaled again before she could help herself. *Of course* Trent Tomlin would smell great.

Man, she had to get a grip. He'd kidnapped her! As she pushed back into her own seat, his earlier words finally registered on her short-circuited brain.

"What do you mean, you saved my life?"

After giving her a brief glimpse of her own confused expression in his mirrored glasses, he returned his attention to the road. "Grab me that baseball cap down by your feet."

Halli automatically leaned forward and swept the floor with her hand. When she sat back with the navy blue cap, she jerked away from his reaching hand. "You put my life in danger, you didn't save it. Because of you, I almost got shot."

"Honey, because of me, you *didn't* get shot," he retorted. "Did you really think you could record those guys and get away with it?"

"What are you talking about?"

"They saw you across the water with your camera."

"I was filming the swans."

He frowned at her like she'd grown a second head. "Swans?"

"Yes, *swans.* You know, big white birds with a long neck and—"

He braked sharply, and she was grateful for the seatbelt that kept her forehead from connecting with the dash as they came to a full stop.

"You weren't videotaping the villa?"

"No. I saw it, even zoomed in on it, but..."

She trailed off with a flash-vision of the person bursting through the villa door. And the man staring at her from the window. Were they the same person? Suddenly it dawned on her why the window had looked odd. It hadn't been shiny from the sunlight glinting off the glass, but dark, as if the glass was no longer there.

The fine hairs on the back of her neck tingled. Trent Tomlin leaned closer, his dark head blocking out the sun. The vision of the man in the window made Halli shrink back against the passenger door.

"You didn't see anything else?" Trent Tomlin prompted.

Her hands trembled. She clasped them together in her lap, absently fiddling with the Velcro adjuster on his cap. After the past ten minutes and the sharp tension in his voice, she was afraid to ask her next question, but forced the words out anyway.

"What do you think I saw?"

He gave a brief glance behind them and yanked up on the hand brake lever. His knuckles brushed along her leg as he reached down into her space. She flinched in alarm, but with her camera now fisted in his large hand, he simply resettled into his seat. He powered it on and hit rewind.

Three seconds later he swore under his breath. "You got another battery?"

"I left the case in the car." *With Ben and Rachel.*

More swearing. He shoved the camera at her and snatched his cap from her death grip. After settling it low over his brow, he released the hand brake, shifted the idling car back into gear and hit the gas.

Her head bounced off the headrest as the car shot forward. Dumbfounded, she stared out the windshield. Comprehension dawned and this time she purposely let her head thump back as she squeezed her eyes shut in dismay. *Stupid idiot.* She'd just missed a chance to escape. Movie star or not, apparent rescue or not, she didn't actually *know* the man. He could be a serial killer for all she knew. Unlikely, sure, but only an hour ago she'd have also said being abducted by him was unlikely. Unlikely did not mean impossible.

What did seem impossible was getting back to her family. The further he drove, the more lost she'd be. Because even if she got away, she hadn't seen any city name signs where they'd pulled off the road and had no idea where they'd left her. Her English/Italian dictionary also sat on the back seat of the blue rental.

"Where are you going?" she asked after a minute of silent berating.

"To my house."

"Your house? Shouldn't we go to the police?"

"*La polizia?*"

His perfect Italian accent threw her for a moment.

"No can do, sweetheart."

"People shot at us! All we have to do is show them your car."

He maneuvered around a corner, their speed sedate compared to earlier. "We can't trust them."

"We can't trust the police?"

"Not here. Didn't notice anyone rushing to stop that chase, did you?"

True, the entire car chase hadn't alerted a single officer of the law, but that didn't mean they couldn't be trusted.

She watched Trent from the corner of her eye. His attention constantly shifted, as if he was keeping watch, and she guessed there'd be no convincing him.

Then again, maybe *he* just didn't want to get caught. That thought didn't make her feel any better.

"Take me to the US Embassy," she said as firmly as

possible, like he didn't have a choice.

"The embassy's in Rome."

Alarm undercut her bravado as she pictured the map of Italy in her mind. "But that's hours away."

"There's a Consulate General in Milan."

"What's that?"

"Basically the same thing as an embassy."

That's right—she knew that. She just wasn't thinking straight with all that'd happened. A deep breath helped quell her rising panic. Giving into her anxiety would get her nowhere. One thing she did know, she didn't want to go back to Milan without finding Ben and Rachel first. She wasn't sure how she'd find them, but she'd have to figure something out. *If* she could get out of this car and away from him.

"You know, you could just drop me off—"

"No."

"It's not like you need me for anything. I didn't see a thing, and I—"

"Until I see what you've got on that video, you and I are best friends, honey."

Her teeth ground together at his fake, condescending southern drawl. "It's Halli."

His head turned, and despite the sunglasses, she felt his gaze rake over the comfortable sweat pants and T-shirt she'd worn for the long trans-Atlantic flight. "That's your name?"

"What else would it be? Look, you can have the video. I don't want it, there's nothing on it that matters to me." She fumbled with the camera as she spoke, but her shaking hands made it impossible to extract the small SD card. Tears stung her eyes as frustration mounted. "Just take the whole thing and let me go."

She shoved it into his lap, hating that her voice wobbled at the end. She'd saved six months to buy the camera, but hopelessness is what made her composure crumble, not the stupid camera. Before she made a complete fool of herself, she averted her head and took a couple deep breaths to get control of her nerves.

"I'm not going to hurt you."

His quiet statement made it worse. She clutched the travel purse angled under her right arm and around her neck, aware the ripples of anxiety grew with each passing moment. Bet Ben and Rachel hadn't figured *this* into their fly-by-the-seat-of-their-pants plan. Heck, even she couldn't have planned for something like this.

A tear slipped from her lashes and out of nowhere, a laugh bubbled up. Was this what hysterical felt like? Didn't matter, she needed some sort of emotional release, and more tears wouldn't get her anywhere.

"Do you have a phone? Can I at least call my brother and sister?"

To her surprise, he set her camera on the console between them and then dug a phone from his pocket. Halli grabbed it like a drowning person latching onto a life-preserver. Shaking fingers forced her to start over twice before she got the number right.

Please, answer, Ben. Please.

Relief swelled when the call connected, but instead of her brother's voice, she got some strange recording in Italian. She tried again with the same result. Biting back frustration, she dialed a third time. This time, all she got was dead air. Then a series of beeps sounded in her ear.

"The call won't go through," she said.

"Service is spotty around the lake," Trent informed her. "You can try again later."

Tears threatened yet again as she slapped the phone against his outstretched palm and leaned her head back against the seat. "I planned this to be the trip of a lifetime. Something to remember."

His answering chuckle held a note of disbelief. "Sweetheart, if you don't remember this, whatever you had planned didn't stand a chance."

"You *know* what I meant."

"What, you're not having fun?"

Halli jerked her head up and straightened in her seat. "No, I'm not. Getting shot at and kidnapped wasn't listed anywhere on my itinerary." *The planned one* or *the windblown one.*

"It wasn't?"

"Of course not," she snapped, glaring at him. "After we landed, right about now, in fact, we were supposed to go right to the hotel to freshen up, then get something to eat and tour the Villa Carlotta instead of listening to Ben's bright idea to stop for a quick look at the lake. Tomorrow after breakfast, I wanted to visit a couple churches headed south and around Como, and after lunch, we were going to explore the village of Careno." She ticked off each day on her fingers. "The next day I planned a drive around the lake until we reached Mandello to see the motorcycle museum—my brother's a motorcycle nut. Then on Wednesday…or was it Thursday?...no, Wednesday, we're going to—"

She halted mid-sentence when his eyebrows became visible above his sunglasses and underneath the bill of his cap. Heat flooded her face as she lowered her hands to her lap.

"You were being sarcastic."

He gave her a patronizing grin. "Yes."

And the pathetic idiot that she was, she'd given him a play by play. To avoid looking at him, she stared out her side of the car and opposite the lake as he navigated south. They were now driving around Lake Como, Italy, and she couldn't even enjoy the scenery.

Heck—alone with *Trent Tomlin*, and she couldn't enjoy the scenery. The man voted Most Sexy by women across America not once, not twice, but *four* times. Most of her female co-workers at PBS had agreed; any woman who didn't fantasize about Trent Tomlin was either blind, or a lesbian.

She snuck a quick peek from beneath her lashes. Yeah, though he hadn't been easily recognizable, he was still hotter than ever with all that rough scruff.

She'd always loved his movies, especially the Shain West ones that were an exciting cross between Indiana Jones and Romancing the Stone, but set in the 1800's. However, things she'd heard on TV and read in the tabloids while standing in line at the grocery store suggested he was an irresponsible, incorrigible, work-a-little-party-too-hard Hollywood playboy.

She wasn't naïve enough to believe everything they

printed, but a picture told a thousand words. Or more accurately, a hundred pictures told a thousand words. The beautiful co-stars, glamorous supermodels and semi-talented pop singers who adorned his arm changed as often as his tie. So while she may have fantasized about the image of the man like the rest of America, it didn't mean she respected him.

And, now that she'd been abducted by him, she certainly didn't like him.

"Where exactly is your house?" she finally asked. They'd passed Brienno and Moltrasio, names she recognized from the hours pouring over maps the past two years. Yet more miles between her and her family.

"Torno."

If only she hadn't wasted so much of her camera battery filming on the plane and in the airports. But she'd wanted to catch every moment to remember later. Trip of a lifetime and all that. Then the town name Trent had said registered and she realized they'd be traveling through more populated areas as they rounded one of the southern tips of the lake.

"Why don't you just stop at an electronics store and buy a battery?"

"Great idea, if you don't take into account that most of the shops close down between noon and three for the traditional Italian *siesta*, and right now"—he glanced at his watch—"it's one-fifteen."

Darn it, that's right. She knew that, too, and had even planned for the inconvenience—just not the rest of this craziness.

"And," he continued, "I can't really drive around town with bullet holes in my windshield, now can I?"

She wished he would. Maybe the police—*la polizia,* she mimicked in her head—would stop them, and she would be free. At this point, she acknowledged it wasn't so much that she was afraid of him, she just wanted things back to normal. Back with Ben and Rachel. They would never believe what'd happened—*she* wouldn't believe it if it hadn't happened to her.

Come to think of it...what had he been doing there? Halli snuck another glance toward his stern profile as they passed the sign for Cernobbio. How did he know she'd been filming and those guys would come after her? Were they really after him?

Halli shifted in her seat to get a better look at his face. "Why were you—"

"*Sonofabitch.*"

She drew back, then followed his gaze to see a large, dark blue SUV-type vehicle up ahead on the side of the road. Two uniformed men stood at the rear, alongside the pavement. One waved a red and white paddle and the other—Halli's heart went nuts all over again—had a very big, very scary-looking gun slung around his neck and shoulders. The kind the bad guys used in the movies.

"Oh my God, who are they?" she whispered.

"*Carabinieri.*"

Even the name sounded scary. Instinctively she cast Trent in the role of protector and leaned closer. "Are they bad?"

"Italian military police."

He flicked on his right turn signal and downshifted to pull over in front of their vehicle with a few short jerks. Halli sat up straighter at the word *police*. Thoughts of protection quickly transferred from Trent to the armed military men.

"It looks like it's just a random checkpoint," Trent added. The tightening of his fingers on the steering wheel and flexing of his forearm muscles belied the casual statement. "You keep quiet, I'll handle this."

Unable to believe her luck, she glanced behind at the two men approaching, then whirled around and reached for the door handle. Trent's hand encircled her wrist before she could open the door.

"I said I'll handle it," he warned in a low, controlled tone.

"Let me go or I'll scream."

She pulled against his hold, but his grip tightened. "Don't do this, for both our sakes."

An unexpected vulnerability in his voice made her pause. He removed the mirrored glasses and their gazes locked for a timeless moment. Her breath caught as she stared into the beautiful hazel eyes that made women's hearts beat madly all around the world.

Darn if they didn't have the same effect on hers.

The voices of the two officers reached her ears. She pulled again and this time Trent let go. She reached for the handle once more, but her hand wavered.

No. She would not be sucked in like a besotted fool.

"Halli. Please."

The husky, desperation-tinged entreaty hit its mark. *Darn him.*

But, then again, he didn't know her. He couldn't know she found it impossible to say no when someone pleaded with such raw, naked honesty. Could it be he was telling the truth and she should trust him? Having been conned by her own parents growing up, she was never quite sure when to trust her instincts.

Yet...those had been real bullets whizzing past her ear as he sped through the narrow streets of Lenno like a maniac. The three holes in his windshield proved that. Did they also prove that he probably *had* saved her life?

She glanced back over her shoulder. The officer with the gun stood back a few feet, weapon not quite raised, but ready none-the-less. The one with the paddle stopped next to the driver's side of the convertible, one hand on the side arm at his waist.

"*Documenti, per favore.*"

Halli met Trent's gaze once more. The plea in his voice reflected in his expression. She gave a silent sigh and released the handle to sit back in her seat. A flash of relief darkened Trent's eyes before he removed his cap and turned a smile to the officers.

"*Si, si,* I got it right here."

The first officer's eyes widened and he let loose an excited stream of Italian. The second relaxed his hold on his gun and stepped forward with a big smile. Halli caught *Trent Tomlin* and *Shain West*. Obviously, they were familiar with the movie star. She watched Trent pump each man's hand with an aw-shucks grin. When the officer holding the big gun beamed at her, she thought about her similar reaction not that long ago. She cringed inside even as she smiled back at the man.

Had she been this star-struck?

She'd stuttered and blushed like a virgin teenager. Yeah, she'd been pathetic.

Squaring her shoulders, she decided it didn't matter. Now that she'd gotten to know him a little, she was over his celebrity status. Humiliation firmly set aside, she focused on the conversation between the three men.

Trent Tomlin really was one hell of an actor. He spoke a combination of English and Italian, just enough, apparently, to bond nice and tight, so that when the paddle officer finally turned his attention to the bullet holes in the windshield, Trent laughed it off with a grimace.

"There was a goof up—*un spaglio*—at the movie set. *Domani,* they will change the glass."

"*Domani?*"

"*Si*, tomorrow, *domani.*"

The other officer pointed to the rear of the car and asked another question. Trent nodded and spouted more words she didn't understand. When the officer looked at her again, she kept smiling, not sure what else to do.

One guy winked at Trent and they shared a laugh before he extended a small notebook and a pen. Halli got the feeling she should be insulted, but not a word had been spoken. Trent flipped to the back of the book and signed one piece of paper and the cardboard with a flourish. After a couple slaps on the shoulder and more handshakes, the officers returned to their vehicle.

Halli glanced at Trent, expecting to see a triumphant grin for his success in fooling the men. The act certainly had been impressive. Instead, he leaned his head back, eyes closed, no smugness to be found. The misery etched in his features made her heart skip an empathetic beat.

Before she could do more than blink, he blew out a deep breath, straightened and shifted the convertible into gear. She choked down any sympathy, grimly reminded by his hands fisted on the wheel and his now inscrutable expression that while he may be known around the world, he was still a stranger.

One very capable of deception.

He donned the hat and glasses once more, effectively shutting her out. The wind whipped her hair in her face as he accelerated and she raised a hand to brush strands from her eyes. Other than a brief glance to her side of the car, he kept his gaze trained straight ahead, his jaw tight, face blank.

Unease rippled through her. The ground alongside the convertible sped by at a dizzying rate and she cursed the stupidity that had convinced her to trust her unreliable instincts.

"So, what now?" she asked over the rush of wind.

"Now we switch cars at my house, find a battery, and see if you caught a murder on that video, sweetheart."

Chapter 2

"There! Ben, that's it, that's the street!"

Rachel's shout vibrated Ben's eardrums. He cranked the steering wheel to the right and stepped on the gas. Halli was going to kill them.

Please let her be okay.

He recalled Rachel's gasp when she'd asked Halli a direct question, then looked into the back seat to see why she didn't answer. Crazy thoughts raced through his head when he'd checked the empty space, and Rachel's horrified exclamation that he might have dragged her when he floored the little rental car to take advantage of a break in the fast-moving traffic didn't help his guilt.

Why hadn't they realized there was never a third door slam? Since discovering her missing, the distinct sound of only two doors reverberated in his head on an endless loop.

Worse than that, they hadn't noticed her absence for almost ten minutes. But Halli never had been much of a talker, and she'd been sulking about her vetoed itinerary off and on since they'd landed. Her silence in the back seat hadn't even registered between the encroaching jetlag and his concentration on the narrow, unfamiliar roads. Much as Rachel wanted her hair dryer converter, he'd wanted a shower and a nap and some food.

Instead, he'd lost his baby sister!

Now he felt like a complete jerk, not even worthy to be a big brother. He prayed they'd find her, safe and sound, right where they'd left her. And from now on, they'd follow her obsessive itinerary. If only they'd done that in the first place, none of this would've happened. Once again, all his fault.

Brake lights flashed in front of him and he rode up on the vehicle's back end. Swerving back and forth, he saw traffic was backed up and pounded an impatient fist on the wheel. "Come on."

"She's gonna be there," Rachel whispered. "She'll be there. Pissed off, I'm sure, but okay. She has to be."

Ben glanced at his watch to see they'd left her behind almost thirty-five minutes ago. Halli was smart enough to wait where they'd left her. Besides, she didn't have the guts to leave all on her own. Much as he loved his sister, reality was, she'd never been able to overcome her desperate need for complete order to combat the effects of their rootless childhood. He and Rachel had agreed to try and show her on this trip how freeing spontaneity could be, but not by leaving her behind.

Around the next bend, Lake Como would suddenly appear, like the last time when its shimmering glory with the mountainous background took his breath away and he'd swerved out of traffic to park on the wide sidewalk. And it did, only this time his lungs seized not from the beauty of the lake, but at the sight of a crowd of people, a half dozen police cars and an ambulance.

With a body on a stretcher.

"*Oh my God, Ben.*" Rachel's hands flew to her mouth, muffling a sob.

His heart pounded against his ribs. A swift jerk of the wheel landed them on the sidewalk again. He barely slammed the vehicle in park and ripped the keys from the ignition before both he and Rachel were out.

Bam. Bam. Two doors. Not three. The sound mocked him as they shoved through curious onlookers. Metal teeth of the car keys bit into his palm.

A uniformed officer caught Rachel's arm, but Ben kept going and made it close enough to see the person on the stretcher had shorter, much darker hair than Halli. And it was a man. Relief eased the tightness in his chest.

"It's not her," he called back to Rachel. He pushed forward again, scanning the crowd, concentrating on the spot where Halli had been filming those damn swans. Where was she?

A hand clamped onto his arm. "*Scusa signori*, but for who are you searching?"

Ben turned toward the heavy Italian accent and met a pair of dark eyes that matched the hard voice behind the question.

Instinctively, he pulled against the officer's hold. "My sister. We accidentally left her behind—"

The man's grip tightened. "You are American."

"Yeah."

"Come with me." The officer pulled Ben through the crowd, close to the spot where Halli last stood. A head taller than most, the officer lifted his chin and nodded to someone across the chaos.

Ben yanked his arm free as he looked around. "Do you know where my sister is?"

"What is her name?" the man asked as another officer escorted Rachel to Ben's side.

Rachel moved close and clung to his arm. "Where is she? Did you find her?"

"Not yet." Ben turned back to the two men watching them. "My sister is about five-foot-three. She's got brown hair—"

"It's more auburn, with red highlights," Rachel interjected. "And blue eyes. Please, you have to help us find her." Tears began to stream down her face. A breeze from the lake stuck strands of her blonde hair to her wet cheeks. "We stopped to look at the lake, and she was filming some stupid swans, but we wanted to find our hotel. She might have been getting into the car when we left. We thought the ambulance was—" Another sob drowned out her words as Rachel buried her face against Ben's shoulder.

"Where is the camera?" asked the light-haired officer who'd come over with Rachel.

Ben frowned at the strange question. "Probably still with her."

"At what hotel are you staying?" the first officer demanded.

"The Grand Hotel in Menaggio," Rachel answered. "But we haven't checked in yet."

"Maybe she will go to the hotel," the blond said, but more to the other officer than to them.

"I don't think so," Ben interjected. Two pairs of eyes pinned him in place and he shifted restlessly. "We weren't gone that long. It seems strange that she didn't wait for us here."

"We have taxi cabs here in *Italia*, eh?" The dark haired officer's tone indicated a less than favorable opinion of tourists.

"You don't know my sister. She's not very confident by herself," Ben explained. "I can't imagine her trying to find her way around all alone."

"Do you know somebody here in *Italia*? You meet friends maybe? Maybe she call someone?"

Rachel and Ben both shook their heads as Rachel said, "She doesn't have a cell phone with her. We're here on vacation. We just flew in this morning."

"This is the first time any of us have ever been here," Ben added.

The officers exchanged a look and then the dark one took out a small pad of paper and a pen from his pocket and said to Ben, "What is the name of your sister."

"Halli. Well, Halliwell is on her passport. Halliwell Sanders."

The man made a few notes, exchanged another glance with the blond officer, then said, "You will come with us."

Rachel nodded, but a twinge of unease settled in Ben's gut. The dark man's demanding tone rubbed him the wrong way. "I think it's better if we wait for her here. Wherever she may have gone, she'll be back—"

"No," the dark haired officer cut in. "*Agente* Mariucci will escort you to your hotel and we will be in contact."

"That car there, it is yours?" The one named Mariucci pointed to the blue car Ben had parked haphazardly on the walkway beside the lake.

"Yes, but—"

"Give *Agente* Casale your keys. We will make sure the vehicle is brought to you."

"I'd rather wait here," Ben repeated.

"We will find her," Casale said. "You will go with *Agente* Mariucci to the hotel."

Ben's frown deepened. His fingers tightened on the keys in his fist. "Why can't you just follow us there?"

"Procedure," Casale stated.

"Don't we need to file a report at the police station or

something? In America—"

"You are not in America, *signori*." Casale cast a pointed glance at Ben's hand and held out his own. "*Per favore*. Your cooperation will expedite the location of your sister."

"Ben," Rachel urged in a confused whisper.

Reluctantly, he placed the keys in the man's palm. He told himself that things were different in a foreign country, but couldn't shake the feeling something wasn't right. Casale departed with the keys, and Mariucci directed them to an unmarked, black vehicle parked on the opposite side of the road.

Rachel slid into the back. Ben hesitated. He turned to scan the spot where he'd last seen Halli. Mariucci stepped forward, his stocky build blocking Ben's view and confining him inside the triangle of the car, the door, and his body.

"I assure you, *signori*, we will find your sister."

Ben looked into the man's eyes. He sounded confident and determined. Releasing a sigh and giving a tired, grateful nod, he slipped in beside Rachel, who hugged herself as she chewed on her thumbnail. She hadn't done that in years—not since dealing with their parents on a daily basis.

The door slammed, enclosing them in the dimness of black tinted windows. Rachel grabbed his hand and he placed their clasped fingers on his thigh, covering both with his other hand as the engine turned over with a soft purr.

"Halli's fine," he murmured, hoping it wasn't an empty assurance.

Rachel sniffed and attempted a smile. "She's probably waiting at the hotel, making copies of her itinerary for us. You *know* she brought a copy."

"Probably," Ben agreed. And if she was, he'd follow the blessed thing to the minute.

Mariucci appeared at the left front window and greeted the driver by the name of Nino. As they spoke in low tones, it occurred to Ben that the man behind the wheel was not dressed in a police uniform. The unease in his stomach did a slow roll and he sat up a little straighter.

Through a pair of black framed glasses, Nino's gaze met

his for a brief instant in the review mirror. The glittering darkness of the man's eyes sent a shiver of apprehension along Ben's spine. He cut his gaze to Mariucci, but the man's emotionless smile failed to reassure. His knee started a rapid bounce.

The front passenger side opened and another man slipped inside. Shoulder-length dark hair, olive complexion, identical in appearance to the driver in that he wore no police uniform. The hairs on Ben's neck prickled, standing straight on end as the car started forward. Gut instinct made him reach for the door handle.

The locks clunked shut.

Ben pulled free from Rachel's grip and felt for the door lock while yanking on the unresponsive handle. The second man turned around and poked his hand through the opening between the front seats. Sunlight through the windshield glinted on the black casing of a gun.

Rachel's shriek pierced his ears a second before she muffled the cry with her hand. Ben shifted in front of her in a hopeless attempt to shield his sister as he met the cold gray gaze of the front seat passenger.

"Shut her up," the man growled in accented English even though Rachel had already gone silent.

"What's going on?" Ben asked. Strain roughened his voice, but he had no control of the terror currently gripping his muscles and robbing him of coherent thought.

"Your sister Halliwell has something we want. Until we find her, you are our collateral."

Chapter 3

Trent keyed in his security code and drove into his small estate after the gates swung open. They closed behind them, as silent as the rigid woman in the opposite seat. She hadn't spoken since the moment he'd uttered the word *murder*. Hadn't asked a single question, hadn't moved a single muscle. He suspected she was in shock, despite her insistence that she hadn't seen anything.

It was better this way though. Bold as his statement had been, he wasn't prepared to answer any questions. Not now that the immediate threat was gone and the reality of Lorenzo Roselli's murder had set in.

Whether Halli caught the crime with her video camera or not, he knew the retired cop was dead. The recording wire his friend had been wearing, the recording *he'd* been listening to and slipped into his pocket, had caught every word up to that fatal moment of Lorenzo's last gasping breath and beyond.

And yet it still wasn't enough. None of it would convict the scumbags on behalf of his brother or his friend Lorenzo. There'd been no names spoken other than the ones Lorenzo himself whispered toward the mic. Not one slip-up by the men at the villa to corroborate Lorenzo's valuable information about the smugglers.

Trent parked in the garage, his hands tight on the wheel as the overhead door reversed direction until it rested against the concrete floor. Would he ever be able to enter this house again without needing a moment to prepare? He'd give anything to go back in time six months ago and refuse his brother's request to use the villa while filming a new documentary about endangered animals sold on the black market.

If he'd said no, without a free place to stay, Sean wouldn't have been able to afford the trip to Italy. Their father had warned him Sean was tackling a dangerous subject, but his younger brother had wanted to make a difference. He *needed* to make a difference to get himself out of his spiraling depression, and had convinced Trent that if he nailed the documentary, he could save lives.

If only he could've saved his own.

The vision of their father's grief ravaged face at the funeral swam before him, but Trent shoved aside the memory and turned toward Halli. He couldn't help Sean anymore, but maybe he could make up for it by keeping this woman safe now. Responsibility weighed on his shoulders, forcing him to take a deep, silent breath before slipping back into character.

Unfortunately, character didn't quell the sudden tremor in the hand he reached across the seats toward her shoulder. "Come on inside, sugar. We both could use a drink."

She recoiled against the door. Trent hesitated, unsure how to handle her reaction. Women never pulled away from his touch. Surely, she understood by now that he wouldn't hurt her?

He opened his mouth to reassure her at the exact moment her chin lifted and her gaze locked with his. The blue of her eyes were lit with a fire the likes he'd never seen before.

"My *name* is Halli."

Those eyes were really quite amazing, even in the dimness of the garage. Trent blinked and focused on her words.

"Right, you did mention that. *Halli*, please come inside and I'll fix us that drink."

Her eyes narrowed to a piercing glare. "I'm not going anywhere with you."

One corner of his mouth crooked up. "Hmm. And yet here you sit, in my car, in my garage. If you think about it, the house isn't that much farther."

She immediately threw off her seatbelt and shoved open her door. Trent followed suit, thankful she'd decided to see reason so quickly. A swift shot, or three, of whiskey should steady his unwelcome resurgence of nerves.

But Halli didn't head for the door in front of them. She bolted for the one leading out to the driveway. Trent caught up as she yanked on the doorknob. She managed three inches of sunlight before his palm above her head slammed the door shut. His other hand gripped the doorframe, imprisoning her between his body and the door. "Where th—"

She threw her head back and her skull connected with his chin. Pain shot into his jaw, accompanied by her low grunt.

"Sonofa—"

A sharp elbow to his ribs on the left side forced the air from his lungs and sent him back a half step. She pushed against him with her body, reaching for the door handle again.

"Dammit, stop!" Trent closed his arms around her, banding them tight to avoid any more vicious jabs.

She tossed her head and kicked at his shins. Pinning her head with his cheek against hers, he growled in her ear, lifted her off the ground, and used his weight to press her against the door. "*Stop.*"

Their labored breathing mingled in the sudden silence. Trent became aware of his heart pounding in his chest about the same time her camouflaged curves registered. The frumpy, baggy clothes concealed a slim body that was a lot stronger than he ever would've guessed. Right now, with her firm, rounded derriere pressed intimately against his front, a twinge of physical response took him by surprise.

Tamping down on the inappropriate reaction, he relaxed his hold the slightest bit while shifting his hips. "I'm not going to hurt you."

Her breath caught on a half-laugh, half-sob. Guilt mushroomed, magnified by his forceful restraint. He sought to reassure her the only way he knew how. "Trust me, sweetheart, you're safe with me."

This time, she outright laughed, minus any humor.

"Trust *you*. With your kidnapping, and car chase, and talk of *murder*."

"I understand you're scared." He took a deep breath and admitted, "So am I."

She gave an unattractive snort. "Shain West isn't scared of anything."

A flash of annoyance overrode his guilt. "Shain's just a character and you know it."

"Aw, sorry, *sweetie*."

Her pointed sarcasm hit home and he *really* wanted a drink

now. "Can I let you go?"

"Dumb question."

Another growl rumbled from his throat. "If I let you go, are you going to try to run again?"

"Smarter question."

He liked her better when she was silent. She hadn't looked like she'd be this much trouble on the sidewalk next to the lake. His clenched teeth made his tender jaw ache worse and a headache began to throb at his temples.

"I'm not kidding around here. I've got a lot of shit to figure out and I don't have time to keep running after you."

Another humorless laugh. "Then don't."

Trent abruptly dropped her on her feet, grasped her shoulders and spun her around. With her back pressed to the door, he leaned in until their noses almost touched.

"You think I'm enjoying this? There's a hell of a lot better things I could be doing right now than keeping your ungrateful ass safe."

She shrank into herself. Her audible swallow reached his ears.

"I didn't ask for any of this. I just want to find my brother and sister and go home."

The waiver in her small voice hit Trent smack dab in the chest with a force greater than her head butt on his chin. His anger vanished on a sigh. "I know," he said softly, eternally sorry this innocent bystander had been dragged into his nightmare. "And I'm going to do everything I can to make sure that happens."

She stared past his shoulder, blue eyes alight with a shimmer of tears. "I still don't trust you."

He lifted her chin with a crooked knuckle and offered a smile that'd never failed him before. "Hey, remember back in the car with the *Carabinieri*? You trusted me then."

She pulled away with a jerk. With her chin raised, her blue gaze met his and held. "Yeah, stupid, gullible me."

Trent frowned. "What?"

"They were nice guys. *They* seemed trustworthy. You could've told them what happened and I'd be at my hotel with my family by now."

That pitiful wobble shook her voice again, but this time he ignored it. "Listen to me, and listen good, sweetheart. This thing goes deeper than you could ever imagine. If the men who were chasing us find out where you are, you'll be as dead as my friend is right now." The reference to Lorenzo roughened his voice.

Her face blanched white, but he cleared his throat and kept talking. "I have to see what the hell you've got on that video before I can even begin to think about who I can trust. Your life *and mine* depend on at least one of us being smart about this whole thing."

She took a shaky breath. "How do I know you're not just acting again?"

"Acting?" he asked in disbelief.

"When the bullets were flying, you had me convinced this was all real, but then you turned around and played those military guys like you were walking the red carpet."

"That's because I've played the movie star to death. It's so second nature I could do it in my sleep. This—" he gestured to the shot-up car and her "—I've never played before. Believe me, *Halli*, I couldn't fake *this* if I tried."

She didn't look convinced. When she fumbled behind her back for the door handle, he lost what was left of his patience. Grasping one of her elbows, he stepped aside and thrust her in front of him, toward the house. Anticipating immediate resistance, he took hold of both her arms, clamping them against her sides before moving close to murmur softly in her ear. "Had this been some sort of elaborate scheme to take advantage of a gullible tourist, I'd have had you inside already."

Her back stiffened against his chest.

"Relax, *sweetie*, I've never been that hard-up."

He reached around her to key in his four digit security code for the house alarm. Once inside, he reactivated the alarm and steered her through the foyer, across the living room overlooking the lake, and to the bar. He pushed her butt into a plush burgundy chair his decorator had picked out a few years ago.

"Sit. Stay."

Her chin took on a mutinous tilt. He waggled a finger in front of her face. "Uh-uh. Be a good little girl and this'll go so much easier." He turned his head, searching, until he noted the sash holding the curtains back. One of those would work perfectly. When her gaze followed his, he raised an eyebrow. "Do I need to take it a step further?"

She sat back in the chair and crossed her arms. Her breasts pushed up, separated by the strap of her travel purse, causing Trent a moment of distraction. Those hidden curves were intriguing.

Abruptly, he spun around to the bar. He took a moment to empty his pockets of Lorenzo's recording device, cell phone, and his wallet, then reached for the full bottle of Glen Grant Single Malt Scotch Whiskey.

"I always suspected you'd be a jerk," she said in a calm, matter-of-fact tone.

Trent downed one shot and poured a second. "Don't you read the tabloids? This is me, sugar."

"I've got better things to do with my time than read about a bunch of spoiled rich people who have everything they could ever want and yet they continually throw it all away."

Considering her condescending tone, he faced her so he could lean back against the bar. She stared out the nearest window, as if the lake were infinitely more interesting. So, Ms. My-Name-Is-Halli thought she was better than him, did she?

He drank the shot and poured another. Well, maybe she was. Bet she didn't have the whole world stroking her ego while at the same time watching, waiting, salivating over any little mistake she made so they could feel better about their own sorry-ass lives. Bet she didn't have a father who never bothered to hide his disappointment no matter how much money her last movie made at the box office.

Bet she didn't have her brother's death on her hands.

He lifted the shot to his mouth, then paused. "Ever think what they have isn't what they want?"

"The grass isn't always greener on the other side."

"Sometimes it is." *Sometimes it's a hell of a lot greener.*

"You all have the world served up on a platter and you still lie and cheat and do drugs and *drink*."

He got that she referred to Hollywood in general, but with her use of *you*, he took personal offense. Holding her gaze, Trent tossed back the whiskey and wiped his mouth with the back of his hand before lowering the shot glass. At least his hand was steady now.

"I've never cheated and I definitely don't do drugs." He let his mouth curve into a smirk and infused as much derision as possible into his next words. "I suppose you don't even drink."

She sniffed her judgmental little nose and he laughed.

Her gaze narrowed to an even deadlier glare. "I'm not a prude."

He poured again, taking measured steps until he stood in front of the chair, whiskey bottle in one hand, shot glass in the other. He lifted one brow in silent challenge and waited for her to chicken out.

She reached up. His initial surprise doubled when she snatched the bottle instead of the shot.

Holding his gaze, she lifted the Glen Grant to her lips and tipped the bottle skyward. He counted three deep swallows before her eyes widened. A second later, her next mouthful spewed all over him and her lap as she doubled over and braced the bottle on the floor. Hacking coughs shook her whole body and turned her face beet red.

Trent shook his head as he leaned down to remove the bottle from her unresisting fingers. He ran a glass of water at the bar and returned to squat in front of her. She guzzled the water as fast as she had the whiskey, only this time her expression reflected relief.

"Thanks," she whispered.

He braced a hand on either side of the chair to look her straight in the face. "Like I said, one of us has to be smart about this."

The red hue tingeing her cheeks deepened and her eyes blazed. Damn, they were something else, framed by those thick, sable lashes.

"I thought we were going to switch cars and then go get a

new battery." Her hoarse voice caught on another cough. "Unless you have a computer the memory card might fit? The sooner this is over, the better."

He wholeheartedly agreed, and averted his gaze to his watch. It was a little after two. "Unfortunately, I fried my laptop last week with a cup of coffee. And no, I don't have a desktop," he added, anticipating her next question. "As for the battery, we've got about an hour before the shops open again."

"Lucky me."

He smiled at her sarcasm and let his gaze roam over her face, taking in her windblown, knotted brown hair and the dark circles under her striking eyes. She might have a nice pair of lips, but it was hard to tell for sure with them stretched in a permanent frown above her small, stubborn chin.

"Much as I'd enjoy your cheerful company for the next hour, you look like hell."

"No thanks to you," she retorted.

"No thanks necessary, sugar pie." He patted her thigh and stood. The flash of lightning in those eyes was worth the stinging slap she gave his hand. He grinned. "Didn't you say earlier that you haven't been to your hotel since getting off the plane?"

"You mean you actually heard something that didn't directly concern you?"

"Shocking, I know. And yet, I bet you'd love a shower right now." When she didn't offer a smart-ass refusal right away, he looked over to see pride warring with the thought of washing away the travel grime after a long flight and the added stress of being shot at and abducted.

Abducted? Crap, she was starting to wear off on him. He'd *saved* her, not kidnapped her.

"A smart woman would just say yes," he pointed out.

Pride took over, but a second later her expression smoothed out and she offered him a sweet smile. Her face transformed and yes, she did have a nice mouth.

A kissable mouth.

"You're right," she said. "A shower sounds great."

Trent hesitated, and then swept his hand in invitation

toward the stairs. At the top, he directed her down the hall to the guest room that connected to his master suite, both of them overlooking the lake. All the while, he couldn't help thinking he'd goaded her into accepting his offer, so why did he get the feeling that she'd pulled one over on him?

At the bedroom door, she turned and blocked the entrance. "I can find the bathroom from here."

She was actually kind of cute, thinking he'd just let her go in there all by herself. "I'm sure you can, but first I need to make sure there's no window for you to climb out of."

Consternation crossed her features, and he bit back a grin at her predictability.

She spun around to enter the room. "It's your house, shouldn't you already know that?"

"I don't use the guestroom bathrooms."

"No, you wouldn't. I suppose your women all come to you, don't they?"

He choked on a laugh. "My women? You make it sound like I have a harem or something."

She avoided the large bed and went to stand next to an antique vanity and chair. "Don't act like you don't crook your finger and women come running. Heck, I bet that door right there connects to your bedroom."

Trent's mouth curved in a slow smile as he crossed the floor to glance into the windowless bathroom. "Careful, sweetheart, you sound curious."

"And you sound conceited," she shot back.

But he noticed a flush working its way across her cheeks. She quickly indicated the tall windows flanking either side of the bed.

"So what about these? You going to sit guard in here while I shower?"

He cast a sweeping glance down her petite length. "You tell me, do I have to?"

With a disgusted huff, she stripped the travel purse from around her neck and threw it at him. "There. My passport and my money. Now quit breathing down my neck and leave me alone."

Trent caught the purse one handed. He focused on the small item in his hands in an attempt to dispel the mental image of her naked body under the hot spray. Halli, meanwhile, grabbed the delicate straight back chair in front of the vanity and dragged it into the bathroom with her. The door slammed, and he heard her wedge the chair under the handle.

He was amused, yet oddly insulted. As if he'd force himself on her. True, he'd noticed a few positive things since pulling up to her on the sidewalk and thinking she was plain, but if he compared her to the women he usually dated, she was the definition of opposite. Picturing her naked in the shower meant nothing more than he was a guy.

He heard the shower door slide open. A second later the sound of water hitting the marble tiles reposted the erotic image in his mind, and reminded him he was a guy who hadn't had sex in awhile. This fact also, thankfully, explained his reaction in the garage, when he'd pressed her against the door from head to toe, his forearms cushioned against her breasts, his hips pinning hers. Who'd have guessed those ugly clothes of hers could hide so much?

Another slide of the shower door, then the subtle change in the sound of the water told him she'd stepped inside. With a low groan, he headed for the hall before his imagination completely took over.

See, she could trust him, damn it. He slapped her purse against his palm in frustration, only to pull up short with the memory of her unexpected meek smile when she'd accepted his offer of a shower. Not to mention the fact she'd handed her purse over a little too willingly.

He unzipped the top and dug out the items inside. Passport, traveler's checks and cash, lip moisturizer and a couple folded pieces of paper. She hadn't lied.

And you know what else? She might not want him to think she trusted him, but handing over her personal stuff told a whole other story. Tension eased from his shoulders, allowing him to relax for the first time in the past couple hours.

****

Wrapped in a luxuriant, navy, terry-cloth robe she'd found

hanging on the back of the door, Halli moved the chair aside and opened the bathroom door to peek into the silent room beyond. She blew out a heavy sigh of relief when she saw her famous kidnapper had not set up camp on the bed. The other emotion tickling her stomach she staunchly refused to identify.

Time to get dressed and set her plan in motion. As long as she had a plan to execute, orderly steps to focus on in her head, she could keep from dissolving into a mindless idiot.

Just before the door clicked shut again, she noticed some items on the bed that hadn't been there before. A single sheet of white paper rested on top. Curiosity got the better of her and she hurried across the floor, her toes sinking into the plush carpeting.

Thought you'd appreciate some clean clothes.

"What, no honey?" She crumpled the neatly printed note in her fist. "Sweetheart? *Sugar Pie?*"

Laid out front and center were skimpy bikini underwear and two satin bras; one black, one white. Heat rose in her face at the thought of Trent Tomlin picking out underwear for her. She didn't even want to know where any of them came from.

Pushing those items aside, she eyed the other choices of tops and pants spread out on the intricately quilted bedspread, wanting so badly to walk away, but at the same time cringing at the thought of putting her smelly, grimy travel clothes back on.

No. She didn't want a darn thing from the man.

She took two steps back to the bathroom before her resistance waffled. The material had felt so soft when she'd brushed the lingerie out of the way. They probably wouldn't even fit, so, what could it hurt to try them on, right? Then at least she could wear her old clothes without thinking twice about the clean ones.

Selecting a pair of lightweight jean Capri's was easy, and they were close enough to her size. The shirts were another matter. A blue, backless halter top she tossed aside without a second glance. The sheer, black button-up blouse was quick to follow. That left her with a white, V-necked, baby doll T-shirt, size small, the least offensive of the three—*if* it weren't for the words *Wet & Wild* emblazoned in blue rhinestones across the front.

Considering she'd seen the women the arrogant jerk dated, she was not surprised by the limited options. At least those women had the body and the confidence for these clothes. Heck, if she strutted around on Trent Tomlin's arm, maybe she would, too.

With an annoyed frown, Halli snatched up the underwear and clothes, and returned to the bathroom, reminding herself she had no time to waste. The Capri's were a little tighter than she usually wore, and obviously made for someone much taller, but comfortable, none-the-less. She rolled up the extra length a few times before pulling the white top over her head.

Flipping her damp hair back over shoulders, she eyed herself in the mirror. The T-shirt sucked tight to every inch it touched; shoulders, chest, stomach and hips. Her breasts stood out, additionally highlighted by the rhinestones that stretched across the shirt's velvet-soft material. Good God, if she got cold, the thin satin bra would hide nothing. Heck, even now, her nipples puckered at the mere thought.

She reached for the hem to take it off when a muted noise reached her ears in the otherwise quiet house. She paused and held her breath. Was that the garage door opening? Chances were Trent was near the garage, too, which put him clear across the house from her. This might be her only opportunity to escape.

Halli bent down and dug into the pocket of her sweat pants for the photo copy of her passport and stuffed it into the front pocket of her new Capri's. A quick flick of her wrist turned the shower back on full blast, and then she scooped up her shoes, ran across the bedroom, and tried the first window. It didn't budge. She bounced across the bed but the pane on the other side was no better.

Muttering under her breath, she hauled butt to the bedroom door and peeked into the hall. All clear. She had to get to a door with a security pad so she could key in the four digit code she'd watched Trent enter. Four years earlier than the year she was born, it was easy to remember. Once out in the yard, she'd bypass his security gates by going down to the lake and around the wall she'd noticed while he was drinking shot after shot. From there, she'd head straight to the local police station.

How?

Halli froze as the question expanded in her mind. How would she get to the police station with no clue where to go and no knowledge of the language?

Stop. She fisted her fingers around her shoes and put one foot in front of the other. Her only choice was to move forward. She'd figure out the how once she was free.

Her heart pounded in her ears with each silent step along the thick carpet in the hall. It nearly leapt from her chest when the muted thud of a dresser drawer sliding shut sounded behind her. Her breath seized. He was supposed to be by the garage so she could sneak past the bar by way of the double doors leading to the lake. Clutching shoes to chest, she ran down the hall and made it to the stairs as the door at the end of the hall opened behind her.

Please let him hear the shower and think I'm still in there.

She rushed down to the first floor, around the corner, toward the bar. Right there, right next to the whisky bottle that'd almost choked her, sat his wallet. She had a flash-vision of her dad and mom, smiling proudly at her, Ben, and Rachel after they'd pulled a successful con. Games, they'd called them. Once she was old enough to figure out what was really happening, she'd sworn she'd never again do those things.

Cheat. Lie. Steal.

Halli hesitated. All her money was in her purse. In Trent's hands.

She grabbed his wallet and bolted for the door. *This is different*, she told herself. This was her life, not some game her parents were playing to beat the system.

And it's not like he can't afford it, Baby. The words were true, but as they echoed in her father's smug voice, they almost made her drop Trent's wallet.

She gritted her teeth and whispered vehemently, "*Focus, Halli.*"

Stuffing the soft leather into her front pocket with one hand, she hugged her shoes against her ribs and keyed in the code with her other.

Her trembling finger slipped on the fourth little rubber square.

Chapter 4

Halli sucked in a breath, wondering what number she'd actually pressed. Three excruciating heartbeats later, the light blinked from red to green. Air whooshed from her lungs, but she had no time to enjoy the relief.

Knowing Trent could spot her at any moment made the sprint past his pool, down some stone steps, across a small immaculate lawn, and finally over the rocky shoreline to the edge of his property seem like a mile. Her headlong rush startled three white swans swimming near the water's edge.

Indignant honks filled the air as they half-ran, half-flew across the water. Halli cringed as they landed near the large white boat house next to Trent's dock. *Stupid swans.* The darn birds would be the death of her yet.

She waded around to the other side of the wall separating his property from the villa next door and paused to catch her breath while taking stock of her new surroundings. Past the front of his neighbor's house there were no gates to block access to the road. *Thank God.*

By the time she reached the sidewalk at the edge of the yard, her feet were dry enough to put on her shoes. She straightened and searched for something familiar. Something...*any*thing to point her in the right direction.

Nothing appeared much different from where Ben and Rachel left her. Pedestrians filled the walkways and cars streamed past.

Her feet refused to move, frozen to the sidewalk. She took in the activity in every direction. So much going on, people going about their everyday normal lives, but she was all alone in this foreign country. Lost. With no clue which direction to turn.

Her shoulders slumped. What had made her think she could do this on her own? She crossed her arms over her stomach, wishing for a reassuring hug from her sister.

That thought brought her up short. Before the debilitating anxiety fluttering in her stomach could multiply, swell, and take over, she dropped her hands to her sides, squared her shoulders and gave herself a stern admonishment.

Quit being such a wimp. You'll fail for sure if you give up before you even try. You got out of the house, didn't you?

A loud wolf whistle to her right made her jump. Two black haired boys waved her over, their wide grins glinting white against tanned skin. A smile quivered on her lips. They looked no older than teenagers, but if they knew English, she could ask them directions to the police station.

The cool lake wind blew a damp strand of hair across her mouth and she reached one hand up to tuck it behind her ear. One of the boys called out in Italian. She couldn't understand the words, but the suggestion in his tone was universal. Didn't even need the vulgar hand gesture in his lap for translation.

"If you are wet, *fighetta*, we can get wild."

The other one stood, spread his arms and then pointed to his crotch with both hands. *Gross.* She flushed straight to her roots and then the heavily accented words registered. Halli glanced down at her shirt with the forgotten shiny blue rhinestoned words. *Frickin' Trent Tomlin.* He'd obviously planned to amuse himself from the choices he'd given her, and now she was the one who had to pay for it.

Both the boys laughed and another whistle split the air. Halli spun away from them to the left, even though it would take her right past Trent's place. She was probably screwed either way.

A taxi cruised toward her, its light on top the roof of the car a blessed beacon of reprieve. She may live in small town Wisconsin, but she'd seen enough movies to recognize that widespread symbol. She practically jumped in front of the darn thing to wave it down, then ran around to slip into the back seat.

"Police. *La polizia*," she implored, interrupting the driver's rapid, scolding Italian mid-stream. "*Please*, take me to the nearest police station."

****

Halli's fingers clenched on the small plastic cup in her

hands. A conscious effort loosened them again. The stupid shirt was bad enough without adding an ugly stain of black espresso.

She stared through the window of the bare-bones room the female officer had put her in. Greco she'd introduced herself. Without a clue how to address the police in Italy, Halli went with Officer Greco.

What was the holdup? Did it really take the woman an hour and a half to call the US Embassy or Consulate to verify the photocopy of her passport was legitimate? It shouldn't take a genius to figure out she was the live version of the black and white picture.

She'd requested to call Ben on his cell phone or at the hotel, but the man in charge insisted on filing paperwork before allowing her a phone call. He hadn't been mean about it. On the contrary, despite taking forever, they'd been nothing but nice to her so far. So she tried to tell herself things were different in a foreign country, that's why where was a delay.

It didn't help. Based on her childhood experiences with her parents, she couldn't help but feel like a criminal.

She wanted to remind the officers that she'd come to *them*. *She* was the missing person her brother and sister were probably frantically looking for. All they had to do was let her make one phone call.

With annoying frequency, a small voice inside her head repeated Trent's insistence that the police couldn't be trusted. *But they're the police*, she rationalized, and this station was half-way around the lake, more than an hour's drive away from where the car chase had occurred. The police were the ones she could trust. Not some arrogant movie star who believed his good looks and fake charm put him above the law.

And yet, for some unknown reason, something kept her from mentioning Trent's involvement. She didn't owe him a darn thing. Well...okay, maybe she did, but he'd been nothing but a bullying jerk once they reached his house. Threatening to tie her up! Would've served him right if she *had* ratted him out.

If it hadn't been for that one moment in the car, when his eyes and voice had begged for her cooperation—

She wondered if he'd gotten the camera battery yet.

Wondered if he'd found the murder on her video. The thought that she may have filmed someone's death scraped across her nerves like nails on a chalkboard. Goosebumps rose on her arms in the wake of the chill that raced over her skin, but she pushed thoughts of Trent Tomlin from her mind with a determined sip from her cup.

Grimacing in distaste at the extreme bitterness of the now cold espresso, she set the cup down and slid it across the table. She rotated her head to relieve sore muscles. Man, she missed Wisconsin. And she was tired. And her head hurt from where she'd hit it in the jerk's car and on his chin. All she wanted to do was find her family, get to the hotel, sleep for a day, then book a flight back home. Maybe even skip the sleep and just head home.

Italy had permanently lost its appeal.

Seeing no sign of Officer Greco, and considering she'd been waved back to her chair with patient words of *"per favore"* and *"fra un momento"* after she'd twice attempted to ask what was taking so long, Halli dropped her head to rest on her crossed arms. Her eyes burned when she closed them. Jet lag, stress and tears were a painful combination.

Voices approached the office and she quickly opened her eyes while lifting her head in hope. Two men, one in uniform and one in business attire minus a suit coat, walked to the door—and kept on going. Halli sighed and resumed her position. After two more false alarms, she didn't even bother looking anymore. She debated pushing to her feet again and trying to get answers, but fatigue crept up on her, despite the hard chair and uncomfortable position. At least with her head buried in her arms, she could block the glare of the lights from her exhausted eyes.

"Alrigo—*aspetta.*"

"Ma lei aveva la video camera?"

The intense, urgent tone of the hushed question directly outside the door roused Halli from a semi-dream state. She cracked open one eye to squint toward the door without raising her head.

"No, solo una copia del suo passaporto."

"Dove cozzo e? Voglio quelle video camera!"

Wide awake now, her heart beating a rapid tempo against her ribs, Halli fought the urge to sit up straight. The words that caught her attention may have been pronounced as *"vee-day-oh kah-mare-ah"*, but even she could figure out that translation. Equally alarming, the speaker sounded pretty upset.

Had she mentioned her camera? She sifted through her foggy memory of the story she gave the officers when she'd first arrived at the station. No, she'd kept it simple; her brother and sister drove off without her, and she took the wrong bus when trying to locate the hotel and got herself completely lost.

Outside the office, the men exchanged more words, but she couldn't understand anything other than the anger in the one man's voice. And even that she didn't understand.

Yes you do.

No. She forced back rising alarm. Trent's dire warnings couldn't be true. She'd done the right thing by coming to the police. They would help her.

Head still down, she stared toward the door through strands of her hair. Only one man's black leather clad shoulder was visible. She willed the men to move, desperate to see who they were, yet hardly able to breathe for the vice clamping her chest. The one with the calmer voice said something, repeated the name *Alrigo*, and she saw a hand settle on the leather jacket.

That man gave a swift jerk and stepped back out of reach, giving Halli a split-second glimpse of his face.

Terror seized her throat. That jaw. The harsh line of his mouth—it was the man from the darkened window of the villa. A tidal wave of panic dragged her into the undertow.

Oh my God, he really is after me! But how did he find me here?

The answer hit with sickening certainty at the exact moment Officer Greco stepped back into the room. No wonder it'd taken so long to process the 'paperwork'.

"Ms. Sanders, if you would come with us, *per favore*."

No. She couldn't. This woman seemed so nice, yet had no qualms about turning her over to a killer.

Halli clutched her arms across her stomach and moaned. "I

don't feel so good, can I use the restroom? Please."

The officer's eyes flooded with concern and she hurried over to help Halli to her feet. "*Si*. I will take you."

Just outside the door, a sharp command halted Officer Greco and froze Halli in her tracks. The woman turned and spoke in rapid Italian. Halli didn't dare look. The man in the leather jacket would know she knew who he was. Heavy footsteps sounded behind her.

She covered her mouth and doubled over with a groan. "I'm going to be sick."

Officer Greco urged her forward, a string of irritated-sounding Italian words flowing over her shoulder. Halli held her breath, expecting a bullet in her back at any moment. By the time they reached the restroom, she was dizzy and truly nauseous.

The whole situation was insane! Thinking some guy would shoot her in the middle of a police station.

Inside the bathroom, she rushed into a stall and threw up the little bit of liquid she'd drank. Dry heaves came next; she hadn't eaten since a light breakfast on the plane hours ago. She flushed and sat back, her stomach still rolling. A hand reached around her, offering a wet paper towel. Halli accepted it gratefully, swiping it across her clammy forehead and face before wiping her mouth.

"Can I get you a drink?" Officer Greco asked.

"Please," Halli whispered with a nod.

She had to get out. Were they the only people in here? She leaned against the toilet bowl and glanced under the walls on either side to find the other stalls empty. Over her shoulder, she said, "A soda, please. White. It'll help settle my stomach."

The officer looked hesitant. Halli turned back to the toilet with dread. This one she was going to have to fake. After she gagged and wiped her face with the paper towel again, she hung her head, slumped her shoulders, and begged, "Please. Sprite or 7-Up."

"*Si*. I will see what I can find."

Halli didn't wait for the door to close all the way before pushing to her feet. She tossed the paper towel in the direction of the garbage and went straight to the sink.

Where were the faucet handles? She waved her hands, looking for the motion activated sensor. Nothing. A quick search located two pedals on the floor, one black, one red. Desperate, she stepped on the red. Water spit out of the faucet, only it was hot. She quickly scrubbed her hands, then pressed on the black pedal, hoping for cold. One chilled handful rinsed her mouth, and two more she splashed on her face.

Groping for a dry towel, she stared at her pale reflection with disbelief. How had her carefully planned life spun so out of control in just a few hours? Not to mention, away from Trent, the whole nightmare was supposed to go away. Instead, it'd gotten worse.

Her mind raced. Working in television, living vicariously through movies, her mind immediately went to the worst case scenario. But maybe they weren't all in on whatever was going on. Surely Officer Greco wouldn't have left her alone if she knew what Halli had filmed? She waivered in indecision. Could she risk trusting her? Would the woman help? Would she believe the real story after Halli's initial lie?

The day fast-forwarded in Halli's mind and her shoulders slumped. Who was she kidding? No one would believe what had all happened to her today. Heck, there wasn't even a single incidence by itself that stood a ghost of a chance of being plausible, let alone the whole of it together.

What she needed right now was a new plan. What did she need to focus on after she got out of here? One step beyond escape was crucial to give her a goal to work toward.

The embassy. No, the consulate. Or the hotel? Ben and Rachel might assume she'd go there, but she quickly decided the consulate was closer and probably safer than finding her way along the lakeshore by herself. Plus, though Trent's wallet appeared well-stocked, she had no idea how far the money would take her. A taxi to Milan was her best plan.

At the door, she took a deep breath, trying to work up the courage for her second bathroom escape in two hours. The thought startled a hysterical laugh. She bit it back before her nerves escalated the reaction out of control.

Focus on the consulate.

Her next breath shook only half as much with a goal set in place. She eased the door open, then quickly stepped back when a visual sweep of the hall revealed a door opening at the end of the corridor. A split-second glimpse of daylight and a green sign imprinted on her mind before the bathroom door shut with a soft hydraulic sigh. That green sign contained a white stick figure running toward a doorway with the word *USCITA* underneath—*USCITA* must mean exit.

Voices reached a crescendo in the hall and then waned. Flattened against the wall, between the door and the paper towel dispenser, Halli prayed Officer Greco didn't locate a white soda anytime soon.

Another quick scan revealed the hall empty. Halli took a second to get her bearings. Left was back to the offices where she'd been held. No hope of escape there. To the right beckoned the exit. Only the hall didn't end at the exit, but T'd in each direction, and between her and freedom stood two doors on either side, the last ones offices with nameplates and windows.

Didn't matter, she had to move. With her first step, the theme music from Jaws began to play in her head. Each step forward increased the tempo, just like in the movie. God, she was losing it!

She made it past the first door. Her sigh of relief was cut short, however, when the second door, not ten feet in front of her swung open, and a short, fat bald man stepped out. The air seized in her lungs.

The man turned to waddle toward the exit sign, reading a document in his hands. Halli watched in amazement as he turned the corner without even glancing in her direction.

Could it be her luck was changing?

A soft noise registered directly behind her just as fingers fisted in her shirt and yanked her backward into a small room. Her instinctive scream was curtailed by a large hand over her mouth. The door clicked shut and a solid wall of muscle forced the air from her lungs. A wall that smelled like leather.

Alrigo.

The distinct, heavy scent assaulted her senses, turning her

queasy stomach. Frantic clawing to remove her living steel gag proved futile. Tears stung her eyes when they confirmed the arm holding her was indeed encased in leather. She screamed again, but the killer's hand muffled it to a moan.

"Shut up, sweetheart, or you'll bring the whole damn building running."

Halli went completely still. *Trent?*

Relief weakened her knees and wiped all logical thought from her mind. She'd never been so glad to hear a familiar voice in her life. She tried to turn and face him in the dim light, but his hold prevented any movement.

"I told you not to go to the police."

Halli stiffened at the unexpected menace in his low growl and his arms banded tighter. She tried to speak, but his venomous whispers overrode her muffled attempt.

"You've screwed up everything, dammit. Everything I've worked on for the past two months, Lorenzo's death, saving your ass—all of it for nothing because *you* had to go to the damn police."

Lorenzo? Was that the friend he'd spoken of earlier?

"Do you know who showed up about fifteen minutes ago, Halli?" Trent snarled in her ear. "While you're wandering around the police station like some lost little tourist?"

She tried to nod her head, but he spun her around so they were face to face. His hand remained glued over her mouth as he pinned her against the door. Beneath the shadow of his blue baseball cap, hazel eyes burned into hers with an anger that scared her almost as much as the man out in the station.

"Your buddy from the villa. The guy who shot up my car when he tried to *kill you*. And what thanks do I get? You turn around and walk straight into his hands. He's waiting out there right now to finish what he started this morning."

Halli couldn't suppress a terrified shiver in the face of Trent's blunt, furious words. A dark, dangerous aura cloaked them in the confined space as she endured his glower. So why, then, was she also completely aware of every inch of his hard, angry body vibrating against hers?

Something fluttered in the pit of her stomach, something

more than fear. She darted her gaze around, desperate to focus on something other than him. They appeared to be in some sort of storage closet, full of miscellaneous items and janitorial supplies.

"I'm taking you out of here right now," Trent stated, compelling her attention back to him. "Despite the pain-in-the-ass you've been, I refuse to let them kill you like they did my brother and Lorenzo. I can't live with another death on my hands, you hear me?"

Halli frowned in confusion at the gruff declaration. His brother committed suicide. It'd been all over the news. Here, in Italy, in Trent's villa, almost three months ago.

"Once we're out of here," Trent continued, "I'll take you to Milan, to the Consulate General. You'll be better off there. Safer. Then *they* can deal with the consequences of what you've done and help you find your family."

Tears threatened, even though he'd just told her he'd take her exactly where she wanted to go. She really was losing it, because though she knew now she'd been wrong to come here, knew she should've listened to him, his recriminations piled on the guilt.

Until indignation reared up and reminded her, what the hell had he expected her to do? Sit in his house like a victim?

"Deal?" he demanded.

She nodded.

"I'm going to move my hand. Don't. Scream."

She shook her head, assuring him she'd be quiet.

His gaze narrowed, holding hers for one last quiet warning. "Understand this, if you don't trust me to get us out of here, if you choose not to believe me right now, then we're both as good as dead."

Trent watched Halli jerk her head in another nod and finally, slowly, removed his hand. He was still pissed as hell, worried as to how they'd even get out of the building, and not the least bit sorry for the fear he'd stirred up in her eyes.

He stepped back, paused briefly at the sight of her slim figure in the tight *Wet & Wild* T-shirt, then spun to survey the contents of the closet. It was time to pull off the act of a lifetime. If he didn't, it might be his last.

"How'd you find me?" Halli whispered.

"Where else were you going to go?"

"I might have gone to my hotel."

"Supposedly, you had no money, and honey, you don't strike me as the type to stick out your thumb on the side of the road. Not that it would've done you any good anyway, since your brother and sister never checked in."

"What? How—"

He tossed her a frown. "Shhh."

She moved closer and grabbed his arm. Lowered her voice to a desperate whisper. "How do you know? I never mentioned the name of the hotel we were going to stay at. How—"

"I found your travel itinerary with your passport and money and called to check. As of about an hour ago, neither of them had registered. Your brother isn't answering his cell, either."

The concern in her eyes told him he probably should've kept that information to himself until after they were on the way to Milan.

"That doesn't make any sense."

Tell him something he didn't know. It had him a little worried, too, but it wasn't his problem. Same as she'd no longer be a pain in his ass as soon as he dropped her at the consulate.

Trent grasped her shoulders, forcing her gaze to meet his. "Forget them for now and concentrate on us. You can't find them if you're dead."

Fear flashed in her eyes again, but she stiffened her spine and determination overrode all else. Good. Maybe she finally understood the seriousness of the situation. He stepped over to a shelf with clothes items folded on it. He'd seen a janitor working during the day at Lorenzo's station once or twice, so this might work. He shrugged out of his leather jacket and tossed it to Halli.

She folded it over her arm, against her stomach. "The female officer who was getting me a soda has probably found out I'm gone by now."

"Yep." He jerked a pair of coveralls out and held them up.

Too small for him, too big for her. As he tossed them aside, he instructed, "Do something with your hair. Put it up. Something so it looks different."

"I'm pretty sure there's an exit just down the hall. That's where I was headed when you grabbed me."

Trent glanced over in surprise. "You were leaving?"

"I saw the guy from the villa, too. I think his name is Alrigo. At least that's what the officer called him—"

His pulse skipped a beat. *Alrigo Lapaglia.* He'd heard of the guy a couple times, and Lorenzo had said his name on the wire, but he hadn't been able to put a face with the name until now. "You're sure he said Alrigo?"

"Yes. He was talking to one of the cops, and he said *video camera* twice, so I pretended to be sick so I could get out of there." She tucked the jacket between her knees as she tied her hair in a ponytail with a piece of string she'd pulled off a shelf. "Did you watch the video?"

"Exactly when do you think I would've had time to find a battery?"

"I just thought…well, it's been a couple of hours since I left your place."

"And I've been sitting outside, waiting to make sure you were okay."

Her turn to look surprised. "You waited for me?"

"Don't read anything into it. I'd have done the same for a stray dog."

"Gee, thanks."

"Right back at ya, baby."

He held up another pair of coveralls. Close enough. As he stepped into them, he directed a new surge of anger toward her bent head.

"You screwed me over real good, you know that? After your story, the police have probably already swarmed my place and found the camera and the video. Not to mention the recording from Lorenzo's wire. That was my only proof—"

"I didn't tell them about you."

His hand halted in amazement, the coveralls half zipped. "You didn't?"

She looked up as she shook her head.

"Seriously? Why not?"

She lowered her gaze and shrugged, her cheeks suddenly rosy red. He zipped the coveralls the rest of the way before stepping close with a relieved smile. She took a half-step back, her eyes wide.

He took hold of her face with both hands and planted a kiss on her forehead. "Finally...you did something right. We just might make it out of here."

A frown creased her brow, accompanied by a look of chagrin. To forestall the expected argument, he took off his cap, put it on her head, and tugged it low over her face. Hopefully the coveralls and his two-day scruff would be enough to throw anyone off. And now that he knew they weren't looking for him, too, his plan had a better chance of succeeding.

He took his jacket from her and draped it around her stiff-set shoulders. A nudge toward the door met with resistance, but he pushed harder. "Listen up, girlfriend Cara. You just found out you're pregnant and came to tell me here at work. Your parents had forbidden us to see each other and your father hates me, so naturally, you're crying at the thought of having to tell them. I'll hug you close and escort you outside to my car, and we're home free."

Her blue eyes were full of apprehension. "You make it sound easy."

"It will be. Just act like you're devastated."

He reached for the door. Her hand secured a vice grip on his.

"I don't understand. How will anyone know what you just told me?"

Trent held back a growl of irritation, pulled free of her grip and swiped his damp palm along the side of his costume. A square shape in one of the pockets caught his attention. "It's back story, baby, so you can act the part better."

"Oh, right—back story. I forgot."

He shook a cigarette from the pack of smokes he'd discovered and lit it with the accompanying lighter. "What do you mean, you forgot?"

"Nothing."

Trent squinted through the smoke curling up between them, wondering about her sudden clipped tone. Her eyes had taken on a bleak, haunted look. He wanted to ask her about it, but they had to get their butts moving.

"You smoke?"

He frowned at her disapproving, wrinkled-up nose. *Seriously?* "My character does. And he's just a tad bit stressed at the moment."

"Oh."

He tucked the pack back in his pocket, took a drag, fought a cough, and exhaled.

Show time.

Halli watched Trent reach for the door, her pulse pumping in permanent overdrive—pretty much since the moment she'd met him. At the last second, she put her hand over his on the door knob.

"Just don't smile, okay?"

He looked at her like she was crazy. "You're upset, you've just told me you're pregnant and your father will kill me if he finds out. Why on earth would I smile?"

Great, now she felt like an idiot. "I don't know. I just thought you should know your smile is very recognizable."

His lips curved into the exact smile she'd seen countless times over the past ten years. His perfect, white, famous smile. "Thanks for the reminder." The smile disappeared in the blink of an eye. "Now start crying."

She took a deep breath as he opened the door. Trent's immediate stream of fluent, dramatic Italian threw her for a moment, but she focused on the part he'd asked her to play. Fear of never seeing Ben and Rachel again and of getting caught by the man from the villa welled real tears in her eyes. A blink spilled them over the edge of her lashes, down her face. She added a soft sob when Trent put an arm around her and drew her close.

Because she didn't understand a word he said, all she could do was cry, her face buried against his chest while he led her toward the exit. The strong scent of bleach from the coveralls filled her nostrils. He'd smelled better in the car.

Voices from one of the upcoming corridors robbed her of any smidgeon of security his embrace gave her. She tensed. Trent's hold tightened, but he didn't stop talking or walking. Smoke curled in front of her from the cigarette in his hand by her shoulder. She lifted her hands to cover her face and sobbed harder.

Trent's lips pressed to her ear as two officers walked by. "Not so damn loud."

She toned it down. A moment later, his other hand cupped her cheek. He halted and lifted her face to his, his thumb swiped across her skin to remove the moisture.

What was he doing? Why was he stopping? They had to keep moving.

Italian words spilled from his mouth, full of heartfelt emotion to match a glowing intensity in his hazel eyes. Halli's heart skipped a beat.

"Shake your head no," he whispered.

She blinked. From the corner of her eye, she noticed the men who'd passed them paused halfway along the corridor to watch their drama. She did as Trent instructed and restarted the waterworks for good measure. He hugged her close again, spouted more foreign lines with a consoling accent, and steered her for the door.

The white little running man on the exit sign near the door beckoned.

Halli fought not to run the last ten feet. Almost there. They were going to make it. Just walk right out. She couldn't believe it was as easy as he'd said. Then she noticed another sign posted on the door and tried to slow their steps.

"That looks like a warning of some kind," she whispered to Trent.

"It's for an alarm." He urged her forward. "But it's—"

Halli sucked in a breath and planted her feet.

"—not activated."

"How do you know?" she asked in desperation.

"How do you think I got in here?"

Trent reached around her and pushed open the door. Halli

cringed, eyes squeezed tight, expecting an ear-piercing warning to announce their escape.

Silence.

She opened her eyes again and breathed. No alarm. The sun was still shining, though it had started its evening decent in the brilliant blue sky. She sniffed away any remaining tears and turned to smile up at Trent from underneath the baseball cap.

A shout behind them wiped away her exhilaration a second before Trent's rough shove propelled her the rest of the way through the open doorway.

"Run!"

Chapter 5

Trent followed Halli out the door. She stumbled and he grabbed the collar of his leather jacket to haul her up from her knees. Too late, he remembered it'd only been draped around her shoulders. The unexpected weightlessness threw him off balance, and he ended up a step ahead of her.

He found his footing, reached back for the hand she stretched toward him, and jerked her back onto her feet. To their right lay a residential area, and to the left, the many quaint shops and businesses that made the village so old-world Italian. Tourists crowded the walkways during the evening dinner hour.

Trent went left, half dragging Halli in his wake. If they could get lost in the crowd, eventually they could circle around to where he'd parked his black Mercedes.

Alrigo Lapaglia and two other men burst through the door seconds before Trent and Halli rounded the corner of the closest building. She slowed up, but Trent pulled her forward. "They're right on our tail, sweetheart, don't quit on me now."

"Where are we going?"

"Anywhere but here."

Trent took every turn he could, dodging people and vehicles. Twice they narrowly avoided being hit when he glanced behind to see how close their pursuers were.

"You watch where we're going," Halli yelled over the ear-splitting screech of tires and blare of the horn after she slammed into his back the second time. "I'll watch them!"

Working together, they made their way through town. His lungs began to ache, his legs burned, and he could only imagine how she felt, with him yanking on her arm for the last five minutes.

"I think we've lost them," she panted a minute later.

Trent eased up, glancing behind to reassure himself they were safe. The immediate area behind them settled back into a walk after their headlong dash, but a block and a half away, the man in the black leather jacket barreled around a corner and through the crowd in their direction.

Renewed adrenaline surged through his body as he urged Halli back into a dead run. Just before they took another turn, Trent checked their progress. He caught sight of a large white truck in the intersection a block away. It slammed on its brakes, but not in time to avoid hitting Lapaglia. His body flew a good ten feet into the intersection. The scream of an onlooker echoed down the street.

Trent felt no remorse for the man who'd killed his friend and didn't wait to see if he got back up, either. He took the opportunity to duck into a shop. Halli gave a small squeak of surprise at the abrupt move, then abruptly clamped her mouth shut.

They both fought to catch their breath as she stood close, pressed against his side while he surveyed the place. It was a gift shop, full of that over-priced souvenir knick-knack stuff tourists loved. Small plastic replicas of the surrounding mountains of Lago di Como, various cathedrals, and of course the unmistakable Leaning Tower of Pisa, cluttered a shelf directly in front of them; kept company by a row of key chains and Italy collector spoons.

Trent propelled Halli in front of him, steering her around the displays to get away from the windows. Along the way, he snagged a brown sweatshirt off a rack and tossed it over Halli's shoulder so he could dig out some cash.

His empty back pocket reminded him he'd never grabbed his wallet when he chased after Halli earlier. Just as quick, he recalled stuffing change in his pocket this morning at the espresso shop and pulled out a handful of Euros. For the first time he was thankful for the annoying coins he always felt should be bills.

Halli frowned at the sweatshirt. "What's this for?"

He leaned down close to her ear while transferring money into her hand. "Pay the girl over there and put the shirt on. Make sure you keep something between you and the window." Lapaglia may have been hit by a truck, but Trent didn't want to take any chances.

"Hey—find out if they have a back door," he whispered after her.

While she took care of the transaction, he stepped behind a mirrored column to remove his coveralls. He couldn't help watching Halli across the room. She looked small, even next to the petite Italian clerk. Especially now that she wore clothes that actually fit her slender frame.

His gaze lingered on the blue lettering stretched across the front of her tight shirt. What a shame she was going to cover up again. A corner of his mouth quirked up. Back at the house, he'd have bet money she wouldn't wear anything he'd left on the bed. He'd figured out Halliwell Sanders was a little uptight. And that was before he'd found the travel itinerary detailing her trip almost down to the minute.

Wet & Wild was a very nice surprise.

The shop girl leaned close to Halli. The two shared a smile, and the girl said something in heavily accented English. Halli laughed and shrugged. The sound, forced though it was, flowed over Trent's taut nerves, soothing even after it faded away. A genuine laugh from her would be something to enjoy.

Halli caught his eye and motioned toward the back with her head before pulling the new shirt on. Once she'd adjusted the oversized hem below her hips, her smile retreated, leaving worry in its wake. Trent scooped up the coveralls and his jacket and made sure the front window was clear before following.

Out in the alleyway, he tossed the coveralls into a dumpster. "What was so funny in there?"

She frowned up at him from underneath his baseball cap. "I'm playing a part, remember? There's nothing funny about any of this."

"Right."

He took the hat from her head with one hand and untied her ponytail with the other. Wispy brown strands settled down around her oval face. A ray of setting sunlight revealed reddish-blonde highlights that he hadn't noticed before she'd showered. The stunning color contrasted with the brown sweatshirt, making the garment appear even uglier. For just a moment, he had the urge to sift his fingers through her hair, to see if it was as soft as it looked.

Shaking off the strange feeling, he jammed his hat on his head. "Let's go."

He led her back in the direction they'd come, careful to retrace their steps, but at the same time, not use the same route. Most especially, he wanted to give the accident scene a wide berth.

After about a minute, she clutched his arm. "Why are you going this way?"

"I parked near the station."

"We can't go back there," she protested when he continued forward.

"We don't have much of a choice."

"But it's not safe!"

"*Now* you realize that."

She let go of his arm and stopped. Trent turned around to find her glaring at him, fists propped on her hips.

"Don't be a jerk again."

He crossed his arms over his chest and leaned back on one foot. "Listen, I don't like the thought of it either, but unfortunately, I've only got two vehicles. One's by the police station, and the other is in my garage, full of bullet holes. Which one would you rather take to Milan?"

She pressed her lips into a thin line and stalked past him. Trent shook his head as he caught up. She still didn't trust him. After he'd saved her butt *twice* already. What the hell would it take?

About ten minutes later, he put a hand on her arm as they reached an intersection. "The station is down that way about two blocks. I'm parked on the other side a couple streets away, so we'll have to go around."

She remained silent, following his lead without resistance or comment. *Finally.* When he looked down and caught a look of exhaustion on her face, he was reminded of the fact that she wouldn't have had any sleep since landing in the country.

A twinge of sympathy increased his step. The poor girl still had a long night ahead of her once she reached the consulate. And God knew she had to be worried sick about her brother and sister.

He breathed a sigh of relief at the sight of his car a few minutes later. "This is it," he said as he dug his keys from his pocket.

She slumped against the passenger side of the Mercedes while he unlocked the door and opened it for her. She straightened, then stepped back with a soft gasp, staring over his shoulder. A quick glance located the reason for her alarm and gave him his own jolt.

Three intersections away, a police car turned onto their street and slowly drove toward them. They had no time to run. Nowhere to hide.

Trent stepped closer to Halli, grasped both her arms and hauled her against him. He brought his mouth down on hers, betting the cop would ignore a passionate kiss and keep on driving. A hell of a gamble, but their only option.

Wide blue eyes staring into his, Halli made a sound of protest deep in her throat. She fought against his tight embrace, but Trent knew it had to look authentic. He moved his lips over hers, trying to communicate his intentions with his eyes. If she'd just relax—

Her foot jammed into his shin.

"*Stop* it."

"Let me go!"

"Just kiss me."

"No way—"

"*Kiss me* before I get arrested for assault," he growled against her mouth. "Or have you forgotten about the damn cops?"

She stopped struggling and her eyes closed. Finally, the little idiot had figured it out.

Trent felt her body relax by degrees, enough that he loosened his arms and rubbed his hands over her back for full visual effect. Her head tilted a little to the right. Her lips softened. Her arms stole up around his neck.

Going into the kiss, he had every intention of keeping it an act. No tongue, all show. Keep his eyes open and once the cop passed, they'd be on their way. But her lips parted ever so slightly with a soft little sigh, and details began to register in his adrenaline-high brain. Her curves molded along his body, soft breasts crushed to his chest, slim hips snug against his.

His peripheral vision recorded the police vehicle gliding by. The officer didn't even give them a second glance. When the car continued down the street and turned a corner, relief tightened his arms around Halli.

God, her lips were so soft. He closed his eyes, savoring the sensation of a lipstick-free kiss. Compared to the women he usually dated, it was a rare, welcome treat. She smelled great, too, after her shower; all fresh with a hint of flowers. No cloying perfume to choke his lungs.

One hand slid up to cup the back of her head, and he discovered her hair was indeed as soft as it looked. He ran the tip of his tongue along her lower lip as a test, uncharacteristically cautious with this mistrusting woman who'd resisted him at every turn. Something else he wasn't accustomed to. Because, as she'd guessed, often all it took was a crook of his finger. A wink. A smile.

Her hold around his neck tightened, pulling him closer as she opened to him without reservation. Trent forgot the cop; forgot their dire situation; forgot that earlier he'd claimed she wasn't his type. He deepened the kiss, pushing his tongue inside her mouth. His taste buds registered a hint of espresso, but underneath, she was sweeter than he'd have imagined. Her tongue slid against his, advancing and retreating, teasing and seducing until his body responded to the rising passion.

Trent spun to lean back against his car, pulling Halli with him. A groan rumbled in his chest. He slid both hands down her back and kept going until her butt filled his palms. Perfect. One swift move lifted her to ride his thigh. Desire pulsed harder and faster. His arms closed around her, pressing her body tight to his. It'd been forever since he'd enjoyed the simple act of kissing so much.

Directly following that thought he became aware of the fact she no longer clung tight to his shoulders. In fact, she'd stopped participating altogether. He was kissing her now, just like at the beginning, but add tongue and minus the resistance. Before he could do more than withdraw his tongue, Halli spoke against his tingling lips.

"Is he gone?"

Trent opened his eyes to find her watching him, her expression calm, cool and collected. Heat flooded his face. He looked in the direction the cop had disappeared and practically dropped her as he straightened.

"Yeah." He cleared his throat and put some space between them. "He's gone."

She smoothed her hair back from her face and squared her shoulders. "Then let's go."

Let's go? That's it?

What the hell just happened?

His gaze narrowed on her face in the dim light of dusk, hoping to see some sort of crack in her stony expression. All she did was bend down and pick up his hat. He snatched it from her grasp and tugged it low over his eyes, further annoyed by the heat creeping up the back of his neck again. *Damn.* How did she remain so cool when hot little flames of desire still licked through his veins from the feel and taste of her?

Trent stalked around to the driver's side of the car as she got in on her side. Hands folded neatly in her lap, she appeared completely unaffected. He bit back a growl. *This* rigid woman was the one who'd typed up that military precision travel itinerary. He'd chuckled when he first read it back at the house. Right now, it wasn't so funny. His knuckles whitened on the wheel in his effort to keep from reaching over to shake her. Something to ruffle her feathers good.

Apparently, it took bullets to do that. He clenched his jaw tight and shifted the car into gear.

Halli thought her lungs would burst from trying to maintain a normal breathing rhythm. She'd freaked when he first kissed her. It'd been awhile, and he was *Trent Tomlin!* Then he'd explained why his mouth was locked on hers, and she'd been embarrassed beyond belief. *Of course* he wouldn't *want* to kiss her. It'd only been an act.

She'd done her best to distance herself from anything her parents had taught her growing up, only to discover in the police station that acting was like riding a bike. Guess you never forget how and a little bit of back story can make it so easy to jump back in with both feet.

She'd jumped alright. Put on a heck of a show for the cop, too, kissing Trent for all she was worth. And oh, God, it'd been nice. *Really* nice. She'd even felt the change in his kiss—kinda hard to ignore the evidence when he'd palmed her butt and ground against her.

For one glorious, mind-numbing moment she was thrilled that she, of all people, could elicit such a response from one of the sexiest men on the planet. But, ingrained from the experiences of her youth was the hard-learned truth that reality was never very far away, and it was better to be prepared than to be blindsided.

Reality was Trent was an international superstar while she was a nobody public television producer from small town Wisconsin. He'd been playing hero all day and was used to women falling at his feet. But no way was she going to be Trent Tomlin's convenient plaything.

No matter how amazing his kiss. No matter how hot his muscled body made her burn. No matter how much his sexy groans of arousal urged her to lend some truth to the T-shirt she wore underneath the hideous brown sweatshirt.

Did it count that she was already halfway there? The second part of *Wet & Wild* would have to wait—*if* the day ever came that she decided to let loose and get a little wild.

Trent drove and Halli stared out the window, determined to ignore the unsettling sensations in her body and focus on their serious situation. That's probably why she'd reacted to his kiss so strongly in the first place. Her senses were super-charged from the last six hours.

Wow. Had it only been six hours ago that she'd met him? Six hours since she'd last seen Ben and Rachel?

And just like that, guilt reared up and smacked her across the face. In the heat of the moment, she'd completely forgotten about them. *Real nice, Halli.*

Trent's comment at the station came back to her, and she worried anew why her family hadn't checked into the hotel.

Maybe they had by now? Maybe once she got to the consulate she'd be able to—

A blue sign whizzed by on her side of the car. Halli sat up straight in her seat and whipped around to stare behind them. "Hey! That sign said *Milano*." She faced forward again. There! Another sign, and an arrow, but Trent was in the wrong lane. She pointed to the sign.

"You need to turn...there."

Disbelief exploded as he drove right past without slowing down. He didn't even glance in her direction, only into the review mirror, then back to the road. *What's he doing?*

"You promised you'd take me to Milan."

"And I will."

"I want to go now." When he didn't respond, she demanded, "Turn around. Right now."

"God, you're bossy," he grumbled.

A red haze blurred her vision. "I mean it!" She hauled off and smacked his arm in impotent frustration.

"*Ow*." He hunched his shoulder and tossed her a glare.

"We had a deal! You promised, you lying, egotistical, conceited jerk!"

Without warning, Trent swung the wheel hard to the right. Halli gave a squeak of alarm as she slammed against his shoulder. Once on a side road, he stomped on the brakes and the vehicle slid to a screeching halt.

She pushed back into her own seat, only to have him lean over and glower in her face.

"At some point in our cozy little relationship here, you're going to have to trust that I know what the hell I'm doing. Otherwise, it's going to get real tempting to leave your ass on the side of the road."

His low tone and precise speech suggested he had a tight rein on his control. Though she was past the point that she thought he'd hurt her or follow through on his threat, it didn't mean she was any less intimidated. Not that she'd let him know that.

She lifted her chin, hoping her glare covered any outward signs of anxiety. "If I'm such a *'pain in the ass'*, why didn't you just leave me at the police station? You already have your precious video."

He stared into her eyes for one more second, then sat back in his seat and stepped on the gas. "Because I need you, sweetheart. It's as simple as that."

Reality bit hard, no matter how much she thought she'd prepared for it. He wasn't helping her because he was nice or even because he liked her. Only because needed her. Halli swallowed a surge of unexpected, and totally unwelcome, hurt feelings and faced the other reality. Like it or not, she needed him, too.

She shifted in her seat and crossed her arms across her chest. "Where are we going?"

"Back to my place."

She opened her mouth to ask why, but he beat her to it.

"To get the video. I also still have your passport and money, *and* I need my wallet. I didn't exactly have time to pack a bag when I saw you hightailing it across the yard."

To avoid any more of his sarcasm, she retreated to silent mode the remainder of the drive. And since they were going back to his house, she decided she'd drop his wallet back where she'd found it. No sense admitting to the jerk that she'd stolen it in the first place. Her twinge of irrational guilt over the money she'd 'borrowed' would go away when she tucked a twenty somewhere after he'd returned her travel purse.

Fifteen minutes later, inside his garage again, the scene played out much differently than before. Halli couldn't help but remember the feel of his body when he'd pressed her against the door. And when he'd kissed her by the car. In both instances, she'd learned first hand the man had the muscles to back up every shirtless photo spread he'd ever done.

Banishing the multiple, vivid images of those photos from her mind, she followed him into the house and watched as he reactivated the alarm.

"How'd you get the code?" he asked on his way to the kitchen.

"You keyed it in right in front of me while holding me hostage, remember?"

He reached into the refrigerator, then shut the door and tossed her a bottle of water before twisting the cap off one for himself. He mock-toasted her. "Lesson learned for next time."

The sight of him lifting the bottle to his lips and drinking three quarters of the liquid in a few deep swallows shouldn't have been sexy, but darn it, she got hot watching him.

Halli quickly turned away. "Year you were born, right?"

"How'd you know?"

"It's only four years before mine, so it's not like I'd have to be a genius to figure it out." She couldn't help but face him again with a condescending smile. "You should never use your birth date for a password."

"I'll keep that in mind," he said dryly. "For now, I'll leave it, in case you need to use it for any reason."

She mock toasted him before ambling toward the living room while taking a drink of her water. If she could get to the bar before him, she'd replace the wallet and he'd be none the wiser. "I'll be gone once you get my passport and drive me to Milan," she reminded over her shoulder. "Completely out of your hair."

"Looking forward to it."

Halli startled at the sound of his voice right behind her. When he brushed past, her jaw clenched. Holding back a growl of frustration, she stared at his back as he headed for the bar. Now how was she going to pull this off without him seeing her?

"However," he continued, "I think we should…"

What she needed was a plausible distraction—

Trent spun and lunged toward her. *"Get down!"*

Chapter 6

Halli dropped to all fours behind a chair, her heart lodged in her throat. Her bottle of water rolled across the hardwood floor, gurgling a wet trail. "Wh-what's the matter?"

"*Shh.*"

Trent pressed close, arm half around her as he moved into a crouched position and rose up slightly to peer above the armrest.

Fear sunk its talons in deep. "Oh my God, did they find us?"

His razor sharp gaze swept the living room and moved to the windows. "I don't know, but someone's been in the house," he whispered. "They might still be here."

"How do you know?" Her heart thumped wildly despite the heat of his body next to hers.

"My wallet's gone. I left it on the bar earlier."

Halli went limp with relief beside him. Tingles spread through her body with the retreat of adrenaline. "It's right here." Without thinking twice, she shifted away for more room and lifted the hem of her sweatshirt to fish his wallet from her front pocket. "God, you scared me half to death."

He glanced down at her hand, then did a double take. "What the hell?"

She started to hand it over, but he stripped it from her fingers in a swift motion. When he flipped it open, she pushed to her feet, scooped up her mostly empty water, and tried to make light of the theft. "I owe you twenty bucks."

He stood as well, still taking stock of the contents of his wallet. "And you talk about *me* with your nose stuck in the air." Finally, he shut it and slid it into his back pocket. "At least I haven't lied or stolen from you."

Halli followed him into the kitchen, guilt overridden by indignation. "Whoa, hold on. You've got my passport and all my money, but now *I'm* the bad guy for taking your wallet?"

"You gave them to me. Threw them at me, remember? I didn't *steal* anything from you." He opened a drawer, withdrew her things, including the camera, and thumped them on the counter.

"Before you get up on your righteous high horse, let's take a look at this from my point of view," Halli challenged. "I was just sitting there minding my own business when you showed up. After your cheesy pick-up lines didn't work, you threw me into your car—"

"Cheesy pick-up lines? They were shooting at you! Would you rather I'd left you there?"

"*My* point of view, remember?" She slammed her water bottle hard on the countertop, surprising even herself with her vehemence. Water splashed from the open top, all over her hand, arm, and the countertop.

He crossed his arms over his chest and leaned a hip against the counter, a look of annoyed resignation tightening his features.

The itch on her palm would go away if she smacked his handsome face right now. She was sure of it.

Resisting the temptation, she clenched her fingers, short nails digging into her skin as she tried a different approach. "You may be used to crazy things like this, but back in Wisconsin, I have a set schedule that I'm comfortable with. I work, I exercise, and at the end of the day, I relax in my garden or by reading a book. The last thing I expected after only a couple hours in a foreign country was to be stranded, kidnapped and shot at. On top of all that, *you* refused to go to the police and forced me into your house. Believe me, I don't make a habit of stealing from people, but I'm just a little out of my element here," she lifted her trembling hand, thumb and forefinger about an inch apart, "so excuse me for not quite being myself."

He snorted. "This version of yourself sounds a hell of a lot more interesting than your regular self."

She scowled at his rude comment.

"I'm curious about one thing, though."

His casual, conversational tone raised her suspicion. "What?"

"When did you plan to go to the bathroom during your trip?" He shoved her purse across the counter. "I didn't see any potty breaks scheduled on that itinerary of yours."

Halli snatched up her purse, annoyed that he'd gone through her things. He sounded like Ben, making fun of her plans. Ironically, if they'd stuck to *her* plans, she wouldn't be in this mess right now, dealing with the likes of him.

"So what if I like a little order in my life?" she muttered defensively.

"You call that *order*? Try obsessive. Or anal. Or—"

"Or shut up."

He smiled, but his expression quickly sobered. "Listen, I understand it's been one hell of a day for you. Despite what you may think, this is far from normal for me, too. But like it or not, you stepped into something very serious. After everything that's happened today, these guys won't care what you've actually got on that video anymore. They'll kill first, and watch it later. I—"

"Thank you, because I needed *that* reminder. This Alrigo guy wants me dead and I don't even know who he is!" She spun away from Trent, tears stinging her eyes from his dire prediction. "I can't believe I came to Italy and got mixed up with the mafia."

A moment later his hands slid onto her shoulders, sending her into the air about three inches.

His fingers tightened before rubbing her tense muscles. "They're not mafia."

"Then who are they?" Tingles radiated along her shoulders from his gentle massage.

"The less you know, the better. It's safer that way."

She rolled her eyes even though her back was to him. "How do you know?"

Suddenly, she felt like she'd been smacked upside the head and twisted away from his hands to face him. She narrowed her gaze. "How *do* you know? About the video, what I filmed, who these guys are? What were *you* doing there?"

He didn't want to tell her, she could see it in his face. She crossed her arms and waited, trying to ignore a growing dread turning her blood colder by the second. Why hadn't she asked these questions earlier?

He ran a hand through his hair, down the back of his head to rub his neck.

She forced the next question into the silence. "Are you working with them?"

"No." His gaze shifted toward the living room.

Suspicion mushroomed and Halli swallowed hard. "That was a quick denial."

"It's the truth."

She watched an inner debate play out in his expression as he stared past her shoulder. Pain shadowed his eyes and drew the corners of his mouth down. Just when she thought he'd explain what was going on, he lifted his arm to look at his watch.

"I've got to get that battery before the shops close for the night."

What was it he didn't want her to know? Her mind raced. He had to be involved; how else would he know about everything?

Trent grabbed his keys and the camera from the counter and headed toward the door. "I'll be back in a little while."

Her stomach knotted, shoving aside suspicion. Despite what she'd just been thinking, the thought of being by herself was scarier than any conspiracy she could dream up right now.

She rushed after him. "You're not leaving me here."

Trent paused, his attention focused on the sudden death grip she had on his arm. "I can't take you with me, what if we run into more cops? One of them might recognize you."

"I'll duck down in my seat." She fought a lump of fear rising in her throat. "Please, Trent, don't leave me alone."

He rested both hands on her shoulders, his gaze locked with hers. "No one knows of my part in any of this. You're safe here. Take a little nap, and I promise I'll be back as soon as I can."

"Why can't we just pick up a battery on the way to Milan?"

His thumbs rubbed up and down her neck in a light, comforting caress.

"Halli, you're exhausted; I can see it in your face. Things

won't magically be over once you're at the consulate. You need to get some sleep."

"I won't be able to sleep." She thought of how she'd almost passed out at the police station, but at that point, she'd considered herself safe. Now he was going to leave her alone after multiple reminders that the bad guys were still out there, guns at the ready. Shoot first, ask questions later.

"You're safe. Fix yourself something to eat and just close your eyes to rest," he suggested.

Mutely, she shook her head, imploring him with her eyes to take her along. He keyed in the security code and gently but firmly pushed her away.

"Make me something, too, would you? I'm starving."

Without waiting for an answer, Trent stepped into the garage and shut the door between them. Halli reached for the handle, then pulled back and swung around to face the kitchen. With one arm hugging her stomach, she pressed her other hand hard against her lips to still the tremble in her fingers. Both hands clenched into fists as she fought the emotions trying to turn her into a helpless puddle of terror.

All she needed to do was think things through calmly, rationally. He'd be back soon and they'd leave for Milan. At the consulate she'd get the help she needed and—

Her gaze swept the room for a phone. There! On the far wall. She could call Ben! Her fingers shook as she dialed his cell phone number.

Answer the phone, Ben. Please, answer.

By the eighth ring it switched to voice mail. Thank God it wasn't the Italian recording like earlier when Trent had informed her cell service around the lake could be spotty after she'd gotten her hopes up. At the sound of her brother's voice, she dissolved into tears, left a somewhat hysterical message asking why and where they were, but when her words came out garbled beyond recognition, she hung up mid-sentence.

Determination made her reign her emotions back under control and the second message was a bit more successful; she apologized for the blubbering, told him she was okay, and she'd try the hotel.

The front desk of the Grand Hotel confirmed Trent's claim that no Sanders had registered yet. Halli hung up, new worry gnawing at her gut.

Why haven't they checked into the hotel by now? When they came back and didn't find me, the next logical step would be to check in at the hotel and wait for me there. They had to come back to look for me, so where are they now?

She redialed the hotel and left a message for Ben in case they showed up later. Then she called his cell phone, forced herself to remain calm as she waited for the voicemail to kick in, and left a third message.

"Me again. Not sure where you guys are or what's going on, but I'm okay." She laughed, knowing Ben would when he listened. "Yeah, I know, not so believable after the last two messages...but *really*, I'm fine, so don't worry about me. I'm going to the Consulate General in Milan. It's like an embassy. Meet me there in the morning by ten. I'll wait out front for you."

She hung up the phone and slumped into a nearby chair, relieved to have a solid plan in place once more. Ben and Rachel would meet her in Milan and everything would be okay.

Energy drained from her like she'd pulled the plug in a tub. God, Trent was right, she was exhausted. Her stomach growled, reminding her she hadn't eaten since arriving in the country.

He had plenty to eat in his refrigerator, but in the end it was easiest to just warm a can of Spaghetti O's. At last, *something* familiar.

As she ate, she thought about Trent's hesitation when she'd questioned his part in the situation. And he'd swiped her camera on the way out, taking with him the only tangible evidence she had of this entire unbelievable day.

After he'd refused to explain his involvement.

"I need you, sweetheart, it's as simple as that."

Why did he need her if he had the video? What use was she to him? None of it made sense.

The canned pasta in her stomach churned, and what was left in her bowl lost its already limited appeal. She returned to the kitchen, dumped her leftovers in the garbage and deposited her dishes in the sink. Leaning back against the counter, she gripped the edge so hard numbing tingles shot through her fingers.

How is he involved in this whole thing?

Impulse propelled her to the drawer where he'd stashed her purse and camera. A quick rummage revealed nothing of significance and she slammed it shut before moving on to another one.

Halli worked her way through the house, not quite knowing what she was looking for, but somehow the systematic progression of her hasty search kept her in a semi-state of calm. Taking action instead of letting things happen gave her a tiny sense of much-coveted control.

One of the bedrooms smelled odd. A combination of fresh paint and the scent of new carpeting mingled in the stale air, suggesting it'd been closed up for awhile. All the drawers and closets were empty save one. When she saw men's clothes along with boxes of cameras and film equipment, something clicked in her mind. Trent's brother had been a documentary film maker, just like their father, Greg Tomlin.

Her gaze scanned the room again, this time comprehending the fresh paint and new carpeting. Of course. This must have been where he'd died. The furnishings looked new. As if they'd been hastily replaced, instead of someone taking the time to find antique pieces like in the guestroom she'd used earlier.

The hairs on the back of her neck pricked and a chill raced down her spine. Backing up, she rushed from the room and slammed the door, unable to stomach the thought of Sean Tomlin's lifeless body on the bed as the newspapers had reported.

In the hall, as she leaned against the wall to take a couple of deep breaths, her gaze focused on the door at the end, the room she'd heard Trent in earlier when she'd made her escape. A likely place to store things he wanted kept private. Heart still pounding wildly, she hurried across the carpet and twisted the door handle.

There was no doubt it was Trent's room. One hundred percent *male* was stamped on the heavy, walnut furniture of the four poster king bed, two dressers, a desk and a black leather chair. On the walls, stark black and white outdoor photos complimented the dark bedding and drapes. The pictures reminded her of Ansel Adams and she wouldn't be surprised if they were originals.

She made it halfway across the room before a part of her balked at violating Trent's personal privacy. Then she thought of him ransacking her purse and quickly forgot her hesitation. She started with his dresser drawers, but the only thing of interest she found there were designer boxer briefs and a box of extra-large condoms.

Lovely. Just what she wanted to know.

Mentally blocking the memory of their earlier kiss and the feel of his hard body, she headed for the desk. In the third drawer, she hit pay dirt. Buried on the bottom, a leather bound notebook sat atop a thick stack of newspaper articles. Articles about Sean Tomlin's suicide. Thumbing through them, she saw a couple she'd read back in the States. She'd been as shocked and saddened as much of the world, especially since it'd never been made public until his death that Trent's brother had fought a battle with depression most of his adult life.

Though not as renowned as their legendary father, Sean Tomlin's last two documentaries had garnered rave reviews from critics and audiences alike. Through her job in public television, Halli had watched and respected his work even before he grew in popularity. He'd been a rising star, unafraid to tackle subjects others shied away from. The world had lost something special when he died.

She set aside the clippings from the US publications and the local Italian newspapers, and opened the leather bound book. Inside were pages of notes printed in bold handwriting that matched the note she'd found on the bed after her shower. The first couple pages seemed to be random thoughts jotted down as they'd come to his mind, though after a page, she began to see a pattern.

Paper crinkled in the silent room as she turned the next page, unable to keep herself from reading. She had to skip a section of blank pages before she found what looked like journal entries. They weren't dated, but it became very clear they'd been started only a few days after his brother's death.

Halli backed up and sat on the bed, her eyes devouring the less concise, more...*passionate* handwriting. His words were at turns angry and anguished; at himself, his brother, and his father. The ink was dark, the indents for each letter grooved deep into the paper as if the hand writing them had pressed hard.

More than once, tears welled in her eyes as she read the emotion he'd poured onto paper. This part of his personality was so opposite the playboy image he presented to the public she could hardly believe it was the same person. He'd laid his soul bare in these pages, and suddenly it was too personal.

She reached up with both hands to wipe her wet cheeks before flipping past his journal entries and paging through the rest of the notebook. A page toward the back snagged her attention with a glimpse of organization and she hurriedly located it again. A detailed outline began at the top of one page and continued for a few more pages. An outline of events leading up to and after Sean's death.

It didn't take long before Trent Tomlin's involvement in this crazy situation became crystal clear.

"I refuse to let them kill you like they did my brother and Lorenzo," he'd told her.

He didn't believe his brother had committed suicide. He was investigating his brother's *murder*.

Chapter 7

Alrigo Lapaglia limped into his lakeside villa, rage simmering in his blood with each stabbing breath he took. Twice the bitch had gotten away. The car chase had caused one hell of a stir with no results. He'd lucked out when his inside guy Stefano called from the Torno police station with the news that a lost American tourist by the name of Halliwell Sanders had turned up at their doorstep. But no more had he had her in his sights, she'd escaped again.

With help.

And he'd gotten hit by a fucking truck.

He was done playing nice. Mariucci and Casale had unsuccessfully questioned the two Americans they'd picked up about who they knew here in town. Apparently, extracting the necessary information would require a professional. The fact that the Halliwell girl had given some story about taking the wrong bus revealed she knew more than she should.

He didn't care that the bullshit story actually helped him, all he wanted was her and the video, and then she could be taken care of for good.

Alrigo stopped at the door to his office, where his right-hand man sat at his desk. "Where's Eva?"

Nino Da Via looked up from his laptop and removed a set of black framed glasses as he sat back in Alrigo's leather executive chair. Placing thumb and forefinger into his mouth, he blew a piercing whistle.

Annoyance and impatience alternately nipped at Alrigo's heels as he made his way across the room and poured a generous amount of *grappa* into a tumbler.

"What's the verdict?" Nino folded his hands across his stomach. "You gonna live?"

Alrigo's gaze narrowed, not fooled by his partner's casual pose or tone. He'd banged up his knee and busted two ribs, but didn't plan to announce the injuries and invite ideas from the more ambitious men in his employ.

Nino's glance dropped from the ten stitches along his hairline to his knee and Alrigo instinctively straightened. It hurt like the devil without the brace the doc had given him, but now he wished he'd fought the pain more to conceal his limp when he'd entered.

He forced a smile, lifting his glass as he answered the question. "For many long and prosperous years, my friend. I see you got the window fixed already."

Nino's nod was as efficient as his actions.

"And the body?"

"I'll take care of it tonight."

Alrigo glared out the newly installed window. He never should've plugged the bastard, but it really annoyed him that the man thought he'd be fooled by such a flimsy cover. As if he was stupid enough to do business with an unknown buyer who was clearly not who he claimed. Yes, Nino would dispose of the body, but the added complication of the man he'd shot being a retired *agente* of the *Polizia di Stato* pissed him off as much as the woman who'd caught the act on video.

Add it all to that damn punk American filmmaker a few months ago and the heat level was rising fast. It wouldn't take long for the cost of keeping his numerous connections loyal to follow suit. His profit margins would shrink. His luxuriant tropical retirement would have to be delayed. Again.

When he closed his eyes, the dark neighborhood of his childhood closed in on his mind. He smelled the rank odor of rotting garbage and heard the rats scurrying around in the dank streets. Suppressing a shudder, he made his daily vow never to go back.

A small amount of alcohol warmed his throat and settled in his gut as he reopened his eyes and contemplated the shimmering water of Lago de Como. Iron control kept his hand from tipping the glass and downing the clear liquid in one furious gulp. He'd painstakingly rebuilt his network and fortune after Frank Gallo destroyed the foundation six years ago. So close now he could taste it, no way in hell some *bastardo Americanos* were going to fuck him over.

His jaw tightened with grim determination. Someone was going to have to pay, and this time it wasn't going to be him. He poured a second glass and handed it to Nino. "Any word on the shipment?"

Before Nino could answer, the door on the opposite side of the room flew open and a small Italian tornado with waist-length brown hair blew in.

"I told you to quit that god-awful whistling! It's Eva. Go ahead, give it a try."

Nino downed his drink, then leaned back in his chair, hands linked behind his dark head as he propped his feet up on the desk. "I can't shout *Eva* through the house."

"I refuse to answer to that whistle again."

"You said that yesterday, *tesoro*."

"This time I mean it," she snapped. "I'm tired of you treating me like—"

Careful to keep his hunger hidden as they argued, Alrigo discreetly slid his gaze along the curvaceous profile of Eva Anelli in her cleavage baring top, skin tight pants, and stilettos. He'd wanted her body since the moment he'd struck his partnership with Nino a year ago and she'd strutted in on his arm wearing a red pair of those heels.

But for all that he trusted Nino with, the man harbored a possessive violent streak that ensured Alrigo kept his distance. If he knew Alrigo lusted after his woman, he'd slit his throat—partner or not. He looked forward to the day he no longer needed Nino's efficiency and Eva would be his. His groin instantly tightened with need.

"Make me something to eat, Eva," Alrigo ordered abruptly before turning to limp back to the hallway. "I'll be in my room after I talk to the Americans."

A sound of outrage erupted behind him. "Make your own—"

"Eva."

The soft warning made Alrigo glance back over his shoulder. Nino was shaking his head at the spitfire. Eva glared at Nino before spinning on one of those sexy heels and storming back to the kitchen. Nino watched her go with the same desire in his gaze that seared Alrigo. The woman must be hell in bed.

Alrigo funneled the heat of unattainable lust into anger and continued to the room where they held the two Americans. After his knock, the door opened and Zucchi stood aside for him to enter. He motioned the guard from the room, then closed the door again and leaned back, arms crossed, carefully.

The girl, Rachel, pushed up to a sitting position on the bed where she'd been laying. Her gaze darted toward her brother by a small table. When Alrigo had walked in, the man's foot had been bouncing in nervous agitation. Now he sat tall and rigid, completely still.

Alrigo transferred his gaze back to the girl. Her expression left no doubt she was terrified. *Bene*. He'd use her if the need arose.

Alrigo took a shallow breath to avoid the stabbing pain of his broken ribs. He inclined his head politely. "Mr. Sanders, Ms. Sanders...or Benjamin and Rachel, if I may." His thick accent coated the English words.

The blond man sat up straighter and faced him. "Do we have a choice, Mr...?"

He debated the pointed question. *Eh*, he decided with a dispassionate shrug. In the end, it mattered not if they knew his name. "Lapaglia. Alrigo Lapaglia. And no, you have no choice."

"Didn't think so."

"The thing is, Benjamin, I am not pleased with your lies."

Ben studied the man who'd held him and Rachel at gunpoint in the car, noting his built physique, square jaw, tense mouth and most especially, his eyes. An unnerving glitter in their steel-colored depths belied the composed exterior the man portrayed. Something to do with the fresh set of stitches zippered high on his forehead?

Because he had no idea what lies the man spoke of, and since he seemed to be waiting for a reply, Ben asked, "What did I lie about?"

"Halliwell has someone helping her."

"We don't know anyone here," Rachel exclaimed from the bed.

"I am not speaking to you," the man stated without shifting his attention away from Ben. "If we are to have a mutually beneficial relationship, I will require your complete honesty."

Ben looked around the room that'd served as their prison for the past eight hours and couldn't help but ask, "Exactly how do we benefit in this situation?"

"I receive what I want from your troublesome sibling, and you all will be allowed to live."

The calm, matter-of-fact delivery doubled the impact of the man's words.

Alrigo Lapaglia straightened from the door, hands lowering to his sides. "Who is helping Halliwell?"

"I don't know—"

In the blink of an eye, the man pulled a gun from the back waistband of his jeans and pointed it at Rachel. Ben shot to his feet as his sister's scream vibrated through the room.

Cold, soulless eyes bored into Ben's.

"Figure it out, fast."

Ben held his hands up, palms out. "I swear, if someone's helping her, it's no one we know." He stepped closer to Rachel. "Please, don't. We don't know anyone in the area, not even in the entire country."

In a breath of silence came the sound of a soft electronic hum. *Shit.* His phone. He'd hid it in his boot while in the backseat of the car and thought he'd also managed to turn it off. His restless tick must've turned it back on and now he had messages. Probably from Halli.

Ben pretended he didn't hear the phone. "Listen, if we can help, we'll help. Just tell us what—"

"Shut up."

The gun swung in his direction as Alrigo stepped forward. Ben did his best to keep a blank expression while resisting the instinct to duck from danger.

"What was that?" Alrigo demanded.

"What?"

Lips thinned and curved in what the guy probably meant as a smile. "Pissing me off is not good for your health."

Acting stupid wasn't working, so Ben went for the bluff.

"It sounded like your cell phone or something."

"At this precise moment, I am not carrying a cell phone."

Heat crept up Ben's neck and slowly made its way to his face. Alrigo stared so hard Ben thought he'd bore holes through his head.

"Need I remind you, Benjamin, benefits require honesty." Anger created an ominous undertone in the man's voice. Very softly, he added, "Rachel, come here."

Ben glanced at her, saw the terror in her face, and swallowed hard. Alrigo motioned with the gun. How long was it safe to carry the pretense? Was it worth the risk? They needed the phone if they had any hope of getting help.

The moment Rachel stood next to the bed, Alrigo's free hand shot out and fisted in her hair. Rachel's scream was cut short when he dragged her to stand in front of him and pressed the barrel of the gun to her neck.

"Okay! All right!" Ben yelled. He bent and dug the phone from his boot to hold it out in surrender.

Alrigo released Rachel's hair and took the phone without lowering the gun from Rachel's shoulder. The guy's skin was pale under the crimson flush of fury.

"Is there anything else?" His breath sounded a little raspy.

Rachel shook her head.

"No," Ben said.

Alrigo lifted the gun to Rachel's temple. "Swear to God?"

Tears streamed down her face and Ben felt his own eyes sting. "I swear," he choked past the lump of fear in his throat.

The Italian shoved Rachel forward and Ben reached for her as she stumbled. Her breath caught on a sob and she clung tight while he hugged her close, cheek pressed to her head as he watched the monster flip open his phone.

Somehow, he had to keep both his sisters safe. He gave Rachel a squeeze, empty reassurance for her as well as himself, before prying her fingers from his arms and shifting in front of her as a shield.

Alrigo lifted his gaze, his mouth curled in a malicious smile. "What do you know, three new voicemails."

It didn't take long for him to access the messages; Ben had

the number and password programmed into his phone. Surprisingly, the guy played them on speaker. First was a jumbled message from Halli in which she sounded twice as freaked as Ben felt.

He worried about her all alone. She'd never been able to handle the fly-by-the-seat-of-your-pants lifestyle their parents had raised them in. At times they hadn't known where the next meal would come from, where they'd sleep, or if the cops would catch up to them. At the first opportunity, Halli set down roots and hadn't changed a thing in her neatly scheduled life, until this trip. She hadn't even visited their parents in prison once over the past nine years.

Halli's message cut off abruptly and Alrigo moved on to the next one. Halli again, her voice slightly calmer as she told Ben she'd try the hotel. Ben felt a brief flare of relief, until he realized she'd call and find out they never showed up. Then what would she do?

He found out with the third message.

"Me again. Not sure where you guys are or what's going on, but I'm okay."

Halli's laugh filled the room for an all too brief moment.

"Yeah, I know, not so believable after the last two messages...but really, *I'm fine, so don't worry about me. I'm going to the Consulate General in Milan. It's like an embassy. Meet me there in the morning by ten. I'll wait out front for you."*

Her decisive, though somewhat shaky, words surprised him. *Go Halli*. Then the triumphant smile on Alrigo's face turned his brotherly pride to something far less welcoming. Halli's message told them exactly where and when to find her. Hoping to figure out a little more of what the hell was going on, he held Rachel back with one hand and stepped closer to Alrigo.

"What does she have that you want? Maybe if you let me call her—"

The hand with the gun shot out and connected with Ben's jaw before he could finish his sentence. Stars exploded on the edge of his vision. Rachel's cry echoed in his ear as he stumbled back a step. She supported him from behind until his balance returned.

Ben gulped back the lump in his throat, warily watching Alrigo suck in a harsh breath, his skin paler than before. When a cough made the man's features twist in pain, Ben knew he was injured more severely than just the stitched gash on his head. Could he use the knowledge to their advantage?

No more had the thought formed in Ben's mind than Alrigo straightened, his jaw clenched tight as he met Ben's gaze. "Do not give me a reason to decide I only need one of you. Your sister is much less trouble than you."

The initial sharp pain of the blow to his jaw receded, replaced by a steady aching throb of discomfort. A trickle worked its way down the side of his mouth and the metallic taste on his tongue confirmed blood. Ben wiped his lip with the back of his hand, but remained silent with Rachel at his back clutching his shoulder.

"*Zucchi!*" the Italian boomed.

The door opened and the man who'd been guarding them stepped back inside. Ben didn't like the stocky little minion any more than he did the ring leader, and he really hated the way the weasel's slimy gaze roved over his sister.

Without warning, Alrigo backhanded the man across the face, then shoved Ben's phone under his bleeding nose. Ben didn't have to know Italian to guess the goon was getting reamed out.

Zucchi looked confused, but he nodded, apparently unwilling to question the boss with a gun in his hand.

Alrigo Lapaglia spoke again, gesturing toward Ben and Rachel. He finished with, "*Capito?*"

Zucchi's "*Si,*" was lost as Alrigo slammed from the room.

Ben made a mental note of Alrigo's limp as he left. If he could get past the man's gun so he didn't have to worry about Rachel, he could probably take the guy down. Then again, he'd still have to deal with Zucchi and Nino, and any other guy in the place. He'd noticed one more for sure on their way inside the villa.

"Are you okay?" Rachel asked softly, her hand lifting toward his face.

He jerked his head back and wiped his bloodied lip again, angry the bastard had caught him so off-guard. "Yeah, I'm fine."

She tugged his arm. After a quick glance toward their guard, who used his sleeve to wipe his nose, Ben faced her.

"What are we going to do?" she whispered.

"I don't know yet, but I'm looking for any chance I can to get us out."

"Halli sounded awful."

Ben gave a soft snort. "Believe it or not, after that last message, I think Halli is actually okay. At least, until *they* show up tomorrow morning in Milan instead of us."

And *if* they didn't find her tonight. But the distress in Rachel's expression told him he should've shut up before mentioning Milan, so he didn't tell her there was a very real possibility the officers who'd handed them over to Alrigo would trace Halli's call. All he could do was pray she'd borrowed a cell phone or used a public phone and then moved on.

"What do you think she has of theirs?" Rachel asked.

"I don't know, but it must be pretty darn important."

"*Basta!* No more talk," Zucchi ordered in barely decipherable English from his chair by the door.

Ben moved further back in the room to sit at the table again, his back to Zucchi this time, and Rachel took the seat opposite him. Speaking in his lowest tone possible, Ben murmured, "I could try to get info from him."

"You're the reason he got hit. I doubt he'll talk."

Ben grimaced.

Her body shifted slightly to the right, her gaze focusing past his shoulder. "Do you want me to try?"

"Absolutely not."

"But—"

"No."

She sat forward. "I can help."

"Rach, please, I know, but the less contact with these guys the better?"

Her gaze flitted over his shoulder again before meeting his.

"Yeah, okay."

"Okay."

Relief that he'd stood his ground was evident in the droop of her shoulders and softening of her lips. Which only served to heighten his tension.

How the hell am I going to get us out of this?

He rubbed the back of his neck; exhaustion weighted his eyelids, making his eyes burn. Rachel had managed about an hour nap, but even so, she still looked as tired as he felt. He couldn't think straight and didn't even know what the hell he should be thinking about in the first place. If he could just find out what was going on; what kind of operation they were running from here. If he could avoid putting Rachel front and center, he might be able to figure a way out. The countless scams they'd run with their parents while growing up had to come in handy at some point.

He cast a surreptitious glance around the room and focused on the window behind Rachel. They were on the second floor, and there appeared to be a balcony along the side of the villa. It was something to consider should they get a chance to escape.

A knock on the door made Ben pivot ninety degrees, his forearm braced on the back of the chair. In his state of fatigue, it was best to face who was coming. Look him in the eye.

Zucchi swung open the door and a dark-haired woman carrying a tray entered the room. Ben blinked twice before making sure his jaw wasn't hanging open. Beautiful, sexy, small, but with generous proportions in the hips and breasts, her skin-tight clothes showed every luscious, curvy line from her proud shoulders down to slim, stiletto-clad feet.

Zucchi's gaze raked down the woman's form, and crawled back up. "*Ciao,* Eva."

The bombshell stopped and arched a brow, her chin thrust out in defiance. Whatever she replied to the man ended with *Nino.* Zucchi's slimy smile disappeared fast. Ben got the distinct impression the studious-looking Nino was as feared in this house as Alrigo. He'd already determined the tall, solid-built driver shouldn't be underestimated, but it was good to have his gut instinct confirmed.

Eva approached him and Rachel, and set the tray on the table. Hm, so the food was for them, not their guard. She served a plate and a glass of wine to each of them. His stomach grumbled, but he didn't trust a single person in this place.

"Thank you." Rachel reached for the wine, her hand unsteady.

Ben beat her to it and held her glass out of reach. Before he could explain that she had no idea what was actually in the glass, a slim, tanned hand lifted it from his grasp. Eva took a sip. Her brown gaze locked with his as she lowered the glass. The tip of her tongue slid across her full, glossed lips to remove any remaining traces of wine. She cocked a challenging eyebrow and without breaking eye contact with Ben, handed the wine back to Rachel.

Reveal no weakness to the enemy. To show his complete indifference to her sexy demonstration of how harmless the wine was, Ben sat back, arms crossed over his chest. The woman shrugged her shoulders at his unyielding pose. Her gaze dipped to his throbbing mouth for a brief moment before she spun and exited the room. It took everything he had to keep his attention focused on the slightly distorted reflection of her departure in the window instead of turning to watch the real deal.

Once the door closed, he shifted his gaze to Zucchi's reflection to make sure the guard kept his distance. Facing the possibility of an oncoming threat was one thing, but showing fear could give the guy a dangerous power trip. He now had plenty to prove to his boss and Ben didn't intend to make anything easy for a single one of them.

"I'm hungry." Rachel stared at the plate of pasta in front of her.

"I know." He picked up his fork, flipped it back and forth in his fingers as he considered, then stabbed a penne noodle. Rachel watched him closely and Ben almost laughed. What the hell did they expect? That something in the food would instantly kill them? They were needed alive, or he had a feeling they'd be dead already.

"Go ahead, eat."

Rachel took a careful bite, only to lay her fork back on the table when Ben heard the door open once more. Muscles tense, he darted his gaze to the image in the window, expecting Alrigo, or Nino, only to see it was Eva who'd returned. His shoulders remained rigid as she approached, but then she set a capped bottle of water in front of each of them, and next to Ben's hand, she laid a cloth covered square.

"For your mouth."

Her soft-spoken words in accented English caught him off guard. His fingers felt a telltale chill through the cloth, and Ben wondered at the considerate gesture. Her brown eyes revealed nothing before she retreated.

Once again, he resisted turning to watch her leave and instead broke the seal on his bottle of water. The carbonation made him frown, but he'd take it since the wine was not an option in his exhausted state. Other than hoping to steal a few hours of sleep through the night, he needed to stay as alert as possible.

Rachel picked up her fork and started eating again, and Ben did the same. The pasta was divine and under any other circumstances, he would've enjoyed the meal. Right now, he ate as a necessity to keep up his strength. Come morning, he might have two sisters to get out of this mess. His foot resumed its rapid bounce under the table.

"She seems nice."

Ben frowned at Rachel's statement. "For someone holding us hostage? Sure. She's wonderful."

"I just meant...oh, hell, I don't know." She picked at her food and mumbled, "Forget it."

He blew out a breath frustrated breath, fisted his hand around his fork, and reached out his free hand to cover her fingers squeezing the bottle of water.

"I know what you meant. I'm sorry, you're right." He met her gaze and gave her hand a squeeze. "We're going to get through this. Okay? We're all going to be okay."

Rachel nodded, but her slight hesitation and hard swallow told him she was as worried as he was. Unsure of what else to say, he withdrew his hand from across the table and lifted his fork for another bite of pasta.

After they'd finished eating, he couldn't stop thinking of the dark-haired woman. She *had* seemed different from the others. And he didn't think it was just because she was a woman in a house full of men. She'd showed a hint of kindness with the ice pack. As he held the cold compress to his swollen lip with one hand and ripped the label from his water bottle into tiny little bits with the other, he wondered...

Did Eva have her own agenda, or could they have a potential ally?

Chapter 8

Trent pulled over two blocks from the camera store and locked the new battery into place on Halli's camera. His free hand shook slightly, but he gave it a couple hard shakes, fisted his fingers, took a deep breath, and thumbed the *Play* button.

A blue screen popped up, and he hit the rewind. After a full minute of nothing but some weird angle that looked like an upside down shot of Halli's black-clad thigh and a stone wall, he stopped the video and used the fast rewind. When he played it again, the screen popped up with a shot of two people walking out of the Malpensa Airport in Milan, lugging suitcases, duffle bags slung over their shoulders.

Neither of them looked much like Halli, but he figured it was a safe assumption they were her brother and sister. Curiosity kept him from hitting fast-forward right away. At first glance, the sister—Rachel, he remembered—was the obvious beauty of the two. Blonde, tall and willowy. Her brother, Ben, was a good-looking sort, also tall and blond. Halli was the odd one out with her auburn hair and short stature.

As Trent watched, Rachel frowned, raised her hand, and told Halli to shut off the camera. She made no effort to hide her annoyance, and Halli shot back a response from off-screen.

"No way. You guys may have talked me into throwing away my itinerary, but after saving six months for this camera, I'm using it every chance I get. Deal with it."

Rachel flipped her off. Ben, a wide grin on his face, quickly grabbed her hand to pull it out of sight of the camera. *Definitely siblings.* A smile tugged at the sister's lips and Trent heard Halli's laugh as the film continued to roll.

Wow. He'd been right about her laugh. Natural and carefree, it was like music to Trent's ears after the day they'd endured. He watched the video for a few more minutes, stealing a glimpse of her ordinary world. Their lighthearted banter started an ache in his chest; made him think of Sean on his good days. The dull pain intensified when when Ben turned the camera on Halli and she made faces at her sister.

Trent's chest tightened. She'd been having fun at the beginning of her vacation. *The trip of a lifetime.*

Then she'd met him.

He shook off a twinge of guilt. Her involvement was *not* his fault. From the moment he'd seen the danger she was in, he'd only done whatever he felt necessary to keep her safe. That had to count for something, even if she didn't put much stock in his motives.

Annoyed with his current line of thinking, he quickly hit the fast forward again. Good God, the woman had filmed *everything*. No wonder her battery had been dead by the time he showed up. Every so often he'd thumb the play button and watch, mostly when her brother commandeered filming rights and Halli appeared on screen.

How in the world had he ever thought her plain? Not with those eyes. Even when tempered by fear, or flashing in anger, and most especially on this film when sparkling with laughter, those blue eyes of hers were amazing. Unguarded, her face conveyed a myriad of expressions that increased her attractiveness ten-fold. And the body revealed under her baggy clothes—

Movement on the screen snagged his attention back where it belonged and finally, he recognized the part he'd been waiting for. His grip on the camera tightened. Swans swam on the lake in front of the villa in Lenno, and the lens zoomed in on them until they filled the viewfinder. In the background he heard Rachel complaining about Halli's subjects.

"I want to see if Lake Como, Italy and Lake Como, Wisconsin have more in common than their names."

Despite the tension infusing his muscles, Halli's snippy reply made Trent's lips tug upward. Every once in awhile she'd made it known she craved her itinerary, even if it was just in the tone of her voice. And if they had followed it? He would never have met her. His smile faded. Better for the both of them.

Wonder how many times she thought that same thing?

A flash of consternation caught him off guard. Ridiculous

as it was, he found he didn't like the thought of her regretting having met him. With a frown, he pushed the thought aside. Halliwell Sanders was nothing but trouble, and it would've been better all the way around had they never met. Most especially for her.

On video, Rachel continued to complain, but Ben appeared to be the mediator between the two.

As her brother and sister conversed in the background, Halli kept taping, and things began to happen on screen. The front door to the villa burst open and he recognized Lorenzo running outside.

Trent sat forward, his attention focused beyond the swans. The camera picked up the distant startled honks of the birds as Lorenzo's body suddenly jerked once, twice, then—

"Hey—" Halli's voice.

The camera swung in a wild arc, catching the tail end of a blue Fiat Punto as it drove away.

"No!" Trent pounded a fist on the steering wheel and willed the camera to turn back across the lake.

Halli's laugh reached the microphone, full of disbelief. *"Real funny, guys."*

Trent hit the rewind and watched Lorenzo get shot again. And again. His eyes burned. The bastards had shot him in the back. *Thirty-five years with Italian law enforcement and this is how you go out. God, I'm sorry I asked for your help.*

He rewound it one last time and played the scene frame by frame. The final moment before the camera veered away revealed a single frame glimpse of a man standing in the shattered window, gun in hand. The same man he'd seen at the police station.

Alrigo Lapaglia.

Trent stared for a moment, committing the image of the man's ruthless expression to memory.

"I got you now, you bastard, and I'm going to nail your ass," he vowed triumphantly in the silent car. "For Lorenzo *and* Sean, you fucking coward."

He set the camera in the passenger seat and dug the heels of his hands into his eyes. What a day. And it wasn't about to get any easier. After he dropped Halli at the consulate, he'd need to go see Simone, Lorenzo's longtime girlfriend. His friend had mentioned she was working the late shift at the hospital all this week, and though the thought of having to tell her what'd happened tore at his heart, it was the least he could do. Over the past year they'd become almost as good of friends as he and Lorenzo.

Turning his mind to less disturbing thoughts, though no more pleasant, he jammed the car into gear and peeled away from the curb. When he got back to the house, he'd make an extra copy or two of Halli's video and put them in a safe place. Maybe mail one to his agent in California. If anything happened during the rest of the investigation, he wanted to make sure Lapaglia got what was coming to him beyond getting hit by a truck.

If they were real lucky, the guy was already dead. But that still left the other lowlifes in his group of associates. Between Halli's video, and the wire he'd recorded off Lorenzo, the evidence he'd gathered would tighten the net on their black market import operations. They would finally pay for the lives they'd ruined, human and animal alike.

Trent anticipated the feeling of vindication when he proved Sean's death was not a suicide as the police had ruled. Sean had been taking his medication. He'd been excited about his new project. Trent had talked to him *that morning.*

If Sean had intended to kill himself just a few hours later, Trent would've sensed the depression. He would've heard something in his brother's voice. Right?

He rubbed a hand over his face as he drove. For the last few months he'd agonized over that question. It didn't matter that he specifically remembered hanging up the phone and thinking how good Sean had been doing lately; nagging doubt hammered persistently at the back of his mind since the day of his brother's death.

Now, he one hundred percent believed what he'd suspected all along. Lapaglia's culpability wasn't wishful thinking on Trent's part as a way to lay aside his guilt. But once he proved the police had covered up the murder, would it be enough?

Enough for his father to finally recognize his oldest son was more than what he read in the tabloids?

And if it wasn't enough for his father, would it be enough for himself?

Surprisingly, that was the tougher of the two questions. He downshifted and slowed for the turn onto his street. His father's disapproval was ingrained, and to be honest, at times Trent had fostered it. Having lived as a disappointment for so long now, if nothing changed, he imagined he would continue on as normal. But the guilt of not being there for Sean ate him up inside. If justice didn't get rid of the guilt, he wasn't quite sure what the hell could.

The added responsibility of Halli Sanders didn't help. Despite being used to pressure, getting her safely into the hands of someone trustworthy was a hell of a lot different than walking the red carpet and hoping the premiere of his current film didn't tank.

Trent pulled into his drive and waited impatiently for the gate to open, then close again after he drove through. He parked in the garage and headed inside with the camera, careful to be quiet in case Halli had been able to fall asleep.

The faint smell of food made his stomach rumble with anticipation. His last meal had been breakfast with Lorenzo that morning while they went over their strategy. Suddenly his stomach churned as a fresh wave of anguish washed over him, magnified by the mental image of his friend's body jerking when the bullets tore into his flesh.

Trent laid the camera on the table and blew out a deep breath before pressing his hand over his constricted chest. He needed to figure out a way to compartmentalize so he could focus. Like when he acted a part. His character would be the guy who didn't care. The guy who put emotion aside, solved the case, and took down the bad guys moments before the credits rolled.

He'd played that guy before, and he'd play him again. Starting now.

Halfway to the fridge, his step faltered. One of the drawers below the island counter stuck out a few inches. He slid it open to see the contents all jumbled around. It was the same drawer he'd put Halli's things in, but he hadn't done that. The neighboring drawer looked identical; everything messed up as if someone had done a hasty search.

Dread snaked down his back. The feeling escalated each step closer he took to the living room. Alarm exploded at the sight of cabinet doors hanging ajar, open closets, and cockeyed couch cushions. There was only one reason for anyone to search his place.

He froze in place, his mouth dry.

Where the hell is Halli?

He caught himself from calling out her name. He'd come in quiet enough, if anyone was still in the house he might be able to take them by surprise. With the living room obviously empty, he flattened himself against the wall to snatch a glance up the stairs. Moving silently on the plush carpet, he made his way up toward the first bedroom.

The room Sean had used.

He hadn't been inside since the day after his brother's funeral, not even to check the quality of the remodeling he'd hired a local company to do. Bracing himself for the living nightmare that plagued his dreams, he twisted the handle and swung open the door.

Relief nearly buckled his knees when he saw the room empty. A part of him had half expected to see Halli's lifeless body where Sean's had been three months ago.

Finding her became imperative. He'd left her alone and defenseless after she begged him not to. If something happened to her while he was gone—*in his house*—how could he not be responsible?

The three other guest rooms were empty, including the one she'd used earlier, which left his at the end of the hall. Heart hammering against his ribs, Trent threw open the door.

Halli lay on the bed, her small body curled around a pillow. Was she dead? Injured? He crossed the room in record time, forgetting to even check if she was alone. *God, please let her be okay.*

"Halli?"

Muttered, unintelligible words faded as she rolled onto her back. Sleeping. *Thank God!* His gaze swept over her, searching for any signs of injury and finding none. He sank onto the edge of the bed; his weight on the mattress shifted her body toward him.

Halli jerked awake, eyes wide with alarm.

As she scrambled backward against the headboard, pillow clutched in her arms, he held out a hand. "It's okay. It's me, Trent."

The sound of crinkling, tearing paper caught his attention even as he noted the fear in her eyes subside. A downward glance made him freeze. In the next second, a white-hot spear of anger shot through him.

"What the hell—?" He reached out and snatched his notebook out from under her thigh. A page ripped out, stark white against his black bedspread. "Are you kidding me?"

"Ah…um…"

Her wide eyes were now full of guilt. She strangled the pillow against her stomach and realization brought a fresh wave of anger. Trent looked at his desk. Newspaper articles were strewn across the smooth walnut surface and the third drawer hung open.

"This was *you?*" He stood and swept an arm toward the desk, then the door. "And out there, too?"

"I thought you might be hiding something."

He swung around at her defensive tone. "So you tore my house apart?"

"It's not that bad."

She released the pillow and set it aside, only to shrink back when he leaned over the bed, the torn page crumpled in his fist. "It looks like I was robbed."

"Geez, relax, I'll straighten everything up."

She swung her feet around to climb off the bed on the opposite side. When she started for the door, Trent took two steps and caught her arm, swinging her around to face him. His fingers tightened with another mental flash of his brother's lifeless body on the bed.

"Christ, Halli, I thought they'd found you! I thought I was

going to find you *dead* in here."

She stared up at him, stiff as a board, and yet sympathy swam in those big blue eyes. Damn it, that sounded like he actually cared. He bit back a growl. Well, so what if he did, it didn't mean anything. She was another human being, after all. It made sense his character would care that much, at least.

"Where do you get off going through my things?" he demanded.

She shook off his hand and rubbed her arm before pointing her stuck-up little nose in the air. "I asked you a question before you swiped my camera and left. A damn important one, too. Maybe next time you'll answer instead of blowing me off."

"I told you I wasn't involved. Besides which, who says I owe *you* any explanations?"

"You kidnapped me!"

He turned to face the desk, eyeing the balled page in his hand. Her expression from a moment ago flashed in his mind. *Sympathy...?*

His journal. Sean. His gut tightened at the thought of her reading his private words and he deliberately made his next words condescending. "We're not really having this discussion again, are we?"

"Oh, goodness, no. Wouldn't want to bore the great Trent Tomlin."

A forward jerk of his knee slammed the third drawer closed with a thud. "Your sarcasm is not appreciated."

"Neither is yours."

"I was serious."

"So was I."

Trent slapped the notebook on his desk and turned to lean back against the polished wood. He ignored the article that floated to the ground and focused on Halli, his hands braced on either side of him, fingers gripping the edge of the desk. "Look, I'm tired and I'm hungry, so can we cut the childish bullshit and be done with this for tonight?"

Red spots appeared on her cheeks as she crossed her arms over her chest. "Aw, poor baby."

"Saving your ass—*twice,* I might add—isn't as easy as I

make it look, so go make yourself useful and whip me up something to eat like I asked earlier."

Her eyebrows shot up and her entire face flared crimson. "Screw you," she spat as she spun toward the door.

"Been happenin' all day, sweetheart," he drawled after her.

The door slammed so hard a couple of his brother's framed photographs bounced against the wall. Trent glared under his arm at the leather-bound notebook on the desk. How much had she read? All of it he'd bet. *Damn her*. She had no right reading his personal thoughts. How'd she like it if he crawled inside her head and exposed her deepest regret?

His hand fisted tighter, his knuckles as white as the paper crushed between his fingers. When the wave of emotion abated and he'd reconnected with his self-assigned character, he smoothed out the page against his thigh, then picked up the book and thumbed the pages until he found where it belonged.

She now had her answer as to his involvement.

And the added danger that went along with that knowledge.

Chapter 9

Childish bullshit?
Make yourself useful?
Halli fumed as she straightened up the mess she'd made in the living room. *What a jackass.*

Slamming the cabinet door hard enough to rattle the beveled-edge glass on the top doors gave her no satisfaction. She'd provided him with the video, hadn't she? The all-important recording he was so desperate to see. That was useful. How in the world could the arrogant jerk she'd just dealt with be the same man whose emotional, written words touched her heart and brought tears to her eyes?

As if her thoughts conjured him, Trent strode into the room. He carried a cardboard box in his arms and she stopped straightening the chair cushion to glare at him, noting his jaw looked to be clenched just as tight as hers. *So what. Let him be angry. Let him be* hungry. *He couldn't pay me to follow his condescending order to—*

He turned his back as he dropped the box onto the couch, completely ignoring her. Halli wondered what he was doing, until he bent to rummage in the box. Then she found herself checking out his butt.

What was wrong with her? She didn't even like the man!

Well, to be fair, she didn't object to certain aspects of him, and his butt was certainly one of those. But movie-star looks and an amazing body didn't make up for his overall…jerkiness. Was that a word? *Who cares,* she decided, still staring at his defined, denim-clad backside. If the pants fit…

It dawned on her when he set aside some lighting gear on the couch that the box he'd brought out contained camera equipment. Most likely from the room his brother had used. She thought of the tortured emotion revealed in Trent's journal entries and the tense set of his shoulders took on a whole new meaning. Her anger melted away.

"What are you doing?" she asked in a neutral tone.

He rummaged through the box with increasing determination. "I'm going to make a copy of your video. I thought for sure Sean's stuff would have what I need." Muttered swear words indicated he'd thought wrong.

She wasn't so sure she wanted the answer to her next question, but asked anyway. "Did you watch it yet?"

"Yes."

"Did it...um...have what you wanted?"

"What I wanted? No. What I need to help put these guys away? Yes."

Meaning she *had* filmed a murder. Halli swallowed hard and moved closer to the couch. Closer to him. The entire day had had a surreal feeling about it—still did, in fact—but knowing he'd watched the murder on her film triggered an instinctive need for security in the form of human contact.

Trent abruptly switched gears and began piling cameras back into the box. When the sound of breaking glass accompanied the next piece of equipment, she reached forward to lay her hand on his arm.

"I'm sorry."

The solid reassurance of his warm skin beneath her fingertips ignited a longing to have his strong arms wrap around her and promise everything would be okay.

He stilled, his gaze dropping to her hand. Her heart beat faster as she imagined him turning those intense hazel eyes her way.

His forearm muscles tightened and bunched just before he jerked away. "I don't need or want your sympathy, sweetheart."

The rejection stung, along with the meaningless endearment. But it was just what she needed to wipe away the strange desire to lean on his strength and comfort him.

To combat a rising, cold loneliness, she clenched her fists at her sides and said, "Is there anything I can do to help?"

"I'm still hungry," he snapped.

As if she would serve him. "Then how about I copy the video while you go eat."

He tossed the last camera into the box and gave her a

skeptical look.

"Back in Wisconsin, I'm a television producer for PBS. I think I can figure it out."

His glance touched on the box in front of him, shifted toward a mirror on the wall across from the couch, and returned to her. "I assume you know where everything is from your private whirlwind tour earlier?"

"Yep." She refused to feel guilty.

"Great. Have at it." He strode toward the kitchen, only to take an abrupt detour to the stairs. Over his shoulder, he added, "I'm gonna take a shower first. Your camera's on the kitchen counter."

Halli stalked into the kitchen, only to freeze at the sight of the camera. What had possessed her to offer to make the copy? She didn't even want to touch the thing anymore, let alone see what she'd filmed.

I've gotten this far through the day without falling apart... surely I can do this one thing more?

Deep breath. One foot in front of the other.

She grabbed the camera and returned to the cabinets in the living room that housed Trent's home theater system. She hadn't really thought about it before, but looking at the mirror above, she realized it was one of those ultra cool, ultra expensive mirror TV's. Of course he'd have one, and with the vintage looking frame, it fit in perfectly with the villa's décor.

"Get the copy made and then you can admire his house all you want."

A quick check of his system confirmed she'd be able to play the video from her camera and record on his DVR. All she needed now was one of the blank DVDs from the spindle stack in his cabinet, and the cable to connect her camera to his DVR.

Which was back in the little blue rental car with Ben and Rachel.

She checked the box of camera equipment Trent had left on the couch, then reluctantly made her way to the bedroom his brother had stayed in. If Trent was right, the same people who'd killed his brother were the ones who were after her.

Halli fortified herself and pushed open the door. Again, the pungent odor of the room's facelift assaulted her nostrils. If she had a hard time coming in here, it must've been ten times worse for Trent. She couldn't imagine losing Ben or Rachel forever.

Not that she saw them every day at home in Wisconsin. Rachel tended to get wrapped up in her jewelry designs and art fairs, while most of the time Ben was flying around the country for his job or traveling on his motorcycle for weeks on end. But at least things stayed ordered and there were no surprises, especially since they both called her on a regular basis. Yes, she'd finally agreed to give up all control of her life for a week, but only because she knew she'd have the two of them as her guaranteed constant during the trip.

But nothing had been guaranteed since they'd stopped beside the lake. And even now, though she'd left the messages on Ben's phone, after the crazy, scary events of her day so far, a small part of her worried she would never see her family again.

Her chest tightened painfully. Before the lump forming in her throat made swallowing impossible, she managed a deep breath. Instead of focusing on how completely powerless she'd been throughout the day, she needed to think of meeting up with Ben and Rachel in the morning. Life *would* return to normal—as soon as they changed their return trip to the states for tomorrow afternoon.

In the meantime, she had a video copy to make.

At the bottom of a second box in the closet, she found a cable compatible with her camera and Trent's system. As she closed the bedroom door quietly, she heard the very faint sound of the shower in Trent's room at the end of the hall.

She paused and closed her eyes, only to pop them wide open and hurry back to the living room. Last thing she needed to imagine was Trent Tomlin naked and wet—especially knowing the size of his condoms.

Her face burned as she set everything up and plugged the cable into his DVR and her camera, then inserted a blank DVD. A quick check showed her video needed to be rewound, so she pressed the button and waited a full minute before hitting play. Her own face appeared on screen.

"*I promise, Halli, you're going to love winging it once you get used to it."*

How ironic she'd chosen that spot to stop the video. Rachel had confiscated the camera while Ben drove. Her sister's words currently prompted a wry smile, even as her on-screen self gave an uneasy laugh. *"I'm not one of the swans on the lake at home, Ben. My wingspan is pretty narrow."*

"Yes, but you agreed to stretch your wings this week," Rachel reminded.

"I know, I know. But you're still going to have to be patient with me and understand my nerves may get the better of me from time to time."

"We'll break you in easy today," Ben assured her.

So much for easy. More like a crash course. Literally.

The laughter in her brother's voice brought the ache back to her chest. Tears welled. And Rachel; what she wouldn't give for a hug from her big sis right now.

Halli sniffed and blinked away the stinging moisture. Tomorrow she'd see them again and get hugs. Lots of hugs.

Ignoring the tiny bit of doubt lingering in the dark corners of her mind, she concentrated on the video and tried to figure out where they were at this point. She didn't think it was too much further along that Ben had parked on the sidewalk so they could check out the lake by that stone wall, so she hit record on Trent's DVD player.

A minute later she prepared to fast forward again, but something Ben said on the video jogged her memory. It was coming up. A tremble wobbled the camera in her hands.

She backed up a step and absently pushed aside a couple of magazines lying on the coffee table so she could sit, still holding the camera. Much as she didn't want to watch, it was impossible to look away. Trepidation remained, but she found herself determined to see what'd happened to Trent's friend. Maybe that's what it would take to make this thing become real in her mind.

On screen, the large white swans moved with graceful ease across the calm water in direct opposition to the current pounding of her pulse. Rachel complained about her filming the swans. Ben offered a suggestion—

A loud, siren-sounding noise pierced her ears. Halli stifled a scream and leapt up from the coffee table. What the heck was that? When it continued to echo through the living room, she knew.

Trent's security alarm!

A shadow moved by the window to the right of the bar area. Halli froze. Was it a tree branch swaying in the wind, or something more sinister?

No way she was staying to find out.

Halli yanked the connection cable from the camera in her hands and ran for the stairs. She sprinted down the hall and threw open the door to Trent's room just as he stumbled from the bathroom, hair dripping, chest wet, jeans low on his lean hips and unzipped. The sight brought her to an abrupt stop, breathless from her panicked run and the fear coursing through her veins.

Trent spotted her in the middle of a hard tug on the jeans' belt loops. He clearly wasn't wearing any underwear. His attention dropped to his zipper as he groused, "I can't take a fricken shower without you doing something stupid, can I?"

Halli tore her gaze away from the dark hair on his lower abdomen and below. She sucked in a deep breath, suddenly too warm for the sweatshirt she still wore.

"I-it wasn't me."

He jerked his head up. "You didn't mess with the security system?"

She shook her head.

Expression tight, he strode to the nearest window as he zipped his pants and peered through the glass, cursing a string of swear words worthy of any thwarted movie villain.

The alarm went silent.

"I saw a shadow outside one of the downstairs windows," Halli whispered.

Trent glanced over his shoulder. "For God's sake, get out of the line of sight then."

Her fingers tightened on the camera clutched against her chest as she hurried to his side against the wall.

"Please tell me the memory card is still in that thing."

"It is."

Trent leaned forward slightly to peer outside. "Did you get a copy made?"

"It's still in your machine."

He swore again.

"What—"

He cut her off with a jerk of his hand. Her heartbeat thundered in her ears in the dead quiet. Somewhere in the house, a door slammed. Halli moved closer, pressing up against Trent's wet back. His muscles tensed.

"Okay, I've got a plan…"

"I like plans," she assured him.

"Assuming this is Lapaglia, we've got to get the hell out of here. My car is out—we won't make it to the garage—but my balcony stairs lead down to the pool deck, which will take us to the lake. Ever drive a boat?"

"My brother's ski boat."

"Close enough. I have a cabin cruiser in the boat house and the key is hanging next to the light switch on the right side of the door. *Don't* turn on the lights. I'll get us in and open the front doors, you untie the boat and get it started. Got it?"

She nodded. Good God, she was still having a hell of a time catching her breath.

Trent reached for the window latch. "Stick right with me, and whatever the hell happens, *do not* lose that camera."

He shoved the window wide open, and Halli slid her arm through the camera strap and draped it around her neck and diagonally across her chest before following him onto the balcony. Faint light from the pool glowed below, but up here, they were enclosed in darkness. Afraid of losing him, she grabbed hold of the back waistband of Trent's jeans. He reached around to remove her hand, wrapping his fingers tight around hers as he led her down the stairs that descended to the patio. The warmth of his large hand gave her a boost of reassurance.

At first they kept close to the villa, and Halli ran her free hand along the cool, coarse stones that made up the outside walls of his home. Surprisingly, the solid mass beneath her fingers offered a sense of safety. Then he pulled her away from the wall toward the pool.

Two strides into the open, she caught a flash of shadow from the corner of her eye. She whipped her head around in time to see a dark figure lunge at them. She screamed Trent's name as the man caught her free arm. One vicious yank tore Halli's hand from Trent's grasp. She cried out again, stumbling backward. An arm closed around her neck, and another rose up, pointed at Trent.

In the glow of light from the pool, Halli saw the outline of a gun in a gloved hand. She threw her head back as hard as she could into her captor's face. Pain radiated through her already tender skull. The man cried out in a hoarse voice at the same time she heard a sharp little clicking noise, followed by what sounded like a kernel of popcorn popping. The arm around her neck loosened.

Trent swore; a vicious, guttural explosion of words. Halli thrust her elbow back, got in a sharp jab to her assailant's ribs, and broke free when the man gasped for air. Trent pulled her out of the way, and she experienced a second of relief that he was okay.

"Go," he ordered with a push, his voice rough and hard. "Follow the plan. I'm right behind you."

Halli didn't need to be told twice. She bolted into the darkness, toward the grayish outline of the white boat house. With every step across the dew-wet yard, her camera banged against her side. Deep grunts of exertion and the drag of metal on stone made her glance over her shoulder toward the patio.

Adrenaline surged at the sight of a short, dark figure only yards behind her—and definitely not Trent. Her lungs burned, legs ached. Fear clogged her throat. She'd never outrun the man in the slippery grass.

Seconds later, a heavy body slammed into her from behind. She cried out as they both tumbled to the slick ground. Labored breathing filled the air. A brutal grip on her arm forced her onto her back. In the sallow light of a partial moon, menace gleamed in his dark eyes and twisted his thin lips. She struggled against his cruel hold, but his suffocating weight pressed her back into the hard earth.

One meaty hand latched onto the camera strap around her neck and pulled hard. The nylon bit painfully into her skin, but held. When he yanked a second time, Halli reached up and raked her nails across his face, digging in as hard as she could. He reared back with a pained roar. Four dark lines appeared on his cheek, all the way to his chin.

She scrambled backward on her hands and feet, constricted lungs sucking in air. Just when she thought she'd escaped, a vice grip locked on her ankle and dragged her back over the wet grass.

Shadows played across the scratches on his face, turning his expression murderous. Absolute terror seized her heart. Lifting her other foot, she aimed for his face and kicked with every ounce of strength she could summon.

A sickening crunch of cartilage imprinted on her memory. The man gasped and then collapsed to the ground face first. The abrupt freedom took Halli by surprise. Until it registered the body in front of her lay completely still.

Unnaturally still.

Oh my God, he's dead!

She shot back a few more feet, her stomach churning. Her eyes had adjusted to the night and the man's outline in the grass seemed to loom higher and higher in her terrified conscious.

"Halli!"

Trent's voice jerked her attention from the lifeless body, snapping her out of her shock. He ran across the murky yard toward her. She pushed to her feet, but stumbled a few steps before gaining her footing.

Follow the plan.

Determination carried her to the boat house and slammed her into the door. Locked. She beat on the wood with rising hysteria. She'd just killed a man. Surreal had become a nightmare.

A hand on her shoulder startled a scream, but she cut it off abruptly when she saw Trent.

"You okay?" he asked.

Leaning against the door, she shook her head back and forth in despair. "I think I just killed someone."

"Yeah? Well, I know I did. You still got the camera?"

What? He knew he did? My God, it just got worse and wo—

His hands gripped her shoulders. "Halli—*please* tell me you still have the camera."

The panic in his voice cut through her dazed thoughts. "Yes, yes, I have the camera."

"Thank God. Now move it so I can get this door open."

"It's locked—"

He shoved her aside and stepped back. Lifting one foot, he delivered a massive kick to the door, bare foot flat against the wood. The sound of splintering wood reached her ears as the door flew inward and slammed against the inside wall. For a moment, Halli would've sworn Shain West stood before her. A lump formed in her throat and she wished with all her heart it was a movie and *not* real.

I killed someone!

"Grab the key, I'll unlatch the front doors."

Trent disappeared inside. Halli glanced toward the villa, reaching a shaky hand inside to feel for the light switch. He'd said the boat key hung right next to it. Her hand slipped down, and when she jerked it back up, light flooded the boat house and spilled into the yard beyond.

"No lights, dammit!"

With a gasp, Halli flipped the switch, plunging them back into darkness. In those few seconds, though, she'd spotted someone bent over the man she'd kicked, helping him to his feet. Duly motivated, she grabbed the key and spun for the boat. Irrational relief combined with fear to send her heart into her throat.

"My guy's not dead! But there's another one helping him!"

Hands outstretched, she felt her way to the boat. In the middle of unwinding the stern's mooring rope from its post, she heard the clunk of wood on wood, and a splash from the water's end of the boat house. As she fumbled her way to the bow, she ran into Trent in the dark. He sucked in a breath but steadied her with a hand on her shoulder.

"Start the boat," he bit out. "When I say go, push her full

throttle."

"What are you—"

But he was gone again, headed for the busted door. Halli took care of the remaining rope, held her camera against her chest with the fisted key, and leapt onto the boat. Noises behind her sounded just like what had echoed in her ear when their first attacker had fired his gun at Trent. Squinting in the shadowy darkness, she saw Trent's outline crouched by the door, arm extended. Another *click-pop* coincided with a slight upward jerk of his hand and arm.

He had a gun? Where the heck did he get a gun from?

The dull thud of multiple bullets impacting the stern of the boat spurred her back into action. She climbed into the captain's chair, but stayed low. Locating the ignition slot in the dark took a few nerve-wracking seconds. Finally, the key slid in and she turned it. The engines rumbled to life, throbbing with suppressed power beneath her feet.

She squinted in an attempt to make out some of the cockpit layout, waiting breathlessly for Trent to give the okay. Her fingers warmed cold metal as she suppressed the instinctive urge to open the throttle right—

"*Now*, Halli, *go!*"

Adrenaline spiked again as she rose up and thrust the throttle forward. The engines responded with a deafening roar. Water churned from the sudden velocity of the propellers, flooding the back doorway. Her head jerked back as they shot forward. A loud *boom* scared the daylights out of her, but the boat kept going so she plowed on. After they'd exited the building, she figured out Trent had unlatched the front doors but not taken the time to push them open.

Driving the cruiser with the running lights off, she searched anxiously to avoid other vessels. Once they were well out of range of the men and their guns on the dock, she'd be able to slow down.

A strange thrill of exhilaration coursed through her as the wind whipped her hair. It'd be frightening if she didn't feel so amazingly, wonderfully *alive*. She couldn't believe they'd pulled off the plan and escaped for a third time. *And* she hadn't killed a man!

After another minute, she eased the throttle back to about ten miles per hour, turned on the running lights, double checked to make sure there were no boats in the near vicinity that she'd run into, and removed the camera from around her neck. As she dropped it on the captain's seat behind her, she laughed and threw a victory smile over her shoulder for Trent.

Her heart anchored in her stomach at the sight of the empty boat.

Chapter 10

Trent didn't have the strength to pull himself up the built-in swim ladder and over the side of the *Scappare* one handed, especially with the heavy drag of the water against his jeans. He'd nearly let go when the boat slowed, but she hadn't stopped yet. He was amazed he'd held on this long.

The boat's running lights blinked on.

"*Trent!*"

Halli's voice was shrill with alarm. Without warning, their forward momentum dropped to nothing. His body slammed into the ladder. Pain blurred the edges of his consciousness as a small tidal wave of lake water washed up over his head, filling his mouth and nose with the nasty-tasting shit. Battling through the haze in his brain, Trent fought to keep his fingers fisted on the ladder rung and his legs clear of the propellers beneath the back end of the boat.

The water subsided as the cruiser bobbed and coasted after the abrupt stop. Over the low growl of the idling motor, Halli called out his name again, sounding even more frantic than before.

Trent coughed and spit a mouthful of water. "Back here." The words scraped his raw throat.

Halli's face appeared over the edge of the stern. "Thank, God!" Her brow wrinkled, despite the relieved smile on her face. "I thought I left you behind."

He summoned a weary grin. "You can't get rid of me that easy, sweetheart."

"I wouldn't have left you on purpose. I swear, Trent, I—"

"Relax. It was a joke." He coughed up more water.

"Oh, right."

She smiled down at him, her brow smoothed this time. All of a sudden, despite knowing only four years separated them, she looked incredibly young. Or maybe it was just that he felt so damn old after the past ten minutes. And tired. And sore.

As much as he enjoyed seeing her smile after so many frowns throughout the day, his arm throbbed with painful insistence. He didn't imagine the polluted lake water was good for an open wound, either. Unfortunately, where he needed to go looked very far away. Clenching his jaw tight, he took hold of both sides of the ladder and secured a foothold on the bottom rung under the water.

"Need a hand?" Halli asked.

"I got it."

Each flex of his left bicep was like a knife stabbing into his arm, but somehow he made it to the top. Prepared to heave himself over the side, his wet hand slipped on the smooth fiberglass and his ribs took the brunt of his weight when he landed on the hard edge of the side of the boat. A deep groan whooshed between his compressed lips.

Halli stepped forward, grabbed hold of his arm and pulled. White hot agony seared along his nerve endings and an involuntary, hoarse shout tore from his lips.

She let go and jumped back in surprise. "I'm sorry!"

Trent fought to breathe. Pain washed over him in undulating waves. It wouldn't have been so bad, except that she'd latched on *right* where a bullet had ripped through his skin. She'd also tipped his balance enough that he slid all the way into the boat with a thud, unable to halt his forward momentum with his injured arm.

"Oh...*God*." Halli stood in front of him, staring at her hands tinged red from his blood. "You're hurt."

"Tell me something I don't know."

The guy on the patio had given him a roundhouse kick in the chest that knocked him on his ass. He'd be dead right now if the wrought iron chair he'd grabbed hadn't deflected the bullet meant for his head. Not only had the chair saved his life, it made an effective weapon, too.

Trent pushed to his feet and promptly dropped onto the back half-bench seat. A sharp jab in the ass reminded him he'd jammed the gun deep in the back waistband of his jeans before hollering for Halli to go. The extended length of the silencer screwed into the barrel is what bit him in the butt.

He leaned forward to pull it free, and Halli stared.

"Where'd you get that?"

"That guy you laid out in the grass didn't seem to need it anymore." He released the ammo clip into his left hand, checked to find four bullets left, and punched the clip back in before setting the gun on the seat. "Nice job back there, by the way."

"Turns out I didn't kill him."

"So you said." He didn't think he'd killed her guy either, though he was pretty sure he'd hit at least one of them before diving for the boat.

With the worst of the agony in his arm having subsided to an insistent throb, he angled toward the rear running lights and gingerly pulled on his left elbow to get a good look at the gash. It hurt like hell, but luckily the bullet had only grazed his bicep.

Halli's indrawn breath made a hissing sound through her teeth. His sideways glance took in her ashen face as she stared first at his arm, then the dark stains on her hands.

"You're not one of those people who freaks out over a little blood, are you?" he asked.

Wide blue eyes rose to meet with his, then dropped back to his arm. A thick, red rivulet had worked its way through the wet hairs on his arm until it dripped off his elbow onto his jeans.

"Uh…that's more than a little."

Another drop hit his thigh as she reached a hand to grip the side railing. He took note of her white knuckles. "Sit down before you pass out."

She blinked before visibly pulling herself together.

"No, it's okay, I'll be fine." She took a step toward him. "I can help. Ah…first thing is to stop the bleeding. Right? What do we need? Bandages. First aid kit. You have to have one on a boat, right? Where would that be?"

She whirled toward the front of the boat and back to him with the last two questions.

Trent picked up the gun again and stood. "Slow down. I'm getting dizzy watching you spin."

"What are you doing? Sit down," she instructed when he tried to move past.

Funny how the blood rattled her, but she didn't seem the least bit fazed by the weapon in his hand anymore.

And she didn't move out of his way. "I can get the kit if you tell me where—"

"Right now, I'm more concerned about how far we are from the house than my arm."

"We're far enough."

"I'm still going to check the GPS." He tried to sidestep, but she moved with him.

"You're getting blood all over the place!"

Her palm pressed flat against his chest as if she thought she could actually force him to sit down. Trent took a hasty step back. Away from the heat of her hand and the unexpected yearning it triggered the moment she made contact with his bare skin. "What do you want me to do about it? For Christ's sake, making sure we're safe is more important than a few drops of blood."

A sound of frustration rumbled in her throat, and the next thing he knew, she yanked her brown sweatshirt over her head and thrust it under his elbow. "There. Now you can check your stupid GPS while I find the first aid kit."

On her way below deck, he heard her mutter, "Like I'm dumb enough to stop within shooting distance of the house."

"It's in the head," he called.

A frown creased her brow as she faced him. "What's in my head?"

Trent held back the smile that threatened. "*The* head. The first aid kit is in the head. That's what a bathroom is called on a boat."

She rolled her eyes and spun away. "Then just call it a bathroom."

This time he gave in to the smile, though it bounced harmlessly off her back. In the next instant, the smile became a grimace as he stooped to pick her video camera up off the floor by the captain's chair. He stowed it in the storage box under the seat cushion before dumping the gun in the cup holder next to the steering wheel.

Still standing, he leaned back against the chair and checked the GPS. She'd gotten them out of range all right, only in the wrong direction. The worrisome question surfaced of how Lapaglia had connected him to Halli, but he shoved it aside to concentrate on getting them to a safe location. He wanted a lot more water between them and Lapaglia's henchmen until he got his arm bandaged and figured out what the hell to do now. Heading south toward the city of Como wasn't going to cut it.

He turned the boat north and navigated to the west shore of the lake so they could pass across from his villa without drawing attention to themselves. Thankfully, there were enough boaters this July weekend that the *Scappare* blended right in on their way up the shoreline to Bellagio.

Another check of his arm revealed the bleeding had slowed some. He didn't mind the blood loss if it washed away the bacteria he knew thrived in the dirty lake water, but Halli had been right about not getting it all over the boat.

What she didn't realize was he enjoyed the added bonus of viewing her *Wet & Wild* T-shirt again. In fact, when she reappeared with the first aid kit, a couple of towels, and a bowl, Trent got a birds-eye view. In the combined illumination of the running lights and cockpit, he noted the blue rhinestones matched her eyes perfectly.

She set up her makeshift triage station on the small refreshment table behind his chair. Then she gave him a small cup of water and a couple of ibuprofen tablets to swallow before instructing, "Give me the shirt and lift your arm."

He sat fully in the captain's seat, but because they were coming up on a couple of boats, kept his concentration on the water in front of them. Or at least tried. As she placed the bowl under his elbow and began washing the blood from his arm with a wet towel, he couldn't help a sideways glance every so often, dividing his attention equally between her face and the cleavage-revealing shirt.

One side of her hair was tucked behind her ear, the other fell forward. Shiny strands blocked his view of her shadowed face save for one glimpse of dark lashes lowered in concentration, lips pressed tightly together. Her administrations were firm, but gentle, and he experienced the same leap of his pulse as before when she'd touched his chest. Something about this woman had really grown on him.

Right now, despite his bleeding arm and the potential danger of Lapaglia and his men finding them again, he wanted nothing more than to pull her close and kiss her. He imagined the press of her chest to his without the bulky sweatshirt to interfere, and his grip on the steering wheel tightened in response to the ill-timed fantasy.

Halli, on the other hand, remained steady, her attention focused on his arm as if she were disarming an explosive. He couldn't remember the last time a woman had intrigued him so much, which made her obvious disinterest in the rest of him more than a little irritating. His macho ego, the one he relished putting on display for the tabloids, sat up and demanded he do something about her indifference.

"Sorry your new sweatshirt got blood all over it," he offered.

"I'm not. It's ugly."

"Wow. Nice."

"Well, you could've at least grabbed something I might want to keep after this is all over."

He smiled at her put-out tone. "You're right. I apologize for not taking the time to shop for you when people were chasing us with *guns*."

Finished washing, now she dabbed a dry towel in a wide circle around his torn flesh, no longer quite so gentle. "Don't do that."

"Do what?"

"Take the jerk route again."

It wasn't the first time she'd made that accusation. He craned his neck to the right and adjusted the wheel to navigate a safe distance around another vessel. "You keep calling me a jerk and I'm gonna start to believe you mean it."

"I do mean it. You're a sarcastic, egotistical jerk." She finished wiping his arm with more force than necessary and set the cloth on the table behind him.

Wow. Her feathers were finally good and ruffled, but damned if he could figure out why. He cast another look in her direction, and when she stubbornly ignored him, his gaze dropped to *Wet & Wild*. A flush of awareness heated his entire body, but there was no doubt she was chilled in the night air.

Forcing his attention back to the water, he chuckled softly. "Since it means so much to you, sweetheart, if we get out of this in one piece, I'll buy you anything you want. And furthermore, I'm not ego—*owww!*"

A severe burning sensation engulfed his bicep as liquid streamed down his arm. His instinctive flinch away from the unexpected pain accidentally swerved the boat at the same time. Halli stumbled and Trent grabbed with his injured arm to keep her on her feet.

"*What the hell is your problem?*"

She pulled free as he straightened the boat and slowed down. After making sure the coast was clear in front of them, he tossed her a dark frown. She quickly positioned the bowl back under the liquid dripping from his elbow. Peroxide he assumed.

The smile Halli lifted toward him was laced with saccharine sweetness. "I'm sorry, did that hurt?"

"Yes, it hurt! You gotta warn a guy before you do something like that. At the very least you—"

"This is gonna hurt."

Another blaze of pain scorched his arm. Trent cursed through his clenched teeth, braced his feet, and throttled back to an idle. From the corner of his eye, he saw Halli drop the bowl to catch the back of the captain's seat when the sudden stop pitched her forward. She made the grab, but still lost her balance. He lifted his left arm so as not to impede the tumble that landed her sideways across his legs.

Hmm. Interesting turn of events. The angry sting of peroxide bled into the background, along with his annoyance.

Halli recognized the aggravation in Trent's tight jaw a second before he brought the boat to a rocking halt. Next thing she knew, she lay sprawled across his hard thighs, and his right arm saved her head from slamming against the throttle. The bowl was a goner, but her fingers remained clenched around the small bottle of antiseptic as she stared up into Trent's narrowed eyes.

She'd pissed him off. Well, who cared? She didn't even feel bad for ambushing the big baby with the peroxide. He'd been *shot*, for God's sake, a little bit of sterilization should've been no big deal.

His warm, masculine scent surrounded her, full of testosterone, threatening to undermine *her* resentment. Desperately, she clung to the emotion like a life preserver while the boat swayed, because anger was so much easier to deal with than outright fear. Anger she could control.

Below deck a few minutes ago, the fact that he could've been killed by that bullet had hit her hard. Hard enough that she'd had to scrub his blood from her hands and take a moment to compose herself or return with the first aid kit blubbering like an idiot.

His fixation on her chest may have heated her from the inside out, like his intense gaze was doing right now, but it'd also given her a convenient channel for her jumbled emotions. And then he'd called her *sweetheart* again. A word he tossed about so casually it made a mockery of the endearment. Her dad had used words like that as if they were nothing, too.

That's it. Don't think about how great Trent smells, or how sexy his body is, or how wonderful it would feel to have his arms hold you close...think about how he reminds you of Dad.

In essence, they were both actors. Both played whatever part they needed to get what they wanted. Having learned that lesson years ago, she didn't trust Trent's act one bit, especially when she wasn't entirely sure what it was he wanted. Told herself she didn't *want* to know.

Before her own traitorous body proved her a liar, Halli grasped the steering wheel to pull herself up and off of his lap. Once she was sitting, he gripped the other side of the wheel, trapping her between his arms. His softened hazel gaze locked on hers, and her breath caught in her throat. Her heart pounded, slow and deep.

This is why she'd avoided looking at him the past fifteen minutes. The man annoyed the hell out of her and yet he could mesmerize a cobra with those eyes. With his heat caressing her skin, she discovered she was much more susceptible than a snake.

It didn't help that the whole time she'd cleaned his arm, she'd had to consciously keep her gaze from lingering on his broad, bare chest. It was one thing to feel those muscles cloaked under a cotton T-shirt and quite another to visually feast upon them unclothed. Not to mention, she couldn't shake the memory that he was commando under the wet jeans that molded his thighs and backside. The same muscled thighs she currently sat upon.

He leaned toward her. Intent shone clear in his eyes, and she suddenly couldn't summon a single ounce of willpower to resist. The gentle rocking motion of the boat enhanced the seductive air cloaking the softly-lit cockpit. Once again, she was awed that *he* would want to kiss *her*.

His warm breath caressed her lips and her breath hitched in anticipation.

"It's so sexy when a woman literally throws herself at me."

Nothing like a dose of of his ego to ruin the sensual fantasy she'd foolishly descended into. Either he was making fun of her, or she was just another convenient, willing notch to add to his proverbial bedpost. Halli turned away from the temptation of his mouth and half-naked body and pushed against the arm holding her captive. There was hope for her yet, if not him.

"This was your fault, and you know it, you bigheaded *jerk*. I rest my case, and your arm's still bleeding."

A light puff of air stirred her hair and tickled her ear. When she hunched her shoulder, he gave another of his deep throated chuckles that made her stomach quiver. Thank God he lowered his arm. She scooted off his leg, the seat of her jeans wet from his.

Trent eased the boat forward.

Resisting the urge to peel the clinging denim away from her skin, she squatted down to gather up the supplies scattered on the floor of the boat and hoped her pants dried fast. For just a moment it had been fun to make Mr. Hollywood lose his cool. Until he turned the tables and proved she didn't have a chance of playing in his league. Nope, it was time to take care of business and get the heck away from him.

She'd given up hope of getting to the consulate tonight, so that meant a few hours on opposite sides of the boat, hopefully a few hours sleeping. Then finally, tomorrow, he'd drop her off in Milan, and she'd never have to see him again.

That thought sent an unexpected ripple of melancholy across the relief she should've been swimming in.

Whoa, no, she *was* relieved. He'd go his way, she'd go hers. Back to Wisconsin and her reliable routine that kept her days sane and secure. So what if they were totally predictable, and—dare she admit it?—a little boring. But so what, if that's the way she liked it? Lord knew she didn't need a sexy movie star kidnapping her every day. Even if he was saving her life. *Especially* if he was saving her life. No one needed that much excitement on a daily basis.

With that in mind, she picked up a clean towel and held out the peroxide to finish the job and get to the other side of the boat. Trent groaned in protest.

Halli rolled her eyes. "Oh, come on, it's not that bad."

"Easy for you to say." He craned his neck around to look at the table. "You got a shot of whiskey back there on your little nurse's station?"

"Watch the water, would you?" When he'd faced forward again, she placed the towel against his arm and lifted the bottle. "Ready?"

He gave a sharp nod and a lock of dark hair fell across his forehead. With the advance warning, his only reaction to the bubbling antiseptic on his raw flesh was the clenching of his jaw and tightening of his lips. His hands flexed on the steering wheel as he released a breath.

She dabbed gently at the wound, relieved to see the bleeding had pretty much stopped. While his skin dried in the wind, she located some butterfly bandages in the first aid kit. Three for sure, maybe four, and then she'd wrap an ace bandage around his bicep to soak up any blood that seeped out.

Increased lights along the shoreline up ahead on the left indicated the location of another small town. They'd passed two already. "Where are we going, anyway," she asked Trent as she unwrapped the first bandage.

"Bellagio."

A map of the lake materialized in her mind. "Why that far?"

"Because it's that far."

"Oh."

"The consulate's closed by now anyway, so we'll get some rest and head to Milan in the morning."

"I figured that much." She lifted the first bandage while releasing a wistful sigh. "Bellagio's across the lake from Villa Carlotta. I wish I could've seen the gardens there."

"You'll still get to see them."

"I doubt it." She touched his arm to warn, "I have to pull the edges together to put the bandages on."

He blew out another breath and nodded. "What's so special about the gardens at Villa Carlotta?"

She gave him a skeptical look. Like he cared about the rare and exotic plants they housed from all over the world.

"Halli, you can talk about the color of your wallpaper for all I care—just give me something to concentrate on, okay?"

She studied his pinched expression, nodded solemnly and launched into a monologue about the flowers at Villa Carlotta and her garden back home as she placed four butterfly bandages to act as adhesive stitches. His jaw clenched tight, and his knuckles whitened on the steering wheel, but he handled the process stoically now that he wasn't jumping at every move she made.

Still talking, she reached back for a package of sterile gauze pads and turned around to the see his chin against his chest while he made fake snoring sounds. Gaze narrowed, she thumped him in the back.

He lifted his head, shrugging his injured shoulder in a defensive move that made him grimace as he laughed. "Ouch."

"Then stop making fun of me. You asked."

He slid her a downcast, sideways glance. A grin revealed his heart-thumping smile. "Something tells me you'd never get away with that shirt back home."

Because her little gardening lecture confirmed what end of the boring scale she tipped. Face it, she was the furthest thing from wet and wild he'd ever meet. Halli gave an inward sigh and, while he was distracted by her breasts, reached up and gave him a slap upside the head this time.

"What? That was a compliment. You've totally pulled it off today." His voice lowered. "Quite well, in fact."

"You're impossible." Her face burned as if she'd spent the whole day in the sun. Men didn't flirt with her for any good reason, much less someone like Trent Tomlin. "Watch where you're going so I can finish this."

She tore open the gauze package and folded one of the pads to press against his wound before winding the ace bandage around his arm. Twice she brushed his rib cage by accident; twice his skin twitched and his stomach muscles contracted. Someone was ticklish? Halli fought a smile and the urge to do it again.

"You're not half bad at this bandaging gig," he observed when she anchored the wrap with the little metal clips.

"I took a class at the Y."

"They teach you how to treat gunshot victims at the Y these days?"

"Just basic first aid. Really, anyone could do it."

"Well, I appreciate your help. Thank you."

His serious tone brought her head up. Sincerity lit his eyes; a look like that made her crave the kiss he'd intended earlier.

She quickly turned away to pack up the first aid kit. "You're welcome," she murmured.

The higher pitched sound of a motor travelling at a fast speed caught her attention. Glancing between them, Trent reached for the gun. "Get down. *Now.*"

She dropped to the floor of the boat as he steered with his left hand, gun palmed in his right, prepared for whatever trouble accelerated their way.

You'd think she'd get used to this; that after the third or fourth time of unexpected danger the instant surge of fear wouldn't seize her lungs and make her heart thump in her chest.

But she wasn't used to it at all.

The approaching boat never slowed. It zoomed past, trailing laughter in its wake. Trent stood in front of the captain's chair, sweeping his gaze around their perimeter before staring in the direction of the fading boat engine. His shoulders relaxed and he put the gun back in the drink holder. "Just a bunch of kids out for a joyride. Sorry I scared you."

Halli wanted to collapse onto her back and let the overwhelming relief wash over her. In the blink of an eye, exhaustion slammed into her consciousness. She'd gotten maybe a half hour nap at Trent's house and as the adrenaline drained from her muscles, her body emphatically told her a half hour wasn't near enough. But instead of succumbing to the weariness, she picked herself up and focused on something else.

"You're pretty familiar with that gun."

Ooh, there you go, distract yourself by asking about the gun.

Trent's gaze shifted to the sleek black weapon. "I've handled my share."

"You said you didn't do stuff like this on a regular basis."

"At the shooting range, my dear, and on set. You've seen my movies."

Every single one. More than twice. Not that she'd tell him that. She pretended to think about it before shrugging her shoulders. "Maybe I do remember a gun or two in the trailers."

"Trailers?" He frowned over at her. "Yeah, right. You called me Shain when we first met. You don't pick up something like that from trailers."

"They played them *a lot*." She headed for the cabin.

"Hey—where you going? We're not done—"

"There's a boat. Eleven o'clock."

"Dammit." He jerked his attention back to the water and she went below deck with a grin tugging at her lips.

Out of nowhere, a particular page in his journal flashed through her thoughts. The one that revealed his sensitivity to his father's dissatisfaction in Trent's work. The choppy, nearly illegible writing and raw emotions on the page testified to how much his father's lack of respect bothered him.

She cringed, sighed, and vowed not to tease him about it in the future. Easy enough, considering their future together ended tomorrow.

Disappointment returned, sharper than before. And what if something happened to him during his search for evidence that his brother had been murdered?

Something more jagged than disappointment grabbed hold of her heart. Halli sank down on the bench seat near the half-stove and mini-sink.

Oh, no. She cared.

Not in the general sense that he was another human being and she wouldn't want something bad to happen to another person, but in a far more personal sense. Somewhere over the course of this crazy day, she'd come to specifically care what happened to *him*.

Darn it all. What part of *movie star* and *unattainable* did her brain not understand?

She shot to her feet and paced four steps across the small cabin. There was nothing to understand. She wasn't looking to attain anyone. Geez. What was wrong with her?

Maybe she could chalk it up to the day she'd had. Or Stockholm Syndrome. It was a proven fact some kidnap victims identified with and became attached to their kidnappers or they wouldn't have named it, would they have?

A quick spin and four more steps returned her to the other side of the boat. Okay, so she knew the real reason he'd tossed her in his car, and it was kind of heroic, and even a little romantic after the fact, but all of that was beside the point. She'd still been kidnapped. That's the part she must be responding to.

Then again, so what if she cared? Every once in awhile, between macho and jerk, she caught a glimpse of the good guy who'd written in the journal. It wasn't a bad thing for her to want that guy to remain safe on his quest to find justice for his brother. After all, he was going to take her to Milan to be reunited with her own family.

She paused in front of the tiny kitchen area. Might not hurt to make the man something to eat, either. He'd been hungry before, now he was wounded, too. He'd need to eat to keep up his strength. Besides, it was the least she could do after he'd taken a bullet for her. Well, not literally for her, but he'd been

protecting her when he'd gotten shot.
You and the video, a negative voice whispered in her mind.
"Oh, shut up," she muttered.

Chapter 11

Trent checked the GPS and figured they had maybe another half-hour before they reached Bellagio. He gradually steered the boat toward the middle of the lake, so they wouldn't pass too close to Lapaglia's villa in Lenno. Much as he'd love to cruise by and see what was going on at this hour of the evening, he was too tired to handle any more high-speed chases or gunfights. A day or two to regroup was in order after the past twelve hours.

He was just thinking he should've taken the chance to eat back at home when Halli appeared at his side.

"I can't believe you live in a country with some of the best food in the world, and you stock Spaghetti O's."

She held a bowl of said pasta and a glass of what looked like wine. What a combo. The pasta evoked a sad smile as he said, "My brother used to ship them in by the case."

In the middle of taking a sip of the wine, she quickly set the glass next to the bowl on the table behind his chair. "Sorry."

"It's all right." His stomach rumbled at the thought of food, even though he didn't particularly care for Sean's favorite fare.

Halli stepped closer to the captain's chair. "How about I drive while you eat."

He glanced back at the bowl and fought a grimace. "Thanks, but you go ahead. I'll fix something after we stop."

"I ate when you went to get the camera battery."

Alarm filled her expression and her gaze did a frantic search of the front seats. "Where *is* my camera?"

"Relax, it's safe and sound under the seat here." He indicated the cushion he'd braced one knee on.

"Oh."

Was that disappointment in her expression? Before he could ponder the strange reaction, she took hold of the wheel with one hand, waiting for him to slide out of the way. Like he could turn down the food now, knowing she'd prepared it just for him. Prepared being a very generous definition for dumping a can of processed food in a bowl and using a microwave.

Trent assessed their positions. Without slowing the boat, he gingerly lowered his left arm to his side and inched back to give her just enough room to slide in and take the wheel. "Best to use both hands out here in the middle of the lake."

She eyed the space he'd allowed for her body between him and the wheel while he did his best to maintain an innocent expression after his bogus suggestion. Although her expression reflected suspicion, she turned her back and eased in, practically hugging the steering wheel. Trent felt a little bad taking advantage of the situation, until her backside brushed against his front.

In that one second, all his guilt was swept away on a wave of hunger. Despite the running around they'd done since she'd showered, a hint of flowery freshness still clung to her skin by her neck. His senses filled, and desire intensified. He leaned in, his chest against her back. Just close enough to brush his lips against the ear she'd tucked her hair behind and pretend he was concerned about her handling the boat.

"Got it?"

Her stiff nod matched her posture.

What would it take to get her to melt against him? Need spiraled to his groin. The enticing sway and brush of their bodies from the movement of the boat became delicious torture. Heat from her flowed into him, magnifying the urge to turn her around into his arms. Struggling for control, he reached his right hand past her shoulder and pointed to the GPS display.

"Keep us headed due north and we'll be there in about twenty minutes."

Another brief nod.

When he shifted back to the left, the dim light of the dash revealed a blush tinted her cheeks. Hmm. Maybe she wasn't as indifferent to him as he thought. Exploring that possibility was highly tempting, but his stomach growled again, reminding him first things first. Satisfy one hunger before moving on to the other.

Trent reluctantly moved out of her space to pick up the

bowl of canned pasta and glass of wine, gritting his teeth at the pain with the flex of muscle in his left arm. He spun the passenger chair around to face her and sunk into a low slouch before propping his bare feet up on the arm of the captain's seat.

The wine, he discovered, was a bottle of his premier Chianti Classico. After an extended sip, he secured the glass stem between his legs and ate while watching Halli. Spaghetti O's had never tasted better.

"I have to admit, there were a few times today I was afraid you might lose it," he said around a mouthful of food.

"The video?"

He chuckled at her indignation. "Your cool."

She surprised him with a low, husky laugh. A genuine one like he'd heard on the video with her family. He liked it even more in person.

"You're not the only one," she said.

"Good to know you can pull it together when the chips are down."

"Any help I managed today was nothing more than dumb luck."

"Don't sell yourself short."

Silence reigned while he finished eating and then set the bowl aside. He took a drink of wine, holding the liquid in his mouth to savor the full flavor. She'd grown on him like the Chianti. A little dry and acidic at first, but the longer the tang remained on his tongue, the more he craved another taste of earthy spices and sweet black cherries with a hint of raspberry. The complex contradictions of Halliwell Sanders were as seductive as the wine.

He shifted in his wet jeans to find a more comfortable position. Maybe he should go change.

She cast him a glance before gazing back over the windshield. "You want to hear something really stupid?"

"Um...it's not about me, is it?"

"Nope—all me." This time her laugh sounded self-conscious.

"Then shoot," he encouraged, content to sit as long as she

was volunteering personal information.

"I know this'll sound crazy, but I was so glad to see that guy get up again back at the boathouse."

Dread stiffened his shoulders. Ramped up the pain in his arm. Of all subjects for her to bring up. He'd purposely avoided any thoughts about the man he'd hit with the iron patio chair. The one he'd left floating face down in the pool. "It's not crazy at all."

"You don't think so? Even if they would've killed us?" She gestured in his direction as she steered around a cruiser twice the size of his boat. "I mean, they shot you. If I *had* killed my guy, you'd think I shouldn't feel bad at all."

"Normal people don't take pleasure in killing another human being."

She stole another glance at him. "Did you really take out the guy on the patio?"

So much for not thinking about it. He swirled the wine in his glass and downed the remainder before giving a curt nod.

"You seem pretty calm about it."

If only she knew this egotistical jerk's stomach was threatening to give back the Spaghetti O's. He dropped his feet to the floor and stood, fists clenched at his side. His flesh burned under the bandage from the flex of muscle, but the pain reminded him of what was at stake.

"The bullet that sliced my arm was meant for my head. I'd be dead if I hadn't defended myself, and most likely, so would you."

"I know."

"These same men murdered my only brother, then took his private hell and turned it against him for the whole world to see. Sean did not commit suicide." He started to head downstairs, but anger swung him back to face her. "And then there's Lorenzo. He was a retired cop. Thirty-five years he put his life on the line, and these bastards calmly shoot him in the back for nothing more than *money*. Any one of them deserved to die."

Her eyes widened at the rage that had exploded in his voice. But it was his only weapon to combat the horror and guilt of taking another's life. His stomach muscles tightened at the hint of fear that'd crept into her eyes, prompting him to take a deep, controlled breath.

"It was either him or me, but that doesn't mean the end result bothers me any less."

Two long strides carried him to the short stairway below deck. He hooked his right hand above the door and swung down into the cabin. He'd had enough of that conversation, and it was time he changed into something dry anyway. Thankfully, he kept clothes on the boat.

Trent unbuttoned his jeans just as the sound of the motor lowered to an idle. The boat rocked beneath his feet. Halli's light footsteps sounded on the steps. He tensed, but kept his back turned, even when her soft touch on his shoulder made him flinch. Though he craved the reassurance of human contact more than anything, he shied away from showing any more weakness. It was bad enough she'd read his stuff in the notebook.

"I know how you feel," she said quietly.

He shook his head no, not trusting his voice to come out strong enough.

"Maybe for only a few minutes, but I do know how awful it is to think you've ended someone's life."

Before he could form a response, she moved in front of him. Right up against him, slipping her arms around his waist, her soft cheek pressed to his chest. Her palms flattened on his back as her arms tightened and held.

The lump in Trent's throat grew painfully large as he stared at the top of her head in astonishment. He could name on one hand the number of people he knew who might've recognized what he needed and then offered it without hesitation. Hell, he hadn't even known how bad he needed this simple comfort until her warmth surrounded him.

Nothing could've kept his arms from closing tight around her. He turned his head to rest his cheek on the top of her head and held on for dear life.

Time stood still until she finally whispered, "I'm sorry, Trent."

"For what?" The question barely scraped past the emotion

clogging his throat.

"Your brother. Your friend. What happened back at your villa."

"None of it's your fault."

"I'm still sorry." Her heartfelt words stirred the hair on his chest.

His arms clenched for a moment, then he relaxed his hold and looked down. She lifted her chin. Long dark lashes rose, revealing deep blue eyes moist with unshed tears. He drank in the compassionate understanding in her shimmering gaze, and in the space of a heartbeat, their moment of companionship transformed into something more.

Air locked in his lungs. Her lips beckoned, parting with a soft intake of breath. Earlier desire surged forward, heating his blood faster than a shot of whiskey or glass of wine. It went deeper than simple lust, unlike anything he'd experienced before.

Because Halli was unlike any woman he'd ever known—and she proved it when he leaned down in anticipation of their second kiss of the day. Instead of melting into his embrace and giving him everything he wanted, she pushed against his chest and stepped back.

A growl of frustrated yearning rumbled in his throat when her palm broke contact with his flushed skin. Her lashes lowered again, sweeping against rosy cheeks.

Suddenly her eyes widened and she spun around. "Um…you need to take over the controls."

Oh, he'd love to take control. Lose himself and the rest of the world in her. But she headed topside so fast he was forced to call after her, "I'll be right up."

His entire body hummed with suppressed awareness, some places a hell of a lot more insistent than others. Maybe it was a good thing she distanced herself. With his heightened emotions, and the bed a mere step away, any encouragement from her would've spun things out of control in record time. She may be different, but he was still just a man.

Trent reached for the button on his jeans in the interest of comfort only to discover it was already undone and the zipper half down from before. No wonder she'd run the other direction.

With a wry twist of his lips, he pulled out a pair of boxer briefs, cotton shorts and a T-shirt from a drawer built into the wall next to the bed. On second thought, he exchanged the T-shirt for a short sleeved button down shirt so he could slide it over the bandage. He left the shirt undone, tossed his blood-stained, wet jeans over the tiny shower rod in the head, and went up to see where she'd stopped the boat.

Halli avoided looking at him as he powered back up and nudged the bow north. A few minutes later, he pointed out the cluster of lights hugging the dark shoreline ahead and to their right. "That's Bellagio."

"So what do we do now?"

"A friend of mine has a place up here where we can dock for the night."

"We're not staying at their house, are we?" Dismay colored her tone. "I'm really not up to facing strangers right about now."

"It's okay, we'll stay on the boat. George is on vacation in France, anyway."

"George?" Sudden interest raised her voice an octave. "Clooney?"

"No, not Clooney." He felt the beginnings of a frown. "I suppose you've seen *his* stuff."

"Of course; I love his movies. Do you know where his place is on the lake?"

Her hopeful question triggered unexpected annoyance. "He's on location until September, so forget it."

"Chill out." She sat back in her seat, arms crossed. "I was only going to ask if we could drive past."

"He lives down in Laglio, near Como, and we're not going back that way."

"Fine. Sorry I even mentioned it."

Of course she'd seen Clooney's movies. Trent knew he shouldn't care if she didn't watch his movies, yet his ego growled in protest. He clamped his jaw tight and tried to forget the whole subject as he'd ordered her to.

A few hundred yards shy of the peninsula of the inverted Y of the lake, he eased the *Scappare* alongside George's long dock with it's yacht and motor boat for water skiing. He cut the engine and maneuvered the cruiser behind the other vessels. Halli jumped onto the dock before he could voice the request forming on his tongue. He tossed out the mooring rope and she secured the stern, then they both moved to the bow.

"Thanks," he offered past the lingering resentment from a moment ago.

Low energy LED's placed strategically around the cabin provided soft illumination without pointing a glaring finger to their added presence in the area. Besides, George's private dock was far enough from the more populated areas that Trent felt comfortable they were safe.

Yet when Halli straightened and looked around from her viewpoint on the dock while hugging her arms across her stomach, he was struck by how small and defenseless she appeared up there all alone.

"Now would be a good time to get some rest," Trent suggested. Judging by mood alone, the day was definitely catching up with him. "Morning will be here before we know it."

"I am tired, but it seems like it'd be impossible to sleep."

"Hmm. And here I am, fresh out of reading material for you."

She made a face at his sarcasm, but he caught a flash of guilt before she turned away and walked to the end of the dock.

An alien sense of vulnerability still remained at the knowledge of her being privy to his private thoughts in the notebook. A part of him wanted to leave her over there, by herself, staring out over the water. The other part, the part that noticed the vigorous rub she gave her bare arms, grabbed the windbreaker he kept stowed below deck, vaulted onto the dock, and strolled along the weathered wooden planks to join her.

Her head turned slightly as he approached, but she didn't face him. He handed the jacket over and felt good when she slipped her arms into the sleeves with a quiet "Thank you."

A couple rolls on each side brought the long sleeves in line with her slender wrists. She stuffed her hands inside the pockets, and he wondered what to do with his as he stood alongside her in the dim light of the partial moon. This feeling of uncertainty in connection with a woman was entirely new to him.

And damned annoying.

His gaze scanned the lights of the various small villages and towns that dotted the lakeshore in the apex of the inverted Y that made up *Lago de Como*. Light spilled from homes, villas, hotels and places of business, shimmering on waves dancing to the tune of a light wind. The occasional ring of a bell echoed across the water that lapped against the boats and the rocks on shore. Romance hung in the crisp night air, just out of reach in their current circumstances.

"Pretty, isn't it?" he asked Halli.

"It's amazing." A heavy sigh lifted her shoulders. "Wish I'd gotten a chance to see more of it."

He angled his head toward her with a frown. "You keep talking like this is it. I'll get you to Milan, Halli, don't worry."

"I'm not." She half-smiled up at him. "Well, not really. What I meant was after I meet up with Ben and Rachel tomorrow morning, I'm booking a flight straight home. I've had enough of Italy to last me a lifetime."

She sounded awfully certain she'd locate her family right away. He felt compelled to caution her against getting her hopes up too high. "I'm sure the consulate will help you locate them, but be prepared that it might not happen right away."

"Oh, geez, that's right." Her palm smacked her forehead. "With everything that happened, I forgot to tell you I called Ben earlier. I'm meeting them at the consulate in the morning."

His frown deepened. "When was this?"

"When you left to get the battery."

At most, an hour before they'd been ambushed. Unease snaked down his spine. "Where were they all day? Why didn't they come to get you tonight?"

She gave a short laugh. "I can try him again if you're that anxious to get rid of me."

"First of all, my cell's back at the villa, and second, that's not what I meant at all."

"Of course you didn't." After that little burst of injured sarcasm, she looked down, rubbing the toe of her shoe on the dock. "I didn't actually talk to Ben. I left a message."

Suddenly, Lapaglia's men showing up at his villa took on a whole new meaning. Then a second realization socked Trent in the gut. *Shit!* The wire recording was back there, too. Right in the hands of Lapaglia's men. And he had no doubt they'd find that extra piece of evidence.

When Trent spoke, he kept his voice calm with effort. "What did you say?"

"I told them I was okay and I'd meet them at the consulate tomorrow. Why?"

"Did you say anything about where you were? Who you were with? Leave my number or anything?"

"No. I didn't even mention anything that happened today, only that I'd meet them about ten o'clock." She turned to face him and repeated, "Why?"

Trent relaxed slightly, realizing his gut reaction assumptions were probably unlikely. All it would've taken was one trip to Lorenzo's house in Blevio to connect him and Trent.

Paranoia and exhaustion were getting the better of him and he tried to make light of the mini-interrogation. "Just want to make sure I can drop you off tomorrow without having to deal with a bunch of fans clamoring for autographs."

She rolled her eyes before spinning on one heel to start back along the dock. "You should get yourself a bigger boat to house that ego of yours. And, my brother and sister hardly constitute a *bunch*."

"I notice you didn't point out they wouldn't want an autograph."

"They don't know you like I do."

"Lucky for me."

"Lucky for *them*."

He laughed and playfully nudged her toward the edge of the dock with his good shoulder. She stuttered a step, then shoved back on his arm with both hands.

At the boat, he braced his weight on his right hand and

jumped over the edge, then turned to offer help down. Her hesitation delivered another blow to his apparently staggering ego. He fought back with a good ol' boy grin.

Her palm slid into his. So small, so delicate, but her grip spoke of a strength easily underestimated.

"I never did actually thank you for saving me today."

Case in point, he hadn't seen that one coming.

The lights of the boat illuminated her face as she joined him on deck, but intriguing shadows darkened her eyes. He tightened his hold on her fingers when she gave a subtle pull. "Three times, now, but who's counting."

"You're a regular knight in shining armor, Tomlin."

"Tell that to the tabloids."

"They'd never buy it."

She tugged harder and he released her hand. "True. And if they did, it would totally ruin my image."

Flip answers came easy, and they were as comfortable as a worn pair of jeans. Better than giving in to the temptation to kiss her again. He might end up head over heels in the water.

She shook her head with a laugh. "In light of your *three* rescues then, I say, thank you, thank you, and thank you."

He dipped his head in a single nod. When she lowered herself onto the bench seat and leaned her head back, he descended to the galley for two glasses and the bottle of Chianti she'd opened earlier. She protested when he returned and poured wine for each of them, but accepted his offer of the glass anyway. He took a seat across from her and sipped.

A few minutes of companionable silence passed before he said, "I'm curious…I noticed it took me getting shot for you to one hundred percent believe I was trying to help. Do you have trouble trusting people in general, or is it me in particular?"

She lifted her hand to cover a yawn, and then took a sip of wine. She did not meet his eyes. "I like things very ordered, and y—"

"No, not *you*."

"*You* are very un-ordered."

"So, naturally, I'm untrustworthy." He acknowledged her statement with a lift of his glass. "I'm impressed with your logic."

"We're not really having this discussion again, are we?" She mimicked his words from earlier at the house.

"Humor me. I was tired, I wasn't listening." He glanced across the lake at the lights of Candenabbia and Tremezzo. Lenno sat slightly to the south. He did his best to focus on Halli and not wonder what Lapaglia was doing right now.

Halli spoke through another yawn. "Typical. It didn't have to do with you, so why bother listening."

Trent turned back to Halli. "I'm sorry, what was that?"

When she started to repeat her words, he couldn't hold back his grin.

"Oh, ha, ha, funny man."

"You walked right into that one."

"Yeah, well I'm tired, too. And this wine isn't helping." The red liquid sloshed around the inside of her glass as she lifted it to point a finger at him. "Another strike against your trustworthiness. First you kidnapped me, now you're getting me drunk."

He arched an eyebrow. "On one little glass?"

She took another drink and rested the glass on her thigh, her head on the seat back. A tired smile curved her lips and her eyelids drooped. "Probably."

He'd argue the wine was helping just fine, just not out loud. She needed more than the short nap she'd gotten earlier. The car chase, the police station, and the attack at the villa would be enough to exhaust anyone, but she also had a hefty shot of jetlag stirred into the cocktail. He was amazed she'd held up as well as she had, not to mention, her impromptu performance at the station had been spot on. Granted, she'd probably been channeling her terror of the situation, but for a rookie, she'd played her character almost perfectly.

He had a brief flashback of their conversation in the station's janitorial closet. Something she'd said had struck him as very odd. Still did now. After a drink from his glass, he asked, "So, you work in television?"

"Yes."

"Have you ever acted before?"

"Not really."

She'd turned to rest her cheek against the seat. Her lowered lashes formed dark fans against pale skin.

"You were a natural back at the police station," he commented, staring at her relaxed mouth.

"*Hmm.*"

"What'd you mean when you said you forgot about back story?"

"My parents," she mumbled, eyes still closed.

He sat forward, bracing his elbows on his knees, curious about her family. "What about them?"

"They used back story."

After setting his own drink aside, Trent got up and rescued Halli's wine glass slowly tipping off her leg. "Were they actors?"

She made a soft negative sound and shifted in her seat. He set the stemmed glass on the floor of the boat, and hunkered down next to her, wishing the wine hadn't taken affect so fast.

"*Halli.*"

With his light touch on her shoulder, her lashes fluttered, lifted to allow a brief glimpse of blue, then lowered again.

"What'd your parents use back story for?"

She mumbled again, forcing him to lean forward to catch her ever softening words. Unfortunately, sleep had finally claimed her.

Settling back on his heels, Trent rested his chin on his hand with a deep sigh. He gazed at her softened features, wondering what she'd been about to say about her parents, and surprised by how much he wanted another glimpse into her world beyond the bits of film with her siblings.

Had she had the ideal childhood growing up in the Heartland of America would suggest, or was it riddled with angst and unhappiness like his? Going off the video he'd watched of her interacting with her brother and sister, he pictured the perfect, All-American family sitting down to dinner like the classic Cleavers or the Brady Bunch. They'd have had a big, sloppy dog under the table, and lots of laughter and fun as they ate pot roast and mashed potatoes with apple pie for dessert. They probably played ball in the yard and had family game nights with popcorn and Kool-aid.

He'd dreamed of that exact scene so many nights after the nanny served him and Sean gourmet French cuisine prepared by their live-in chef. The fancy food made no sense with their father on the other side of the world filming his latest award-winning documentary, but François had refused to prepare food he considered unworthy of his self-proclaimed five star talents.

It was only in weak moments that Trent admitted to himself he still resented being left at the mercy of hired help who had no patience for two boys craving attention after the sudden death of their mother. Greg Tomlin repeatedly touted the fact that he'd provided a luxurious roof over their heads and anything they needed, but Trent felt his father's absence was nothing short of abandonment.

When they got a little older, Sean sought and gained approval by following in their father's footsteps. Trent, on the other hand, had rebelled by entering the very profession that'd stolen their mother. He and the old man hadn't seen eye to eye since, especially when he succeeded despite his father's predictions of failure. To Trent's knowledge, the elder Tomlin had never once admitted when he was wrong.

Banishing the dark thoughts back where they belonged, he picked up Halli's glass and stood, debating his options. She was light enough to carry below deck, but he didn't want to wake her. Since the temperature was mild, with no rain forecasted, he decided it would be better to make her comfortable where she was.

He drank the remainder of his wine, but dumped hers overboard. Much as he would love the numbing affect more alcohol would provide for his thoughts and the steady throb of pain in his arm, he needed to stay alert. Although he wasn't too worried about their location, Lapaglia had been resourceful enough through the day, even if he hadn't been successful. Trent would sleep topside tonight, too, just in case.

Chapter 12

Ben woke in his clothes, with a crick in his neck, and a sore jaw. Nothing new since he was used to sleeping in odd places and had been known to get into trouble at the bars on occasion. This morning, it was his surroundings that threw him off completely. Cheap hotels and country campsites didn't have plush velvet chairs and four poster beds.

It only took a moment for the nightmare to come crashing back. He tensed, but refrained from making any sudden movements. A slow stretch in the chair he'd occupied for the night allowed him to take stock of the room with a careful sweep of his gaze. Rachel slept soundly on the bed nearby, and their watchdog Zucchi still sat at the door.

Through a part in the curtains, he saw dawn had broken across the water. The sun peaked over the snow tipped eastward mountains that made up part of the alpine region surrounding Lake Como. It was absolutely breathtaking, and he wondered if Halli could see it from wherever she was at this moment. Worry stirred in his gut. Was she safe out there all alone, or possibly still with the mysterious stranger helping her?

He hoped he'd get to meet the man some day and thank him. But not today. God, he wished there were some way to warn Halli before she went to the consulate in Milan.

A snore erupted from the bruised face of the guard at the door. He shifted in his chair, snorted once more, then silence returned. Ben listened carefully. It seemed the rest of the house slept along with the guard so he sat up to reevaluate the balcony he'd assessed the day before. The one story drop might be a problem for Rachel, but it couldn't be helped. This might be their only chance to escape.

Movement in the courtyard below caught his attention. He leaned forward and nudged aside the curtain for a better look. The Italian woman from the night before stood on a small cobblestoned area of a corner garden. Eva balanced on one leg in a difficult yoga move his last girlfriend had attempted a time or two. Spandex clad curves flowed lithely from one pose to the next, her control of movement remarkable.

Damn. She posed a problem out there. As if sensing his scrutiny, her head lifted toward the second story window. Ben ducked back behind the curtains and shifted toward the door. Forget the woman for a moment, he had to concentrate on disabling Zucchi. Better yet if he could secure the gun hanging limply from the man's lap.

He looked around for something to use as a weapon. Something quiet, but effect—

His gaze swung back to the sleeping guard and focused on the weapon. His heart began to pound. Could he really go and just pluck it from his grasp? And would the guy stay quiet with a gun in his face? Hopefully. He wouldn't want to have to make the decision to pull the trigger.

One smooth movement brought him to his feet. He allowed no time to think before crossing to Zucchi's side and snatching the gun. The guard came awake with a start, but Ben pressed the barrel hard against his cheek. *"Shh."*

Zucchi's dark eyes widened, but he didn't make a sound.

"One word and I'll blow your head off. *Capiche?*" Good God, he even nailed the Godfather accent. The guy nodded. Ben stepped back and jerked his head toward the bed where Rachel slept. "Up. Move slow and don't make a sound."

Once they were near the bed, he shoved Zucchi to the chair. Without taking his eyes off the man, he leaned over and gently shook his sister. "Rachel, wake up."

She groaned softly and he felt her shift away. She wasn't a morning person and didn't usually become coherent until after a couple cups of coffee. After one swift glance, he returned his gaze to Zucchi before shaking a little harder.

"*Rach,* wake up."

From the corner of his eye, he saw her roll over, blink a few times, then she jolted upward with a gasp.

"*Shh,*", he warned. "Come on, let's go. We're getting out of here."

She scrambled off the bed, in no need of liquid stimulants

this morning. "I'm all for that. What about him?"

They both looked at Zucchi, glaring at them above his bruised, swollen nose.

"Tie him up," Ben told his sister. Then he caught the guy's eye. "You even think about touching her, buddy, you'll be singing soprano for life. *If* you live that long."

Rachel moved toward the curtains.

"Stay away from the windows," Ben ordered. "That woman was out there. I don't want her to see we're awake."

"I need the sashes to tie him up." Rachel removed the restraints and gave a quick peek out the window. "Looks clear."

Ben kept the gun trained on Zucchi's lap as she approached the chair. He hated having Rachel do the hands on work, but she had no experience at all with guns.

While she tied the man's hands to the arm chairs, Ben felt behind him for a pillow. "Tight as you can, sis, and hurry up."

The pillow slid from its case when he upended it, and he tossed the material to Rachel when she was done. "Gag him."

Confident he had a little breathing space, Ben eased over to the window. The courtyard did appear deserted. Did they chance their escape that way, or try the hall? He turned back to Rachel to see her unlacing one of her shoes. "What are you doing?"

"Tying his feet so he can't kick something and make noise after we leave."

"Good thinking."

The yard remained empty and he decided they'd go that way. Rachel finished tying Zucchi's feet and stood. Ben walked behind the chair and tipped it back on two legs.

He pressed the tip of the gun to Zucchi's forehead. "Is there any security on the windows?"

Zucchi's Adam's apple bobbed frantically. He soundlessly jerked his head back and forth.

"If an alarm goes off when I open that window, I will shoot you before we run. Understand?"

Zucchi nodded.

Ben lowered the chair backward, all the way to the floor, and stepped over him to the window. He held the gun chest high and reached to unlatch the window. It swung open with the slightest of squeaks. Rachel sucked in a breath and their eyes met for a charged moment. The absence of an alarm did not allow for relaxation, and Ben took a deep breath before stepping out onto the balcony, his sister close behind.

They crept steadily along the length of the villa, crawling under each window while Ben tried to figure out the best place to jump down. It was hard to see what was underneath and the last thing he wanted to do was drop directly in front of a lower window. The very end looked to offer the best protection. Ben debated giving Rachel the gun, but decided to tuck it against his back instead.

He pulled her close and breathed in her ear, "I'll let you know when to jump, okay?"

She gulped and nodded agreement. Ben judged the distance, grabbed the railing, and vaulted over the side. He landed on his feet and immediately dropped down into a squat to do a quick visual sweep of the surrounding area. *All clear.* Rachel had climbed over the rail and stood on the edge, waiting for his signal. He waved her down.

She bent her knees, leaned forward, and jumped. One of her unlaced shoes fell ahead of her. Her landing was far from elegant and she gave a soft cry as she tumbled to the ground. Ben rushed to her side and helped her to her feet. One step and she nearly fell again. A barely perceptible moan escaped her compressed lips. "My ankle."

Ben swore under his breath. Seconds later, shattered glass sounded from the second floor. Somewhere in the house, a dog barked. Ben swore again, pulled the gun, and braced Rachel's arm around his neck. As they started forward, he was struck with a sense of déjà vu. He couldn't help but crack, "Just like old times, hey sis?"

"Been a long time."

"Sure has. But we're old pros. We can do this."

She soldiered on with him, but her ankle slowed them down. At the end of the villa wall, Ben took a quick look around the corner and spotted their Fiat rental in the drive. It'd been years since he'd hotwired a car, and never a foreign one.

Shouts from inside the house indicated their absence had been discovered. A door slammed on the bottom level. There was no time for him to even try the car.

"Come on, this way."

Rachel stumbled as they ran across the drive toward the neighboring property. Ben held her upright and saw she'd lost her other shoe. He fought against impatience and focused straight ahead. If they could get past the six foot high privacy hedge surrounding the villa, they might be able to get help.

A deep, ferocious growl halted them in their tracks. Ben whirled, gun raised as he pushed Rachel behind him. Rachel's shriek vibrated his eardrum at the sight of Nino pointing a gun at them while holding the leash attached to a huge black Rottweiler. The dog's white teeth gleamed beneath curled, snarling lips. Drool dripped from massive jaws.

"Drop the gun," Nino ordered.

Ben's fingers clenched on the handle of the pistol. *Damn it.* They'd been so close. A indecisive glance around convinced him he had no other choice than to toss it aside.

"Benjamin, you insult my hospitality." Alrigo approached in Ben's peripheral vision. "If you are in need of fresh air, you must ask nicely."

He swore silently and smiled at the man. "We did. Zucchi wasn't very accommodating."

Alrigo leaned to pick up Ben's discarded weapon as he laughed. The sound chilled the blood in Ben's veins.

"You still wish to run this beautiful morning?" Alrigo taunted. "I am sure Bruno would be happy to...accommodate."

Ben eyed the now panting dog and lifted his gaze to the stone-faced Nino while Alrigo circled behind him. "No, thank you."

"Excellent decision."

Without warning, a forceful blow on the back of Ben's skull knocked him to his knees. Rachel cried out as pain radiated through his skull and the dog went wild, barking and snarling.

Reflexes stunned, Ben tried to turn toward his sister, but Alrigo moved in front of him. The man grabbed a handful of his hair and jerked his head up while the other fist slammed into his jaw. Agony exploded across Ben's face. A second strike nearly made him pass out and when shoved to the ground, he was too disorientated to brace his fall.

Gravel bit into his already throbbing cheek. Eyes squeezed shut, he swallowed hard and tasted blood. The dog's bark echoed in his throbbing head.

Get up!

He gave his head a shake, trying to clear all thought but the one, and opened his eyes to fight his way to his feet. His gaze registered a booted foot a split second before the rock solid force connected with his ribs. Air rushed from his lungs on a whooshing grunt. Fire seared his mid-section. Ben coughed and gasped for oxygen as another kick had him instinctively curling into a ball.

Blackness crowded the edges of his vision. Rachel sobbed and begged the Italian to stop.

Distantly, Ben heard another female, speaking in curt Italian. *Eva.*

"Basta." Nino's firmly voiced command brought everything to a halt.

Rachel knelt at Ben's side. Tears ran down her cheeks. "Ben, are you okay?"

Holding back an agonized groan, he pushed himself to his knees, turning his head to the side to spit out a mouthful of blood. He felt with his tongue for the gash inside his cheek and smoothed the jagged skin back in place. When he lifted his gaze, Eva stood next to Nino, still in her spandex yoga suit, hand resting on the Rottweiler's head. Bruno stood perfectly still and silent.

Eva's concerned brown eyes connected with his, but he had no chance to wonder about the emotion before she spun on her bare foot and retreated to the house. He resisted raising his head to watch her leave.

"Get up," Alrigo bit out.

Rachel helped him to his feet. He was sore all over, and they made quite the pair, him partially doubled over and her limping on her sprained ankle. With each step closer to the stone doorway leading them back to their prison, frustration and anger mounted. They should be free right now.

At the door, he urged Rachel ahead of him, and cast a covert glance back toward Alrigo. The man's attention was diverted by a vehicle that'd just turned in between the gates of the villa. Ben bent low and took a step backward at the same time. His elbow connected with Alrigo's ribs, eliciting a hoarse cry of pain.

He smiled his revenge and spun to face their captor, prepared to beat the prick to a pulp. He'd pulled his arm back, fingers forming into a fist, when something struck him from behind again. The world went black before he hit the floor.

****

Ben came to on a soft surface. Gentle fingers pressed a cool cloth to his throbbing face. His head pounded as if punishing him for an all day bender and his body ached as if he'd gunned his bike off the side of a cliff and landed on rocks.

Still…if Rachel was taking care of him, that meant she was okay. He cracked an eye open. Steady brown eyes regarded him.

Eva.

Ben stilled in surprise, then cast his gaze about the room and moved to sit up. His upward momentum was cut short with a painful bite and a metallic jangle on his wrists. He twisted his head to discover his arms were handcuffed to the bed. A jerk of one arm did nothing more than rattle the metal chain and wrench his wrist.

"Rachel?" he called, searching the room again as fear squeezed his chest. His gaze sliced to Eva. "Where's my sister?"

Eva's hand lowered. She turned to dip the cloth into a bowl of ice water sitting on a table next to the bed. "Rachel is fine."

"Where is she?" he demanded again.

"Resting in a different room to repair her ankle."

"I want to see her."

"That is not possible."

"I want to see that she's okay." Ben glared his insistence. When Eva leaned forward to press the cold cloth to his cheek once more, he jerked his head away. Her lips compressed. Emotion flashed in her eyes, but her long black lashes lowered too quick for him to identify it. When her gaze met his once more, her shuttered expression revealed nothing.

"Stubborn American. Let me help where I can."

He tried a different tactic, banking on the concern he'd glimpsed in her expression outside. "Do you have family, Eva?"

She regarded him for a brief moment before turning back to the bowl and dipping the cloth again.

He pressed harder. "Parents? A child? A brother or sister? *Anyone* you care about?"

He knew he'd hit a nerve when she caught her lower lip between her teeth. Finally, she admitted, "A sister."

"Do you love her?"

"Of course."

"Then you understand."

Her gaze returned to his, direct and unwavering. "I understand you must not anger Alrigo again if you and your sister wish to leave here alive. I assure you, for now, she is fine."

Her sultry accent made the sincere sounding words all the more convincing. This time, he didn't move when she reached to apply the icy compress. He studied her face, appreciating the dark beauty of her Italian heritage. A thick shiny mass of ebony curls framed her small, rounded jaw line and high cheekbones, a shade lighter than the impossibly long eyelashes that highlighted her brown eyes to perfection. Her straight nose led down to a set of lips that promised a sensuous cushion for a man's demanding mouth.

His gaze strayed lower, resting on the abundant swell of her breasts at the top edge of her skin-tight spandex leotard. As he watched, her nipples stood out against the tight material. Ben swallowed hard and averted his attention in time to see her tongue slide across that full bottom lip. Her awareness of his appraisal sent a surge of lust to quicken his pulse. It was followed almost instantly by a tide of disgusted guilt.

Wrestling his hormones back in line, he asked, "Tell me, Eva, how is my buddy Alrigo?"

"Very unhappy."

"Got him good, didn't I?"

He caught a flash of a smile on her glistening lips a split second before she turned away.

"You are too arrogant. You must be careful."

"Will you help us?"

Surprised brown eyes met his. "No."

Dammit. He'd intended to feel her out, get an idea of how deep her loyalty ran, not ask her outright. But he couldn't take the request back now, so he tried to appeal to the kindness he'd glimpsed in her eyes.

"You're different than them. I saw it last night. I can see it right now, otherwise you wouldn't be taking care of me."

Her spine stiffened and she shoved off the edge of the bed. She scanned the empty room before leaning forward, her eyes lit with an internal fire. "You are mistaken. I do what is necessary, nothing more."

Ben stared at the door after she'd slammed out. He wasn't that far off base. Her gaze had blazed with anger and something more. An emotion he could easily identify, because over the past twenty four hours, he'd become familiar enough with the feeling to recognize it in someone else.

Fear.

Time dragged for what felt like hours, and the sun told him the morning had advanced before the door opened again. Rachel entered with Nino and Alrigo. Ben caught a glimpse of the stress lines bracketing Alrigo's mouth. His lips were pressed so thin there was no doubt the man was in pain. *Good.*

Nino released Rachel's arm and she quickly limped toward the bed. Alrigo gave them a menacing smile. "Take a good look, *carina*. Your brother's life hinges on how well you follow instructions."

Rachel sat next to Ben, her light blue eyes full of worry and unshed tears.

"What's going on?" he asked.

She wiped a tear that spilled down her cheek. "They're taking me to Milan. I'm supposed to wait outside the consulate for Halli."

Realization sent a combination of dread and anger through his aching body. They were going to use her as bait. Halli wouldn't think twice about running to Rachel, and Alrigo would grab her in a heartbeat. The man had no conscience.

Looking at the bastard's stony expression, Ben highly doubted he had any intentions of letting them go. They knew too much. Once he had Halli, and whatever it was she possessed that he wanted so desperately, they'd be nothing but a liability.

It was up to Ben to make sure his sisters stayed safe. But what the hell could he do, laying here in fucking handcuffs? He wanted to kill the men in front of him with his bare hands.

When Rachel leaned over to kiss his cheek, he turned his head and pressed his lips to her ear as the Italians conversed in their native language.

"Promise me something?"

"Anything," she breathed softly.

"Take Hal and run," he whispered. "Don't worry about me."

She pulled back to look at his face, her eyes wide as she shook her head. "Ben—"

"Do it, Rachel," Ben ordered, his voice raised on purpose. "For me."

"What do you know, Benjamin finally shows some sense." Alrigo pulled his pistol out and made a show of ejecting the ammo clip, surveying the bullets, and shoving the clip back into place with a loud click. "Listen to your brother, *carina*."

Rachel stared at Ben in abject misery until Alrigo took hold of her arm. "We go. Now. You must not keep Halliwell waiting."

****

Evalina Gallo, aka Eva Anelli to Alrigo and his associates, watched Raphael pull out of the drive with Tony and the American girl in the back seat of the Lancia. Oddly enough, her first inclination was to go see the brother again. However, Alrigo and Nino had remained at the villa to finalize some details on the shipment due in two days, and showing too much interest in the American would be unwise. Nino would not understand.

Besides, did she really want to spend more time with a man who was too intuitive for her own good? If she wasn't careful, Benjamin Sanders could blow the foundation she and Nino had carefully laid with Alrigo over this past year.

And that she could not risk. After six long years, she owed it to her father to finish what he'd started.

Chapter 13

Details registered on Halli's mind as her consciousness slowly surfaced from sleep. Like the tantalizing aroma of fresh brewed coffee wafting by her nose. A nose that was chilled, while the rest of her was toasty warm. Not entirely comfortable, but warm.

Soothed by the gentle rocking motion of the seat beneath her, she listened to the soft slap of water against the side of the boat and the rocks on shore. The echo of bells across the lake, and the cries of the seagulls added to the morning symphony.

She shifted underneath a soft blanket she didn't remember tucking around her shoulders and wiggled her toes to discover her shoes were gone. A plump pillow cushioned her head from the firm bench seat of Trent's cabin cruiser.

Another whiff of coffee teased her nostrils, tempting her to open her eyes, stretch and sit up. She resisted. This moment of sensation was hers to fantasize of a fun, relaxing day on the lake with a gorgeous man who wanted *her*, not the SD card in her video camera. To pretend yesterday hadn't happened, and that today did not stretch endlessly into an uncertain future.

It was just the simple here and now. One selfish moment.

But all the day-dreaming in the world could not hold reality at bay. She sighed softly and stretched her arms up over her head. Muscles protested, sore from being tackled by the thug on Trent's lawn.

"Morning, sleepyhead."

Her fantasy man's deep voice rumbled through her and awakened the butterflies that'd cropped up last night when he'd leaned in to kiss her. She pushed to a sitting position and finger-combed hair from her eyes before lifting her gaze to Trent's. His smile made her heart stumble. How long had he been sitting there watching her?

"Hi," she said self-consciously. Where was a darn mirror when she needed one?

He lifted a black mug and one dark eyebrow. "Coffee?"

"Yes, please. With sugar."

He headed below deck. Another stretch wrung a groan from her. "What time is it?"

"Quarter after six," Trent called from below.

Halli scrubbed her hands over her face and rubbed sleep from her eyes. Ran her fingers through her hair before smoothing the sides. The sound of Trent's footsteps made her drop her hands back to her lap. When he handed her a forest green mug identical to his, she concentrated on not spilling it , nervous to look at him.

"You're up early," she said.

"Didn't sleep much."

He sat in the chair opposite her, much the same as last night with the wine. Steam curled up into the cool morning air and the hot coffee warmed her hands through the ceramic. Its robust aroma cleared any remaining cobwebs. She lifted the mug up to her mouth and blew softly.

It was impossible not to notice how wonderful Trent looked in the morning sunshine. The whiskers darkening his jaw had been trimmed, but not close enough to eliminate the scruff look. He wore it well. It was hard to recall if she'd ever really seen pictures where he wasn't clean-shaven, and she understood exactly why he didn't shave now. He blended well with the many dark-haired Italians and was hard to recognize. So long as he didn't smile.

Like now. That smile was a dead giveaway. Her heart thumped and she dropped her gaze from his. Clean jeans encased his long legs—and the question of what he may or may not have on underneath was firmly ignored.

Her face warmed anyway. *Darn it.* She switched her focus and noticed he wore the same short sleeved shirt from last night, though it was buttoned now. *So what.* Better if she didn't have to avoid staring at his bare, muscled chest. The material of the left sleeve stretched tight over the bandage and she seized on that detail like she'd been thrown a life preserver.

"How does your arm feel this morning?"

He shrugged his right shoulder. "I'll live."

"You should go to a hospital and have them stitch you up."

His smile vanished. "Too many questions at a hospital."

"But what if your arm gets infected?"

"I'll be fine."

"Trent—"

"No hospitals." His abrupt tone closed the subject.

"Then at the least I'll change the bandage before we leave for the consulate."

He nodded and she finally took a sip of her coffee. The strong brew woke up her taste buds and she closed her eyes with a low, appreciative, "*Mmm*." One more drink made her slump down in her seat as she savored the flavor on her tongue. In the ensuing silence, it dawned on her she enjoyed the drink a little too vocally.

Trent stared at her as if he'd been in the desert for a week and she was a cold glass of water. *Oh God...* how she wanted to be the water.

She straightened and stated in a matter-of-fact voice, "Good coffee."

He blinked and rose to his feet. "We should get going. I've got a surprise for you before we head to Milan."

His gruff, abrupt tone and the word *surprise* set her nerves on edge. Halli shoved aside the blanket covering her lap. "Surprise? What is it?"

"Not a surprise if I tell you." He vaulted up onto the dock.

"I'm still not so sure I can trust you."

He spun around with a frown, clearly not appreciating her attempt at humor to diffuse her own unease.

She held up a hand. "I'm kidding. Geez."

"There's a new toothbrush on the sink and a towel if you want to freshen up while I go get us some breakfast. I didn't want you to wake up all alone."

But she could be alone now? She turned away to hide an instant, overwhelming surge of panic and told herself she'd be fine. No one knew they were here. Perfectly safe.

Of course, that's what they'd thought about his villa, too.

"I'll be right back," he added.

A firm nod did nothing to alleviate her anxiety. Her fingers clenched on her mug. *Stop. You're not helpless.* She took a drink, mentally straightened her spine and reminded herself they'd be separated in a couple hours anyway, so she may as well get used to being by herself. Well, she'd have Ben and Rach—

"Halli."

Trent's softened tone made her turn around.

"I'll be right over there." He pointed down the shoreline. "And I'll be able to see the boat the entire time."

For the first time she noticed an open air market near one of the wharves. She rose up on her tiptoes for a better look. Hopeful curiosity took a stand next to her apprehension.

"Can't I just come with you?"

"Ah…" He squinted toward the market while pulling a black ball cap from his back pocket. As he tugged it low over his eyes, he shrugged. "Sure, why not."

She grinned with anticipation. "Give me five minutes."

Before he could change his mind, she hurried below deck and did what she could to freshen up with soap and a washcloth, a comb she found in a drawer, and the very welcome toothbrush. She took an extra moment to survey her hair. Oh well. At least it was still shiny-clean, not greasy-shiny. Thankfully, she had an easy style that didn't require a hair dryer like Rachel.

Had she found a converter last night? Probably. She'd find out in a few hours, wouldn't she? Halli smiled to herself. Today was already better than yesterday in so many ways.

Back on the deck, she paused before joining Trent on the dock. "Maybe I should take care of your arm first."

"Halli, the Spaghetti O's wore off about midnight."

Her own stomach growled and she laughed. "You're right, let's go."

He reached out a hand to pull her up, but didn't let go when her feet hit the wood. Her lips parted in surprise when he caught her close and his mouth covered hers for a breathless, all too brief moment. She didn't even have a chance to close her eyes, though he had.

When he released her, it took a moment to remember to

breathe. "What...was that for?"

"Hell if I know." He grinned, draped his good arm across her shoulders and steered her toward shore. "Let's go eat."

God, he smelled good. Just like all day yesterday whenever she'd gotten close. It wasn't fair. *She* needed deodorant.

When they reached the edge of the market, she tried to distract herself by drinking in every nuance of the busy street laid out before them. Trent slid his hand down along her arm and laced their fingers together.

"Cover," he whispered in her ear. "We don't want to stand out in case any of Lapaglia's police connections are around."

Alarmed, Halli jerked her head up from where she'd been staring stupefied at their hands. His lips began to curve upward, but before his white teeth could flash, she moved close and placed her hand over his mouth.

"Don't smile."

Their eyes met beneath the shadow of his baseball cap and he smiled anyway.

Wow.

Her stomach fluttered as his lips moved against her palm to finish the expression in his eyes. She thought it'd been hard to resist his magnetism last night, but today he was really getting to her.

"Wud ooh aunt to epth?" he asked.

Lessening the press of her hand on his mouth, she tried not to smile herself.

"What do you want to eat?" he repeated.

She considered for all of two seconds. "Something sweet."

"Mmmmm. Me too."

The low, exaggerated growl vibrated his lips against her skin and she quickly lowered her hand. His eyes were still smiling; locked on hers and lit with an inner fire. The man was like a chameleon all of a sudden. Brusque on the boat, playful here.

She tilted her head. "Are you sure you're feeling okay?"

"Oh, yeah."

"You're starting to freak me out."

His hands lightly grasped her hips and urged her closer.

"Not *quite* the affect I was going for."

He was flirting his ass off.

"Whatever you were going for, knock it off." *Before I throw myself at you and embarrass us both.*

She averted her gaze only to see a young couple stop in the middle of the marketplace to do exactly what she'd just imagined doing to Trent. No one batted an eye at the R-rated kiss.

"Sorry." Trent's dejected tone and little boy face made her feel bad. His hands dropped to his sides, his smile gone. "It was a stupid idea. I just thought we could have a little fun before the rest of the day takes over."

When he put it like that, she felt like a total killjoy. *Live a little, Halli. He's being nice. Enjoy your limited time together.* She sighed. "No, Trent, I'm sorry. You're right, again. Any fun on this nightmare vacation would be nice."

"Yeah?"

Hopeful, boyish charm did her in the rest of the way. A sheepish smile lifted her lips. "Yeah."

His hands returned to her hips as he waggled his brows. A tug brought her flush up against him. She gave a nervous laugh, putting a restraining hand against his chest. "I said fun, not sex."

Trent's eyebrows arched skyward. "Whoa-ho-ho. Who said anything about sex?"

Not her. No. *God, please let me take it back.* Her face flamed redder than an over-ripe tomato straight off the vine, and she didn't need a mirror to know it.

He leaned back, which only served to put his hips in more intimate contact with hers.

"Get your mind out of the gutter, sweetheart, I'm not that easy."

She fought the urge to bury her face in her hands. "I—"

"Who am I kidding? Yes I am." He gave her a roguish wink. "And believe me, I can make sex fun."

Of that she had no doubt. Sizzling heat had already zipped along her nerve endings, leaving a tingle of anticipation in its wake. But she was in way over her head here and nowhere near sophisticated enough to play this cool. She glanced around self-consciously. "Shut up."

"You're the one who wanted to talk about sex."

"I did not!" She prayed no one was actually listening to their conversation. And if they were, hopefully they didn't understand English. Still, she lowered her voice and spoke through clenched teeth. "I didn't mean I wanted to...I mean, I...oh, *darn it*. Just forget it."

She shoved free of his grasp and lost herself in the crowd. Embarrassed didn't even begin to cover how she felt. Mortified was closer. Combine the two and add some humiliation. She wandered past half a dozen stalls only to discover she'd separated from Trent and now what the hell was she supposed to do?

Her feet stopped moving. Someone bumped into her from behind, sending her pulse into overdrive. A quick spin brought her face to chest with Trent. Relief warred with the full force of her embarrassment.

Then he had the nerve to grin.

"Talk about fun. Was that as good for you as it was for me?"

She frowned in amazement. "My God, what are you on?"

"I'm a little dizzy from pain, lightheaded from hunger, and weak from—"

She smacked his good arm.

"Aw, come on, Halli, you make this way too easy." He pulled her into a one armed hug and turned her around. "Breakfast is this way, along with your surprise."

"I hate surprises."

"I'm pretty sure you'll like this one. In fact, I predict you'll kiss me for it."

Yeah, right. She had no plans to kiss him, what with trying to retain even a tiny scrap of common sense. Not to mention they came from completely different worlds, and they'd be saying goodbye in another three hours. At the most. Let's face it, her chances of never seeing him again beyond the silver screen were one hundred percent.

But then he bought her the most tantalizing, melt-in-your-mouth pastries she'd ever tasted. And a new shirt, thank God.

Dyed a rich royal blue, the silk, wrap-around blouse had short filmy sleeves and tied mid-point at her ribs before flaring just past her hips. First thing when they returned to the boat, she planned to change out of the *Wet and Wild* shirt.

Bag in hand, pastry in the other, she reconsidered kissing him.

Only he led her in the opposite direction of his boat as they left the market. She licked the remnants of a third pastry from her fingers, following him up a long set of stone steps. He knocked on the door of a quaint home tucked on a hill overlooking the lake and part of the town, then removed his ball cap as he turned to smile down at her.

What was he up to? Was this the surprise? Apprehension over the unknown rushed to the forefront.

When the door opened, a small, weathered Italian grandma straight out of the cliché beamed at Trent. He greeted her warmly in Italian, placing a kiss on each weathered, wrinkled cheek. After another brief exchange between the two, Halli found herself enfolded in the ample arms of the woman Trent introduced simply as Concetta.

Concetta ushered them inside where Halli met a gentleman named Giovani, who sat at a small kitchen table finishing his breakfast. Trent either missed Halli's discreet questioning look, or he ignored it as he and Giovani settled into a discussion, also in Italian.

She sipped the unsweetened tea Concetta placed in front of her, hard pressed to conceal her rising frustration. Trent's masculine voice in a foreign language would've been about the sexiest thing she'd ever heard, except she wanted to know what they were saying. Especially when each of their elderly hosts took a turn to smile in her direction. Neither spoke nor understood English, Trent had deigned to inform her at one point.

Giovani pushed to his feet and motioned Trent to follow. When Halli rose, Concetta stepped close to place a hand on either side of her face and spoke very seriously. Halli looked to Trent for translation.

Trent's lips quirked into a small smile. "She says you will be lucky in life and love."

Perfect, but currently proven *so* untrue. The kindness and conviction in the woman's faded eyes prompted Halli to smile anyway. "Thank you. Um…*grazie*."

Trent placed his hand against the small of Halli's back as he brushed another kiss on Concetta's cheek. His touch remained steady on their way out the back door; Halli's pulse did not.

"What's going on?" she asked to distract her hormones.

"We now have a car to get us to Milan," he told her.

"We're going right now?"

"Shortly."

She was taken aback by an internal warring of emotion. She couldn't wait to see Ben and Rachel again, God she longed for that. But the thought of saying goodbye to Trent brought a sharp ache to her chest. Completely crazy, given she'd only met him yesterday, and more than half the day she hadn't even liked him.

I ask you, Concetta, how lucky is that?

Trent opened the passenger door of a small black car identical to the blue rental Ben had driven yesterday. Halli waved to Concetta, who watched from the doorway, and slid into the seat, thinking the woman was a little touched in the head. Giovani settled in behind the wheel, while Trent folded his long frame into the back.

She looked at him over her shoulder. "He's driving us to Milan?"

"Not exactly."

"Where are we going?"

"You'll see."

"I wasn't kidding when I said I hate surprises."

Trent simply smiled. The vehicle lurched forward and Halli faced forward in confusion. She didn't like this at all. Surprises made her nervous. She didn't know how to plan for them and the lack of control freaked her out. Hadn't he figured that out by now?

A minute later, the little car squeezed between two

buildings lining the old cobblestoned street. An ancient, vine-covered stone wall rose up before them and Giovani brought the car to an abrupt halt. Halli leaned forward to search for a way out of the dead end, but Trent exited the car and reached for her door. Apparently, they'd arrived.

Giovani withdrew a set of keys from his trousers and opened a door she hadn't noticed under the leafy camouflage covering the wall. He pressed the car keys into Trent's hand. They spoke only long enough for Halli to recognize Trent's words of appreciation. Giovani responded with a low chuckle, nodded politely to her, and left them with the car and the open door in the wall.

"Where's he going?"

"Don't worry about it." Trent faced her with a grin of anticipation. "Ready?"

"No."

"Close your eyes."

"Absolutely not."

His hands landed on her shoulders and forced her gaze to meet his.

"Do you trust me?"

Despite all his outlandish teasing of the morning, his now sober gaze convinced her he wasn't joking. She swallowed her uneasiness and answered honestly. "Yes."

"Then close your eyes."

She stared at him a moment more, took a deep breath, then did as he asked.

"Okay, now breathe."

At the smile in his voice, a nervous laugh released the air from her lungs. He urged her forward, careful to forewarn her of any steps or uneven areas of the pathway beneath her feet. Still uneasy, she relied on her other senses to reveal clues as to what might be in store. They were outside, still near the water, since she could hear the gulls and bells and activity of the local wharves in the distance. A hint of something exotic teased her nostrils, but proved too elusive to identify.

As they continued, though, everything slowly faded into the background. Everything except Trent. The low timbre of his voice. The warmth of his body against her back. The alluring scent of whatever understated cologne clung to his skin. It dawned on her that maybe it was just him. He'd been dunked in the lake last night and still his heated masculine scent nearly overwhelmed her good sense when she'd given him that comforting hug.

"Okay. You can open your eyes."

The rest of the world rushed back in, overloading her brain. She allowed a few heartbeats to settle her nerves, then lifted her lashes. Unexpected beauty robbed her of adequate words. Only a soft gasp passed her lips.

"Halliwell Sanders, I give you the Japanese gardens of Villa Melzi."

They stood in the center of a stone bridge spanning the middle of a long, narrow lily pond. Intricate scrolled ironwork provided railings on either side. Colors from shoreline flowers and surrounding trees reflected on the glass-smooth surface of the murky, sun-lit water.

Hand over her mouth, she slowly spun in a circle to take it all in, noting they were completely alone. Too early for the popular tourist attraction to be open to the general public she distinctly remembered from her hours of trip planning. Through the red, yellow, and green leafed branches, she could just make out the mountains standing sentinel over the small villages and shimmering waters of Lake Como.

Lago de Como the Italian's preferred, and today, it sounded better to her, too.

"Good surprise?" Trent asked from behind.

She blinked away the mist blurring her vision. "The best ever."

"You said you were hightailing it back to the States, so while it's not the Villa Carlotta, I thought you might still enjoy it. We've got about a half hour to explore before we have to leave for Milan."

Still slightly breathless, she turned to face him, hands clasped together in front of her. "Believe me, it's so much better than the Villa Carlotta."

He lounged casually against the railing, thumbs hooked in

the front pockets of his jeans. Standing there, sunlight glinting off his tousled hair because he had yet to put his baseball cap back on, he rivaled the magnificence of their surroundings.

He also looked like the cat that ate the canary, thoroughly satisfied with his good deed. She decided she didn't care.

"Do I get my kiss now?"

His cocky confidence brought her up short. "No."

"You know you want to."

Maybe she did care. She'd seen the women he dated and knew she didn't come close to their beauty or sophistication.

Again, she reminded herself his interest was nothing more than an answer to the challenge she presented and she did her best to resist his magnetism. "You're a real piece of work, you know that?" She kept her tone light.

"What?" he asked innocently.

"Don't *what* me. Once we get to Milan, that'll be it, we won't ever see each other again. You'll continue your investigation, I'll go home. Just because you've charmed me with this last ditch effort to get a little something doesn't mean I'm going to simply fall into your arms." *No matter how much I want to.*

"Are we talking about sex again?"

Her face heated, but she forced a smile while walking across the bridge. "We weren't talking about it the first time."

He laughed after her. "You know, I think I might actually miss you."

She snorted.

"I'm serious," he insisted as he fell into step beside her.

"You said I was a pain in the ass."

"Well...yeah."

"You're no picnic, either."

"I believe the correct terminology is *egotistical jerk*."

Did she detect a hint of bruised ego under his smiling sarcasm? No. Of course not. Trent Tomlin wouldn't care what she thought of him, though it wasn't even true anymore.

The two of them walked together, enjoying the quiet, perfectly manicured gardens for a little while before she asked, "So how do you know Giovani and Concetta?"

"They're George's parents."

"The non-Clooney George?"

"Yeah. Giovanni has tended these gardens since he was a teenager."

Explained where Giovani had disappeared to. "Everything is just so beautiful."

Rounding a corner of the walkway, Halli stopped short at the top of a long stone stairway, lit by sunlight. The view over the lake took her breath away and her hand rose to her heart. "Oh, *wow*."

"Tell me about it."

He'd descended the first step and she shifted her gaze to see he stared at her, not the view. Their gazes locked. Nothing but complete honesty glowed in his hazel eyes. Until a spark lit and flared. Suddenly, every argument she'd used to keep herself from kissing the man became the very reasons why she should.

He didn't move and she knew the next step was up to her. *Carpe diem*. A term she was familiar with in theory, but not in practice. Her heart raced erratically. She shifted to the edge of the stair. Even with the added height of the step, he still had a good two inches on her. She lifted her arms to rest on his shoulders, linking her hands behind his head. He remained so still she'd swear he held his breath.

The entire world narrowed down to just the two of them as she leaned in until her lips hovered above his. "Thank you for this morning."

"I'd say anytime, but—"

She pressed her mouth to his, cutting off the unwelcome reminder of their limited time.

Now that she'd made the first move, he slanted his mouth over hers, demanding entry with his tongue. Rough whiskers rasped against her skin, but she didn't mind his dominance. Being wanted by this man was a heady sensation, one that no longer had anything to do with his international fame.

Trent's fingers splayed across her back, strong and sure and warm. Hers twined in the soft thickness of his dark hair, urging him ever closer. He tasted of the coffee and sweet pastries they'd enjoyed for breakfast. She craved more as her tongue explored the smooth line of his teeth. Rising on her tiptoes, pressed against him from chest to hip, she sought to gain back some control. After all, it was *her* kiss.

But he pressed back, dueling with her; giving little, taking more. And when he blocked one of her advances and countered with his own, she felt his mouth curve into a grin. He was cocky even in the middle of a kiss. But it felt so good to give in. Live in the moment and enjoy what was right in front of her, without having planned things out to the last detail.

At some point, the dynamics changed. He eased his possession, delved deeper, laved slower until the sensual glide of his tongue against hers made it impossible not to imagine what he would feel like inside her.

Passion rose, robbing her of oxygen, leaving her lightheaded. Desire throbbed in her most sensitive places, all the more acute for the firm press of his growing arousal against her belly.

A soft, helpless sound of pleasure vibrated in her throat. Had his arms not supported her, her weakened knees would've betrayed her, leaving her in a melted puddle at his feet.

He answered with his own groan of raw need, burying his face against her neck. "God, Halli, we should've done this at the boat."

She dragged air into her aching lungs, clearing the fog from her brain. She'd never experienced such a forceful, primal reaction to anyone. If they had kissed on the boat, she knew exactly where it would've led. Another notch on the bedpost for the playboy—in the easy conquest column, no less—and nothing but heartache for her.

One amazing memory to haunt her dreams for years to come.

In the ensuing silence, Trent wished he could take the words back. She hadn't moved from his embrace. With her arms wrapped around his neck, every luscious curve still clung to him, heating him almost beyond endurance. Every chest-heaving breath she took sent fresh spikes of desire screaming through his veins. And yet, he sensed her withdrawal as if she'd physically stepped ten yards back.

The interlude was over. Reality returned with a huge dose of regret. Not for kissing her, but because they'd say goodbye and he wouldn't get to do it again.

He ran his hands up the length of her back, over her shoulders, and along her arms as she eased her body away. Her lips were slightly swollen, red, and glistening. They begged for more, but he wasn't so sure he could handle another kiss without spontaneously combusting, or taking her right here in the garden. He bit back a groan at that thought.

Down swept lashes hid her blue eyes, and color stained her cheeks. The contrast between her blushing shyness and that fiery kiss turned him on even more.

He dipped his chin, caught her eye, and summoned a teasing smile. "Now that wasn't so bad, was it?"

She laughed softly, breathlessly. "Not bad at all."

At least she didn't deny having enjoyed herself. That might have pissed him off. As it was, this time his smile took no effort at all. He secured her hand in his and didn't let go as he led her down the steps to loop around Villa Melzi, back to the car.

"I think we made some great progress here today," he said matter-of-factly. "You trusted me. You enjoyed a surprise. And most importantly, you finally came to terms with how much you want me."

"Your conceit knows no bounds."

He discovered he'd do just about anything to keep her laughing as they finished their private tour. It was pathetic, really. He felt like a horny teenager on the two minute drive back to the boat so she could change and get her camera. All he could think about was carrying her below deck and picking up where they'd left off at the top of the garden steps.

But time ticked relentlessly, and though she didn't say it, he knew she was anxious to meet up with her family again. He wished he had equal enthusiasm. There was no reason not to, since he'd be rid of her and the responsibility of keeping her safe. That alone should have had him running for the car to be on their way.

That, and his investigation, like she'd said. He needed to go back to his place and see if by some miracle the voice recording was still there to back up her video. He had to figure out exactly how much Lapaglia knew about his involvement. He wanted to follow up on a comment Lorenzo had said into the mic yesterday morning about a new shipment of animals. And he couldn't do any of that with her at his side.

Take any *one* of those reasons and he should have no qualms about saying goodbye to the uptight Halliwell Sanders.

Unfortunately, she'd gotten under his skin. And no matter how much he tried to convince himself not to worry about the meeting in front of the consulate, after their surprise guests last night, his gut told him to proceed with caution.

Chapter 14

To Trent's relief, Halli sat mute on the way to Milan. After the sensual energy that pulsated between them as she carefully changed the bandage on his arm, he needed some distance. Physically, that problem would be solved in the next twenty minutes, but it unnerved him that his earlier teasing about missing her was completely true.

Didn't help that the blouse he'd bought her brought out the blue in her eyes in the most amazing way. Not to mention, with its cross wrap and side tie, the silky material molded her breasts almost as much as the *Wet & Wild* shirt.

He fought against a sideways, downward glance. She was a distraction he didn't need right now, damn it. The emotional distance her silence created was definitely for the best.

He'd been to the US Consulate General in Milan a time or two since purchasing his villa, and only took two wrong turns on the confusing one-ways before getting them on the right track. A couple blocks from the government building, he pulled the car over near a pay phone. Removing his cap, he ran a hand through his hair and resettled the hat, keeping the visor low over the spare pair of sunglasses he'd snagged off the boat.

Halli leaned forward to look at the buildings around them. "Is this it?"

"Not quite." Trent chose his words carefully. "I think we should try your brother's cell again. He may not have gotten your message."

"They'll be there," she stated. And then he thought she added under her breath, "*They have to be.*"

"Then let's find out where they want to meet. It'll save some time driving around."

"I told them in front of the building. It can't be that big. I'd rather just go see if they're there. How much farther is it?"

"A few blocks, but—"

"Then let's go."

The ball of lead in Trent's stomach refused to budge. In fact, it'd gotten heavier the closer they got to the city. He wasn't sure if it stemmed from the imminent meeting with her family, or the idea that she was about to walk out of his life for good.

His hands tightened on the steering wheel. This was absurd. He made friends with people and said goodbye all the time in his line of work. A few months, weeks, sometimes only days, on set and everyone went their separate ways. Halli was no different.

Yes she is.

He ignored that voice, turning his attention to another issue that'd occurred to him during the drive to the city. The reason he'd secretly hidden the video SD card, his one remaining concrete piece of evidence, back at the boat. When he got justice for Sean and Lorenzo, he'd find a way to return her family memories.

"Listen, even if your brother and sister are here—"

"They are."

"—have you thought about the rest of your situation?"

"The rest of my situation?" she repeated with a frown.

"I don't want to scare you, but you do realize that after what happened at the Torno police station, these guys know exactly who you are, right?"

Silence.

"You gave them a copy of your passport." Voicing that fact out loud triggered a click in his brain. *That* must be why he didn't feel right about leaving her. Because even after she was back with her family, she wouldn't be safe. *Not* because he didn't want to say goodbye. Not because he was going to miss her. "They've got your full name, your address back in Wisconsin, everything. And they know what you recorded."

"Stop."

"I'm serious, Halli. You'll still have to—"

"*Trent.* I want to go now."

"No, damn it!" He struck the steering wheel with the heel of his hand. Tension pulsed through the interior of the car, stimulating the hairs on his arm. "You need to listen to me and understand—"

"I understand, okay? *I get it.*" She took a deep breath, but stared straight ahead. "Now quit ruining everything and take me to the consulate like you promised."

Ruining everything? All he was doing was trying to look out for her. His frustration mounted, but if she didn't want his help, what could he do? He was done forcing anything on her.

After a quick check of the mirrors, he shot back out into traffic and made the final turn onto Via Princepe Amedeo. Buildings rose up along either side of the narrow, one-way street. Five stories high on the right, with the consulate up ahead on the left in a more modern high-rise.

Halli obviously spotted the American flag flying above a first-floor, side entrance, because she needlessly exclaimed, "There it is!"

She sat forward, and he just knew she was scanning the area for Ben and Rachel. He slowed down on his way past the consulate entrance, but didn't see anyone resembling either of her siblings in the video.

"Pull over and I can wait for them here." She'd already unbuckled her seat belt.

He kept driving. "Hold on. I want to take a drive around the block first."

"Why?"

"Just humor me, okay?"

She sat back with a huff, arms crossed over her chest.

As he made a left hand turn onto the one-way Via Montebello, he noted his windbreaker folded on her lap. "Do me a favor and put that jacket on."

"I'm not cold."

"Just do it. And put the hood up." He reached up to tug at the bill of his hat, though it really couldn't go much lower.

"You're acting like we're on some sort of covert operation," she complained.

That was just it, he wasn't acting at all. Surprisingly, though, she did as he asked, and pulled the hood up over her head without further prompting.

Coming up on the next intersection, he eased his foot off the gas and flipped the lever for the left turn signal again. Like many larger cities in Italy, the narrow streets were hell to navigate with the number of cars and the endless confusion of one-ways merging into two-ways. Looked like they'd have a wait up ahead before the two-way traffic allowed them to continue.

A pedestrian with a backpack slung over one shoulder darted between two parked cars. Trent braked hard to avoid hitting the guy, automatically reaching a hand to brace Halli. Good thing, since she hadn't refastened her seatbelt. However, his palm collided with the silky blouse and soft curves of her chest. In a different situation, he might have enjoyed the accidental contact. Now, he jerked his hand back lest she think he did it on purpose.

That's when he spotted her sister, sitting on one of the cement barricades partitioning off the small plaza in front of the building that housed the Consulate. She sat straight and stiff, one forearm across her middle to brace the elbow of her other arm as she chewed on her thumbnail. Halli's brother Ben was nowhere to be seen.

Red flags exploded like fireworks.

Trent's gaze darted to the traffic ahead and back to Rachel again. Maybe Halli's sister routinely indulged that particular nervous habit. Then again, maybe she had a specific reason to be edgy. Trent kept driving. Given the past twenty-four hours, he preferred to err on the side of caution.

"There! That's Rachel right there." Halli bounced in her seat like an excited kid. "I told you they'd be here!"

Trent stepped on the gas and switched the signal to a right hand turn. A horn bleeped, conveying the annoyance of the driver on their rear end who'd darted over to go around them. Rachel's head jerked in their direction, but she focused on the car behind him. Thankfully his lane scrabble drew no more notice as more horns blared ahead and behind them.

Halli spun around as Trent drove past her sister. "What are you doing?"

"Just hold on a sec." Trent took the right turn, checked traffic, his review and side mirrors. No one seemed to be following them. He pulled over in the first parking spot he saw and jammed the car into park. A yank on the review mirror confirmed her sister hadn't moved.

Halli, on the other hand, dove for the door and had one foot out of the vehicle before Trent caught hold of her arm.

She fought him. "Let me go!"

"Jesus, Halli, stop for just a moment." He hauled her back into the car and growled, "Shut the door."

She rounded on him, blue eyes snapping with fury. "What the heck is your problem?"

"Something doesn't feel right."

"Tell me about it. You're holding me hostage again!"

"Don't start. Now shut your door until I can figure out what the hell is going on."

"There's nothing going on—"

He felt below his seat, located the pistol with its silencer, and brought it up to wedge between his thigh and the seat, the grip free for an easy grab. Halli's eyes grew round as saucers. He hadn't let her see him stow the gun in the car when they'd left the boat.

"Shut the door."

The car rocked with the force of her compliance. Trent drew a deep breath, glancing around to see what kind of attention they'd drawn. Apparently, they were nothing out of the ordinary, because no one cast them anything other than a cursory glance. Especially now that she'd finally listened to him.

For good measure, he thumbed the automatic locks. "Now look," he commanded. He sunk lower in his seat and twisted around to focus on Rachel, who was just barely visible beyond the corner of the building at the end of the block. "What do you notice about your sister?"

Halli stubbornly remained facing forward. "That she's sitting there all alone probably scared to death wondering if I'm okay. This has nothing to do with—"

"Dammit, Halli, *look at her.*"

She turned her head to glare at him, then sighed with annoyance, grasped the headrest, and pulled herself around. "Just like I said. She looks worried."

"She's wearing the same clothes she had on in your video. And where's your brother?"

"They were probably looking for me all night. Ben's probably checking inside right now while Rachel waits outside so they don't miss me."

"Clearly they got your message to meet here, so they knew you were okay and would've had no reason to stay up all night looking."

"Maybe they didn't get it until this morning."

Trent held his frustration in check at her single-minded belief that today would be the end of her troubles. Unfortunately, he'd bet a hell of a lot of money they were far from over. And, unfortunately, it was up to him to spell it out, letter by un-sugar-coated letter.

"Okay, then, tell me this. Where's their Fiat?"

"Their what?"

"The blue rental car your brother was driving. I don't see it anywhere."

"Maybe they parked around the corner—I don't know! Trent, *please*, let me go to my sister."

Halli didn't know what else to do other than beg, but Trent was relentless with his suspicions, hurling question after question after each explanation she lobbed back.

"I watched that video yesterday," he stated in a low, ominous tone. "Your sister was obsessed with a hair dryer. Don't you think she would've changed her clothes at the *very least?*"

A ripple of fear cascaded down her spine. Oh, God, he was right. She stared through the back window at Rachel across the street, all alone, and suddenly looking more terrified than worried.

"What are you saying?" She knew the answer, just couldn't wrap her mind around it.

"I'm saying, we can't rush in there after Lapaglia's goons showed up at my villa out of the blue last night. Somehow they connected you to me. Now how exactly do you suppose that happened?"

Her hand covered her mouth. "Ben's phone."

"Exactly."

"But…I never said your name, and I didn't leave your number because I didn't know it. How could—"

"My guess is your brother and sister came back looking for you yesterday morning and found Lapaglia instead. After you left that message for Ben, and assuming his phone records incoming calls, Lapaglia easily could've run a check with his police contacts for the info on where the call came from."

Her eyes burned. She squeezed them shut, but it did nothing to relieve the pain or the guilt. This was all her fault. Her brother and sister were in the hands of murderers all because she had to film a couple of swans that she'd known darn well were no different from the ones back home. How she wished she could go back in time and shut off the camera when Rachel asked her to.

Opening her eyes again, Halli pressed her cheek against the headrest, staring at Rachel. "She's just sitting there."

"Think about it, Halli. They want you. They want your video."

"And if I'd have run out there…"

"They'd have you, too."

His blunt statement skimmed another icy chill across her skin, leaving goose bumps in its wake. She was safe for the moment, but what about Rachel, sitting there like bait? And where was Ben? She turned to Trent, wishing she could see his eyes through the dark sunglasses shadowed even more by his baseball cap. One glimpse of the man who'd surprised her with the garden walk would really help right now, because this stranger left her cold.

She swallowed hard and willed her voice to work. "So now what?"

"I'm working on it." He swung around in his seat again and shifted the car into gear.

Halli grabbed for the steering wheel in mindless protest. "We're not *leaving*."

Trent pushed her back in her seat with one hand, ducking his chin to check the left side mirror. "The longer we sit here the more dangerous it is."

She fought against his strong-arm tactics with one hand and fumbled for the door lock with the other. "Rachel is in danger, too."

He whirled around, locking his grip on her left wrist to pull her away from the door. When she swung at him with her right hand, he caught that one, too. Applied pressure brought her face within inches of his, but stopped just short of being painful.

"You're not going anywhere right now so *stop it* before whoever put your sister out there sees this little scene you're making."

Helplessness overwhelmed her. "What do you care anyway? Just leave me. You can have the video either way."

"Fuck the damn video, Halli."

"No, fuck you!"

The moment she screamed the harsh expletive, tears flooded her eyes. How easy it would be to fall apart right now. Give in to the terror trembling in her limbs and let whatever was going to happen, happen. But something in his dark, granite carved countenance challenged her. She stiffened her spine. Sucked in a huge lungful of air and refused to let the tears fall.

"You done?"

Her gaze narrowed at his callous tone, but she gave a stiff nod.

"Thank God." He released her as if she were nothing more than an irritating fly.

Anger rose up, engulfing everything inside her in fiery flames. To think just an hour ago, she'd actually believed she'd developed feelings other than dislike for the insufferable jerk.

Trent swerved back onto the street, talking as he drove. "As I see it, we've got a couple options here. One, we get into the building through a side entrance or something, then access the consulate, and enlist the help of the officers inside."

"I like that option *very* much."

"Problem with that is," he threw her a reproachful glance, "we still don't know where your brother is. We could put him in more danger."

Grudgingly, she acknowledged that was the last thing she wanted. Silently, she recognized her current anger toward Trent would only be a hindrance, and released a frustrated sigh. Better to work together, especially given the fact he kept speaking in 'we's' instead of driving back to dump her at the consulate so the US government could take over.

"What other options are there?" she asked.

"We wait and watch...see what they do when you don't show."

She shook her head. "Uh-uh."

"No? Just like that?"

"What good will watching them do?"

"For one, I'd be able to ID some of these guys, and then we could follow them, find out where they're holding your family."

"And what then?" she demanded when he didn't continue. "Rescue them? You and *me*?"

"It's an option."

"You're crazy."

"Maybe." He'd driven back around the block by now, and at the farthest corner, pulled over on the right side of the road.

Halli sat forward, craning her neck to get a glimpse of Rachel down and across the street. Trent reached over and tugged her hood back up. She straightened it, realizing it must've fallen down during their earlier struggle. She'd love to remove the jacket in the rising heat, but she understood the reason for its bulky disguise. Felt a tiny bit safer in it, too.

After she caught sight of her sister still sitting on the cement block, she looked at Trent. "Listen, I'm all for doing whatever it takes to get them back, but let's be realistic here. I'm no good at stuff like this."

"You're better than I would've guessed," he muttered toward the windshield.

Sticking with realistic, she knew she'd gotten lucky more than once. Starting with his arrival. "Still, what could you and I do against God knows how many of them?"

He sighed through his nose, a sound of pure, controlled frustration. His hands gripped the wheel in front of him and a muscle ticked along the hard line of his unshaven jaw. "Probably not much."

Her stomach sank. After a moment of silence, she ventured

hopefully, "Any other ideas?"

"Nothing viable," he bit out.

Acute despair formed a lump in her throat. The hopeless feeling churned in the pit of her stomach. He was supposed to have a solution. He'd gotten them this far.

And as suddenly as if someone had flipped a switch, anger flooded back. Not at him, but herself. Since when had she become a helpless wimp, completely dependent on a virtual stranger? The night her parents were arrested for the first and last time, she'd vowed to make a life for herself without resorting to the tricks of their dishonest trade. At sixteen, she got herself a job, finished high school, worked her way through college and established a pretty darn good career.

She sat up straight in her seat, decision pulsating through her body. *No more acting like a victim.* Granted, this was a lot more intense than striking out on her own. And though yesterday may have vaguely resembled one or two fuzzy-edged incidences in her childhood, she was still amazed at what they'd managed to escape. But sure as the sun rose each day, nothing would get better if she crawled in a hole and waited for Trent to rescue her. Or Ben and Rachel, for that matter.

The wheels in Halli's brain finally kicked in and began to turn. Scenarios played in her mind and she faced Trent's profile with a surge of hope. "What if we call Ben's phone and see who answers? If it's one of these guys, we could offer to trade the video for Ben and Rachel. After all, that's what they want."

"I already thought of that, but…"

She frowned at his hesitation. "But what?" Then she gave a short laugh of disbelief. "I get it. You don't want to lose the video."

"For starters."

"My brother and sister are worth more than that video."

"I won't argue that, but with Lorenzo's wire-recording only God knows where by now, your video is the only evidence we have of his murderer."

"You've still got me," she pointed out. "I could be an eye-witness."

His head swiveled toward her. "You said you didn't see

anything."

She shrugged.

"Did you watch the video?"

"I didn't get that far," she admitted. "But I believe it's there if you say it is."

"You know damn well that's not good enough."

"Why not?"

"Because the Halli I know couldn't testify *under oath* that she saw who pulled the trigger if she didn't actually see it."

"You don't know me that well," she argued.

"Well enough."

His gaze returned to the street as she fumed beside him. Darn man was right about one thing—she wouldn't lie under oath. But he was wrong about the other. Calling Ben's phone was a better idea than anything he'd offered.

"You said for starters. What else do you have against my idea?"

"If they agree to the exchange, there's still no guarantee we'd get both of them back. One, maybe, but two would be pretty hard. Two bargaining chips gives them too much leverage."

"So we grab Rachel now and trade the video for Ben. Besides, even with the odds stacked against us, negotiating for an exchange is smarter than rushing in like Remington Steele and Mrs. King."

His gaze narrowed as he stared out the windshield. "Scarecrow."

"What?"

"You're talking about two different TV shows. Remington Steele did not partner with Mrs. King."

"Who cares? You know what I meant." Now that she'd decided to do something instead of let things happen, Halli's annoyance grew by leaps and bounds. She hated sitting here while her sister sat at the other end of the block.

"How do you even know those shows?" Trent asked. "Weren't they way before your time?"

His, too. But her retort about reruns on TV Land was forgotten when his entire body suddenly went on alert. He leaned slightly forward, his attention focused down the street. Halli instinctively mirrored his movements.

A man carrying a newspaper had stepped from a vehicle parked on the left side of the street, not far from Rachel. Nothing unusual, other than the fact that the blond man wore black pants and a black jacket that probably made him sweat like a pig in the bright July sun. Halli watched his casual stroll toward her sister, who rose to her feet, then abruptly sat back down.

"You see that?" Trent asked.

Intent on the action, Halli nodded.

Rachel's head jerked in denial to something the man must've said. He walked past, did a quick scan of the immediate area, and sat on the cement barricade near her. It was definitely not Alrigo Lapaglia. She'd gotten a good enough look at him at the police station.

"Do you recognize him?" Halli asked Trent.

"No."

Her sister didn't turn to look at the man who now appeared to leisurely read his paper. She simply stared straight ahead, or down the block, in their general direction. Not that she'd see them this far away, sitting in the car.

When Rachel began chewing on another nail, Halli wished she could do something. Anything. The situation was definitely bad if her sister was ruining the very nails she'd paid to have professionally manicured before their trip.

Halli shifted her attention. "There's only one other guy in that car now—and he's in the passenger seat."

"I noticed." Trent said under his breath. His fingers drummed out a staccato beat on the steering wheel. "You know…with the right diversion, we just might be able to pull this off."

Wait—when had they come to a decision about what they were going to do? She ground her teeth against the helpless feeling of always being two steps behind. "Pull what off?"

"Grab your sister and bargain for your brother."

Chapter 15

Ten minutes later, Halli was expecting him, yet she still nearly jumped out of her skin when Trent appeared next to the driver's side door of their borrowed car. Because he'd had her move behind the wheel while he was gone, *"just in case,"* she scrambled back across to the passenger seat so he could get in.

"All set," he said, flashing a newly purchased, throwaway cell phone. "Anything new going on over there?"

"No." She hadn't taken her eyes off her sister more than a few seconds every so often to check the mirrors around the car. Trent had caught her in between sweeps and in the middle of a prayer, since she was still unsure of his plan.

"What if there's more than just those two?" she worried out loud.

"Have you come up with a better idea in the past fifteen minutes?"

"No."

"Then let's hope to God there isn't."

"That's reassuring."

"Anytime I can help."

He didn't look at her, but she saw the corner of his mouth crook up. Her back teeth clenched together. Easy for him to joke when it wasn't his sister and brother dangling on the hook. Just as quick, she thought of his deceased brother, Sean, and his cop friend, and took the thought back.

After a deep breath, she eyed the phone and asked, "You really think it's okay to involve the police now?"

"For a distraction only, we'll have to chance it. Besides, the phone call will be completely anonymous and I don't plan on saying anything more than it looks like a drug deal going down." He lifted the phone as if to make the call.

"Do you think it'll take long for them to get here?"

"Illegal activities this close to a foreign consulate? I suspect they'll be here in minutes. In fact, you should get in the back now."

A frisson of resurgent fear threatened to override her earlier determination. She climbed between the seats and sat directly behind Trent like they'd talked about, so she'd be on the side closest to Rachel. The deep breath she sucked in and immediately released ended up much louder than she expected.

Trent's head jerked up, catching her gaze in the review mirror. "What's the matter?"

She hated to admit it after having just decided to stop being a victim, but there was no denying the tremble in her hands. "I'm scared."

A split second smile softened his expression. "*I'd* be scared if you weren't."

She tried to smile back, but it felt all wobbly. *Focus, Halli.* She looked past Trent at Rachel to bolster her courage and resolve, only to have her heart thump in her chest. Clenching the headrest, she pulled herself forward.

"Something's going on."

Trent's attention shifted as well. Rachel stood in front of the blond man, hands on her hips, in what Halli recognized as her stubborn stance. It appeared the two were arguing. It also appeared Rachel won when the blond man spoke toward the car his partner sat in and pointed across the street, down the block away from where Trent and Halli were parked.

The man in the car turned his face and Halli gasped. "That's the guy from last night! I scratched his face when he tackled me."

Trent straightened in his seat as the blond man took hold of Rachel's elbow and escorted her in the direction he'd pointed. Halli immediately noticed her sister's pronounced limp. Rachel jerked free of the man's grip, but continued walking at his side.

Halli's attacker from the night before remained in the car, even after Rachel and her guard disappeared inside a corner café.

Without warning, Trent started the car and navigated back into the one-way traffic. "Change of plans, sweetheart. Give me the jacket and get down on the floor."

Halli ducked down below the window level and struggled

to remove Trent's windbreaker in the close confines. "What are we doing?"

"I'm leveling the playing field to one on one. If I can get inside that shop, maybe I can take out one of these guys without drawing the attention of the other. Roll down that back window a little so you can hear when your sister is on her way."

She pushed the jacket to him between the seats before spinning the handle for the window a half dozen times. It was hard to resist the urge to poke her head up to see where they were. A second later, Trent braked hard enough to throw her against the front seats. Once she stabilized herself, a peek through the seats revealed him knotting the jacket sleeves around his waist. Over the gun.

When she heard the driver's door open, she said, "Trent?"
"Yeah?"
"You're not going to shoot that guy, are you?"
"Not if I don't have to."
Shocks creaked as his weight lifted from the car. "Trent?"
"*What?*"
"Be careful."

Trent appreciated her concern, but slammed the door and strolled around the front of the car, keeping his back to the guy parked a short twenty or thirty yards behind them on the opposite side of the street. He'd double checked twice, but still found his hands itching for reassurance that the windbreaker completely concealed the gun stuck in his front waistband.

There were four bullets left. He didn't want to use a single one.

The difficulty of maintaining a relaxed pace tightened his muscles. He fought the urge to run inside, grab Halli's sister, and get the hell outta Dodge. Unfortunately, the situation required a tad bit more finesse. Hopefully, that's all it'd take.

A trio of young girls exited the café and he ducked his chin with a tug on his cap. It wouldn't do for anyone to recognize him. Out of the blue, Halli's frequent reminders not to smile had him struggling not to do exactly that right now. Until he noticed one of the girls had fallen a step behind her friends to flash him a grin.

He scowled discouragement at the tall, flashy blond, and she immediately scurried to join the others. One bullet dodged, now he hoped to maintain his percentage with real lead.

Inside the cafe, Rachel's watchdog stood off to one side, pretending interest in a nearby display. Trent did a quick scan for Halli's sister, but she was nowhere to be seen amidst the half-dozen or so customers. He stepped up to the counter and ordered an espresso in Italian while digging a couple coins from his pocket. From the corner of his eye, he saw the blond man glance toward the back of the café.

Trent's gaze followed and located the door to the women's restroom. The reason for this opportune distraction became clear. The barista slid his cup across the counter at the same moment Rachel stepped from the restroom. He reached for the cup with an absent smile, his attention on Halli's sister. "*Grazie.*"

A gasp from the barista wiped the smile from his lips and he whipped his head around. She'd covered her mouth with both hands, her eyes wide. Trent immediately thought something had happened with the blond guy or Rachel and spun back. No. They'd just turned for the door.

"You're Trent Tomlin!" the barista exclaimed.

Trent's gaze snapped back to her. *Damn.* Without even taking into account Halli's warnings, he'd used his smile enough that he should've known better than to let it slip. He made a face and summoned his best Italian accent to speak in the barista's native tongue.

"No, but I get that a lot. Too bad the guy's such a prick."

The coins bounced on the counter as he swiped up his cup and started for the door. In two strides, the gaze of the blond man met his. After what the barista had said, a flash of recognition darkened the guy's ice blue eyes. His hand reached for the inside of his jacket.

Trent lunged forward, popping the lid off his cup as he went. Before the man could draw a weapon, Trent threw the steaming espresso in his face.

Rachel leapt back at the man's pained shout. Hot drops of liquid pelted Trent's bare skin and shirt, but he ignored them along with the alarmed exclamations of the café customers. He thrust a surprised Rachel toward the door.

"Halli's outside in the black car. Go!"

He spun back to the guard. An oncoming fist super-charged Trent's reflexes, and he flung his left arm up to deflect the blow. His wounded arm screamed with the effort required to hold the heavier man back until an adrenaline-boosted swing of his own connected with the man's jaw. His head snapped to the side. He stumbled backward, flailing for balance. Two tables and a number of chairs gave way at the last moment, and the back of his head hit the wall with a resounding thud.

Trent had no time to see if the man was out cold—Rachel's frantic exit from the café would not have gone unnoticed by Blondie's partner. Trent shoved past a startled pedestrian in the doorway to see Halli had opened the back door of the car. Hand outstretched, she emerged from the vehicle, beaming at Rachel limping toward her.

Glass shattered behind him. Needlepoint shards rained onto the sidewalk. Screams erupted all around. Trent ducked at the same time Rachel's body jerked. Halli cried out as her sister crumpled to the ground. On hands and knees, Trent fumbled for the gun at his waist. Halli fell to her knees beside her sister.

For one heart-stopping, unbearable moment, he thought she'd been shot. Until her tear-filled eyes lifted to his amidst the chaos. He waved her back, fingers clenched on the grip of the gun. "Get in the car!"

No more than he started to spin around to take out the man in the café, the half rolled down window of the open back door exploded. Trent ducked again in the midst of more screams. He caught sight of the second man from the Fiat sprinting toward them, gun extended. When Trent raised his gun, the man immediately dove behind a vehicle three cars away.

He checked Halli and saw her working with her sister to get them both into the back seat. Trent fired a shot into the back end of the car the man hid behind and cast a glance over his shoulder to make sure Blondie in the café didn't pose a double threat. His blood froze at the sight of café customers helping the guy to his feet.

"Halli—we gotta go!"

"Then let's go!"

He surged to his feet, firing two more cover shots down the street. Quick spin, aim, fire, and the window above the door of the café exploded. A running leap launched him feet first across the hood of the car. The rivets on his back left jeans pocket screeched across the metal until he landed on his feet on the other side.

Halli slammed the rear passenger door as he slid behind the wheel. He'd left the keys in the ignition, so a twist of his wrist brought the engine to life. The left side mirror revealed a miracle break in traffic and the running approach of the sidewalk gunman with the scratched face.

The image shattered in a flurry of glass.

"Hang on and stay down!"

Trent jammed the car in gear, wrenched the wheel and stomped on the gas. Noise bombarded him from all sides. Blaring horns. Squealing tires. Rachel's harsh breathing laced with sobs. Halli's low voice attempting to reassure her sister. His own pulse pounding in his ears.

He drove. Down the block, hard right, quick left, and keep on going. The review mirror offered some relief. Thank God no one followed. He wasn't up to a second car chase in as many days. Especially since he was completely out of bullets.

"What are we going to do?"

Halli's shrill question rang out from the back. Trent didn't answer. He had no clue.

"Trent, she's bleeding bad." She sounded on the verge of panic. "We have to get her to a hospital."

He reached up until Rachel's pale face filled the review mirror. *Christ.* He'd known something like this was possible, but hadn't prepared mentally. He dragged the windbreaker from his waist and tossed it over the seat.

"Do what you can to stop the bleeding. Where was she hit?"

"There's too much blood. I can't tell."

"My leg," Rachel gasped. "But Ben—" An anguished cry ripped from her throat. "Oh, God, Ben."

Halli's trembling hands froze, her heart lodged in her throat. "What about Ben?"

"They said they'd kill him if I didn't do exactly what they said." Rachel buried her face in her hands, her entire body wracked by fresh sobs.

A conflicting surge of relief that he was still okay and a stab of alarm that he might not be for long ripped through Halli. She thrust one jacket sleeve under Rachel's leg and knotted it with the other just above the torn fabric of her pants. Rachel bit off a scream with a sucked in breath.

"Sorry." Still, Halli yanked on the knot. It couldn't be helped. It had to be tight, to act like a tourniquet and stem the flow of blood.

"We need to call Ben's phone *now*," Halli told Trent as she folded the bulky part of the jacket over the welling wound. "Before they do something to him."

"He told me to go." Rachel said.

She collapsed against the back seat with a cry when Halli pressed hard on her leg. At first Halli thought she'd passed out, but she took shallow breaths, speaking in between.

"Said not to worry about him…to run with you. We almost escaped…this morning. But I twisted my ankle…" Fresh tears streamed down her face.

"It's okay," Halli reassured her. "We've got a plan."

A plan that wasn't going the way it was supposed to. Still pressing down with her left hand, Halli used her other hand to brush the tangled strands of blond hair from Rachel's face. Tears stung her own eyes as she gazed at her sister's pale, pain-pinched features.

"We're going to get him back," she vowed.

Rachel simply closed her eyes and let her head rest against the seat.

"How's her leg?" Trent asked.

Halli lifted the compress for a quick look before meeting his somber gaze in the review mirror. "The jacket helped. The bleeding's slowed a lot."

"Good. I'll pull over to make the call as soon as we're out of the city. We'll be no help to your brother if those guys catch up with us. I'm out of ammo."

Halli nodded. She couldn't argue his reasoning no matter how desperate she was to secure Ben's safety or get help for Rachel.

"A hospital is out of the question right now anyway," he continued. "That's the first place they'd look."

Rachel's lashes fluttered, then opened to stare at the back of Trent's head. "Is that really *Trent Tomlin*?" she whispered.

"Yeah."

"How'd you manage that one?"

"He showed up after you guys drove off without me."

Halli's basic explanation sat in an unexpected silence. She cringed, wishing she'd chosen better words. Rachel shifted in the seat. She groaned in pain as she turned anguished eyes to Halli. "I am so sorry. This is all our fault. We thought you were right behind us. We never meant to—"

"It's okay. I didn't mean it the way it sounded. I don't blame you guys."

"First I left you, and now Ben," she cried. "I'm an awful sister."

"Don't you dare say that. You were always there for me when Mom and Dad weren't. If this is anyone's fault, it's mine. I'm the one who kept taping. I'm the one who filmed something she shouldn't have. I'm the one they're after."

"That's what they want? Your video? What the hell did you film?"

"Someone was shot and killed right as Ben drove off."

"Oh my God. You saw it happen?" Rachel asked in a horror.

"No, but the killers saw me with the camera across the water."

"But if you didn't see it, how do you know?"

"I saw the video," Trent stated as he pulled over on a quiet, tree lined road. "It's on there, and as you already know, they'll do anything to get their hands on it."

Halli shivered at the certainty in his voice. Not that she hadn't seen proof enough of Alrigo Lapaglia's determination, but the grim reminder made her wonder if the trade for Ben could even be accomplished successfully.

Phone in hand, Trent faced Halli and Rachel from the front seat. He locked his gaze with Halli's. "Ready?"

She nodded.

He read a trust in her eyes that hadn't been so forthcoming yesterday. Funny how he'd wanted her faith so bad, and now that he had it, it scared the shit out of him. She was counting on him to get the job done and he was terrified he'd let her down like everyone else in his life.

His heart pounded after he'd dialed the number and counted the rings. It was a bit of a surprise when the voicemail clicked on. Damn it. Now what? The beep sounded in his ear and he said the first thing that came to his mind. "Ben Sanders better stay alive or I'll send the video to the police and every major television network in the country."

Halli's eyes widened when he flipped the phone shut. "What was that?"

"Voicemail. I improvised."

"What if they don't check it?"

"They will."

Rachel's whispered words drew his attention. She lay slouched against the back, her head now on Halli's shoulder. She didn't look good. Hell, he'd been improvising so far, but this shit had seriously gotten out of control. Especially since Rachel's injury wasn't a surface wound that could be patched up with butterfly bandages.

Halli caught his eye and jerked her head toward her door. Trent got out of the car, automatically doing a visual sweep to make sure they were still safe. When she joined him outside and shut her door, he left his open, ignoring her pointed frown. He got that she didn't want to talk in front of her sister, but he didn't want to be caught unprepared.

"What do we do now?" she asked quietly.

He shrugged, answering her while attempting to unseat the guilt riding his shoulders that he didn't know exactly how to fix this new complication. Then he offered the best answer he had. "We wait. If they don't call us back, I'll try the number again in a little while."

"I meant about Rachel. I'm scared she's lost a lot of blood."

She sounded more than scared and he knew exactly how she felt. He ran a hand through his hair; somewhere along the way he'd lost his baseball cap. Halli's blue eyes beseeched him, tightening a vice inside his chest. If her sister died, she'd blame him. *He* would blame him. The thought left him with no decision at all.

He reached to open her door. "Get in the car. I'm taking you back to the consulate."

"What? No. What about Ben?" She stood her ground.

"We have to trust the video is enough to keep him alive."

"But—"

He gripped her shoulders. "Your sister needs medical help. You know that. Once we're close to the consulate, I'll get out and continue with the original plan. You take Rachel to the consulate and get her the help she needs. You'll both be protected and I'll get Ben."

Rachel stirred in the back seat. Halli glanced inside, before facing him with obvious indecision.

"I have to go this alone, Halli, but I also have to know you're safe. If I'm worried about you it's going to get us all killed. The consulate is our only option right now."

"No."

The feeble denial came from Rachel. She reached for the door handle, only to collapse onto the seat. Trent ducked inside, over the driver's side as Halli yanked open the back door. She helped her sister back into a sitting position.

"You need to rest. Don't move," Halli cautioned.

Rachel's labored breathing doubled Trent's alarm. After a moment, though, she caught her breath. "We can't go back to the consulate."

"We have no other choice," Trent said.

Rachel shook her head. "Ben."

"Leave him out of it. Make up a story about the café shooting, and I'll take care of your brother."

"Listen to me," Rachel insisted weakly. She grasped Halli's hand and looked from her sister to Trent. "There's someone inside. We can't go there."

Trent's fingers tightened on the seat. Halli's gaze met his as she asked, "What do you mean by inside?"

"One of the consulate guards. He talked to Tony. They knew each other."

"Who's Tony?"

"The blond asshole in the coffee shop. If we go back to the consulate, *they'll know*, and Ben is dead for sure."

As if the words sapped the last of her strength, Rachel sagged back against the seat. Her lashes fluttered, her eyes rolled back, and air whooshed from between her dry, parted lips. The hand that'd been holding Halli's went limp with the rest of her body.

"Rachel? *Rachel!*"

Trent reached across the seat to feel for her pulse, heart in his throat. A moment later, he gave Halli a tense nod and sat back. "I think she passed out. Surprising she didn't do it sooner."

Halli checked the wound on Rachel's leg and Trent was relieved to see the makeshift tourniquet was working. Tears swam in Halli's eyes when she lifted her gaze again. "Now what?" When he didn't answer right away, she dipped her chin to catch his eye. "Trent?"

"I don't know." It killed him to admit it out loud, but there it was. Rachel had shot his solution all to hell, and he didn't know which way to turn next. He couldn't look Halli in the face and turned away with the pretense of another check of their surroundings.

"We've got to figure something out," Halli hounded. "There has to be somewhere we can get help."

If Lapaglia had someone in as deep as the consulate, there was no way they could risk a hospital. The cops would show up in a heartbeat, especially if hospital officials had been alerted to watch for a gunshot victim. But they wouldn't know which side those cops were on until it was too late.

For lack of anything better to do, he started the car and began driving. Halli kept talking.

"What about a smaller clinic, they have facilities like that here, don't they, like in the US? Or...I know! What about a veterinarian?" She sat forward, hugging his seat back so that her chin hovered just above his right shoulder. "Remember that movie—*Bird on a Wire*? Mel Gibson was treated by a veterinarian when he was shot in the butt."

"Too bad I don't conveniently have a veterinarian ex-lover here in Italy."

"It's an idea," she retorted with distinct annoyance when he flicked his gaze to hers in the review mirror. "Sometimes it helps to talk things out with someone. Like in *High Lonesome*, when Shain and the sheriff figured out a way to save Emma."

"You're not seriously comparing this to one of my movies, are you?" If she'd just shut up, he could—

"Why not? Shain does stuff like this all the time. What would he do?"

"I don't know!" he shouted.

She sat back abruptly and he braked. Took a deep breath.

"I'm sorry. Just give me a minute to think, will you? This is a hell of a lot different than reading a script written by someone else."

A memory struck like a bolt of lightning. Simone, Lorenzo's girlfriend who was a nurse, had offered to read lines with him after dinner one night. And he recalled Lorenzo had told him yesterday she was working the night shift all week so she'd be at her city house. After mentally placing the next couple street signs on a map in his head, Trent recognized they weren't that far away.

He didn't say anything to Halli lest she restart her inquisition, and she actually kept quiet as he drove. A glance in the mirror wasn't enough time to tell if she was pissed or worried about her sister. Probably both, but since they were almost there, he refocused on the road and once they arrived at Simone's small house, he simply said, "Wait here." No sense getting her hopes up if Simone wasn't home.

Urgency, hope and dread all took their turns tying his stomach in a knot as he knocked on the door. A full minute went by and he knocked again. He'd begun to think their luck had permanently changed for the worse when the door swung open.

Simone stood before him dressed, ironically, in her nurse's scrubs. The unflattering hospital garb did nothing to diminish her beauty, still stunning in her mid-fifties. Her eyes lit up when she saw him. "Trent! *Ciao*. How good it is to see you."

"Simone." He leaned down to kiss each cheek she offered, a painful lump in his throat. One of the sweetest, most generous people he'd ever met, her kind heart had balanced Lorenzo's brusque demeanor to perfection. Based on her happy smile of welcome, Trent knew she had no clue what'd happened yesterday morning. He wanted to hug her tight and tell her right then—get it over with—but that would be too much of a shock. Hopefully, a more sensitive opportunity would present itself.

"Renzo's not here, but please, come in," Simone offered. "I need a moment to change from my work clothes."

Trent took her hand before she could back away from the doorway. "Simone, I need your help."

She answered with a puzzled smile, but no hesitation. "Of course I will help you. Tell me what you need."

Trent took a deep breath and battled a twinge of duplicity for not telling her about Lorenzo first. But Rachel might not have time. "A friend is in trouble. She was shot, but we can't go to a hospital. People are searching for her."

Simone's eyes went wide. "Where is this friend?"

He nodded toward the car. Simone cast a furtive glance around, as if the people he'd mentioned would suddenly appear. "Bring her inside. I will prepare in the kitchen."

Relief swept through him. "Thank you, Simone. You have no idea—"

"Go." She waved him away. "Get her."

Trent did a quick scan of his own as he jogged back to the street. Thankfully, it appeared to be very quiet this late in the morning and there'd be no nosey neighbors to watch them carry Rachel inside. He opened the back door closest to Rachel and was relieved to see she'd regained consciousness.

"Let's get you inside."

"Where are we?" Halli demanded.

"A friend's house. She's a nurse," he explained briefly,

reaching for Rachel.

"Remembered an ex-lover after all?"

Halli's judgmental tone raised his hackles. "Simone is Lorenzo's girlfriend of sixteen years."

He saw the instant she understood the complication of their arrival when her contrite gaze met his.

"Does she know?" Halli asked.

"No," he said, taking the brunt of her sister's weight so she could close the door. "And I'm still trying to figure out how the hell I'm going to tell her, so keep your mouth shut."

The sympathy in her eyes dampened from an infusion of indignation. "I wouldn't say anything on purpose to hurt her, so don't start acting like a jerk again."

Trent bit back a retort as she opened the front passenger door and leaned inside. That word was starting to get on his nerves. She was right, though, his comment was uncalled for. Picking a fight with her right now would only serve to redirect his stress, not relieve it.

Seeing Halli had grabbed her camera only added to his stress with a flash of guilt. *Shit.* She hadn't checked the memory card since they'd left the boat. For one, he had no doubt he'd have heard about it, and two, she wouldn't have bothered with the useless, empty camera. Something told him now was not the time to bring it up; as they carried her wounded sister inside and waited for a call from her hostage-held brother.

Simone was all business as they entered the kitchen. Trent and Halli followed her instructions to help Rachel sit on the blanket-covered kitchen table and stretch her legs out. He made very brief first name introductions then hurried outside to move the car to the side of the house. Not completely out of sight, but out of the way for now.

When he made his way back inside, Simone had just finished cutting away Rachel's red-stained pant leg. Halli held her sister's hand. If she thought he'd bled a lot last night, how was she handling this?

He studied her face, but she seemed to be holding up okay.

Simone kept up a running commentary as she worked. "Bullet went straight though. That is good. And it is not near the femoral artery—also good." She glanced up from the wound toward Rachel. "Or you would be dead right now."

Trent winced. Halli drew in a sharp breath. If possible, Rachel paled even more as she leaned back against the kitchen wall.

"How long ago did this happen?" Simone asked.

Trent looked at his wrist, only to remember he'd removed his watch to shower last night and it still sat on his bathroom counter at the villa. So he guessed. "About a half hour."

"Maybe forty-five minutes," Halli added.

"Good job stopping the bleeding." Simone worked quickly to clean and bandage the wound.

Silent tears trickled down Rachel's face, and more than once Trent noticed Halli switch hands and flex her freed fingers. Finally, Simone handed a couple of pills to Rachel with a glass of water and a professional, reassuring smile.

"This will dull the pain. You will recover, with antibiotics to prevent infection and much rest. This bandage is temporary, until I return from the *ospedale* with adequate supplies."

Trent tensed at the Italian word for hospital. "Simone—"

"I know." She rubbed Rachel's arm, then walked over to deposit the empty glass on the counter next to Trent. "Discretion is of upmost importance, *si*?"

"*Si*. Lives depend on it."

"So be it." She picked up a set of keys from the counter and glanced at Halli on her way to the back door. "We are close in size. Choose some clean clothes from my room and use the bathroom down the hall to clean up, if you wish. Rachel, wait for my return. I will hurry, but do not expect me sooner than at least one hour."

"*Grazie*."

Trent's thank you was lost under Halli's, "Trent was shot, too. Last night."

She might as well have shined a spotlight on him.

Rachel's eyes widened. "You were?"

He threw Halli a dark look as Simone pinned him with a frown. "Why do you not tell me this?"

"It's just a scratch and Halli already patched me up."

"It's more than a scratch," Halli contradicted. "If Rachel needs antibiotics, it stands to reason you do, too. Especially after being dunked in the lake water."

"Show me this *scratch*."

Simone's tone brooked no argument so he reluctantly unbuttoned his shirt to shrug free of the sleeve. He'd gotten used to the constant ache, but with nothing else to claim his attention, the sharp twinge that accompanied the flex of his bicep made him grimace.

Simone unwound the Ace bandage, and clucked in disapproval. "*Si*. Antibiotics, *idiota*." Her gaze shifted. "And what is all this?"

Trent didn't have to look down to know she meant the large black and blue blotch about the size of a boot print in the middle of his chest. More bruises colored his left side where his ribs had taken his full weight when he slipped on the side of the boat. He slid his arm back in his sleeve and pulled the shirt edges closed. "Nothing I can't handle."

She rolled her eyes and departed without another word.

After the click of the door, Trent buttoned his shirt and prepared to meet Halli's I-told-you-so expression. But she'd already moved on. "You should try the phone again."

His second call to her brother's phone went straight to voicemail. Either the battery had died, or it'd been turned off. If it was the latter, someone had listened to his message. He didn't want to speculate why they hadn't called back, but hoped they heeded his warning.

The worry on Rachel's face read like an open book, while Halli's was more subtle. What struck him was an inner strength he saw today that hadn't been there yesterday. Amazing considering her obsessive compulsion for order and control in this situation where chaos reigned.

Somewhere in the other room, a clock ticked off the minutes until Simone's return. Lost in his own thoughts, Trent let Halli and Rachel's quiet conversation flow over him. Simone had pushed the kitchen table up against the wall earlier, and Rachel rested her head back, eyes closed. He saw Halli look down at her hands. A further glance took in her blood-stained clothes and she deposited the camera next to him on the counter before murmuring she was going to make use of Simone's offer to clean up.

As she walked down the hall, he wished the phone would ring and dreaded it at the same time. More than anything he wanted to give Halli confirmation that her brother was alive. If only he could take her in his arms and promise everything would be okay. Take the burden off her shoulders. Bring a smile to her face. Make her laugh again.

If only life were as simple as wishing.

He wished he'd gotten the chance to meet her under different circumstances. Wished *his* brother were still alive. Wished he'd never asked his friend to help him, that Lorenzo would walk through the door, and that he didn't have to tell Simone the man she loved was dead.

Full of restless energy, Trent wandered into another room in search of that infernal ticking clock to see how much longer before Simone returned. The sound of the shower shut off, and about ten minutes later he heard the door open in the hall.

He felt Halli's presence beside him where he'd braced his arms against the back of Simone's sofa.

She laid a hand on his forearm, gave a soft squeeze. "You have to tell her."

His hands fisted in tension as much from her touch as from her words. "I know."

"If there's any way I can help…"

The urge to hold her, to draw strength from her, overpowered all else. He turned and pulled her close, wrapped his arms around her slim frame. She stiffened for a moment before relaxing against his chest, her arms folded between them.

Fresh from the shower, she smelled like heaven. A distant part of him recognized he was digging himself in too deep where she was concerned, but he came alive with her body against his. She was the one bright spot in the darkness. Shifting position, he spread his feet so that when he leaned back against the sofa she stood between his legs.

His pulse sped up, making his heart thud in his chest, directly beneath her cheek. He loosened his hold and she eased back a few inches, palms flattened against his chest. When she lifted her gaze, he was lost.

"Just you being here will help, Halli."

Cradling her face between his hands, he reveled in the silky slide of her damp hair against his fingertips. Her lashes drifted closed as his mouth covered hers. He took his time exploring her soft, sweet lips, watching the wondrous expression on her face as he did so. His kiss pleased her.

Her breath did that little catch, unleashing a sliver of the morning's desire into his veins. She pressed closer, the invitation of her parted lips irresistible and the perfect incentive to close his eyes. As he savored the kiss with his other senses heightened, he acknowledged he could get used to kissing her on a regular basis.

"Figlio della putan!"

The violent Italian curse hit Trent like a bucket of ice water. He jerked his mouth free of Halli's to find Simone standing in the doorway between the living room and kitchen. Her beautiful face twisted with rage.

In her trembling hands gleamed a gun.

Chapter 16

"Simone."

Careful not to make a sudden movement, Trent stepped forward and maneuvered Halli behind him. She resisted. Teeth clamped hard in frustration, he tried to push her back with one hand while extending the other toward Simone and the gun. Tears filled the Italian woman's eyes and streaked down her face.

"*Bastardo!* How dare you come here and ask for my help after what you did," she accused.

Lorenzo. She could be talking about nothing else. Now he recognized the grief mixed with her anger. "I'm so sorry I didn't tell you right away, I just didn't want it to be a shock. If you put down the gun, we can talk about this."

"I will talk to you about nothing."

"Simone, *per favore*...put the gun away."

"So you can kill me, too? I do not think so."

"*What?*"

"He considered you his friend. How could you?" Her voice broke at the end.

"What are you talking about?" The confused question came from Halli. "Trent didn't do anything."

"*Si!*" Simone yelled with a jerk of the gun. "He shot my Renzo. Do not deny it—*la polizia* came to the *ospedale* as I retrieved supplies. They are searching for you right now. After that shooting at the United States Consulate, they know you are armed."

Halli's fingers gripped Trent's forearm as she gave a soft gasp beside him. "You told them about us?"

"No. I do not get *my* justice if I reveal your location," Simone said. "This way, I am defending myself from *assassino.*"

Trent eyed the gun, wondering where she'd gotten it, if it

was loaded, and did she really know how to use it? Knowing Lorenzo, the answer to the last two parts was yes. Next question—*would* she use it? He prayed that answer was *no*, but grief did strange things to a person and if he was wrong, a sudden move could prove fatal. He wasn't willing to risk it with Halli at his side.

"I didn't shoot Lorenzo, Simone—"

She gave a wild shake of her head. Her hand trembled even more than before. "They found him in *your* swimming pool. They want to ask you questions about his death. But I see your arm. He shot you when you betrayed him, did he not? I ask you *why?* What did he do to you?"

"I swear to you, I did not betray him. He was my friend. He was helping me—"

"And for this, you murder him?"

"No! Do you really think I'd come here if I'd killed him?"

"Simone—"

Halli's plea was cut short by the ring of the cell phone in Trent's pocket. He stiffened, his gaze slicing to Halli's. Lapaglia calling back about Ben. Returning his focus to Simone, he reached for the phone.

"*No*," Simone ordered.

"He has to answer it," Halli argued.

The phone rang again. Trent slid his hand into his pocket. "The men who killed Lorenzo have Halli's brother. We have a video that proves *they* shot him, not me. They're setting me up."

"*Basta!* Stop lying to me."

"They'll kill my brother if you don't let him answer." Halli took a step forward, but halted when Simone's hand wavered in her direction.

Rachel had worked her way off the table to brace herself in the doorway. "Please," she begged over the fourth ring. "It's true. They have our brother—"

The second Simone's attention shifted to Rachel, Trent lunged forward. He grasped Simone's wrist with his right hand and twisted it behind her back. Using his body to pin her against the wall, he simultaneously answered the phone.

"Who is this?"

Halli stepped forward, and Trent's firm squeeze on Simone's wrist made her release the gun into Halli's possession.

"Let us not play games, Mr. Tomlin."

The cold, calm voice across the cell phone line sent a chill down Trent's spine. Simone tensed and he knew she heard both sides of the conversation.

"Fine, Lapaglia. We both have something the other wants, so I'll keep this short and sweet. A simple trade. My video for Ben Sanders."

"As I understand, the video does not belong to you. Neither does Benjamin. Why do you concern yourself in this matter?"

"You know why, you bastard. Like you said, no games. Just make the deal and this can be over."

"Your arrogance exceeds your brother's."

Mention of Sean gave Trent absolute confirmation that the man had been involved in his brother's death. Fury engulfed him. His fingers clenched so hard it was a miracle the phone didn't snap in two.

"You will not last the day with the police searching for you," Lapaglia taunted. "Too bad some of them will shoot first and ask questions later. Curious event, *eh*? Roselli's body turning up at your villa?"

Lorenzo's surname brought forth a soft gasp from Simone. Trent controlled a violent urge to punch the wall as if it were Lapaglia's face and calmly stated, "Sucks for you that the video doesn't reveal my face behind the trigger finger."

Silence.

"That's right, it's all on there. Now, let me speak to Ben, and we'll set up the exchange."

"That is impossible at the moment."

Trent swallowed hard, his gaze cutting to Halli's rapt expression. "He better be alive."

Anguish clouded her eyes.

"He is," Lapaglia said.

Trent nodded to Halli and relief flooded her tense features. "Give him the phone," he demanded of Lapaglia.

"I am a business man, I have meetings to attend."

"And I care, why?"

"I do not babysit," Lapaglia snapped. "You must take my word he is alive, the same as I trust you will not try to make any more copies of Halliwell's video."

Trent wasn't surprised they'd found the partial copy at his house, but he stood his ground. "I'm calling the shots here. Setting me up as Lorenzo's killer gives me plenty of incentive to use that video to prove my innocence, so don't give me a reason to rethink my offer. I'll give you one hour. If you don't call me back with Ben on the phone, I will release the video to a trusted source."

"I need two hours to return where we hold him."

"One."

"Then release the video. Benjamin will end up as dead as your brother and your *agente* friend. And do not forget, I know where Halliwell lives."

A broken sob shook Simone's shoulders.

"Two hours." Trent flipped the phone shut and slid it back into his pocket as Simone collapsed in his arms.

****

More than an hour and a half later, Trent sat with an arm around Simone on the edge of her bed while Halli shadowed the doorway. The older woman had fallen apart, but with Trent's help, was slowly pulling herself back together.

Watching them grieve over the loss of his friend and her lover, Halli felt like she was reading Trent's journal again. And yet, a part of her could care less. After what Trent said about using the video for himself, her confidence in him faltered. It'd shattered when she checked her camera and discovered the SD card missing.

It didn't matter that she recognized the tactic for what it was, the moment he'd made the threat, it struck her that since Lapaglia and the rogue police officers had set him up as Lorenzo's killer, the video was his only hard proof of innocence. Clearly, he was keeping it close, too. Her gaze strayed to his hips, wondering which pocket he'd slipped the digital card into.

With his own life on the line, he didn't really owe her and her family anything. She hadn't seen the video, damn it! Not that she believed for one second Trent shot his friend, but she didn't actually see Lapaglia pull the trigger, either. Believing and seeing were two different things in a court of law. Both, she'd wager, in The United States of America and Italy.

When the choice came down to him or Ben, what would Trent do? Earlier, he'd tried to convince her to take Rachel to the consulate, insisting he needed to follow the plan alone. Was it really for her own safety, or so she'd leave the camera with him and he'd have sole possession of the video?

She hated the suspicion that ate at her earlier blind trust.

Simone raised red-rimmed, tear filled brown eyes to Halli. The woman was still beautiful.

"Please forgive me. I did not know—"

"Oh, please, no—don't apologize." She hurried over, and after a slight hesitation, leaned to hug the grieving woman. "I'm so sorry for your loss."

Fresh tears overflowed Simone's lashes as Halli straightened, but she didn't break down. "Thank you." After a moment, she blew her nose and sniffed with determination. Looking from Halli to Trent, she said, "I will help any way I can. They must pay for what they have done."

Instead of being relieved, Halli's stomach churned. She clasped her hands together, her knuckles white. If they exchanged the video for Ben, there might never be a way to prove the identity of Lorenzo's real killer. How would Simone feel about that? Would she try to convince Trent to turn the evidence over to the authorities no matter what?

"You've done enough already, we couldn't ask for more," Trent said.

"You do not have to ask. I freely offer."

"*Grazie.*" Trent brushed his lips across her cheek before rising to his feet.

Simone stood as well, and put a hand on his arm. "I will be out in a moment to properly bandage Rachel's wound and administer the antibiotics."

Trent rubbed her shoulder. "Take your time, I know this is hard."

"*Si*, but better if I keep busy, or else I will stare at the door, wishing him to enter."

Halli preceded Trent out of the room, but stopped in the living room. After a glance to make sure Rachel wouldn't overhear, she faced him. "What are you going to do?"

"About...what?"

"The video. The cops suspect you shot Lorenzo, and *my* video proves you didn't."

Confusion drew his brows together. She hesitated voicing her suspicion outright, but for Ben's sake, she had to know exactly where they stood. With effort, she put some backbone into her next words. "I need to know you're not going to suddenly decide to save yourself at the last minute and my brother gets the short end of the stick."

Indefinable emotion flashed in his eyes, was eclipsed by anger, and then his expression went completely blank. "I cannot believe you just said that."

When he moved to brush past her, she caught his arm. It was his left arm, and his jaw clenched as he jerked free.

"You're the one who pointed out the possibility to Lapaglia," she reminded. It took everything she had not to add, *You're the one who stole the card from my camera.*

"I need him to believe he's got the most to lose here, or he'll never make the trade. It's as simple as that, sweetheart."

I, not *we.* Halli held her chin high even though she wanted to cry in despair. Trent stalked away, leaving her stranded in the same spot she'd started yesterday. Desperate for help but unsure who to trust. God, this was exactly why she hated being dependant on someone other than herself.

A touch on her shoulder made her jump. Simone murmured some words in Italian, then said softly, "Do not worry. Trent is an honorable man. He will do what needs to be done."

Hardly reassuring coming from the woman who'd accused him of murder and pointed a gun at them less than an hour ago. Had she figured out yet that saving Ben meant giving up the evidence that could convict her lover's killer? Halli followed her into the kitchen and saw Trent had picked up her camera. Had he put the card back?

Please, let him have put it back.

"Explain for me what is going on," Simone requested as she started Rachel on IV antibiotics.

His gaze flicked to hers for a split second before shifting to Simone. Halli read his shuttered expression and spoke before he could.

"Yes, please, explain for all of us. Or are you going to pull the '*it's safer if you don't know*' bullshit again?"

He glared at her, and again, she read his expression. *Pain in the ass.*

Jerk, she silently replied.

He set aside the camera, faced Simone, and boosted himself up to sit on the kitchen counter. Halli frowned at his presumptuous choice of location, but Simone didn't give him a second glance as she began to apply a new bandage to Rachel's leg.

"My brother came over here about five months ago to film a segment for his latest documentary on the black market trade of exotic and endangered animals," Trent began. "As you know, two months later, he was found dead in my villa and the police ruled it a suicide. Blamed it on his depression, said he wasn't taking his medication. But I talked to him that morning and he was fine. I grew up with him, I knew the signs."

Halli's chest tightened in unavoidable sympathy. The combination of grief and anger that'd appeared on paper in his journal was twice as potent when it bled into his gravelly voice.

"Still, I questioned my judgment, wondered if maybe I had missed something…until I remembered a conversation we'd had a few days prior. He'd gotten footage of a smuggler based in Lenno importing illegal animals from Switzerland, via Lake Lugano."

"Alrigo Lapaglia," Halli stated.

Trent nodded. "Sean was excited about following the lead and I was on location on the last day of a hellish shoot that was three weeks behind schedule. I barely listened, gave him a virtual head pat, told him his film would be great, and went on my way."

"This was revealed to the police?" Simone asked the question before Halli could.

"Yes. And their response is what started me digging deeper. All Sean's camera equipment had been confiscated at the beginning of the police investigation—if you'd even call what they did investigating. When I requested everything be returned, there wasn't a single bit of film for the two months my brother had been in the country. His notes, contact list, cell phone, all of it was gone. Sean was meticulous about stuff like that. He filled notebooks for every film he ever made, even as a kid. So I laid it all out for Lorenzo to see what he thought."

Simone's hands paused over Rachel's leg as she looked up at Trent. "And he offered to help you?"

"Yes."

She took a shaky breath. "He has been so unpredictable and on edge these last few months. *I knew* he'd started something, but he never told me it was with you."

Trent frowned. "When I asked, he seemed happy to help. He said retirement wasn't what he expected."

"*Si.* For years he planned to buy a boat and fish away the 'good years'." Fresh tears gathered in her eyes. "But the last time I asked him about it, he told me to mind my own business."

"I'm sorry, Simone," Trent said softly. "If I'd have known…"

She shook her head. "It is not your fault. Please, continue."

He scrubbed his hands over his face and raked his fingers through his hair with a deep sigh. "We started the investigation about a week after Sean's death, and it didn't take long to realize these guys had a network of connections extending beyond what we'd ever imagined. The market for these animals is in the billions."

"What kinds of animals?" Halli asked.

"Tigers, leopards, monkeys, lizards, birds—you name it. Endangered and exotic animals are the third largest smuggling commodity in the world, right behind illegal drugs and firearms."

Quiet up until now, Rachel said, "Really? I had no clue."

"Many people don't. Lapaglia's got guys scattered around both lakes and the entire Lombardy Region. Local police, town officials, *Carabinieri*—and that's not counting his regular guys."

"Or the guard at the consulate this morning," Halli added.

"That's one we didn't know about," Trent admitted. "Anyway, we got word a shipment was due in sometime this week. Lorenzo went into the villa wired, posing as a buyer, hoping to get some names on tape. I didn't like the idea, but he insisted, said just because he was retired didn't mean he'd lost his touch for undercover work."

A sad smile touched Simone's lips. She finished with Rachel's bandage and pulled out a syringe, attached a needle, and stuck it into an upside down bottle of clear medicine.

"Unfortunately," Trent continued, "one of the officers working with Lapaglia had transferred to Lorenzo's district just before he retired. He showed up at the villa yesterday morning, blew Lorenzo's cover, and…well…"

"And that's where I come in," Halli supplied so Trent wouldn't have to say the obvious. "I was filming swans on the lake and caught more than I bargained for in the background."

Simone listened as Halli continued with a brief rundown of events leading up to their arrival on her doorstep. Trent interjected a comment here or there, but for the most part was quiet. Halli noticed he leaned forward every few minutes to look into the living room. She guessed he was watching the clock. Waiting for Ben's call, just like her. She kept talking, trying not to think of the minutes crawling by.

Simone returned her attention to the syringe in her hand. She tapped it with her finger, squirted out a small amount of liquid, and approached Trent.

"Renzo's cousin, Luca, works for the *Carabinieri* here in Milan," she said. "He might be able to help you."

"Maybe." Trent's attention zeroed in on the needle. "What's that for?"

"Antibiotics."

"Don't you just have some pills you can give me?"

"Discretion has limits. I secured what was at hand."

His jaw clenched, released. "Right. Sorry. You need my shirt off, or can I just push up my sleeve?"

"You can drop your pants."

His mouth opened and just as quick, clamped shut again. With a sigh, he slid down off the counter and reached to unbutton his jeans. Heat crept up Halli's neck at the thought of seeing his ass right there in the kitchen. She averted her head as he turned around, only to find Rachel watching the proceedings with unapologetic interest.

Halli couldn't help another look of her own. Big deal, right? She'd seen it before. Larger than life on the big screen, no less. Unfortunately—or thankfully?—she wasn't quite sure, Simone's body blocked her view.

"Relax," Simone instructed Trent.

A moment later, she stepped back and Halli got a glimpse of one taut cheek before he yanked up his briefs and pants. When he turned around mid-zip his gaze happened to catch on hers. One corner of his mouth lifted in a smirk.

It wasn't fair. He didn't look the least bit uncomfortable, and here she sat, caught looking, and feeling like *her* butt had been exposed.

She abruptly stood and stalked down the hall to the bathroom. Anything to escape his scrutiny, which she still felt all the way down the hall. Inside the privacy of the small room, Halli splashed cold water on her face a few times before wiping dry. It helped the heat in her body, but not the uncertainty frazzling her nerve endings.

Exhausted from the events of only this half day, she sat on the toilet lid and buried her face in her hands. She wasn't going to cry. She'd meant it when she vowed to quit being a victim. She just needed a moment to fortify herself and put things in perspective. Take a few deep breaths. Form a new plan.

And how have all those plans worked out for you so far?

She ran her fingers though her hair and dropped her hands onto her lap at that sobering question. Who was she kidding? Any plan she made needed input from Trent, especially if the video was in his pocket. They had to talk before Alrigo called back.

If he called back. She refused to think about that possibility and forced herself to her feet. Not that Trent would be very receptive to her input right now, but none of them had the luxury of time.

Back in the kitchen, her gaze was drawn to him like metal to a magnet. A look of concern in his eyes surprised her, but he straightened from where he leaned against the counter and turned toward the sink. Away from her.

Not far from his hand rested Simone's gun and the cell phone. Both ready for use in the blink of an eye.

An uncomfortable ache settled in the region of her chest at this evidence of his willingness to help when he had so much to lose. Not to mention all he'd done already. Without her asking. Heck, without her even knowing she needed him most of the time.

She knew her responsibility to her brother, but she owed Trent a debt of monumental proportions. He'd saved her life three—no, now it was four—times. Not to mention Rachel. The only thing that could ever hope to repay a portion of that debt was the video that proved his innocence. Did she dare let him keep it?

If he refused, her trust in him would be secure.

If he accepted, her obligation would be wiped clean and they'd have to find another way to save Ben. Maybe with the help of Lorenzo's cousin Simone had mentioned. That thought brought no reassurance.

Until a glance at Rachel spotlighted the right choice, if not the solution she desired.

An exchange was Ben's only chance. The video wasn't hers and it certainly wasn't Trent's. She owed it to her brother, and her sister, both of whom had protected and watched over her ten times more than their parents ever had. They were all each of them had.

So why, with the decision effectively taken out of her hands, did guilt sharpen the pain in her heart?

The ring of the cell phone shattered the oppressive, expectant silence. Everyone froze. On the second ring, Trent simultaneously answered and spun around to face Halli. His gaze locked on hers as he spoke.

With a curious light in his eyes that made her heart pound,

he walked forward.
 Extended the phone.
 "Your brother wants to talk to you."

Chapter 17

"Ben?"

An unbelievable tide of relief swept through Ben at the sound of his baby sister's small, hopeful, shaky whisper. "Halli. You okay?"

"I'm okay."

Ben pictured her tear-filled blue eyes and his eyes squeezed tight like his heart.

"How are you?" she asked.

He'd exchanged handcuffed to the bed for tied to a chair, but kept that information to himself so the worry in her voice didn't increase. "I'm fine. Where's Rachel?"

"She's okay, she's here with us."

More relief, just as profound. The pain in his swollen right eye was nothing now that he knew both his sisters were safe. He opened his eyes and lifted his narrowed gaze to the man who'd caused so much misery. Alrigo'd had Zucchi give Ben another round of bruises after Rachel's escape, but it was worth it knowing the man's plans had been screwed yet again. Until that bastard with claw marks on his face came in and gloated about shooting his sister.

"Is she hurt?" Ben asked Halli.

"She was shot in the leg, but we got help. She'll be okay."

He took a deep breath and began speaking fast. "Listen to me, Hal, you and Rach stay out of this now. Don't worry about me and don't you dare come—"

Lapaglia pulled the phone away from Ben.

"—*anywhere near them!*"

Ben glared as the man listened to his sister's voice on the other end of the line. A grin spread his thin lips across his darkened face. "Hello, Halliwell. Clever escape back in Torno, *carina*." He chuckled, then his grin faded fast. "Careful, Tomlin," Lapaglia warned with soft menace. "Sounds like you have come to care for the girl."

The man's expression of pure pissed-off matched his earlier one when he'd explained why he needed Ben to speak to Halli.

When Eva had brought him breakfast shortly after their first conversation, he'd worked on charming information from her and succeeded when she'd let it slip that the movie star was the man helping Halli. He had no clue how a guy like Trent Tomlin had become involved in this crazy situation, but would be eternally grateful for the help the man gave his sisters.

Rachel's rescue made it at least three times Tomlin had bested Lapaglia in the past twenty-four hours. No wonder the Italian was pissed. Ben hoped to God he got a chance to shake Tomlin's hand when this was over.

"You have your proof, now we make our deal," Lapaglia said. "We meet tonight. On the lake."

Ben waited to hear details of this deal and the meeting, but was distracted when Nino and Eva entered the room. He tried to catch Eva's eye, but beyond one glance, she coldly ignored him. So different from the woman who'd gently washed the blood away after Zucchi finished using him as a punching bag.

Nino said something in Italian and Lapaglia turned to him with a frown. He barked something into the phone, then held a hand over the mouth piece. The three of them conferred softly, their speech rapid and quite heated. Eva threw up her hands in the universal sign of frustration. Lapaglia began to raise the phone, but Nino spoke again.

Both Alrigo and Eva went still. Lapaglia's face registered interest; Eva's surprise. After a few more exchanges, Lapaglia cut a hand through the air and lifted Ben's phone to speak in his heavily accented English once more.

"I have determined your offer is inadequate. If Halliwell wishes to see her brother alive again, I will not only require the video, but additionally, a sum of one million US dollars. Cash."

Ben's jaw dropped in shock. *A million dollars?* "We don't have that kind of money!" he protested.

Lapaglia ignored him, concentrating on the phone in his hand. After a moment, his grin made another appearance. "That is precisely what Benjamin just advised. But *you*, my friend, have sufficient funds to make the deal."

Again Ben sat in amazement. He actually expected Trent Tomlin to pay a million dollars for a complete stranger? The man may have been nice so far, but nobody would be willing to help out *that* much.

So what then, with no one to pay? His parents were in prison. He had no rich friends, and no one besides his sisters would value his life that high. They certainly couldn't hope to come up with the money. Lapaglia's next words made him wonder if he'd read his mind.

"You may not believe Benjamin is worth more than a short video of questionable evidence, but I am positive Halliwell would agree with the value I have put on his head."

A video? That's what this was all about? Ben thought of Halli filming at the lake. She must've seen something other than swans after he and Rachel drove off without her. How many times more would he wish he could go back in time and change that monumental mistake?

Lapaglia grunted into the phone. "Then we have nothing more to discuss and I have no further use for him."

Ben didn't think it possible, but his muscles tensed even more when the man's hand moved to rest on his weapon. He'd known Trent Tomlin wouldn't agree to pay.

Eva moved forward. Ben noted her expression of protest with surprise. Lapaglia's gaze narrowed on her and her step faltered, then stopped.

Into the phone, he said, "You screw with my business, I require compensation." He turned to the window. "Do not play me for a fool. We both know you can get the money."

Ben couldn't see his face, but the undercurrent of steel in the man's voice didn't bode well for him. He wished to hell he could hear the other half of the conversation, but Lapaglia's words made it clear Tomlin was stalling.

"I think not. You have twenty-four hours." Quiet fell in the room. Lapaglia moved aside the curtain to look at the lake. He made a humming noise deep in his throat. "No. However...to prove I am a reasonable man, I will give you until five p.m. tomorrow before I call with additional instructions."

He flipped the phone shut and pivoted toward Ben. "It appears all of you lucked out when the superstar showed up."

Ben drummed his fingers on the arm of the chair he was tied to. "Yeah, there's my silver lining."

The phone rang in Lapaglia's hand. He ignored Ben's sarcasm and checked the display. With a chilling smile, he headed for the door, hand at his side. Just when Ben thought he'd let the call go, he answered. He narrowed his eyes after a moment.

"*Si*, I will have my men retreat, but…I have no further control over *la Polizia*. Furthermore, a word of warning…my connections are many. You do this alone. If you seek assistance, I *will* know, and then neither one of us will have use for your money."

Another pause, and then the Italian chuckled. "You insist I will pay, but your brother committed suicide, remember? It is no fault of mine he was weak."

He disconnected the call with a downward slap of the phone against his palm. As if snapping the phone shut flipped a switch, he began an angry tirade in Italian as Nino followed him from the room.

Lapaglia's last comment finally gave Ben another clue as to Trent Tomlin's connection. Had the Italian been involved in Sean Tomlin's suicide that'd been all over the news a few months ago? The possibility wasn't a stretch; Ben wouldn't put anything past the bastard.

Eva moved to stand in front of him. It was just the two of them in the room now, not that he'd complain. She was something else. And a hell of a lot easier on his swollen eye than Zucchi. His hands were losing feeling from lack of circulation and he rotated them as best he could within his bindings. He was rewarded with a slight tingling in his fingertips.

"So…will you get a cut of that million dollar ransom he just demanded?"

His question caught her off guard. Confusion and uncertainty clouded her eyes, but she recovered with determined, "*Si*."

"Damn. I was still kinda hoping you'd help me."

"I have helped."

He gave a short laugh. "Oh, right, I'm sorry. Thanks for that ice pack so my eye won't be so swollen when they kill me. All the easier to stare down the barrel of the gun with."

"Sarcasm is unattractive."

Ben tipped his chin. "I apologize again. Maybe our problem is that the definition of *help* has gotten lost in translation."

"When Mr. Tomlin pays, you will be free."

Ben laughed at her choice of words. "*If* Tomlin pays a million dollars for a complete stranger he's never even met. Tell me Eva, after all I've seen, all I've heard, what's the likelihood I'm still going to get out of this alive?"

She turned around to straighten one of the pillows on the bed, but the brief glimpse of her expression gave him an answer without a single word passing her lips. The ball in his stomach knotted tighter.

"Help me."

The pillow received a thorough fluffing. She thumped the pillow once more and then faced him with her arms crossed under her breasts. He struggled to keep his gaze on her face.

"Are you hungry?" she asked.

Looked like he'd have to approach this a different way. "Are you cooking?"

"*Si.*"

He curved his sore mouth in a slow smile. "Then yes, I'm hungry."

Her head tilted. She returned his smile with a dazzling one of her own. "I bet that works when you are not black and blue."

"You mean it's not working now?"

She rolled her eyes, but his vision wasn't so bad that he missed a promising flicker in her eyes just before she turned for the door. If he could just get her on his side, he might have a fighting chance here. He pitched his voice low and husky. "Eva."

She paused. Pivoted on those toned, sexy legs.

"I can't feel my fingers anymore."

Her gaze dropped to the rope securing his hands to the arms of the chair. He wiggled his fingers again to ease the pressure and gain sympathy. The resulting grimace was completely genuine. After a glance at the door, she sighed and returned to his side.

She leaned over to begin loosening the ties on his right wrist. He kept still, hoping she wouldn't notice his muscles tensed in a play for additional movement within the bindings. A spicy exotic scent that completely fit her enveloped his senses. He drew it into his lungs.

Tough but feminine. Sizzling yet aloof. Erotic and innocent.

Seeking to ground his wavering focus, he said softly, "If it's about the money, I can pay you."

She raised her gaze to his. His heart thumped in his chest.

"You said you do not have the money."

"Not a million dollars, but what I can get you won't have to share with the other bastards."

Her eyebrows lifted. "Other bastards? Meaning I am one, too?"

Crap. "I didn't mean it like—"

"It is not about the money." With that brief statement, she shifted to his other side, now standing directly in front of him, practically between his legs.

Her attention focused on his left hand, he discreetly tested his right. Unbelievably, his plan worked. With very little effort, his hand slid free. Before she could do more than begin to turn her head, he'd fisted his hand in her long hair and drew her close. She braced one hand on his left forearm, the other on the right arm of the chair. He clamped his legs together on hers, holding her captive.

He stared into her brown eyes, only inches from his. Flecks of glittering gold mesmerized him.

"If not the money, then what? Why are you with these guys?"

Her attention dropped down to his lips. When her lashes lifted again, no fear registered in the depths of her eyes, despite her vulnerable position. Irritation poked his ego. She may imagine herself relatively safe with his one hand still restrained, but he didn't doubt his superior strength would secure his freedom.

"Why else does a woman stay with a man if not for money?" she countered in a low, throaty whisper.

Heat sufficed his body in a split second, though he recognized the fact that she was playing him as much as he played her.

"In that case..." He deliberately focused on her exposed cleavage. "I'm more than willing to pay for your assistance in any manner you desire."

"Yes?" A slow sensuous glide of her pink tongue wet her lips.

Ben bit back a groan. "Hell yes."

Then the most unexpected thing happened. She leaned forward and pressed her mouth to his. A warning bell rang somewhere in the distant recesses of his mind.

Do not respond.

He closed his eyes to focus. She angled her head and slid her tongue between his lips, into his mouth. With his senses in a heightened state of awareness since realizing Halli was missing, every nuance of the woman in front of him was magnified. His tactical error registered too late for him to recover.

A half-hearted effort tightened his fingers in her hair, but he didn't drag her away. Not when he'd entertained more than one brief fantasy of this exact experience since seeing the woman yesterday. Red hot desire overrode common sense. The stimulating combination of her scent and taste triggered his response with a vengeance. And not just in the thrust and parry of his tongue with hers. His body hardened damn fast, too.

Eva deepened the kiss. Pressed her chest to his. A moan erupted from deep in his throat. Partly from arousal, partly from her sensual, yet painful assault on his swollen bottom lip. A frustrated tug on his still captive left hand yielded no result. He wanted to crush her against him with both arms. Feel her ripe body and the pleasure-pain of her hips against his straining erection.

Her hand slid along his right arm, skimmed over his bare

forearm, and found his hand, fingers still entwined in her hair. The other curled around his head before her nails raked along his scalp. The passion in this one kiss promised incineration in bed.

Oh, but what a way to go.

All thoughts of her naked body writhing under his fled with the sudden jab of her knee to his groin. Pain registered. In his crotch and in the middle fingers of his right hand that she pulled from her hair and bent back almost to the breaking point. He jerked forward in an attempt to relieve the pressure on his hand. Her knee pressed harder into his groin.

"Jesus," he gasped. "Easy."

Her breathing was as unsteady as his, but her brown eyes regarded him without apology. "Do not attempt to take advantage of me again."

"You kissed *me*, dammit. *Ow*."

Her brutal hold on his fingers directed his hand back to the arm of the chair. Once the restraint was back in place and tight enough to prevent another escape, but not so snug as to cut off his circulation, she finally removed her knee.

Instead of moving away, she placed that knee on the chair against the outside of his thigh. His pulse began a steady increase when her other knee mimicked the first on the opposite side, and she straddled him on the chair. He fought the insane urge to thrust upward. What the hell was wrong with him? The woman was a sadist!

Starting at his hairline, she ran the fingers of both hands through his hair, down to the nape of his neck. Her nails stimulated countless nerve endings on the reverse trip. Tingles worked though his entire body. That's when she settled her weight onto his lap and smiled.

"You are easily excitable."

Ben choked back a tortured groan. "You're a very exciting woman."

He barely recognized his own voice. Never had he been aroused to such a fever pitch before. He'd heard danger could be a wild aphrodisiac, but this was nuts.

With a husky laugh, she rotated her hips in a slow circle.

"*Grazie.*"

His body throbbed. The groan broke free. "God, woman, what are you doing?"

"Exploring my power." Her throaty whisper gave the statement twice the punch.

He found himself pulled forward for another mind-numbing kiss that ended way too fast. A ragged breath did nothing to bank the fire burning him from the inside out. Staring into her darkened eyes, he admitted, "I'm completely at your mercy."

"A fact you must not forget." She braced her hands on his shoulders and pushed off the chair. While he scrambled to form a coherent thought, she smoothed the snug hem of her shirt over the curve her hips. "Now that we have that settled, I will do what I can to satisfy your hunger."

Was she serious? He waited in breathless anticipation for her next move.

She spun on her heel and exited the room. Somewhere in the distance a church bell rang the noon hour. Ben gave a self-mocking laugh that ended in a low, agonized growl.

She was referring to hunger of the non-carnal variety.

****

Evalina's knees wobbled the moment she closed the door, but thankfully, the wall offered necessary support. Sweet mother of God. What had come over her in there? Anyone could've walked in. Nino. Zucchi. Alrigo.

She shuddered at the last possibility. His eyes made her skin crawl. They'd undressed her too many times since hooking up with Nino here at the villa. With God's help, this would be over soon.

They needed that video. It was imperative it didn't fall into the wrong hands. Ensuring their remaining bargaining chip did not escape was also crucial. No matter the cost. Or so she tried to tell herself. Against her better judgment, she liked the American more with each visit to his room. Sure, he was brash, and cocky, but when his sister had been here, she'd caught a glimpse of a pure heart. He'd protected her more than once, and at great risk to his own life. In her line of work, men like that were rare.

It did not help that he could make her insides quiver with a single look. And that kiss. Would she have had the same out of control reaction to him in a different setting? Or was it just the unusual circumstances they were trapped in?

The lip-lock had started as a necessary move to get him restrained again, but…what came after. On the chair. She got warm all over again just thinking about her rash behavior. Not to mention, his scalding response and the feel of his hard body beneath hers.

She leaned her head back against the wall and closed her eyes.

"Where the hell have you been?"

Nino's annoyed question jerked her head up. Erotic thoughts fled, leaving a flush of heat on her cheeks. Aw, hell, when had she become such an amateur?

She straightened and hurried away from the door, self-consciously smoothing her messed hair. Nino's gaze narrowed as it swept over the length of her body.

"What's going on?" Nino asked.

She took a deep breath and fisted her hands on her hips. "You tell me. What the hell were you thinking suggesting a ransom? Are you deliberately trying to screw this up?"

"Easy money," Nino stated. "A sure bet Alrigo would go for."

"Well, I don't like it."

"The ransom was to buy us some time. We aren't ready and you know it."

Evalina stalked forward until she was right in his face. "And what if Tomlin can't come up with the money? What if he changes his mind?"

She stopped herself from asking a third question, but it didn't matter. The emotion that seeped into her voice allowed Nino to read between the lines with ease. *What if Alrigo killed Ben?*

Nino grasped her shoulders and pushed her against the wall. "That man in there is a means to an end, nothing more."

"He didn't do anything to anyone."

A door further down the hall opened, and Eva saw Tony step out. She'd heard about the espresso Trent Tomlin had tossed in his face at the cafe and the guy's face still showed the effects of the scalding liquid. Knowing he was in league with Alrigo, she couldn't find it in her to care about his pain.

He paused when he saw the two of them. Nino leaned in close to Evalina, threading his fingers into her hair while his thumbs rested along her jaw. His lean, muscled body unnecessarily held her in place. She knew she had to keep up appearances, though the longer they were here, the harder it became to endure his touch.

Nino's lips brushed hers, and then skimmed across her cheek to rest against her ear. She closed her eyes against the sight of Tony watching.

"Careful, Eva," Nino breathed. "Or you'll be the one to screw everything up."

His hot breath sent a shiver down her spine, but it chilled to the bone where Ben's had warmed and excited.

Proving Nino was absolutely right.

Chapter 18

Halli paused in the doorway of Simone's front room as Trent spoke into his cell phone.

"No, I figured you'd heard the news already, but I swear to you, I did not kill that cop. We were friends. He was helping me investigate Sean's death."

The muscles in his back were as tense as his voice, but then his shoulders relaxed a bit.

"Thanks—your belief means more than you'll ever know," he continued. "Which is why you're the only one I trust with the money. I don't care what you have to do, just so it's ready when I call tomorrow. I'm dead serious about this, Brad. Waterproof bag, and someone *you'd* trust with your daughter's life. Yeah. Thanks."

The ransom money. Hearing him make the arrangements solidified Halli's growing remorse for doubting him. If he intended to keep the video for himself, he'd have been gone already, right? She watched him flip the phone shut and slip it into his jeans pocket, his back still to the doorway. She searched for an opening line, but he spoke first without turning around.

"Are you here to accuse me of ulterior motives again?"

She'd intended to apologize, but instead went on the defensive. "I had to ask."

He ran his hands through his hair, frustration evident as his fingers clenched at the nape of his neck. Was that an existing habit, or newly formed, she wondered, stepping into the room. Then he pivoted to face her as he leaned back against the window sill, and she forgot all about the errant thought.

"I'd like to say I've looked at it from your point of view, Halli, that I get where it came from, and, dammit, I do. It's just…I thought we were past that."

He couldn't really be as offended as he sounded, could he? Unless he didn't truly understand where she was coming from.

"I'm sorry." She lifted her hands, then dropped them back

to her sides with a feeling of helplessness. "I'm more grateful than you'll ever know for what you've done for me, and Rachel, but I still have to think about my brother. Can you honestly tell me you didn't consider the fact that you'd be turning over the one piece of evidence that proves you're innocent?"

"Of course I considered it. Can *you* honestly tell me you think I'd choose to let your brother die?" His hand rose, palm out. "Forget it, you already answered that question."

Heart pounding, she lifted her chin and stated, "No, *you* answered that question when you stole the SD card from my camera."

"*What?* You think that's..." He leaned his head back, and swore at the ceiling. Then he met her gaze dead on. "I did not steal the card. It's in a safe place."

"And where's that, in your pocket?"

Hurt flashed, then his gaze sharpened as his features turned to granite. "On the *boat*, Halli. I had a bad feeling about the consulate so I hid the card to ensure *your* safety in case anything happened."

"Oh." Remorse was an understatement now. "Why didn't you say something?"

"You were excited about seeing your family. We'd had a good morning and I didn't want to ruin it by worrying you in case I was wrong. And God do I wish I would've been wrong."

When he pushed away from the window and walked past her toward the living room, she cleared her throat to find her voice. "Trent..."

He kept walking.

"*Trent.*"

This time he stopped, and when he swung around, his expression was cautious.

"I'm sorry."

All she got was a tight nod.

Blinking away the moisture blurring her vision, she smoothed her damp palms down the sides of her newly borrowed jeans. "About the money..."

"What about it?"

"I'll probably never be able to repay you, but I'll do

whatever I—"

"Christ, Halli, I don't give a damn about the money!"

"It's a million dollars."

"Which is peanuts compared to what I make on one Shain West movie. Hell, I'd pay ten times what the bastard asked for. What does it take for you to believe in someone?"

A sound in the doorway brought them both around. Simone stood behind the couch where she'd settled Rachel to rest after giving her a mild sedative. The petite Italian woman's gaze shifted between them before settling on Trent.

"You need a new bandage," she said quietly.

"Okay if I shower first?"

She nodded and Halli stared after his back as he walked away from her yet again. After she forced her gaze from his long stride and the ripple of muscles across his shoulders, she caught Simone watching her watch him. The older woman offered a sad smile, fresh tears in her eyes.

Halli walked over and gave her another hug. Despite being strangers, she felt Simone's loss and feared what she and Rachel might face in the next twenty-four hours if they didn't get Ben back. The comfort worked both ways.

Neither of them said a word as they cleaned up the mess in the kitchen. After they'd finished, Halli returned to the living room by Rachel. Her sister slept, leaving her alone with her thoughts and guilt.

The first sixteen years with her parents taught her to look for ulterior motives, especially when money was involved. The past ten years struggling on her own taught her to only depend on herself. So it wasn't that she didn't *want* to trust Trent, but a lifetime of hard lessons was almost impossible to set aside in two days. She'd done it once and was already second-guessing herself.

Trent's footsteps in the hall brought her forward in her chair, but he didn't even look in her direction as he strode past, shirt fisted in his hand. She rose and circled around the couch, only to pause out of sight when Simone's voice reached her from the kitchen.

"You will get justice for my Renzo?"

"I will," Trent answered. "I promise they'll pay for what they've done."

Halli stood there, the conviction and tenderness in his voice resonating in her heart. It reminded her of the gentle kiss she'd shared with him in this very spot just a few hours ago. The man who'd kissed her like that had to be someone she could trust.

"I do not work for two days," Simone said. "I will help with anything you need. You can stay here and I will see to the sister."

"A computer would be very helpful," Trent asked, a hopeful lift to his voice.

"Sorry, no computer."

"It's okay. Any chance I can use your car?"

"*Si.*"

"Thank you," Trent said. But then his next words were low and indecipherable.

When Simone's response was just as quiet, Halli's inner skeptic quickly reminded, *that man you want to trust is also an Oscar-winning actor.* And he'd said *I* again, not *we*. She entered the kitchen just as Simone pointed Trent to a chair.

"Let me bandage that before you go."

Halli narrowed her gaze on Trent. "Where are you going?"

He rolled his eyes as he removed his shirt and sat down. "Here we go again."

Halli crossed her arms over her chest and waited.

"I'm heading back to the boat to get the memory card."

"You mean *we*."

"No." His jaw clenched. "I mean *I'm* going to get the card, and you're—"

"Going with you."

"—staying here with your sister. Where it's safe."

"It's my video, Trent. My brother."

He watched Simone work for a moment. She noticed his fingers curl into a fist on his thigh but didn't think it had anything to do with pain when his gaze lifted to hers.

"Yesterday you didn't trust me to stay with me. Today you don't trust me to leave you."

She gave him a fake smile, no longer sorry about her doubt

when he clearly intended to ditch her. "Don't take it personally."

"How can I not?" he muttered. As Simone finished with his arm, he shrugged his uninjured shoulder and rose to his feet. "Fine. Come along and guard your damn video. You can watch your own ass while you're at it, too."

That argument was over much quicker than she expected. Instead of being relieved, she wondered what'd changed his mind. Nothing she'd said—she hadn't said much—so what was he up to?

Simone handed him his shirt and then turned to Halli with a wrapped syringe and a bottle of clear medicine. "He requires a second shot tomorrow. Fill the syringe three milliliters and—"

"Me?" Halli's gaze found Trent's again. "We're coming back here, aren't we?"

"Not until we have your brother. I don't want to risk leading anyone here until this is all over." He paused a beat. "*Now* will you stay?"

Her stomach flipped at his ominous tone. "No."

Trent held out a hand toward Simone. "I can give myself the shot."

"I'll do it." Halli quickly took the supplies. If she hadn't argued, the jerk would've left her behind and not come back. She'd give him a shot alright. When Trent's gaze narrowed toward her, she maliciously added, "It might even be fun."

"We'll just see about that," he warned softly as he pulled his shirt on. He jerked his chin toward the living room. "Say your goodbyes and let's go."

Halli made her way to the couch and looked down at Rachel. She hated to wake her, but didn't want to leave without saying goodbye. Yesterday everything had seemed so surreal. Today it was harsh reality. As she moved around to sit on the edge of the couch, it struck her that there was a chance this could be the last time they saw each other.

Instant tears sprang to her eyes. She covered her face, took a deep breath, and wiped away the moisture on her cheeks. When she opened her eyes, she found Rachel watching her.

Halli forced a smile. "Hey, how are you doing?"

"I feel like I'm more than a little out of it, but I s'pose that's a good thing. Not much pain."

"That is good." She took Rachel's hand in hers. Noticed the broken, chipped nails that two days ago had been manicured to perfection, and prayed everything would turn out okay. "Listen, Rach, you're going to stay here with Simone, and I'm going with Trent. We'll be back tomorrow night with Ben."

"That last part sounds good to me." Rachel's fingers tightened on hers. "Halli...I need you to know how sorry I am about all this."

"I told you, it's not your fault."

"But we left you. None of this would've happened if we—"

"If *I* hadn't insisted on filming those stupid swans," Halli interrupted.

Rachel's eyes widened. "Hal, this is not your fault."

"I should've shut off the camera when you asked."

She tried to pull away but Rachel held fast and ordered, "Stop it."

They stared at each other until finally Rachel heaved a weary sigh. "We can't change what happened, so this isn't helping at all."

"No, it's not." Halli squeezed her sister's fingers. "But we're gonna get him back, so you concentrate on getting better, and pray for Ben, okay?"

Rachel nodded.

"Halli."

Trent's low voice in the doorway drew their attention. She'd just seen him in the kitchen, and yet when she glanced over her shoulder, Halli's breath caught in her throat.

He hadn't shaved after his shower and wore the same black shirt and jeans. His dark hair was still damp, its tousled disarray sexier than if he'd taken the time to comb it. The man's effortless appeal stirred butterflies in Halli's stomach and annoyed her at the same time. She should be completely focused on her family right now, not noticing his sex appeal.

Rachel's tired gaze transferred back to Halli and she gave a pitiful excuse for a smile. "On the bright side, we got to meet Trent Tomlin, right?"

I got to kiss Trent Tomlin, but she wasn't going to tell Rachel that right now. Maybe never. Instead, she rolled her eyes. "Not such a big deal when you consider what a jerk he can be, but I try to look past that."

"While I deal with her neurotic, bossy brattiness," Trent countered.

Rachel smiled for real. "He knows you already."

"Shut up. You're supposed to be on my side." She leaned over and hugged Rachel. "We'll all be on our way home before you know it. Years from now, you, me and Ben will laugh about our big adventure."

"You cook, I'll bring the wine," Rachel whispered.

"Deal."

Rachel's hold tightened. "Be careful, Hal. I love you."

"I love you, too." She sniffed back tears.

On their way out the door, Rachel called out, "Take care of my sister, Trent."

He nodded once and they left.

****

Trent's impatience grew by the minute and there wasn't a damn thing he could do about it. Halli's need for essentials made sense, he just hated being cooped up in the car while she shopped. He tugged on the bill of one of Lorenzo's caps and adjusted his sunglasses. She'd claimed it'd only take her a few minutes, and she'd only been gone five, but past experiences told him his wait had barely begun.

Damn it, the clock was ticking. If someone recognized him and alerted the authorities, his arrest would put her brother in more danger. Not to mention, the fact that Simone had given him Lorenzo's gun wouldn't help his case one bit. He should've stressed all that to Halli before she went inside the store.

It had crossed his mind to drive off without her. But as quick as the thought formed, he knew he'd never leave her alone without her safety guaranteed. Besides, with the money he'd handed her to shop with and the backbone she'd found over the past twenty-four hours, he had no doubt she'd figure out a way to follow him back to Bellagio.

If he was going to leave her behind, he should've done it at

Simone's.

So why the hell didn't you?

Her sister would've talked some sense into her after he left, and he wouldn't have another fight on his hands when he told her in no uncertain terms that he'd make the exchange alone. Leaving her at Simone's would've forced her to trust him to do the right thing.

The hell of it was, he didn't want her forced trust. He wanted her to trust him of her own free will. That she thought he might rank his freedom over her brother's life cut deep, and pissed him off. It shouldn't. In her shoes, he would've asked the same question. Would've thought the same thing she did when the memory card came up missing. But all they'd been through so far should count for something—right? He finally played the hero for real; a little faith was not too much to ask for payoff.

Besides, she should know he had the resources to defend himself if it came right down to it, so of course her brother came first. Hell, even without the money to hire defense lawyers, he'd like to think he'd still make the right choice. Good thing for her he had his movie star fortune, or paying the ransom would be impossible. What would Halli have done then?

Trent shifted in his seat, trying to stretch his legs as the second phone call from Lapaglia replayed in his mind. At first, he'd been so shocked by the demand for money, he hadn't thought beyond doing what was necessary to ensure her brother's safety. Now that he'd had time, he kept thinking how Lapaglia had been ready to deal, then told him to hold on.

Something about the whole thing didn't sit right. Nothing he could actually put his finger on. The men sold near-extinct animals for money, they *murdered* for money, so it was no surprise they'd use any opportunity presented to make a fast buck. A million in cash in twenty-four hours was a no-brainer.

And yet, gut instinct said someone else had suggested the ransom. He hadn't heard it directly, but the muted conversation on the other end of the phone had indicated a heated discussion. Then Alrigo's smug stipulations. Not that it really mattered who suggested the ransom, did it? The end result would hopefully be the same. In their favor. His and Halli's and Ben's. After he paid.

Now all he had to do was figure out a way not to get killed in the process. More than anything, he wanted to take a trip up along the west coast of the lake and check out Lapaglia's villa. See what they were up against. But something told him Halli wouldn't let him go alone, and taking her that close to the hornet's nest was a risk he wasn't willing to take. He'd have to make do with the information Rachel had provided to coincide with Lorenzo's headcount over the wire recording.

The back passenger door of Simone's silver Lancia opened, bringing him out of his thoughts with a jolt. He immediately went for the gun, until he saw Halli. His tension eased as she tossed a couple bags onto the backseat and then got in the front.

She buckled her seat belt. "All set."

Starting the car and checking for traffic before pulling out, he then glanced at the clock. Ten minutes. "That was fast."

"I told you I wouldn't be long."

"I've heard that before."

"Yay for me. Yet another way I'm the complete opposite of women you're used to."

More than you know.

"Here's your change, by the way."

A wad of bills landed in his lap. Change? *Really?* He stuffed the money into his pocket without looking to see what she'd spent. He shouldn't even care if she spent all or none, damn it. Why was it that, despite the fact she drove him crazy and annoyed the hell out of him with her sarcasm and distrust, she was the first woman in a long time to interest him beyond sex?

Come to think of it, where the hell was that detached character he'd assigned to himself back at the villa yesterday evening? The one who set everything else aside and simply did what needed to be done to take down the bad guys. New roles came easy to him, but getting a handle on *that* guy was proving to be very difficult.

"Rachel said they hurt him."

Halli's soft words jolted through him. She didn't have to

say her brother's name for Trent to know who she was talking about. So much for staying aloof. His fingers tightened on the steering wheel.

"It's not your fault, Halli."

She stared out the window long enough that he wondered why she brought it up in the first place. A quick glance revealed no tears, and yet the need to offer reassurance took hold. "I'm going to do whatever—"

"Do you think they're holding Ben at the same villa that I filmed?" she asked, cutting him off.

He hesitated before answering truthfully. "Based on Rachel's description, probably. Plus, it's the only place I know of that Lapaglia operates from on this lake, and he specified we'd meet by boat."

"Any chance we can get inside?"

His brows lifted. "You want to pull a Remington and Mrs. King?"

"I'm serious."

"That's what I'm afraid of. It'd be a suicide mission for all of us."

"You didn't think so this morning."

"I wasn't wanted for killing a cop this morning. Have you stopped to think about what happens to you if I get arrested? What happens to Ben?"

Her silence confirmed she hadn't.

"Our best bet is to trade the video and pay the ransom."

She rubbed a hand over her face, propped her elbow on the door and chin in her hand, and sighed. "Are you going to contact that guy with the military police?"

Lorenzo's cousin Luca, the *Carabinieri* officer. "Simone gave me his number, and God knows we can use all the help we can get, but I worry about how far Lapaglia's arm reaches, especially after finding out he's got an informant at the consulate. If he gets wind we contacted the authorities…"

No amount of money would save her brother.

He also didn't tell her one or two of Lapaglia's comments made Trent wonder if the ransom would do the trick , even if they followed instructions to the letter. The man's arrogance confirmed he believed himself above the law, no matter the evidence they had against him. During their phone conversation, he hadn't even reacted when Trent brought up Lorenzo's murder. With so many men of authority in his back pocket, a few more added to the body count wouldn't faze him.

As he slowed for the turn that would take them along the lake up to Bellagio, Trent glanced over at Halli. "But he's your brother, so it's your call. Do you want to contact Luca?"

She looked surprised that he'd given her the decision and it took her a moment to answer. "I think we should figure out how the exchange is going to take place without these guys just killing us after they have the video and the money."

He held off on initiating the argument that he'd be alone during the exchange, but he was all for making sure he and Ben were still alive on the other side. "Great idea. Seeing as I don't think well on an empty stomach, let's say we stop for dinner and see what we come up with."

"Let's say we skip the chance of you being recognized and arrested and I'll make something on the boat," she countered.

Trent grimaced even though she had a damn good point. Still, he couldn't help thinking with his stomach instead of his head. "Cops or Spaghetti O's…man, that's a tough call."

"I can cook if I have ingredients."

"Yeah?"

She lifted a noncommittal shoulder. "It'll give me something to do."

In the name of safety, he gave her the benefit of the doubt and kept an eye out for the first market he could find. Two detours later to avoid *Carabinieri* checkpoints, he spotted a market not far from Bellagio and pulled over.

Proving true the statement that she was the complete opposite of women he was used to, Halli took twice as long picking out food compared to clothes. After she returned with the sack of groceries, he drove the last few kilometers to George's place where the boat was docked.

"What are you going to do about Giovanni's car?"

Trent recalled the shattered left hand mirror—he hadn't had much luck with mirrors the past two days— and blown out back window and shrugged. "Buy him a new one."

Surprise lifted her eyebrows. "Just like that?"

"Just like that." He parked out of sight of the road behind a small shed then looked over at her raised eyebrows. "What? You want to clean up all that blood?"

"I can."

Trent shook his head on his way around to her side of the car, Lorenzo's gun tucked neatly into the back waistband of his jeans and covered by his untucked shirt.

Halli closed her door, ever-present camera in hand. "After we get Ben—"

"You're going home, remember? Don't worry about the car, Halli, I'll take care of it." After a moment of enjoyable distraction while she retrieved the bags from the back seat, he took the overloaded grocery bag from her arms.

"Must be nice to have that kind of money."

He gave a short laugh as she preceded him along the path to the dock, carrying her small handful of other bags.

"It has its advantages." *Some days more than others.*

She stopped suddenly. Busy doing a quick check of their surrounding area, Trent almost ran her over when she turned to face him.

"That sounded bad—like I'm envious or something."

"You mean you're not?"

He meant it as a joke, but she immediately replied, "God, no."

He lifted his brows, mimicking her earlier expression. She whirled and quickly started walking again. "What I meant was, I wouldn't want your problems."

"Huh," he mused. His problems included her. Trent swept his gaze down the length of her back, taking in the fitted navy T-shirt and low-rise jeans she'd borrowed from Simone. "And your life is so perfect."

Over her shoulder, he received a roll of her eyes, softened by a small smile. "Obviously not. But do you think Lapaglia would've asked for the money if you weren't who you are?"

"Probably not." He stepped past her onto the dock and leapt down into the boat.

"That's all I'm saying," she explained as he grasped her hand to help her aboard. "And more for myself than anything. It's a reminder that, sure, the money's probably nice, but it's not everything. Most times it's more trouble than it's worth."

Her unexpected bitter statement at the end spoke of hard-earned experience. The vessel swayed gently beneath their feet, and while he would've liked a chance to study her expression, she pulled free as if she didn't want to touch him. Then she set the camera atop the groceries in his arms, took the bag, and went straight below deck.

Trent retrieved the SD card from where he'd stashed it in a waterproof compartment under the the captain's cushion and joined her. There may be some way to dig deeper into her last words while he figured out how to make a backup copy of the video for insurance. He wouldn't risk Halli or Ben by using it if the exchange went well, but if something went wrong…well, better to be prepared.

After she put the antibiotics bottle from Simone in the refrigerator, the small galley table became her workstation to unload the camera, Roma tomatoes, a long loaf of French bread, pasta, parsley, basil, garlic, fresh mozzarella, parmesan, and one onion. He palmed the camera as he slid along the booth-style bench and propped his feet up on the seat cushion.

The answer was obvious, but he asked anyway. "Whatcha makin'?"

"Spaghetti. I know, cliché, but I could easily recognize all the ingredients without having to speak Italian."

"And how about dessert?"

The moment the words left his mouth, he could've kicked himself for not keeping the question to himself. In the close confines of the boat, with her recently showered fresh scent lingering in the air like it had in the car, his mind immediately flashed back to the scorching kiss at the Villa Melzi that morning. The one at Simone's had been nice, too, but it'd ended badly—how could it not with a gun involved?—and, that one certainly didn't make him crave a long, slow, hot dessert like the one in the garden did. His mouth actually watered as he fiddled with the camera in his hands.

"Sponge cake with fresh fruit and cream."

He made a noncommittal noise, still vying for control over his over-imaginative mind.

"You want something else?"

She was bent over, digging pots and pans and a cutting board from his small cupboards. He eyed her tempting curves and said, "Nothing you'd go for."

A sauté pan banged onto one of the two stove burners. She put a hand on her hip and turned to give him a challenging look. "You don't think I can handle your dessert?"

Now was the time to lay on the playboy charm and let her know they were talking about two entirely different things. See where it led. It's what his character would do to help pass the time until tomorrow. Ease the stress. Get their minds off things.

He snorted softly. *Yeah, right.*

"You might be surprised," she said.

Oh, there'd be surprise all right. He flipped open the viewfinder of the camera and powered it on. "I don't think we've got the right ingredients." Oil and water didn't mix anyway, right? No matter how hot the fire burned.

"Just tell me what you want. I'm very good at improvising."

Irritation had crept into her tone.

He paused with his finger above the play button. "Forget I asked. I don't need dessert."

"For a million dollars cash, dessert is the least I can do."

Fine. Trent slowly and deliberately slid his gaze up the length of her body until their eyes locked, leaving no question as to his definition of dessert. Color flooded her cheeks and she quickly turned toward the stove.

To grab a knife.

He smiled, wondering if he should take the move as a pointed warning. After her suspicion at Simone's and cool attitude since, he'd be stupid not to, even though she applied the razor sharp steel to the onion and garlic, not him.

When both ingredients were sizzling in a pan with a liberal splash of olive oil, she turned her slicing skills to the tomatoes and he started digging.

"So when was money ever more trouble than it was worth to you?"

The blade cut through a tomato and hit the cutting board beneath with a thud. "When isn't it?"

"Uh, uh. One million's got to buy me more than that."

The look she gave him clearly said it didn't. He dropped his hands and the camera to rest in his lap and played dirty. "You read, in intimate detail, how I feel about certain things." In particular, his father. No one had known how much the man got to him except Sean.

The journal reminder stilled her hands. They restarted in sharp, choppy jerks. "I didn't have what you'd call the typical all-American childhood."

"No apple pie, a big ol' dog, and family game nights playing Monopoly?"

This time she gave a soft snort. "I wish."

"I hear Monopoly isn't all it's cracked up to be."

He received a small smile, but it didn't last, and he still didn't know what made her think money wasn't worth the trouble. If she'd grown up without it, he'd assume the hard work involved in reaching financial security would be more than worth it. It had been for him after he struck out on his own.

Or…was it more that he could shove his success in his father's face through the tabloids?

Her chopping had intensified, the rapid sounds punctuating the silence. She quartered the Romas and removed small clumps of seeds before dicing and tossing the tomatoes in the pan with the onion and garlic.

Normally, he'd take the hint at her obvious discomfort and change the subject. Except he hadn't acted what he'd call normal around her since they'd met, and his curiosity was truly roused after her comments the day before.

"What do your parents do that have to do with back story? You said they aren't actors."

"Not like you, that's for sure."

When she didn't elaborate, he prompted, "Were they in sales? Starving artists? What?"

"Artists. Hah. They'd love that."

Trent was losing patience. "What exactly do they do?"

She finished with the tomatoes and swept her gaze across the table as if she wished there were more. With nothing else to chop, she braced her hands on the table and looked him straight in the eye.

"Unless the federal government took time off for good behavior, they're probably making license plates somewhere in Ohio."

Surprise held him completely still.

"When I was with them, their sole focus was money," she continued. "Didn't matter how much we had at the time, or what they had to do to get it, they always wanted more. *That's when money was more trouble than it was worth.*"

Resentment, anger and hint of vulnerability shimmered in her dusk-blue eyes. "Anything else you'd like to know?"

Chapter 19

Trent ignored the thud of his heartbeat and held her gaze. "Not at the moment."

Not actors, but they used back story; currently locked up in federal prison. For robbery? Fraud? Were they con-*artists*?

She turned away to begin running water into a pot. Her shoulders rose and fell with a deep breath. "Just let me know if anything else trips your trigger. I wouldn't want you to feel like you're not getting your money's worth."

He sat forward, setting the camera on the table. "In that case..."

She slammed the faucet handle off and transferred the pot to the stove with a loud bang. Once the burner flamed and water sizzled on the underside, she faced him with her arms crossed. Prepared for whatever he threw at her. Ready to fight.

He didn't want to fight with her at all—and he missed the *Wet & Wild* T-shirt. "Which underwear did you pick yesterday?"

Her brow furrowed even as color bloomed in her face. "What?"

He shrugged, wondering himself where the question had sprung from. Not quite the mood lightener he'd intended, but hard to take it back now. He tried for an innocent smile. "Easier than the last question, isn't it?"

"You're on drugs, aren't you?"

"Antibiotics."

She rolled her eyes and reached to give the tomato sauce a vigorous stir. Red droplets spattered onto the stovetop. A couple landed on her arm, making her hiss in a breath and drop the spoon in the pan. Trent resisted the urge to jump up and make sure she was okay as she ran water over the scalded spots.

"Aren't we supposed to be discussing tomorrow?" she said.

"After we eat."

A quick flick of her wrist turned off the faucet, and then the burner under the pot of water. "The sauce is going to take at least an hour." She started cleaning up from her earlier preparations, throwing a glance at the camera before rinsing a wash cloth in the small galley sink. "Do you really need to watch that again?"

He picked up the camera and turned it in his hands. "I'm hoping to figure out a way to make a copy. Not—" he added when she looked over in alarm "—to use for myself. For insurance. Back up. Just in case."

"In case what?"

Their eyes met. She dropped her gaze and the collapsible table shuddered under the force of her sudden scrubbing. The surface wasn't dirty, and he didn't really need to give voice to the answer that hung in the air between them. *In case everything goes to hell and one of us ends up dead.*

"I should watch it," she said, then scrubbed harder.

"No."

"But then I can testify—"

He reached out a hand to stop hers. "It's not going to come to that."

Distracted from taking the finish off the table, she pulled away and scanned the cabin walls. "Do you have *any* video equipment on board?"

"Stereo only. The boat's my getaway. No TV, DVD, computer, or internet."

"What about Giovanni and Concetta?"

"Simone didn't have a computer, you think they do?"

She sighed her frustration. "No."

"Besides, with me being a fugitive and all, I'd rather—"

"No, I get it. Better not. What about your friend George's place?"

He shook his head. "Security alarms."

Her attention returned to cleaning. Trent didn't see any difference between the before and after, but Halli didn't let up. She moved from table, to sink, to the tiny bathroom. Her constant movement made it impossible for him to concentrate. Every time he started thinking about a strategy, something she did would distract him.

When he heard the shower running and the door remained open, exasperation finally got the better of him. "Damn it, Halli, relax, would you?"

The water shut off and one step brought her into sight.

"The boat's not going to get any cleaner," he stated.

"When I'm stressed at home I work in my garden."

"You want me to talk to Giovanni anyway? See if he's got something for you to dig up?"

She ignored his joke and gave him a quizzical look. "How do you stay so calm?"

"Do I look calm?"

Her expression immediately reflected his own frustration. "Like you're kicked back on the beach with your third margarita in hand."

"My old acting coach would be so proud." Again he rested the camera in his lap. "Just come and sit. Or stand and stir the sauce. But your constant"—he waved a hand in the air—"flitting about is getting on my nerves."

"*'Flitting about'?*"

He shrugged. "My last role was a Regency romantic comedy. It's the first thing that came to mind."

She returned to the stove and set the water to boil again. French bread was cut as she muttered about forgetting to save some garlic. Trent was fine with warm bread and fresher breath. Next she whipped up what he guessed was the previously mentioned sponge cake with more ingredients pulled from her bottomless grocery sack. While the cake baked in the tiny galley oven, the pasta was added to the water, tomato marinara stirred more carefully this time, and fresh fruit sauce and homemade whipped cream set in his small refrigerator.

Despite the fact that she no longer 'flitted about' like a bird on speed, his concentration came no easier with her precision completion of each task. He slid from behind the table and removed himself from her disturbing presence by heading topside.

A swift scan of the area revealed nothing out of the ordinary. Strange that security had become a habit already. He touched the pistol at his back for reassurance and then, despite having just told her he'd rather not contact Giovani, he dialed the phone.

The older gentleman didn't sound surprised to hear his voice and listened as Trent gave him the abridged version of the situation. Giovani and Concetta had always treated him as if he were their son, ever since George had introduced them after their first movie together. He felt he owed them the explanation and was relieved he'd called when Giovani assured him they didn't believe the lies on the news, offering faith and support in a way Trent's father never had.

After also confirming they did not have a computer or video equipment he could use, he pocketed the phone. Then he tried to avoid thinking of his father and the fact that he felt no obligation to call him despite the news reports that were sure to have reached the location of his latest project. After their last phone conversation about Sean's death, he seriously doubted the Great Greg Tomlin would believe anything else he had to say, so why even bother?

Warm evening air brushed against his bare arms and Trent doubled his effort to banish his father from his mind by surveying the untamed Italian vista before him. The sun rode a downward descent in the cloud-free sky toward the surrounding mountains, casting a golden hue across the rippled lake and everything else in its reach.

The bustle of the morning markets on the wharves had quieted to the ever-constant bells that echoed over the water. He'd spent enough time on the lake that they were normal, predictable, relaxing. Occasional carefree laughter of children, or the call of a parent added to the end of day tranquility. Mixed in with the damp, musty smell of the shoreline soil was the more pleasing scent of dinner simmering below. His stomach growled in anticipation.

A brief sense of peace washed over his unsettled nerve endings and ironically, he immediately thought of Halli. This was the Italy she'd come to see and experience. Not the one with murderers and guns and her sister getting shot while her brother was being held for ransom. To think he'd envied the Midwest upbringing he'd imagined she'd had. Parents in prison made his father look like a saint. She deserved so much more, like the garden tour this morning.

Their kiss replayed yet again.

That'd be a nice bonus—*really* nice—but this was about giving her experiences to remember beyond the bad stuff. It was the least he could do in exchange for the tantalizing aromas wafting up from the galley.

"How about we eat up top?" he called down to her. "It's a nice night."

"Sure. This'll be done in about ten more minutes."

Trent used the time to set up the table, then made a few trips below for a small linen table cloth, dishes, wine, water, and two long, tapered candles. Once everything was ready, he stood back to survey the scene. The wine glasses sparkled in the flickering candlelight and the seat Halli would occupy faced the lake where lights were starting to wink on across the water.

Perfect. Ambiance…lighting…he snapped his fingers. *Music.*

He met Halli at the short set of stairs. Flattening against the side to allow her room to pass with two covered serving dishes, he said, "I'll be right back."

Once the smooth, seductive tenor of Luciano Pavarotti flowed from the *Scappare's* speakers, Trent returned to find Halli staring at the romantic setting, a dish still in each hand. He took one on his way past, set it on the table, and started to turn back for the second.

She was already beside him, setting the dish on the linen covered table. "What is all this?"

Suspicion underscored the casual question. Trent knew exactly what it looked like, and he'd be lying if he didn't admit—to himself—the thought of seducing her made his pulse beat faster. But he could honestly say his intention here was nothing so selfish. He wanted and expected nothing more than to give her an evening to take home to Wisconsin.

"A truce," he declared. "A few hours to put everything aside and not worry about tomorrow."

For a moment, she stood there, staring at the table, her bottom lip caught between her teeth. Then she shook her head with dismay. "Ben can't put anything aside. How can I just forget what he's going through? Or Rachel? In fact, I should call her."

Trent caught her arm when she would've gone back down below. "I'm not saying you forget, Halli, you just let it rest. Give your mind a break and clear your head so we can come up with a strong plan of attack for tomorrow. There's nothing better you can do for Ben right now, and Simone promised to call if there were any problems with your sister. Let her rest, too."

She didn't look completely convinced, but at least when she pulled free from his light hold, it was more of an afterthought, not a jerk. Her gaze swept over the picture-perfect scene and he glimpsed longing in her expression.

"You really think this will help?"

"It's worth a try. Besides, a trip to Italy wouldn't be complete without an authentic Italian dinner. While I apologize that you had to make your own, I figured the least I could do is provide the rest." He gestured to the small bench seat facing the water. "After you."

One last, slight hesitation and she sat with a quiet, "Thank you."

Trent uncorked the bottle of Chianti and scooped up both glasses.

"Oh, no." She held up a hand and he stopped pouring with her glass only a quarter full. "You think better on a full stomach, I think better without alcohol. You saw what happened last night," she protested when he set the glass in front of her, half-full.

"You were stressed, jet-lagged, and exhausted, of course it knocked you out."

"Sure, o-kay. That was it," she said with a wry grin.

He poured himself three quarters of a glass. Before sitting down, he reached back to pull the gun from his waistband and laid it on the table within reach. Much as he hated the reminder, he wanted protection ready and available.

Halli stared at the weapon as he sat. Without a word, she transferred her attention from the gun and removed the covers from the dishes to serve. Trent found he couldn't look away from her face. Candlelight softened the pink tint across her cheekbones and picked up the reddish highlights in her hair. Their knees brushed under the cramped table, sending instant warmth through him.

Latent desire flared in his veins like a match to gasoline. He shifted, and then immediately wanted to press his leg back against hers. He second-guessed his noble gesture of a friendly romantic dinner. This was going to be torture without the sensual promise of his definition of dessert afterward.

But it was a torture he'd endure again and again if it would put a smile back on her face. Whenever she smiled, truly smiled, those blue eyes sparkled and her whole face lit up with an inner beauty that took his breath away. His chest tightened, and without warning, his heart thudded hard. Suddenly, it felt like he'd just tossed her into his convertible and stepped on the gas all over again.

She glanced up, caught him staring, and gave a questioning lift of her brow and a self-conscious smile. He quickly took a gulp of wine before leaning forward for an appreciative sniff of his full plate of steaming pasta.

"Smells great."

Her shy smile came a little easier, and his heart beat faster. He picked up his fork and twirled pasta onto the tines. Time to stop acting like a virgin teenager; he hadn't played that part in years. Maybe he should channel Shain.

Shain West appreciated and enjoyed the women in his scripted life, but he never actually fell for them. Trent straightened, shoved that last thought as far away as possible, and concentrated on his plate.

His first forkful brought forth an involuntary moan of approval. "Tastes even better."

"It's just spaghetti."

Savory flavors of basil, tomato and just the right amount of garlic lingered on his tongue. "Doesn't change the fact that it's *really* good."

"Thank you."

Heightened color in her cheeks told him she was pleased

with the compliment.

Pavarotti's Italian opera combined with the seemingly distant sounds of the town behind them, and the serenity of the lake in front of them. The night closed in, wrapping them in a sultry blanket of intimacy lit by candlelight, the quarter moon, and the stars in the clear sky above. Unattainable romance from the night before suddenly seemed attainable, and Trent fought not to take advantage of the unbearably sensuous situation he'd unintentionally created.

"Tell me about your last movie," Halli prompted after a minute or two.

Safe subject. *Thank God.* Between bites, Trent gave her the DVD back cover blurb. Her revealing comment in the car after Rachel had been shot echoed in his memory—the scene with Shain West and the sheriff discussing Emma's rescue had never appeared in any trailer. As the star and a producer on the film, he'd have known.

Lifting his wine glass, he watched her carefully as he said, "Hopefully they don't give away the entire plot in the trailer like *High Lonesome* did."

Her hand stilled, and then her guilty gaze met his. "Okay, *fine*, I watch your movies."

"Why lie about it?"

"Your ego's big enough, what do you care if I like you—*r* movies?"

His heart did a little flip at her slip up, but he covered with a mock-scowl. "Is there a compliment somewhere under that insult?"

She only laughed softly and took a sip of her own wine.

More than halfway through the meal, she'd finished most of the glass she'd earlier protested and had visibly mellowed. Either she'd taken his advice to heart, or the alcohol completely lowered her guard. His first inclination was to refill her glass, and she didn't object.

While topping off his own, Trent's hypocrisy slammed home with a jolt. Noble intentions? *Un*intentional seduction? The woman enticed him like crazy, and he'd plied her with wine, music and candles in the most romantic country in the world. Who the hell was he kidding? One crook of her finger and he'd be all over her.

In his head, Shain laughed his ass off at him and told him to go for it.

Trent set the bottle down and sat back, his appetite for food or drink gone, his mood equally demolished. She'd been right to call him a jerk all along.

Halli pushed her plate aside as if she were also done. "I'd like to make a toast."

His fingers curled around the stem of his glass as she lifted hers. Her blue gaze found his in the candlelight and the warmth in her eyes told him he wasn't going to like what she had to say.

"First of all, thank you. For all you've done so far, and...this." Her hand made an all-encompassing sweep of the table, boat and lake, though her voice wavered, as if she were uncertain. He felt worse than ever and hoped that was it, but she suddenly sat forward. Soft light shimmered in her hair, framing her earnest expression.

"I really am sorry about earlier...at Simone's. I want to trust you, Trent. I *do* trust you, it's just... so much has happened, so fast, and without any warning...it...takes me a little time to regroup each time, you know? Does that make sense?"

Unfortunately, it did. And unfortunately, understanding how she ticked did him no good. He needed to hold tight to his resentment over her mistrust, not sympathize with her emotions. Resentment would help him keep his distance much more effectively than sympathy.

"You were right about the quiet dinner clearing my mind. Maybe a little too much."

A soft laugh and her embarrassed smile socked him in the gut.

"I feel like a complete idiot for doubting your intentions when you were only trying to be nice."

Yep. Jerk with a capitol J. His grip tightened on the glass. "You were going to make a toast?"

She blinked at his clipped question and straightened before lifting her glass a little higher. "To success tomorrow. And bringing Ben home."

Damn. He didn't need the reminder that she was depending on him. Sean had depended on him, too. Not in anything specific, but still, he hadn't been there when his brother needed him most.

He saluted Halli with his glass and then downed his wine and stood. The gun he shoved against the small of his back and then yanked his shirt over it. Her blue eyes widened in confusion, piling on the guilt.

"Did I say something wrong?"

"No." He stacked their dinner plates together, tossed on the silverware, and grabbed his glass.

"Yes I did. I'm sorry, I shouldn't have brought it up. I didn't mean to ruin everything."

"You didn't." He'd ruined it by being a self-serving ass. "I'll clean up since you cooked."

"But there's still dessert."

Trent left that statement completely alone and went below to wash dishes. If he was lucky, she'd remain up top until he talked some sense into himself.

Luck was not his friend. Halli's appearance made him squeeze the soap bottle too hard and bubbles mounded under the running water in the small sink. Tiny iridescent spheres floated into the air when he plunged his hands in to begin washing. She brushed past to scoop up a towel and take the first dish he rinsed.

A brief slip and slide of her fingers against his soapy hand sent a spark of electricity up his arm. He barely contained a reactive jerk. Between her close proximity in the cramped space and the tantalizing citrus-vanilla scent of the warm sponge cake, his frustration mounted. The dishes ended up cleaner than they'd ever been.

More than once he heard her inhale like she was about to say something, but each time he tensed and waited, she let the breath back out and remained silent.

He released the plug in the sink and turned for a towel in time to see her stretch to put one of the wine glasses back in the built-in rack. She could barely reach, even with one hand braced on the counter and raised on her tiptoes. Normally, a cabin cruiser wouldn't require even a five foot three person to reach further than arms length, but he'd special ordered the boat for his height.

 The subtle sway of the boat threw her off balance. Trent jumped forward. He caught her with one arm around her waist and the other steadied the glass before it toppled to the floor.

 Being classified an international super star didn't make him any less of a man. She smelled like dessert and the soft curves against his body overwhelmed his already stimulated senses. Once he secured the wine glasses in the wooden rack, his arms closed around her, his will-power drained like the dishwater.

Chapter 20

Halli's breath caught in her chest with the warmth of Trent's embrace. She started to turn around, but his voice sounded harsh in her ear. "Don't."

The strength of his hold said he wanted her right where she was. The tone of his voice said the opposite. Ever since her stupid toast, he'd been acting strange.

"We were going to talk about our plan for tomorrow anyway, so why did what I said make you so mad?"

"I'm not mad."

"You sound mad." She was starting to get a little annoyed herself. The wine may have relaxed her, but it also boosted her bravado. "Look, I'm sorry that I—"

"Stop apologizing!" He spun her around and braced an arm on either side of her.

"It wasn't a real apology..." She trailed off at the fierce look in his eyes as he leaned close.

"What did you think I'd planned when you saw the table?"

A telltale flush heated her face, fueled hotter by the press of his hips and thighs holding her in place. Not that she wanted to go anywhere. And, since she'd been willing to drink the wine to loosen her inhibitions, and her face surely already gave her away, she might as well be honest.

"I thought you were looking to get lucky." His jaw tightened, and she took a figurative step back. "Stupid, considering we both know you don't date women like me. I'm not your type."

"Right on all three counts, sweetheart."

The blunt confirmation and distancing endearment put an ache in her chest. As if she expected him to deny ulterior motives, despite where they stood right now.

Yes, darn it, she had. Or she'd hoped, anyway. Because during dinner she'd fallen under the spell of his thoughtful gesture and the romantic atmosphere. With the slightest encouragement and her growing feelings of respect and trust, she'd have said yes to anything he asked.

Faced with the truth, she felt like an idiot who'd been set up. Why the heck couldn't he have kept up the farce for both their sake? Stupid actor.

"You said dinner was a truce."

"See how good I am? I even fooled myself."

His crooked smile sent her heart skipping, but didn't make her feel any better. The wine prompted her to ask, "So…would you have looked to score with just anyone or me specifically?"

His expression became serious. "Just *anyone* isn't standing in front of me. You are."

She laughed. At her own stupidity, because she wanted to believe him. "Yeah, you are good."

"I'm not just saying that, Halli."

"I might buy it if I were a good five inches taller and model gorgeous."

"At first glance, it's easy to mistake you as plain, especially in those God-awful clothes you were wearing when we met."

"They were travel clothes," she defended.

"Hideous."

She shrugged. Refused to give in to vain disappointment from his less than flattering description. She knew she wasn't going to win any beauty contests, but didn't mean she wanted to hear *him* say it. Apparently, all he really did need was his looks to get women into bed with him.

Case in point, she still wanted him. *How pathetic.*

He brushed her hair back off one cheek with his knuckles. "It's the second look that gets a guy. And the third. And the fourth." He lifted a lock of hair, rubbed it between his fingers. "Highlights in your hair. The sparkle in those beautiful baby blues. A set of kissable lips that transform your entire face with just one smile."

Her stomach quivered in response to his low, gravelly voice and the way his gaze travelled over her face like a caress. Hurt and disappointment disappeared as if they'd never been. Hazel eyes locked with hers and for the first time in her life, she felt beautiful.

His head lowered toward hers. She closed her eyes in anticipation of his kiss, only to have a picture of him in 1880's western wear and a worn brown Stetson appear like her eyelids were a movie screen. Her eyes flew open as she gave an outraged gasp and shoved him back a step.

"When did Shain show up?"

He grinned. "You really *do* watch my movies."

"I already admitted I did, so why are you feeding me a line now?"

"I was just playing around, and that line was practically written for you."

She glared at him, arms crossed over her chest. Couldn't believe he'd stoop that low, and worse, that she'd almost fallen for his act.

"Wow, I didn't know you'd take it so personal. You want my own version?"

"Can you manage?"

His grin widened as he gripped her shoulders. A smart woman would twist away, but she couldn't make herself move. He squared his shoulders and cleared his throat as if he were about to make an important speech.

"Ready?"

"Probably not."

"Probably not," he agreed.

Halli found herself pulled into an unexpected kiss. His lips were firm, yet undemanding. Beneath her hands wedged between them, his heart pounded a rapid rhythm that rivaled hers. He couldn't act that, could he?

It suddenly hit her how exhausting it was to be so defensive all the time. Dinner had given her a glimpse of peace in the storm. She liked him. He was kissing her. What the hell was her problem?

Impulsive decision made, she relaxed and parted her lips. He groaned softly and lifted both hands to frame her heated face. His tongue slid past her teeth, igniting a need deep inside that she'd never felt before his first kiss. After a last lingering moment that shifted emotions inside her chest, he pulled back to gaze down at her.

"Definitely not ready for that," she breathed.

"Halli Sanders, you are a pain in the ass, you drive me completely crazy…and I've wanted you from the moment you smashed your head into my chin in my garage."

Mind still reeling from the kiss, she frowned. "Violence turns you on?"

"No," he said on a laugh. "That's when I figured out what you were hiding under your travel clothes."

"I distinctly recall you saying you weren't that hard up. I'm nothing special compared to what you're used to."

As if she'd flipped a switch, annoyance flashed in his eyes. "Stop doing that."

"What?"

"Selling yourself short. You're—"

"I am short," she quipped.

"You're the only one making comparisons to women I've dated and finding yourself lacking. I'm attracted to you, Halli. Not just your body, but the whole obsessive, compulsive, patience-trying package."

Another backhanded compliment. Man, he was so good at those. Then again, why did she care so long as he wanted her?

His hold tightened on her shoulders a moment before he pushed away. His fingers raked through his dark hair before he braced against the sink. "I was mad before," he admitted, head hung low. "But at myself, not you. If anyone's not good enough, it's me. I have no business taking advantage of you. Especially after you've been drinking."

Halli stared at his back in amazement. "Seriously? You think that's what's happening here?"

"I know that's what's happening. You're completely out of your element with everything you've been through the past couple days. You said so yourself."

That much was true. Sitting across the table from him at dinner she'd accepted the fact she had no idea what tomorrow held. They could succeed wildly, or fail tragically. The upside down trip her life had taken scared her to death. At the same time, unbelievably, she'd never been more aware of the world.

Colors in the garden, in the city, along the roadside and surrounding the lake were brilliant and vibrant. Food tasted better, smelled better. She was thankful for every breath of air and even for the scant few hours she'd spent with her sister this afternoon.

What a wild realization that, threatened with her own death, she was learning to live for the first time since she was sixteen. Trent was a part of that, and she wanted more.

From him.

With him.

Ironically, it sounded as if she'd have to do some convincing. The perfect idea waved its hand wildly in front of her warm face. She leaned against the small bar counter behind her and put the plan in motion, ever thankful for the extra bravery from the wine.

"You know, you're right."

He straightened and turned. His expression of resigned disappointment bolstered her courage further.

"And thank God you're so honorable," she continued. "I had no idea how defenseless, innocent, drunk little me would be against your grand, movie star irresistibility."

His gaze narrowed. "Spare me the sarcasm."

"Then spare me the ego. Yes, I had a little wine, but I am more than capable of saying no."

After a moment of steady contemplation, his cocky smile surfaced. "I can be very persuasive."

That's the ego she was looking for. She spread her hands wide, palms up. "Give it your best shot."

"Don't tempt me."

Halli deliberately lowered her gaze, shrugged a shoulder, and looked back up. "If you're not up for the challenge..."

Trent pushed away from the sink and took the two steps that separated them. He leaned forward and whispered in her ear, "I'm always up for a challenge. You sure you want to be it?"

Yes. No.

Oh, God, she was ready to chicken out. *So much for the wine.*

He didn't touch her. Didn't need to. Her pulse raced out of control, stunned she'd actually gone through with the split-second decision to invite his seduction.

Live, Halli. Live.

She turned her head to meet his gaze. Their noses almost bumped. "I'm sure I know my own mind."

His low, sensual laugh about melted her where she stood. A deep breath should've shored up her will-power to present token resistance for appearances sake, but she only got a heady, seductive dose of Trent. *Great.* He'd win before the challenge even began.

He was going to win, she just didn't want to stroke his monumental ego by caving so soon.

A soft kiss touched on the corner of her mouth. She kept her eyes open, afraid if she closed them, sensation would completely overwhelm her determination. Their only physical connection was his lips on hers, but she felt the heat of him from her shoulders to her toes. Anticipated the moment she'd feel the full effect of his lean, hard length.

His mouth feathered across her cheek, whisper light, warm on her skin. Somehow, she remained stock still as he brushed her hair back off her shoulder, baring her neck for his exploration. Oh, her heart pounded, stomach quivered, knees weakened and fingers clenched the counter so hard she nearly lost feeling in them, but she didn't so much as whimper her consent when he located her weak spot under her jaw, just beneath her ear.

His tongue swirled a pattern over her pulse, drew her earlobe between his teeth, then soothed away the sting of his sensual nip. He stepped back. By some miracle, she managed a cool, inquiring lift of her brows. He considered her with eyes darkened to a combination of moss green and burnt amber. She held his intense gaze, and her breath.

He shifted to her other side and started all over again.

She wondered if ten more seconds was long enough to hold out.

When she reached a mental count of nine, he lifted his head with a frustrated growl. "God, you are hell on a guy's ego."

The rough edges on his words were her undoing. She sucked in a gulp of air and reached up to pull him back down. Full on, mouth to mouth, no more teasing. Her hands threaded in his hair, pulling closer, closer still. Surprise held him stiff for only a second or two before he wrapped his arms around her and returned the kiss like a drowning man who'd been thrown a life preserver.

But she was the one who'd been drowning. In her rigidly planned, boring, predictable life. She just hadn't known it until she'd met him.

Halli dragged her hands down, over the taut ridges of his shoulders, wedged her arms between them, and fumbled with the buttons on his shirt. For one wild second, she entertained an urge to grab each side and yank them apart. Would the little round plastic discs pop and fly free, or would the material tear? Either way, the wine only went so far and regular bravery didn't cover ripping his clothes off.

But wouldn't that be fun?

He gave her some room to work and caught his breath at the same time. "What happened to *'I'm more than capable of saying no'*, and *'I'm sure I know my own mind'*?"

"I can still say no anytime I want to…right?"

A stillness settled in his body and wariness shaded his eyes. "Right."

She undid the last button, flattened her palms on his hot skin, and watched her hands slide up the wide expanse of his chest. The bruises on his torso gave her a moment's pause, but she pressed on. Just the right amount of dark hair tickled her palms, and underneath, the strength and hardness of him felt so good. So did taking charge. Having control of this situation gave her a sense of…freedom.

Completely unlike herself.

Scary, yet exhilarating.

She smiled without a single flicker of uncertainty over her actions. "Then I'm sure I know this is what I want."

His mouth slanted across hers in an all-consuming, wet, wild kiss that ratcheted the heat between them to an impossible level. They turned, spinning the few feet from the counter to the panel that concealed the sleeping berth. Trent slid it open with one hand, spinning again to pull her down on top of him as he lay back on the bed.

He sucked in a gasp and arched his back. "*Ow*."

Halli braced her hands on the bed and levered her weight off him. "Sorry, what—oh."

In the dim light filtering in from the galley, she saw he'd pulled the gun out from underneath him. His long reach deposited the weapon on a tiny shelf at the head of the bed, while his other arm kept her from moving too far away. The constant reminder of danger only served to reinforce her decision.

Knees on either side of his hips, she straddled him, hips snug against his hard arousal. He drew her down for another kiss. The auburn cascade of her hair was brushed out of the way, only to glide back along her cheeks when his touch skimmed her shoulders, back, and waist, to grasp her hips. Fingers flexed, then sought bare skin under her shirt.

Halli sat up and criss-crossed her arms over her stomach to grab the hem. His hands caught hers, stilling her action before dropping to rest on her thighs. He lay beneath her, completely still.

"There's something I need to ask, and I want the truth."

Her stomach protested his serious tone, but she waited for his question.

"Does this have anything to do with the money?"

Relief released her tension. She wasn't sure what she'd expected, but this was easy. Her hands splayed on his flat stomach as she leaned forward with a soft laugh. "As if. Even Julia Roberts only got three thousand in *Pretty Woman*."

Abdominal muscles tightened beneath her touch just before his hands snatched hers and he moved to sit up. "Damn it, Halli—"

In a quick movement, she linked her fingers with his and used her weight to keep him horizontal.

"I'm kidding—geez. No, it's not about the money."

He had the strength to overpower her easily, wanted to by the look in his eyes and rigid arms, and the way he held them both mid-way off the bed. She got right up in his face. "Frankly, the suggestion is insulting."

His gaze held hers without apology. "I don't want you to feel obligated, or that it's the least you can do. Then *I* would be insulted."

The words she'd said about desert earlier caught her off guard. *For a million cash, it's the least I can do.*

Halli quit pushing and abruptly sat back on his thighs. He rose up and braced his hands behind him. As they faced each other in the intimate position, she took a moment to honestly analyze the motivation behind her out-of-character decisions tonight. The result kept her from climbing off his lap.

"Am I thankful? Yes. Amazed at your generosity? Yes. Do I feel like I have to have sex with you to show my appreciation?"

He seemed to hold his breath.

"No."

His expression told her he wasn't sure she told the truth and she huffed in annoyance. "You're the one who keeps saying how boring I am, so—"

"I didn't say you were boring."

"You've said it more than once."

"I said *Wisconsin* Halli sounds boring," he corrected. "Italy Halli is anything but."

"Then chalk this up to Italy Halli's decision to enjoy what life has to offer before the moment passes her by."

She took a deep breath, suddenly nervous again. Somewhere along the way, he'd stopped being Trent Tomlin, International Movie Star. The man in front of her was so much more than the selfish playboy the public read about in the tabloids, and she wanted to be as close to this man as a woman could be.

"Tomorrow's going to come soon enough," she said. "Give me something else to think about. Something else to feel other than scared to death."

The plea nearly stopped Trent's heart in his chest. "You're sure?"

"Obligated is the last thing I'm feeling right now, so,

unless you're looking for an excuse to stop...?"

He flipped her onto her back so fast she barely had a chance to gasp in surprise. Looming over her, he nudged her legs apart with one knee and covered her body with his. Need pulsed through him, centered where her hips cradled his.

"Does it feel like I'm looking for excuses?"

She shook her head. A small smile curved her kiss-swollen lips and he couldn't help but claim them again, thinking he could drink her in for hours and not get bored. Moments later, she dragged his shirt off his shoulders and down his arms. As he wrestled his bandaged arm free of the sleeve, she did the criss-cross move again and arched her back to drag her shirt over her head.

Yeah. Getting naked was good, too. He stared at the lace-edged, white satin bra he'd left on the bed for her back at his villa. "Damn, I was hoping for the black."

"Excuse me?"

"The underwear you picked. I was hoping for black."

"Oh."

He located the spot along her jaw where her pulse raced, and now that she wasn't fighting to prove a point, he succeeded in eliciting a sexy purr of pleasure from her lips. The sound deepened when he brushed his palm over her satin and lace covered nipple, teasing it to a hard peak before cupping her breast through the material. She fit perfectly in his hand, but he couldn't wait to take her in his mouth.

"Wait a second," she protested. "After all the staring you did at my chest last night, you never noticed my bra wasn't black through that white shirt?"

Kisses feathered across her collar bone and the exposed curve of her breast brought him closer to his goal. "I was more focused on the *Wet & Wild*."

"Typical."

"I won't apologize for being a guy, Halli."

With one finger, he pulled the lace aside and closed his mouth over the pebbled tip. The first deep pull of his mouth on her sensitive skin made her arch off the bed. Her involuntary sound of pleasure quickened his pulse and he took advantage of the opportunity to unhook the bra.

Halli's hands fisted in his hair after he'd removed the satin and lavished attention on first one firm, warm mound, then the other. The sensual rub of her bare foot along the back of his calf and up his thigh reminded him to toe his shoes off. As she continued to rub, up and down, up and down, their hips ground together.

God, she made him so hot. The sounds and sighs and soft gasps coming from her lips only increased the fire raging within. Pooled blood in his groin pounded relentlessly, almost painfully, demanding relief.

He rolled off her and skimmed his hand down across her belly to the button of her jeans. She pushed his hands aside and undid them herself, apparently as eager to have them off as he was. He braced a hand on either side of her, then lightly dragged his whiskered chin along the same path his hand had taken. Muscles quivered when he stopped to dip his tongue in her navel.

"I was wrong."

She lifted up on one elbow. "About what?"

He ran a finger along the edge of her panties, noting the shadow of dark curls under the silky wisp of fabric. "White's just as sexy as black."

Halli drew in a shaky breath as he removed her last piece of clothing and just looked. Completely exposed to his gaze, she reminded herself Italy Halli lived in the moment. When he leaned forward and pressed his mouth to the inside of her thigh, she couldn't help but jerk in surprise. Heart pounding impossibly hard, she gulped and squeezed her eyes shut. His warm breath and lips skimmed up her leg, closer to where she ached for his touch.

"Trent…I, ah, I've never, um…"

Air chilled her skin where his mouth had just been. "Never what?"

Heat of an entirely different kind took over her body. She should've kept her mouth shut. She squirmed, and when he moved to lie beside her, pulled her knees together and threw her forearm over her eyes.

"Are you a virgin?"

The surprised, gentle question prompted a smile, but she didn't move her arm. "No. I've done that before, I've just never done...*that*." She waved her hand in the general direction of her waist and below.

"Well, now that's just not fair," he said sternly. Yet a smile colored his voice. "What kind of selfish jerks have you been with?"

She shrugged. Strong, insistent fingers curled around the wrist draped over her eyes. Face still burning with embarrassment, she let him pull her arm down and opened her eyes. His gaze met hers, completely serious.

"Do you want to?"

Desire and curiosity warred with apprehension over the unknown. He must've read her hesitation because he leaned forward to kiss her. Slow, deep, sensual; a mating of their mouths as if they had all the time in the world. Trepidation had completely receded by the time he lifted his head again.

"You said you trust me."

"Yes," she breathed.

"Let me show you how good it can be."

A nod was the best she could manage before giving herself up to the pure sensation his kisses evoked as they moved back down her body to center in that one spot. He was right. It was good. Better than she could've ever imagined.

All sense of time and place disappeared, and for the life of her she couldn't keep quiet. Biting her lip did no good. Tension built inside, unlike anything she'd felt before. He took her higher, and higher still, until she couldn't take any more, pleaded with him without even knowing what she wanted. *Needed.* She gasped his name and then cried out as he sent her cresting on a wave of such ecstasy her world seemed to explode.

Halli lay in amazement, thinking she should be mortified at her loss of control and how uncharacteristically vocal she'd been. Energy to care deserted her. Mini aftershocks continued to pleasure as Trent propped on one elbow to grin down at her.

"Good?"

A deep sigh of contentment accompanied her smile. He roamed his free hand over every reachable inch of her body, following it with his gaze. Halli's heart sped up again at the look of appreciation his eyes. It gave her the courage to reach down and tug on the waistband of his jeans.

"Why are you still half-dressed?"

"Thought you'd never ask."

He wasted no time undoing the button and zipper. Halli rolled onto her side and watched, still slightly dazed from what he'd just done to her. When he lifted his hips to shuck the denim, she splayed her fingers across his taut stomach.

"Damn. I was hoping for commando."

His laugh came out low, tense, and completely sexy as her hand slid lower.

"That's only when I'm surprised from the shower by thugs. Otherwise it's too dangerous to zip—"

His words dissolved into a growl when she brushed across the soft material of his boxer-briefs and felt the length of his erection. Extra large condoms, indeed.

The boxers followed the jeans and, channeling Italy Halli, she took her turn exploring his body. All hard planes and angles and sinewy muscle beneath velvet skin, with a faint salty taste to compliment his intoxicating male scent. She kissed each bruise as if she could erase them; ribs, sternum, forearm and even the faint shadow the back of her head had left on the side of his chin.

Heat shimmered off him in waves, spiking with each groan she wrung from his lips. She'd finally given in to the fact that her life was out of her control, and yet she'd never felt more in control than at this moment.

When Trent couldn't take anymore of her wicked tongue and teeth, he dragged her up and flipped their positions again. She continually surprised him. Shy one moment, wonderfully eager the next. He took the necessary moment to put on a condom before sliding into her heat. So hot, so tight. It took everything he had not to take her fast and furious, but he managed to hold on by a thread.

Slow. Make it last.

She was beautiful, lying beneath him, hair fanned on the navy bedspread. Those blue eyes of hers were unreadable in the dim light, but going by her expression, she wouldn't be complaining any time soon. He'd make sure of that.

Her hips lifted, taking him deeper with each thrust. Heat built again, one tantalizing degree at a time. Soft, breathy moans emanated from her parted lips. They turned him on like nothing else and his control began to slip.

Faster. Harder. She urged him on, her voice desperate, relentless, reaching, until suddenly she cried out, louder than before. Trent followed her over the edge with a jerk of his body and a mind-blowing release.

His arms trembled from the extended time supporting his weight. Fighting to catch his breath, he eased to the side. He couldn't resist a kiss on her smooth neck and a taste of her sweat-slick skin with the tip of his tongue. He should be satisfied, tired. Instead, he wanted to start all over despite the dull ache of his injured arm.

"Mmm," she murmured, eyes closed.

"Never figured you for a screamer."

"Never was before."

Her eyes popped open and a flush spread across her face; a captivating, unexpected return of shyness.

Trent grinned with pure male satisfaction. "That was all me?"

She quickly shook her head side to side. "No."

"You can't take it back."

"I can if I don't want the boat to sink under the weight of your ego."

He chuckled. "I special ordered the boat to handle my ego."

"In that case, your earlier comment about not being good enough is completely unfounded."

He smiled slightly, but didn't hold her gaze. He hadn't been talking about sex when he'd said that. Aware of cooler air on their damp, heated bodies, Trent shifted and urged her under the covers. She curled up on her side, head pillowed on her arm. He propped up on one elbow, watching her eyelids droop.

"Ready for dessert?"

"Isn't that what we just had?" she asked with a sleepy smile.

After a heartbeat or two, Trent managed a soft, cocky, "By my definition, we sure did, sweetheart."

Her brow furrowed slightly, but relaxed as her breathing deepened.

"I'll be back in a minute," he said, pretty sure she was already sleeping and didn't even hear him as he climbed off the bed. After a trip to the bathroom, he pulled his briefs on, palmed the gun, and took a quick turn topside.

Just past midnight, everything was quiet. Everything but the panicked, confused, hopeful, terrified tangle of emotions constricting his chest. He braced his hands on the railing to stare out over the water, drawing in long, slow breaths and letting them out with equal control. The dull ache in his arm became a painful bite with each clench of his fingers on the smooth metal rail. An ineffective distraction during the damned hopeless battle to keep the truth at bay.

He gave in with a low groan of surrender.

That last sex-satisfied smile of hers grabbed hold of his heart with the strength of a bald eagle snagging a fish. He hadn't seen it coming. Didn't want to be caught.

It was more than obvious they were all wrong for each other. She craved order and dependability; events in his life proved he was far from dependable. In time, she would resent him for disrupting her neat little life, and he'd succeed yet again in being a colossal disappointment. And that wasn't even taking into account his Hollywood lifestyle.

Clear as the star-filled sky above, as opposite as their worlds were, as different as they were, it'd never work.

Wouldn't it?

That insidious little voice in his head refused to be swayed by logical reasoning. Earlier, Halli had made a decision to live in the moment before it passed her by. He understood that sentiment wholeheartedly.

Maybe you aren't completely different.

He considered that and thought, *maybe not*. He had no idea

how the day would end. Plans could go awry, as they often did. Rules could be broken. Murderers couldn't be counted on to follow any particular code of ethics. These moments with her could be all he had. Did he really want to waste them by arguing with himself as to why they'd never be together?

Though not normally a snuggler, Trent returned to the bed, replaced the gun on the headboard, and snuggled with Halli. Held her small, fragile, amazingly strong body close to his and prayed to God he didn't let her down, too.

Chapter 21

Foot twitching a mile a minute, trying to contain his restless energy, Ben glared across his luxurious prison, wondering how the day would unfold and thinking if he was this unnerved, Halli must be going crazy between taking care of Rachel and worrying about him. If only he could talk to her again. Tell her not to worry, that someone must've decided he wasn't such an escape threat and untied him from the chair. He had a guard outside the locked door and on the balcony, but at least he could move around again. Maybe even make a plan. Halli loved a good plan.

He surged off the bed and headed toward the window, anxious for the sun to rise above the mountain peaks and get this day over. Hopefully, Trent Tomlin had reassured his sisters and kept their minds off the whole nightmare. Halli'd always had a thing for the guy's movies, and being in television herself, maybe they'd wiled away the sleepless night hours talking shop.

He, on the other hand, had been cursed with erotic dreams of his sexy Italian captor on his lap and woke to discover dawn had yet to break. Now, fifteen minutes later, the sky was just beginning to lighten to the East.

In mid-reach to sweep aside the curtain for a view of the lake, a low-pitched voice on the balcony made him draw back against the wall. An *English*-speaking, Italian-accented voice. These guys didn't speak English without good reason, and some didn't speak it at all. Why was this one?

Ben strained to make out the words.

"…standing guard like one of his fucking flunkies. I believe he has suspicion, so the sooner this is done the better. Is everything set up like we agreed?...Good. After the trade and money transfer, I will finish the job and make sure it looks like a deal gone bad…No, do not worry about him. It is a simple matter to insert doubt in his mind."

He lowered to the floor and crawled to the other side of the busted window. Back to the wall, he peered through the slim opening provided by the curtain lifting every few seconds in the morning breeze. No lights lit the balcony. The weak glow of impending day revealed only a shadowed profile, dark hair, and dark rimmed glasses. A cigarette tip burned bright, providing brief illumination before arcing down out of sight, and a thin plume of smoke streamed into the cool morning air.

Nino.

"No...she poses no more problem than we anticipated...Relax. I said I will take care of her and Lapaglia, and I will."

Ben's heart thumped hard against his ribs. *She.* Halli? Rachel? Oddly, he didn't think so. Something about the man's tone. The only other woman he'd seen here at the villa was Eva. Given the reference to Alrigo Lapaglia, the logical conclusion was the bastard plotted to double cross the others. Indignation rose up on Eva's behalf, until it hit him he could play this information to his advantage.

"*No*," Nino stressed out on the balcony. "Follow the plan and remain out of sight. Do not fuck this up Roselli."

Who the hell is Roselli? Ben leaned his head against the wall and noticed the darkness of the room had faded to gray. He returned to the bed and considered the scant but useful knowledge he'd gained. Yes, this could definitely work in his favor.

His first instinct was to tell Eva, get her on his side, use what he'd learned to 'buy' her help. Question was, would she negotiate?

Or did he put his money on Alrigo? Surely he'd like to know his right hand man was planning a con larger than Ben's own parent's had ever attempted. What he'd just overheard could save his life, if the heads-up resulted in Alrigo being grateful enough to set him free.

And if he'd read things wrong? Though what he'd heard was pretty hard to misinterpret, if he had, his gut and his head told him Eva was the better bet. The easier con, if it came to that. She couldn't have been faking every emotion he'd read in her eyes yesterday. The first kiss made sense; a distraction until she could restrain his arm again. Humiliation over how easily she'd accomplished *that* was firmly thrust aside so he could focus on the second kiss.

After his lust had dulled, allowing for clear thinking, he'd bet his freedom the second one had been more than her simply showing him who was boss. He'd sensed an honest attraction sizzling in the air between them. Real desire warmed those almond colored eyes of hers. And when he'd asked her the likelihood of him surviving this damn thing, she'd seemed genuinely distressed before retreating behind her mask.

Alrigo's cold, flat, black eyes chilled in comparison.

Eva was definitely the better bet.

He took a shower, surveyed his battered ribs, chest and face in the mirror and hoped with an absurd grin that he didn't die today looking like he'd been on the losing end of a fight. If he died, he'd have lost, but still. Shirt in hand, he stepped from the bathroom to see Eva setting a breakfast tray on the small table Zucchi had kicked into the window the previous morning.

Ben's morbid humor faded, but he kept the smile in place. "Good morning."

She turned around, her expression tight with suspicion. His grin widened when he noted her gaze journey down and up before lingering on his bare chest. Her expression softened, probably without her even realizing it. Either she admired his build, or she was taking pity on his numerous bruises. Both possibilities were to his favor, though his ego preferred the first.

By the time she lifted her gaze, he'd performed his own appraisal of her black leggings and silky, shimmering red top belted at her lush hips before ending mid-thigh. He did nothing to hide his appreciation of her figure as pulse-spiking attraction flared. She immediately broke the connection by turning to leave.

He swaggered across the room, pulling his shirt over his head as he went. "I was hopin' you'd keep me company while I eat," he suggested conversationally.

She spun around with a frown. "You insult my intelligence with your false charm."

He conceded her point with a quick dip of his chin. "I

apologize."

Her glare pierced across the room before she reached for the door.

"I have something you might be interested in."

Again she faced him. Again she frowned. "I am not interested in you at all, Mr. Sanders."

Increased defensiveness in her voice raised his hope another notch. He smiled, sat, and reached for the bitter cup of espresso he'd discovered the Italians preferred over regular coffee. "I didn't say you were interested in me. The *information* I've obtained, well, that's a whole other matter."

Her fingers wrapped around the door handle.

"Life and death."

She didn't move.

"Mine *and* yours," he added softly.

"Is that a threat?"

"I'm trying to protect you." He took a bite of one of the pastries on the tray, but underneath his calm façade, he discovered he really did want to protect her. The thought of Nino *'taking care'* of her made the food hard to swallow, no matter how good it tasted.

Eva spun around. "I need no man's protection."

"Everyone needs protection at some time or another, Eva."

She strode closer, mouth opened to protest, no doubt, but he kept talking.

"Take me for example. I'm a pretty tough guy, normally more than capable of taking care of myself, yet here I sit. I admit I need you, so it's not beyond the realm of possibility that if what I've learned is true, we could help each other."

She slapped both hands on the table with a loud jangle of bracelets and leaned forward. No fair. Her cleavage distracted him to the point that he almost didn't hear her question.

"What information could you possibly have that I would find helpful?"

Ben swallowed his lust with a gulp of espresso. *Ow. Damn. Still hot!* He sucked in a cooling breath and then cleared his scalded throat. "Keep your voice down, please."

Her gaze darted to the window and then back to him.

"Who's out there right now?" he asked quietly.

"Tony. Zucchi stands in the hall. *Perche?* Why?"

Ben leaned closer, lowered his voice. "Nino was outside on the balcony not more than an hour ago. Before it got light."

"So?"

"He was on the phone with some guy named Roselli."

Eva's eyes went wide. She shook her head. "Impossible."

"I heard him through the window—saw him, too."

"Roselli is dead."

"Not from what I heard. Now listen, your *'partner'* is planning something all on his own. He told this guy he'd take care of you and Alrigo and that you, specifically, wouldn't be a problem. My parents landed in jail when they trusted someone better at the con game than they were, so believe me, I know a double cross when I hear one."

Her gaze narrowed as she considered his words. Watching her face, he could practically see the wheels turning in her head.

He reached out to cover her small hand with his. "You can't trust him, Eva, but you can trust me. Let's help each other."

She jerked from his touch and straightened. She'd gone poker-faced again, retreating behind an indifferent mask.

"You misunderstood. I know where Nino's loyalty lies. Say nothing more to anyone."

Again with the door. Damn it, she was going to get herself killed if she ignored him. Ben surged to his feet and followed her across the room. Two steps from the door, he reached for her shoulder.

Next thing he knew, he was kissing the wall, arm twisted mercilessly behind his back. Christ, she was fast. With the painful vice grip she had on his arm, her slight weight had no problem holding him in place.

Twisting his head to the side, he uttered a few choice words and then demanded, "How the hell'd you do that?"

"A woman in my line of work learns to take care of herself."

"What exactly is your line of work, by the way?"

"That is not clear?"

The only thing that was clear right now was her warm body tight against his. Her spicy exotic scent wafted up to tease his nostrils. Damn it, he needed to focus here.

"It's clear you can cook like nobody's business, and equally clear you have exceptional defense skills, but none of that tells me what a nice, smart girl like you is doing with scum like Alrigo and Nino."

"You are so sure I am a nice girl?"

Her voice had dropped a notch and Ben turned his head as far as possible to see her face over his shoulder from the corner of his eye. "You want to help me. I've seen it all along in those beautiful brown eyes of yours, Eva, and the eyes don't lie."

She applied pressure to his arm, her gaze downcast. When her lashes lifted again, the warmth he was so sure he'd glimpsed had shriveled under a thick sheet of ice.

"You have no idea what you are involved in, but trust me when I say if you wish to survive the next twelve hours, you will cease your arrogant attitude and *keep your damn mouth shut*."

It was more of a warning than a threat, yet a shiver ran down his spine anyway. Fine, she wanted to trust the scumbags, let her roast her own ass.

Yeah right. Cheap talk, buddy.

"My arm's going numb."

Her grip loosened a fraction. Ben shoved away from the wall, throwing her off balance enough that he was able to wrench free. Moving as fast as she had, he grabbed her and spun so her back pressed against the wall, wrists imprisoned above her head. A preemptive hip swivel blocked her knee to his groin. Not going there again.

He fought the urge for a long, deep inhale of her unique scent and focused on meeting her furious gaze.

"Just like that, the tables turn," he murmured.

Uncertainty flickered in her eyes, only to be blinked away. "You said I could trust you."

"You can." His gaze dropped to her lips, pressed together in determination. *No kissing. Look up.* "I can't get out of here alone, I know that. I'm equally certain Nino is not who he seems and you're going to get screwed."

"Why do you care?"

Good question. He was still searching for an answer when her expression softened slightly and she tilted her head.

"If I agreed right now to help you…you would trust me?" she asked.

"Yes."

"I could be lying to obtain my release."

Staring into her eyes, heat simmering between their intimately aligned forms, his body began to react. There's no way she didn't feel the insistent pulse epicentered below his waist. But damn, the woman was good; her gaze never faltered.

He leaned his body further into hers, pressing his chest to hers. "We both know if you wanted to be released, all you'd have to do is scream."

"You do not think I will?"

"You would've already."

"You are much too…how do you American's say? *Cocky*."

Ben gave a slow smile, bent his knees slightly to align his hips with hers and pressed closer still. "Guilty as charged."

Her gaze narrowed. "You walk dangerous ground."

"You won't hurt me, Eva."

"Do not be so sure," she warned.

A decidedly dangerous glint sparked in her eyes. What the *hell* was wrong with him that he was more turned on than ever? Her lips beckoned, recently moistened with a torturous swipe of her tongue. A slip of his gaze caught a rapid flutter beneath the tanned skin at the base of her throat.

His smile widened to a grin. "My gut tells me deep down you've got a good heart. You won't let anything happen to me. Over the years, I've survived a number of close-calls by trusting my instincts."

Another flicker in her eyes, only this time he couldn't define it. Before he could sift though possible emotions in his mind, her lashes lowered and her attention focused on his mouth. Whether he closed the distance or she did, he didn't know. Didn't care. Rational thought deserted him the moment their lips met.

He released her arms to pull her closer, taking full advantage of having free hands for this kiss. As her tongue swept along the seam of his lips, her hips brushed against his, back and forth, and back again. It registered that she'd hooked her left leg behind his calf a split second before she pushed on his chest and swept his feet out from under him.

He tightened his hold, bringing her to the floor with him. Expecting a strike where it'd hurt most, he tensed for an onslaught of pain. Instead, she slid up along his body and covered his mouth with hers again, hands braced on the floor alongside his head. She put her whole body into the kiss. Surprise held him immobile for only a few seconds, then he kissed her back, lifting his head, using tongue and teeth. His palms swept down her back to squeeze her butt as he surged up against her.

A move to roll her underneath was hindered by her firmly planted hands and then completely halted when she straddled his hips. Despite the frustrating barrier of clothing between them, the intimate contact stimulated a low growl of approval. She pulled back a few inches and stared down into his eyes. One hand lifted to gently thread her fingers through his hair, brushing it back from his forehead. He swallowed hard as his chest tightened with her unexpected gesture of tenderness.

"Are you a man of your word, Benjamin Sanders?" she whispered with that throaty Italian accent of hers.

"Yes."

She shifted her weight, slid her hand down between their bodies and cupped his erection. "Promise you will speak of what you heard to no one."

With her warm breath caressing his lips, her sexy scent filling his nostrils, and her nimble fingers stroking his desire higher, he'd have promised her anything.

"My lips are sealed."

A smile curved along her delicious mouth. "Thank you."

She planted a quick kiss on his lips, then rocked back on her heels and rose to her feet. He pushed up onto his elbows as she slipped through the door and disappeared.

When it dawned on him that she hadn't actually agreed to

help him despite his promise, he dropped his head against the floor with a groan. God, he was so damn cheap.

****

Evalina strode through the villa, seething with anger and anxiety. She'd known all along this would be difficult, but the wheels had been set in motion that fateful night six years ago and no way was she going to back down from her chance to even the score with the bastard who'd killed her father.

The game had turned upside down with the involvement of Ben and his family, and for the first time she was scared. She hadn't anticipated having to deal with a physical attraction beyond anything she'd ever experienced. She certainly hadn't expected to care for someone in this scam, even if the American was an unwilling participant. But worst of all, she hadn't planned on having to examine Nino's motives.

She rounded the corner just before the kitchen and found herself face to face with Nino and Alrigo. Her heart slammed against her ribs. Avoiding the lust lurking in Alrigo's cold eyes, she kept her gaze focused on Nino. Ben's suspicions echoed in her head and she thought of Nino's absence from their room when she'd risen at six a.m.

"Breakfast is laid out in the dining room," she managed to say casually. "I brought the American a tray."

"And how is our guest this morning?" Alrigo asked with a narrowed gaze.

Hard. She battled against an unfamiliar blush, casting him a glance as she sidled up to Nino. "He anticipates reuniting with his sisters later."

Alrigo's evil chuckle chilled her blood.

Evalina pressed against Nino's side and placed a hand on his chest to gaze up at him with a pout on her lips. "I was lonely this morning in bed."

He smiled down at her, because they shared a room, but never a bed. "In that case, breakfast can wait," he said suggestively.

His hand palmed her ass, not unlike Ben's a few minutes ago. With Ben, she'd fought to make herself move away. With Nino she had to fight to stay close. Playing the same character with different urges was wearing her out.

She forced a sexy little purr and pulled Nino's head down toward her. Before they kissed, Alrigo made a sound of impatience.

"We have plans to discuss."

"Give me a minute," Nino stated.

Evalina seized her chance as Alrigo walked away, but was still in earshot. "Why didn't you wake me up this morning?"

"You looked exhausted after last night," he returned.

Since her back was to Alrigo should he turn around for one last look, she rolled her eyes at Nino before standing on tiptoe to press her lips to his ear. "Where were you?"

He stiffened at her tone and she cringed. Yes, she needed to know she could count on him so the whole damn thing didn't go south and Alrigo Lapaglia got away with yet another murder, but she couldn't let her nerves tip him off that she had doubts.

"I took a turn at guard for a few hours outside the American's room."

So Ben hadn't been lying about that part. *What about the rest?*

Nino began kissing her neck. His fingers clenched on her butt again, then roved over her back and spanned her ribcage. Evalina endured his touch on the off chance that they still had an audience.

"Alrigo's waiting," she reminded breathlessly.

He licked her neck, hands inching upward. Lolling her head back as if overcome by passion, she scanned the hall to find it empty just as Nino's hand cupped her breast and squeezed hard. With a gasp, she shoved against his chest and glared at him. Nausea rolled in her stomach.

He gave a shrug of innocence. "I heard someone coming."

Her gaze swept the hall again in both directions. Assured they were still alone, she hissed, "Is everything set for later?"

He gave her a confidant, satisfied grin. "All set."

Unfortunately, she was not reassured. The moment he disappeared around the same corner Alrigo had, Evalina clenched her fists at her side and tried to rationalize her morning. The last few minutes meant nothing. Of course she despised the liberties Nino took with their situation, but they went with the characters they played.

Just because he'd crossed the line, she couldn't discount the fact that they'd worked well together since discovering their common goal. Each success along the way had brought them a step closer to that goal.

"Believe me, I know a double cross when I hear one."

And maybe that's exactly what Ben's warning had been. A double cross. It made perfect sense after what he'd said about his parents being in jail. Although...the guy thought he was fighting for his life, so it couldn't really be counted as a double cross. Still, that alone confirmed she couldn't trust a word he said. He'd do anything to turn her against the others.

Her gut insisted differently as she headed into the kitchen and opened the refrigerator to plan ahead for lunch. Had to keep up appearances until all the pieces fell into place.

Ben's comment about trusting his gut instincts had struck a chord, because she was alive today for exactly that reason. Why in the hell did the guy trust her? Other than cleaning blood off his face, she hadn't been *that* nice to him.

Unbidden, the memory of his kisses swamped her with sensation. She grew warm thinking about his tall, hard body pressed to hers. Such a different feeling than when she was forced to touch Nino.

Ben's voice sounded in her head again. *"I can't get out of here alone, I know that. I'm equally certain Nino is not who he seems and you're going to get screwed."*

A chill snaked down her spine as she remembered the pain of Nino's fingers squeezing her breast. She prayed she'd read Ben right and he'd keep his mouth shut.

Bottles rattled on the refrigerator door when she slammed it shut in frustration. Damn them both. Ben had planted the seed of doubt, and Nino had watered the hell out of it.

****

Alrigo pushed his half-empty breakfast plate aside and declined a cigarette from Nino. By the end of the day, he'd have just about everything he wanted.

Enough money to start over somewhere else.

Nino out of the picture.

Eva.

She wouldn't be willing, but he relished the added excitement of her resistance.

He sipped his espresso and contemplated the fact that they'd been in his house for almost a year, yet over the past two days his repressed desire for Eva Anelli had mutated into a consuming need to possess. Part of the acceleration resulted from the loathing she mistakenly thought she'd managed to conceal. For that, he would thoroughly enjoy teaching her to show some respect.

And the rest of the transformation had been triggered by her subtle increase of aggressive belligerence. He'd first noticed it during his phone conversation with Tomlin to verify Ben remained alive. The moment he'd threatened to kill Sanders and reached for his gun, Eva had reacted to protect the man. As if she could've stopped him. She'd caught herself, but he'd since taken note of a slight difference in the way she treated him and Nino, and even in the way she stared down their American hostage. He didn't like it.

In the past she'd used her brash, icy demeanor to put any man who dared challenge her in their place, but this was different. He'd observed from afar long enough to recognize her defense of something hidden, something he'd bet not even Nino knew about, because his gut told him this change was directly connected to Benjamin Sanders.

He kept his doubts to himself as Nino drew on his cigarette and squinted through the smoke. If Nino suspected anything between Eva and Ben, even if there wasn't, Alrigo would lose his human collateral in a heartbeat. Hell, if he didn't need the prick, if he wasn't the key to the entire exchange, he'd get rid of Sanders himself before Eva had a chance to do anything to fuck things up.

He supposed he'd have to bring her along to keep an eye on her. His men hadn't been able to handle a couple of American tourists, there's no way they'd contain a dynamite like Eva. His fingers tightened briefly on the cup in hand. Originally, he'd only wanted the evidence on the video. Then they'd all made the mistake of screwing with him.

Tomlin snatched the video from his grasp. The sisters' escapes made his entire operation look incompetent. Sanders made the fatal mistake of hitting his broken ribs and exposing weakness in front of his men.

Alrigo forced himself to relax, keeping his ever-growing impotent fury hidden as he set his cup in its saucer with a steady hand. He just needed to keep control and everything would work out as *he'd* planned. That nosy cop Roselli had paid for his stupidity, so would the rest.

The same as Frank Gallo had six years ago.

Chapter 22

Trent cracked an eye open, squinting against the light piercing the small starboard window above his bed. Bright sunlight, not the soft glow of dawn. The past couple days had *definitely* caught up with him. A smile tugged the corners of his mouth when he thought of the activities that'd added to his exhaustion last night.

With a contented groan despite the aches in his sore body, he turned his head to find he'd sprawled across much of the otherwise empty bed.

Alarm sent him reaching for the gun, only to come up empty. His stomach lurched at the sight of the bare shelf and he sat up with a jerk. The digital time on the microwave in the galley read just after ten. Other than a brief wince at the sting in his bullet-torn bicep, he focused on Halli.

Details registered as he shot off the bed. Her clothes no longer littered the floor. Through the half-open door of the head he glimpsed a towel hung over the shower rod. Coffee aroma lingered in the air, and the pot was half-full.

His urgency abated slightly.

Halli making coffee didn't suggest trouble. And anyone who would've taken her and the gun would've probably shot him as he lay oblivious to the rest of the frickin' world. God, he couldn't believe he'd slept through her getting out of bed, showering, and making coffee.

Some protection he was.

His waking contentment had now vanished completely, replaced by fear seconds ago, and now guilt. He raked both hands through his hair and fisted them tight, welcoming the pain. There was a very real possibility that he'd fail her today like he'd failed Sean. The responsibility of keeping her safe had been an unexpected, unwanted burden, but now the thought of not living up to it scared the hell out of him.

Halli's hushed voice from above sent a wave of relief

crashing through him despite having rationalized there was no immediate reason to worry. He braced a hand on the wall at the opening to the deck and drank in the sight of her slim form by the boat railing. Dressed in a snug black T-shirt and tan shorts, she stood with her back to him, talking on his disposable cell phone.

Sunlight filtered through a tree along the shore, its dappled rays glinting off the golden-red highlights in her shoulder length hair. The longing to once again feel its silky softness skim across his stomach set his blood pumping.

He closed his eyes against the gut clenching need and took a deep breath, last night's emotional realization still raw and not entirely welcome. Silent arguments flooded back, gaining strength in the light of day.

Somewhere, he recalled reading that people formed emotional attachments in dangerous, stressful situations. That had to be what he felt, considering they'd depended on each other to stay alive during the past couple days, and it wasn't over yet. Once the danger was gone, the emotion currently constricting his chest would reveal itself to be nothing more than a coping mechanism.

She'd go home to Wisconsin; he'd head back to L.A. to begin shooting his next Shain West film in less than two weeks. Life would return to normal. It'd take longer to achieve normal without his brother, but eventually it would happen.

A sharp ache near his heart undermined his confidence. He clenched his jaw and ignored the pain to focus on Halli's conversation.

"We're all better than mom and dad; you, me and Ben, and don't forget that. They're the ones sitting in jail right now, not us."

Trent marveled at the strength in her voice and was glad she was on his side.

"Rachel, stop it," Halli ordered. "Everything is going to work out just like we've planned. Once Trent pays the ransom and trades the video for Ben, this'll all be over and we can go home."

Her words drew him up short and tightened his muscles

like the string on a bow. *Work out like they planned?* Having become otherwise occupied, they hadn't worked on their plan yet. At least he and she hadn't.

So who *had* she been planning with?

Halli shifted to lean one hip against the railing, presenting him with her profile. Uneasy, he pressed back into the shadows. She held the phone low enough that he could see a smile lift the corner of her mouth.

"You haven't spent the past couple days with him."

Her body stiffened all of a sudden, and he noticed she held the gun in her right hand, resting against her thigh.

"He said he'd pay it and he will. You just worry about Simone, okay? Call if anything else strange happens."

Fingers of dread crawled along his skin as snippets of conversation hurled through his memory.

"We're better than mom and dad." The con-artists. So…better how?

"They're in jail, not us." Ben, Rachel and Halli were better because…they'd never been caught?

More pieces fell into place. He remembered thinking something about the ransom demand had been odd, that someone other than Lapaglia had made the suggestion. Someone like…her brother, perhaps? Had that been what *they'd planned*?

Her refusal to stay at Simone's took on a different light. And last night. Christ, last night, she'd flipped back and forth enough times he was unclear who'd seduced whom.

"For a million dollars, it's the least I can do."

He thought she'd been talking about dessert when she said that, but in the end, she'd slept with him. Another case where money was more trouble than it was worth?

Anger began a slow simmer. Shy, cute little Halli had been playing him the entire time? While he agonized over the possibility of falling in love with her, she'd probably been laying in his bed dreaming of how she and her brother and sister would spend the money she guaranteed he'd pay. He was so gullible. He'd been had by the whole damn lot of them!

The knife in his back twisted brutally.

Halli had hung up and now lifted her hands to her face, phone in one hand, gun in the other. Trent's gaze narrowed on the weapon. If he wasn't careful, he just might have a bullet in his chest, too. But he couldn't bring himself to care at the moment.

He moved into view, leaned his injured shoulder against the wall and crossed his arms over his bare chest.

"You look worried."

Halli startled with a small shriek and spun to face him. The gun bounced at her feet with a couple of dull thuds.

"Oh *God*...sorry. You scared me!" She pressed the hand holding the phone to her chest, the other over her mouth, and stared at the gun. Her gaze lifted to his. "W-what did you say?"

Trent joined her on deck, scanning the area for anything suspicious. He bent to pick up the weapon, surprised when she did nothing to stop him. With effort, he tempered his tone. "You look worried."

She actually looked like she was about to cry as she lifted her small shoulders. "Yeah, well, it's tomorrow now, you know?"

Her words brought back memories of last night. How she'd decided to put aside her worries for one night. His jaw tightened in tandem with his grip on the gun, and he made a small questioning gesture with the weapon. "Why'd you take this?"

"I started thinking about later and got so claustrophobic I couldn't breathe down there." She motioned below deck. "I had to get some air, and thought I'd feel safer up here by myself if I had the gun. Stupid, since I don't even know how to use it."

His gaze narrowed at the wobble in her voice. Damn, she was good. "Why didn't you wake me?"

"I know you didn't get much sleep the past couple nights."

He immediately pictured why he'd lost sleep last night. Judging by the increased flush coloring her fair skin, her thoughts travelled the same path. He forced the erotic images from his mind and asked, "I take it that was your sister on the phone?"

She nodded. Trent leaned against the railing, gun held casually at his side, ready for anything. He did another scan of the immediate area around the dock and George's house but noted nothing unusual. "What's going on? Is she okay?"

Halli sidled past him to sit at the table where a mug of coffee rested. "She's feeling okay, but said Simone got a phone call this morning that really shook her up. Not that she could understand Simone's Italian, but Rachel said it looked like she'd seen a ghost. And when she asked if something was wrong, Simone completely clammed up. Wouldn't even look her in the eye. Rachel said it was very strange and freaked her out."

Trent frowned. He didn't like the sound of that. Halli distracted him with a downward sweep of her gaze, reminding him he wore nothing but navy boxer briefs. Betrayal had effectively taken care of his morning hard-on but her attention threatened to bring it back. He was an idiot.

More color stained her cheeks when she raised her gaze to his. It wasn't possible to produce blushes on demand, was it?

"Do you think it's strange?" she asked.

Yes. Everything in his life was strange these days.

He shrugged. "Hard to say since I wasn't there."

Halli lifted her coffee, only to *thunk* the mug back down without taking a drink. "I realize they're not friends or anything, but Simone really seemed like she wanted to help yesterday."

Trent kept his own concern hidden to see how far she'd carry the act. "It could've been a call from the hospital."

"Yeah." Her fingers gripped her mug, knuckles white.

"Would you feel better if I called her?"

Those blue eyes pleaded. "Would you, please?"

He extended his arm for the phone. She handed it over with a thankful smile that lit her eyes and wrenched his gut.

Was she really playing him, or did he have it all wrong? A moment ago he'd been certain, now he waffled. Shouldn't he, the actor, be able to figure out if someone was genuine or running a con?

Simone sounded a little out of sorts, but assured him she was just tired. With miles separating them and the day marching forward relentlessly, he was forced to give her the benefit of the doubt. He asked about Rachel again, and then made Simone promise to get some rest when she could before hanging up.

"Everything's fine."

Halli's relief was palpable, until their eyes met and her smile faded. She took her still half-full mug and brushed past to go below deck. Trent followed, watching her dump out the coffee while he reached for his jeans on the floor. The phone bounced where he dropped it on the unmade bed, but the gun he set on the corner of the rumpled comforter farthest from her while he dressed.

"Exactly how are you and your sister and brother better than your parents?" He cringed at the slight note of accusation. Nothing like telling her he was on to her.

"You heard that?"

"And the rest," he stated, buttoning his jeans.

She turned around, hands braced against the counter behind her. She looked nervous, but met his gaze directly. "Rachel's just worried about Ben, please don't take her doubt personally. A million dollars is a lot to ask even a close friend to fork over, let alone a stranger."

Not quite the angle he'd expected. Trent tugged a clean white T-shirt down over his stomach and let his gaze linger on her curves as he stuck the gun into the back waistband of his jeans. "We're hardly strangers, Halli."

Color deepened in her cheeks and neck again. Trent's heart insisted she couldn't fake that, or the shyness he swore he saw in her eyes when he stepped closer. It was unnerving how bad he wanted back what they'd shared last night. So bad that he couldn't keep from crossing to her and reaching out to touch despite his insidious suspicions.

He brushed the back of his knuckles along her jaw and tucked her hair behind her ear. One moment she looked up at him with such a pure expression of trust, and the next she wrapped her arms tight around him. He tensed with the instant thought she was going for the gun, but all she did was lay her cheek on his chest and lean against him.

Forcing himself to remain somewhat vigilant, he removed the gun and laid it within *his* reach on the counter before returning Halli's embrace.

"Rachel doesn't know you. And I did mean what I said last night. I trust you completely."

Her words were muffled against his shirt, but no less effective.

"Only you."

He squeezed his eyes shut in despair. Did she have any clue what she did to him?

"What I said about my parents..."

Her chest expanded and relaxed within his arms. With trepidation, he waited for her to continue.

"Rachel thought maybe with us getting mixed up in all this...that maybe that meant in some sense we were more like our parents than we thought. That despite us trying to live normal lives, there was no escaping the past, or who we are. But I *know* we're nothing like them. It may have taken Ben and Rachel a little longer to escape their influence, but it's true."

Her voice rang with steel conviction. He wished he could see her face. Instead, he kept her talking. "What was it like, growing up with them?"

A long minute passed before she spoke. "For the most part it was fun, like a never-ending adventure that once in awhile got a little scary. Us kids were always part of whatever elaborate scheme they were running and they'd make each one into a game. I guess you could say they conned us, too, because I thought we were close, until that one time we didn't leave town before I saw the result of what they'd orchestrated." She leaned back in his arms with a sigh and slight shake of her head. "I was twelve, and though I don't know the specifics of the con, I was old enough to know I'd played a part in my new best friends' parents losing their jobs, their house, their savings...*everything*...because of my family."

Her voice had grown hoarse and she sniffed.

"I couldn't bring myself to turn them in, even though I wanted to, but I refused to help anymore and things were never the same between me and my parents. Ben and Rachel took up the slack and watched out for me. Then, shortly after my sixteenth birthday, someone beat them at their own game and they were convicted less than six months later."

Trent frowned at the thought of her being alone so young. "What'd you do?"

"Got an honest job, finished high school and worked my way through college."

She rattled off her accomplishments as if they were no big deal, but there was no mistaking the underlying determination and pride in her voice. He thought she'd gained strength on this wild ride they'd shared, but in truth, he saw she'd had it all along.

"Ben was already out of school, working for some courier service that took him all around the country. Rachel always had a flair for art and she started her own business not far from where I live now. She travels to art fairs all over during the summer and creates in her studio through the winter. Ben helps her out with the books whenever he's around."

Call him gullible, but Trent was well on his way to reforming his hasty conclusions from a few minutes ago. Why would she tell him any of this if she was playing him?

He took one moment of clear, rational thought to consider Sean and Lorenzo's murders and everything else they'd been through the past couple days. The twisted tangle of events leading up to this exact spot convinced him there was no way anyone could plan what they'd been through. Too many variables would've made it impossible, and he felt like a jerk for even going there in the first place.

Thank God he hadn't openly accused her.

Relief clogged his throat, but he managed to ask, "And your parents...has prison made a difference for them, or you?"

"I haven't spoken to them since the trial almost ten years ago and I don't want to. They'll never be a part of my life again."

As if suddenly uncomfortable with the conversation, she brought her arms around to push against his chest. He released her with reluctance.

"What about your brother and sister?"

She shrugged. "I know they've kept in touch, but we don't talk about them." She reached up to brush moisture from her cheeks, turning her back as she did so. "I've never even told anyone about them. I can just imagine what people would think or say if they knew."

Trent made her face him. "Like you told Rachel, you're not your parents." He saw that now without a doubt.

"Still doesn't mean I want anyone to know."

"Your secret is safe with me," he promised.

He was rewarded with a brief smile. His stomach chose that moment to grumble for breakfast and Trent decided to get the morning back on track where it should've been.

He lifted her chin to give her a thorough good morning kiss. After a moment, her palms flattened on his chest as she rose on tiptoe to kiss him back. With effort, he sidelined thoughts of taking her back to bed and ended the kiss.

"Hungry?" he asked.

Before he could pull away, she wound her arms around his neck with a shy grin. "Very."

His pulse leapt, but he avoided the temptation of her mouth for a peck on the tip of her nose. "That's Italy Halli talking. And while I look forward to speaking with her again tonight, right now I need Wisconsin Halli's attention."

Her smile faded and she pulled her arms down. He gave himself a mental kick in the ass and pressed a quick kiss to her lips. "I didn't mean—"

She pushed away, shaking her head. "No, you're right. Here I told Rachel we had a plan and we haven't even talked about anything yet. Coffee's made, and it's sponge cake for breakfast, so—"

"Halli…"

She paused in the middle of handing him a clean mug.

"Will you have dinner with me when this is all over?"

Trent's question was the very last thing Halli expected. He'd been in a strange mood since sneaking up on her earlier and she was still trying to read him. The 'morning after' situation only made things more awkward because, from the moment she'd woken up next to him, she'd wanted thousands more 'morning afters' with him.

For a speechless moment she simply stared at his serious expression. Her heart said yes, but common sense pointed out when this was over, she'd be Wisconsin Halli no matter where her feet were located, and he'd see she really *was* boring.

Thrusting the mug into his hand, she reached for the cake with her other hand and tried to make light of his question. "Let's get through breakfast and the rest of the day before talking about dinner."

"I'm serious."

"So am I."

Cake on the table, she opened the small refrigerator door to get the fruit and whipped cream and spotted the antibiotics bottle from Simone on the door. Thankful for the distraction, she grabbed the bottle.

"You need your second shot of antibiotics."

He poured himself a cup of coffee and leaned back against the counter as he took a drink. "So that's the way it's going to be?"

"That's how it has to be," she confirmed.

Last night had been a great distraction—the best distraction of her life—but if she continued down that road, she'd start looking beyond the next twelve, twenty-four, and even forty-eight hours…and that would only lead to heartache. She was pretty darn sure heartache was in her near future anyway, no sense magnifying it with a voluntary dinner that would only highlight how completely different their lives were. Plus, he could say she wasn't her parents, but the tabloid press would have a field day with Trent Tomlin's girlfriend's parents residing in federal prison.

She almost laughed a second later. Listen to her. Assuming she'd be his girlfriend with one dinner. Talk about setting herself up.

After retrieving the syringe, she faced Trent. "Ready?"

He set down his mug and reached for the button of his jeans. "Just remember, this is not fun for me. It bites like a sonofabitch."

Halli couldn't hold back a smile as she filled the syringe and then coaxed the air bubbles to the top like Simone had done. Trent bent over slightly, presenting her with one bare ass cheek. That's when the nerves struck, and she hesitated.

"Simone pretty much just jabbed it in, right?"

"That's what it felt like," he confirmed between clenched teeth.

"Okay."

The hand she braced on his back trembled. So did the one holding the syringe.

"Is your hand *shaking*?" he asked incredulously.

"I'm a little nervous."

"*You're* nervous?"

"I've never done this before."

He jerked to his full height. "Christ, gimme the damn thing!"

"I got it." She held the syringe behind her back and met his gaze as he faced her. "I can do it, just give me a minute."

"I appreciate that you've been looking forward to *jabbing* me with the needle, but I prefer not to have it broke off in my ass."

He had a point. She carefully set the syringe in his extended palm and then watched him pull a contortionist act to give himself the shot. He'd pulled his pants down further so they didn't slide back up and she got a good look at his firm muscles as he stuck the needle in. Heat warmed her face as she recalled running her hands over them last night.

Trent glanced up and caught her staring. He pulled the needle out with a grimace and set the syringe on the counter so he could refasten his pants. His teeth flashed as he cut his gaze back to her. "Enjoyed that anyway, didn't you?"

There was no use denying it, so she simply smiled at his egotistical grin and then laughed when he waggled his brows and asked if she'd rub his butt for him.

Yeah…heartache definitely lurked right around the corner.

The cell phone rang with a sobering dose of reality. Halli followed Trent's gaze to where he'd left it on the bed. He crossed the space in three strides, checked the number, and flipped it open. The rigid line of his jaw told her it wasn't Simone.

"I'm working on it. You gave me 'til six…don't worry, you'll get yours as long as we get Ben." He paced to the bar counter and yanked open a drawer to pull out paper and a pen. Then he wrote while repeating out loud a set of GPS coordinates and the time. He ended that call and immediately began dialing again as he faced Halli.

She started to speak, only to have him hold up a silencing hand.

"Figured you'd be up," Trent said without any other greeting. "Where are we at with the money? Good. Don't forget, waterproof bag, and tell him to meet me at the Villa Melzi gardens at four, on the steps leading down to the waterfront. Can't miss 'em."

His gaze shifted from Halli to the gun on the counter.

"You're absolutely sure I can trust this guy? Thanks, Brad, I owe you one."

After an abrupt disconnect, he slipped the phone into his pocket, his mouth set in a grim line. Halli blew out a shaky breath when he picked up the gun and tucked it in place against the small of his back before meeting her gaze.

"Time to make that plan."

****

Numerous ideas had been suggested and discarded, and Halli was beginning to think they'd never figure out how to pull the whole thing off. They had about an hour before meeting the guy delivering the ransom money. Three hours before the exchange with Lapaglia. Time was running out.

Head buried on her crisscrossed arms, she mumbled under her breath, brainstorming to herself about the lake, boats, meeting on the water. Trent had insisted a minute ago he was *not* pacing, but since then he'd resumed wearing a path in the carpeting. He didn't even see her glare, so she dropped her head again.

Stupid boat. They needed more space. For the first time since yesterday, she actually wanted to be separated from—

Halli stiffened. She lifted her head from her arms. "I've got it. We need a second boat."

Trent paused in his pacing. "A second boat?"

"A second boat," she repeated, smiling. "That way we can keep our bargaining chips separated and stack the odds in our favor."

His gaze narrowed as he considered her suggestion.

She got up from the table and went to stand in front of him. "Think about it. The money on one boat, the video on the other."

"They get one when they release Ben, and the other when the boat with Ben is a safe distance away," he expanded, nodding, warming to the idea.

"Exactly," she agreed. "You asked for a waterproof bag, so we hold that back until we've got Ben. Since there's no way for them to know for sure if we've made another copy of the video, I think the money's the better incentive."

"Good point."

Excitement pumped up her pulse. *Finally* they had a workable plan the two of them could realistically pull off.

Trent reached past her to grab the notebook she'd been using at the table and turned toward the bar area. "Renting a boat shouldn't be too much of an issue around here, but the driver is a whole other matter. We can't just ask anyone—"

"We don't have to ask anyone," she interrupted. "I'll drive it."

"No, you won't."

"Yes, I will. If I can drive this one, I can drive—"

"I said *no*."

Gaze fixed on his back, she waited for him to face her and explain his reasoning. A full minute passed, during which he didn't even bother with a glance over his shoulder. As if he'd said "No," and that was it. Disbelief combined with rising anger.

"There is no way you're leaving me—"

He banged a fist on the counter and swung around so fast she took a step back before she could help it.

"Damn it, Halli, I knew this was going to be an issue. Why the hell do you think I wanted you to stay at Simone's? You are not going, so let's end this argument right now. I'll ask Giovanni to drive the boat."

"You can't drag him into this. It's not fair to Concetta or your friend George and you know it. Or me for that matter, because if something happens to him..."

The flexing of muscle in his jaw told her she was right. She crossed her arms over her chest in satisfaction. "You got no one but me to drive that boat."

"I'll call Simone's cousin."

She shook her head. "That was my choice, and I'm not risking Ben's life by involving any police."

"Then I'll find someone else," he vowed. "I'm not taking you in that close to these guys."

"And I'm not letting you go in to rescue my brother alone."

"Because you still don't trust me, do you?"

"That's not it at all," she shot back, annoyed he'd play that card. "And after last night, you should know that."

That made him pause. Emotion flared in his eyes but he quickly turned back to the bar and pulled the cell phone from his pocket. "No. End of discussion."

Determination ground her teeth together before she forced a deep breath and said calmly, "Doesn't matter how many times you say the word, short of tying and gagging me, *I'm going.*"

He braced his hands, hung his head and regarded her with a rigid sideways look. The unwavering force of his piercing gaze bored between her shoulder blades on her way up the stairs to the deck.

An hour later, Halli sat on a sun-warmed wrought-iron bench, a nameless book in her hand that did no more to hold her interest than the splendid view of Lake Como and the lush, colorful gardens of Villa Melzi surrounding her. She only had eyes for the tall, dark haired man some twenty yards away.

Trent could insist she stay behind all he wanted, didn't mean his decision was final. She was here now, wasn't she? Not back at the boat like he'd also tried to dictate. Lack of trust wasn't the issue any longer, like he'd accused in an attempt to guilt her into complying. No way she'd let him go into such a dangerous situation without any form of back up.

Besides the fact he needed her, it was her responsibility to help rescue Ben.

Trent didn't look around as he sat with a newspaper and a to-go cup of espresso on the stone wall by the steps some twenty yards away, but Halli would bet he hadn't read any more than she had. Beneath that tattered baseball cap, behind those mirrored sunglasses, she knew his razor-sharp hazel gaze scanned the garden's visitors, locals and tourists alike, searching for the man who held the key to her brother's survival.

Somewhere in the distance, church bells chimed the four o'clock hour. Halli looked around for anyone with a bag that could be holding cash. Her unsuccessful gaze doubled back to Trent as he flicked down one corner of the paper. After a casual glance, he returned his attention to the newspaper.

Amazing how he blended in with the other Italians in the area despite being U.S. born and raised. An air of sexy mystery surrounded him, and she forgot she was mad at him. She knew she'd never look at a magazine picture of him clean-shaven without imagining the shadow on his jaw and the look in his eyes as he made love to her. Would looking at those pictures in a few years hurt as much as the live version now, knowing their time together was almost over?

She forced the question from her head and wondered about the man delivering the money. Anxiety ate away her outer layer of calm as the minutes ticked by. Worry mushroomed when Trent gave up all pretense of reading to openly scan the area. No one approached, and he gave no indication of recognizing anyone.

Halli shut her unread book with a thud and headed in his direction. The tilt, hang, and slight shake of his head conveyed his annoyance at her deviation to this supposed simple plan, but she didn't care. The stone warmed her hip and palm as she leaned against the wall next to him.

"What if he doesn't show?"

"He'll show," Trent ground out.

"You're that sure you can trust your buddy Brad?"

"I'm that sure."

Was the taut line of his jaw conviction or doubt?

Thirty-five minutes later, Trent snapped the cell phone shut with an emphatic curse. He didn't need to explain Brad hadn't answered and Halli's stomach knotted tighter than a wet shoelace. Trent's firm grip on her hand led her down the garden steps and back toward the boat.

"I promise you, it's not over," he said. "I'm going to get Ben back no matter what."

Emotion thickened his voice, and in a startling moment of clarity, Halli realized his vow had as much to do with helping her and her family as him making up for the fact that he hadn't been around to protect his own brother. She tightened her fingers around his when they reached the dock, drawing him to a halt.

Nerves attacked out of nowhere, and she blurted, "It's not your fault."

He pulled free and strode along the wooden planks. "How do you figure? You depended on me for the money and we've got squat."

She jumped down into the boat after him, grasping the rail to keep her balance as it rocked beneath their feet. "I'm talking about Sean."

He whirled on her. "You don't know anything about Sean."

"I know you blame yourself for his death." He'd as much as wrote it in that leather bound notebook of his.

He sucked in a breath as if she'd struck him. Then a blank mask slipped over his expression and he gave her a small smile. "Read a couple pages and you think you got me all figured out, don't you, sweetheart?"

She recognized the defensive, distancing tactic. "Don't, Trent, not now."

His gaze shifted. The mask slipped as he turned away. "Exactly. Not now."

"Now is the only time we have," she persisted.

His fists clenched at his sides when she laid a hand on his back. Muscles tensed and held beneath her fingertips.

"Nothing you do in the next couple hours will bring your brother back."

"You think I don't know that?"

"I think guilt and revenge make a dangerous combination."

One corner of his mouth lifted as he faced her again. "Bad guys and guns make a dangerous combination, Halli. *My* combination equals the odds."

"Your combination is going to get you killed, trying to help me. What do you think I'll be writing in *my journal* then?"

"Do you even keep one?"

She narrowed her gaze, but stuck to the subject. "You said yourself Sean was determined to finish the documentary."

"And I knew it was dangerous." His fists balled at his sides. "I should've been watching his back."

"You can't blame yourself for living your own life."

"I should've been there," he repeated, his expression grim once more. "Whatever happens tonight—"

A muted thump below deck halted him mid-sentence. Trent whipped around, pushed Halli behind him and reached for his gun at the same time.

Chapter 23

No more than the reassuring weight of the pistol filled his palm and he'd steadied his aim with his other hand, Trent heard a voice that put him even more on edge.

"She's right, you know."

A tall figure stepped from the shaded interior of the boat. Trent didn't lower his guard or the gun when he recognized the khaki-clad man.

"Good way to get yourself shot, Dad. What the hell are you doing here?"

The Almighty Greg Tomlin moved forward, unconcerned with the weapon in his son's hand. He was a little heavier around the middle and a lot grayer on top since the last time Trent had seen him. Halli's body relaxed from where she'd pressed close against his back. Trent dropped his hands to his sides in resignation.

Great. He was not in the mood, nor did he have the time to deal with this particular family dysfunction right now.

"I heard you needed some money," his dad said.

Halli stepped up, hope lighting her eyes. "You have the ransom money?"

Trent recognized an annoying combination of relief and dread. Of all people, why'd Brad pick his Dad to bring the money? If he failed, his father would be right there—

"Ransom?" his father questioned, his light brown gaze bouncing from Halli to Trent.

"I didn't give Brad details."

"Obviously."

Trent re-tucked the gun, wanting nothing more than to demand his father leave. Instead, he indicated they should all go below deck. He checked how they were doing on time as Halli and his father sat at the galley table. One more hour.

"What do you need ransom money for, Trent?"

"It's for my brother," Halli supplied.

When his father lifted an eyebrow toward her, Trent sighed in defeat and leaned back against the counter. "Dad, this is Halli. Halli, my dad, Greg Tomlin."

"I know."

Of course she knew. He gave his father a hard stare and folded his arms over his chest. "How'd you find us here and why didn't you meet at the designated spot?"

"Despite appearances to the contrary, I'm not completely clueless when it comes to your life and your friends." His father leaned his elbows on the table and linked his fingers together. "I put two and two together when Brad mentioned Villa Melzi."

"Doesn't explain why you didn't meet us there."

"I've had two shadows since arriving in the country last night."

Trent stiffened. He reached for his gun as he moved to the opening leading to the deck. "So you came here instead?"

"Relax. I lost them this morning." When Trent glanced over his shoulder, his father lifted his brows. "I do have some experience losing tails, you know. I just wanted to be extra cautious."

Given his dad's experience in war zones, and a fair number of his own criminal activity documentaries, Trent silently acknowledged they likely weren't in any immediate danger. "Why'd Brad call you?" he asked.

"*I* called him when I saw the news and didn't hear from my own son."

Trent countered with a pointed dig of his own. "I specifically asked for someone I could count on."

His father's gaze dropped to the gun in Trent's hand. "Want to tell me what's going on?"

"No."

Halli frowned. "Trent, he could help."

"Cut the concerned parent act." Trent stalked over and slapped his palms on the table. It wobbled under his weight as he leaned forward. "You've *never* been around when it mattered. Why show up now?"

His father met his gaze, his brown eyes brightened by an unnatural sheen. "Because I wasn't around when it mattered."

A lump formed in Trent's throat.

"*I should've been there for Sean, not laid it on your shoulders,*" his father said in a low, hoarse voice. "I'm the one who argued how dangerous it was. I knew what he could be facing. I should've been here with him."

Halli's hand slid over to cover Trent's. He couldn't risk a glance at her. As it was now, he had to turn around to blink away the stinging sensation in his eyes. What the hell was with the two of them ganging up on him now? He resumed his cynical stance against the counter.

"Sean committed suicide, remember?"

"I don't believe that now anymore than you do."

"What changed your mind? It sure as hell wasn't me."

"I thought about what you'd said and decided to do a little investigating of my own. I assume whatever's going on with you being wanted for questioning by the Italian police has something to do with whoever killed Sean?"

Trent seized on the opportunity to redirect the conversation. "Halli accidentally filmed the shooting of the cop found dead at my place, and in about an hour we'll meet the killer to exchange her video and the one million dollars for the release of her brother."

"Same man who killed Sean?" Greg pressed.

"Yes."

His father's lips thinned, his fingers tightened until is knuckle were white, but he nodded calmly, his gaze transferring from Trent to Halli, and back to Trent again.

"What's our plan?"

After one beat of hesitation, Trent swallowed his pride. With his father added to the mix, Halli's argument that Trent needed her to drive the second boat was null and void. She could stay behind where it was safe and he could focus on rescuing Ben. He explained Halli's idea.

Color rose in her cheeks as he spoke. In the middle of a question from his father, she gave a sharp shake of her head.

"*I'm* driving the other boat."

Trent clenched his jaw. "Halli, I told you that discussion is over."

"Since when does your order qualify as a discussion?"

"Since your safety is my first concern."

"The damn video has been your first concern all along."

Trent ignored the sting of that accusation. "Nice try, but I'm all guilted out."

She pushed to her feet, blue eyes snapping. "You try to leave me behind and I'll raise holy hell."

Quiet settled after she'd stomped up the short set of stairs to the deck.

"She's got some fire."

"Yeah, I know," Trent muttered.

"Reminds me of your brother."

Trent cast a quelling look at his father and followed Halli above deck. A peek into the family closet of skeletons was enough for today. Right now, he had more important things to focus on. Like the woman strangling the railing as she stared across the water.

When she spotted him, her chin lifted in that defiant way of hers. Just as he expected; reasoning with her would be out of the question. He stood beside her without saying a word, biding their limited time.

She glanced sideways and shifted her stance. "I'm sorry I said you only cared about the video."

"You've ranked above the video from the moment I tossed you in my car."

Her chin lowered a notch. Not quite a nod of agreement, but it was something. He leaned over to bump shoulders with her. "If I say please, will you stay?"

"No."

Another bump. "Pretty please?"

"No."

"God, you're annoyingly stubborn."

"When it matters, yes. You're annoyingly dictatorial."

"When it matters." He allowed a small grin and turned to lean back against the rail so he could see her face better. "So, here's the deal. You ride with my father and stay out of sight. Completely and without a word. If you can't agree to that…"

He revealed a length of rope he'd lifted from a hook by the

stairs.

She gasped in outrage. "You wouldn't dare!"

He met her wide eyes. "Try me, sweetheart."

"Your father would never allow you to tie me up."

"My father has absolutely no say in this matter. I shouldn't have to remind you Lapaglia is not a nice man. He's ruthless and vindictive. Not only did you video him murdering a cop, but you've evaded him enough times to make him look like an incompetent fool. I don't trust the man to let bygones be bygones if he sees you."

She lifted her chin again. "Ben would never sit back and wait if I was in trouble."

"You've more than done your part."

She shook her head in denial.

He growled in frustration. "Make your choice, then. The deal, or the nice soft rope that'll keep you safe."

"Great choices."

"They are what they are. At least I'm giving you one."

She huffed and glared back over the water. "Sometimes I really—"

"Love me? I know." He forced a laugh at her startled look, and then looked up when the drone of a motor caught his attention. "Look at that, the boat's here. Show time, baby. I need an answer right now."

Trent rubbed the smooth nylon rope against her skin, wishing he could replace it with his lips. She jerked her arm away and swung around to watch Giovani guide the rental boat around to their side of the dock.

If he thought he could get away with leaving her here, he'd do it in a heartbeat. Unfortunately, she had that whole noble, stubborn thing going and he didn't doubt her ability to raise hell to a holier-than-thou level. They couldn't afford the attention with the clock ticking.

Maybe, just maybe, she'd stay behind of her own free will.

She set her jaw and shoved away from the rail. "Deal."

Par for the course he'd been playing on the past couple of days. She wouldn't be completely safe as he'd hoped, but at least she'd be out of the way.

After Giovani left, Trent took a few more minutes to make sure they were all completely clear on the plan. Then he turned for the rental boat before his father voiced the concern etched in features Trent didn't remember looking so old the last time they'd seen each other. The switch from his father's usual disappointment or anger threatened to undermine the detachment Trent needed to successfully survive the next hour.

"Trent."

Halli's low voice stopped him with one hand on the rail. His gut clenched. Much as he wanted to ignore her, he couldn't help but turn around.

"Be careful, okay?"

Despite the fact that he'd just threatened to tie her up and leave her behind, trust radiated from her darkened blue eyes. Nothing like reminding him how much was riding on this exchange. How much she depended on him to save her brother. How much they both had to lose.

He struggled to summon the character who put emotions aside and got the job done. "I'll do everything I can to keep Ben safe."

"I'm not just talking about Ben."

His heart lodged in his throat, but he managed a cocky smile. "Don't worry about me, sugar, I can take care of myself."

He started to pull himself up onto the dock, but she grabbed his arm, right on the injury she'd rewrapped less than an hour ago. His breath hissed through his teeth.

"Don't do that," she snapped.

"How else do you expect me to get to the other boat?" He shook her hand from his arm.

"I'm talking about the *sugar* and *sweetheart* crap." Her words vibrated with anger. "You do that when you want to distance yourself, or pretend you don't care."

"I do care. About you getting your ass down below and keeping your mouth shut. You want to help your brother so bad, don't screw this up."

"Resorting to being a jerk again. Why am I even surprised?"

"According to you, I'm a jerk all the time, so what does it

matter?"

Her gaze wavered, then held his with a glimmer of vulnerable hope. "You weren't a jerk last night."

Behind them, his father cleared his throat. Trent ignored him and absolutely refused to let his character slip despite the crushing tightness in his chest. He crooked one corner of his mouth upward and let his hand brush Halli's breast as he lifted it to run a knuckle along her jaw.

"Don't go reading anything into last night, sweetheart. We both know exactly what that was."

She paled beneath the flush in her cheeks. The hurt in her expression nearly did him in, but then she lifted her chin and her eyes chilled. Without another word, she spun around and walked below deck, her spine as rigid as the jaw he clenched to keep from taking the words back.

One glance at the disapproval etched in his father's face brought everything in Trent's world back to normal and he climbed up onto the dock.

"Let's do this."

He pushed nagging thoughts of Halli from his mind and focused on the upcoming exchange as they motored toward the meeting coordinates near the less populated end of Isola Comacina. The sun had begun its downward decent in the cloudless sky, though it'd be at least another hour before the fiery ball slipped behind the snow tipped mountains on the west side of the lake.

It was the perfect time, actually. Light enough to see someone face to face, but with enough shadows on this side of the island to camouflage their activities from any distance across the water. Clear evidence not to underestimate Lapaglia.

They were a few minutes out when Trent spotted the man's boat through a pair of binoculars. Five people on board. Damn, he didn't like those odds. Seconds later, his cell phone rang. Expecting it to be Lapaglia, he frowned when he recognized a different number. "Simone?"

"Trent, thank God."

He slowed the boat and raised a hand for his father to do the same, fifty yards behind him.

"What's the matter?" he asked Simone.

"I have to tell you something. I should have said something earlier, but…" Her voice caught on a sob.

Trent's heart skipped a beat. "Is it Halli's sister? Did something happen?"

"No, no, Rachel is fine. It…it is Renzo."

Christ. He didn't have time to console her right now. "Simone, I'm sorry, but I can't talk right now. I'll—"

"No, you do not understand. He—" Her words cut off when a beep indicated another incoming call.

A glance confirmed the first number he'd expected and Trent spoke over Simone when her voice reconnected on the line. "I'll call you back when we're done." The phone beeped again and he clicked over to the other call.

"Stop where you are, Tomlin. Who the fuck is with you?"

"Relax." Trent kept his tone casual, but slowed the boat even more. "I've got the video, he's got the money."

"Where is Halliwell?"

"Safe from you." *Bastard.* "Once you and I conclude our exchange, and Ben and I are a safe distance away, your money will be dropped in a nice tight waterproof bag, and our business will be done."

"That was not our deal."

"You're greedy, I'm suspicious. Anything happens with this first exchange and you can kiss the other half goodbye."

"I warned what would happen if you contacted the authorities."

Trent's pulse jumped but he kept his voice steady. "The man in the other boat has no connection to the law. Don't be too hasty now. It'd be a shame to give up all that cash when it's only a few minutes away."

Trent powered down to an idle. The rental boat bobbed in the water as he waited for the man's greed to gain the upper hand.

"If you attempt to fuck me over—"

"Human life is worth more to me than money, Lapaglia. All I want is Ben."

And revenge for Sean, but right now Halli's family took

precedence.

In the ensuing silence he wished he'd kept his mouth shut. Last thing he needed was to give the guy more leverage.

The phone beeped for an incoming call, but returned to Lapaglia in time for Trent to catch his clipped, "Proceed."

Trent throttled forward and checked the phone. Simone again. Knowing Lapaglia watched him, and unwilling to rouse the man's suspicions even more by answering, he shut the damn thing off and slid it into his pocket.

Chapter 24

Alrigo's anger simmered at a dangerous level as he watched the two boats approach, a good thirty to forty meters apart. Tony had confirmed the driver at the helm of the cabin cruiser was in fact the famous elder Tomlin, but who might lie below the deck still had him uneasy.

All along, Alrigo figured luck played a big part in the past couple days. Now, he understood the Hollywood playboy was smarter than he'd anticipated. To get the money—and Tomlin was right, it was too close for him to say 'fuck it' now—something else was going to have to give.

Nino stood directly to his right. Tony covered Eva; who covered the American at the back of the boat. Eva didn't know she was being watched, but Tony had his orders. Alrigo's gaze flicked back to find her watching him. Same as Benjamin. The ring of a cell phone split the silence and Lapaglia noted all eyes shifted to Nino.

Nino dug the phone from his pocket and turned his back to answer. Alrigo's gaze narrowed at the action. Though Nino's body language said casual, his hushed tone made it obvious he wanted no one to overhear. Not even Alrigo.

Instinct told him something was off. His control strained, but held. Nino's time was coming.

Tomlin's boat drew closer and Alrigo focused on the first order of business. His plan to verify the video and money and then eliminate the Americans and Nino would no longer work with the money on another boat. If he chose revenge, he'd forfeit the money. Unfortunately, the bulk of his savings was tied up in off-shore accounts and he needed this cash to disappear fast. His inside connections hadn't reported hearing so much as a whisper on their side, but that didn't mean Tomlin hadn't managed to contact someone on the right side of the law.

He decided right then to screw the shipment of animals due in tomorrow night; this was over today. Once he had the money in hand, he'd deal with Nino, give Tony a cut, and head into Switzerland with Eva. Or without, depending on her cooperation.

Nino sidled up on his right. "We've got a problem."

Damn right you do.

Trent's boat slowed for final approach.

"Can it wait?"

"Eva's been acting strange," Nino answered, his voice low so it didn't carry. "And the other day, something she said got me to thinking...so I—"

"Get to the point," Alrigo bit out.

"Her real name is Evalina Gallo."

The name slammed into Lapaglia like a sledgehammer. Frank Gallo's daughter. *Fuck.* He was screwed all over again.

****

Ben straightened in his seat as Trent Tomlin's boat drew alongside theirs. Alrigo tossed a rope across to lash the boats together as Ben took stock of the situation. Halli wasn't with Trent, and even at a distance in the evening light he could tell the figure at the helm of the second boat was too big to be his little sister.

Good. He'd worried when Alrigo asked about his sister, but at least some things could still be counted on; like Halli's fear of the unknown. Without a guaranteed outcome, she'd stay far away.

Far away and safe.

"Keep your hands where I can see them," Alrigo ordered Trent in his accented English.

Ben shifted. Somewhat reassured Halli was safe, now he battled mixed feelings about what would go down in the next few minutes. Strangely enough, Eva was his guard, but then he'd noticed the red-faced blond guy, Tony, watching the both of them. His suspicion that she was in danger intensified and he hated the thought of leaving her on the boat with these men.

Nino's phone call and his subsequent whispered conversation with Alrigo didn't help matters. Alrigo had noticeably stiffened as if jolted with electricity.

But what could he do? Halli and Rachel depended on him

to return with Trent. Eva made her own choices, and she'd assured him she could take care of herself, hadn't she?

"Eva."

Alrigo commanded their presence with one word, never taking his eyes off Trent. Ben rose to his feet without any prompting from Eva or Tony.

Trent Tomlin looked rougher than Ben had ever seen him in the movies, even when playing Shain West, the Robin Hood gunslinger of the Wild West. If he didn't know the man was on his side, the murderous glint in his eyes would scare the hell out of him. The intensity of his gaze dimmed a bit when Trent made eye contact with Ben and gave a barely discernable nod.

Alrigo motioned with his fingers. "Show me the video."

Across the small expanse of water between the boats, Trent faced the camera toward Alrigo and pushed play. Ben watched the video Halli had shot of the villa across the bay where they'd parked their first day in Italy. Thirty seconds later Alrigo nodded his acceptance. The Italian had a strange look on his face as Trent stopped the video and hit eject.

Ben's stomach gave an uneasy twinge. If Trent noticed Alrigo's expression, he gave no indication in the gaze that flicked to Ben and back to Alrigo.

"Send him across and I'll toss it over. We leave, you get your money."

Alrigo's hand jerked up in denial with Ben's first step forward. Ben sensed increased tension in Eva's body slightly behind him, and his own edginess multiplied.

It was never that easy, was it?

He held his breath as Alrigo backed up a few steps. Color rose in the man's face and calm disintegrated in an explosion of rage. For the first time, Ben understood the saying, *"he just snapped"*.

Alrigo's arm flung toward Nino. Two muted discharges registered as Eva shoved Ben aside so hard he stumbled against the side of the boat. Alrigo's body jerked violently. Ben surveyed the stunning reality before him, time suspended in slow motion.

Alrigo crumpled to the ground and lay bleeding on the

deck of the rocking boat. Eva and Tony had their guns trained on each other, and Nino bent to retrieve Alrigo's gun.

Eva and Tony yelled at each other in Italian, but Trent's English overrode their words. "Nobody move!"

Ben blinked at the sight of a gun in the movie star's hand.

Movement registered to his right. He swung his head back to the others in time to see Nino's weapon leveling out—straight at *Eva*. His heart stopped. *This is it.*

He didn't think twice; just shouted her name and threw himself in front of her. Another muffled discharge. Pain exploded in his chest. The bottom of the boat rose up to meet him in a dizzying rush.

Muffled popping noises collided and merged with shouts of his name. One sounded far away. Like Halli. He had to be hallucinating. Nothing made sense in the confusion. Darkness crowded the edges of his vision.

Eva's face wavered above him as an excruciating pressure bore down on his chest. He narrowed his focus on her beautiful brown eyes and fought to stay conscious.

****

It was like a scene on a movie set Trent had been on countless times; only none of this had been scripted, and the blood was real.

Halli screamed her brother's name from the *Scappare*. Lapaglia wasn't moving. A grotesque hole in his head said he wouldn't move again. The dark haired man who'd shot Ben slumped on the back bench, face ashen as he gasped for air while blood spread across his gray button down shirt in two different spots.

Halli's scream tore into Trent's heart, but he forced his attention to her brother, trusting his dad to take care of her. He had to make sure Ben was alive. Had to make sure he *stayed* alive. At all costs.

Tony, the blond guard from the coffee house, surged forward at the same time Trent vaulted from his boat to theirs. The vessel rocked, throwing Tony off balance as he reached for the wounded man's gun. Ben groaned as the woman named Eva leaned over him. She had one hand pressed to his chest, the other trained on Tony, gun steady as she shouted in Italian.

Translating her frantic speech proved difficult as Trent debated who posed the most risk to Halli's brother.

"I'm a police officer, Eva, like you," Tony said. He spoke in English and shifted his gaze to Trent. "I'm on your side. It's over. We can all put down our weapons."

The woman named Eva demanded to see a badge. Trent's hand wavered between them, gun still ready. What the hell was going on?

"Trent—call for help," Eva ordered without looking away from Tony as he slowly reached into his pocket. "Have them send medical teams to the dock at Via al Lago off Via Statale."

Ben's head lifted toward Eva. "You're a cop?"

Tony flashed an official looking badge and Eva immediately lowered her gun to focus solely on Ben. "Nino and I were undercover. Alrigo Lapaglia's been under investigation for years."

He dropped his head to the boat with a thud. Groaned as he sucked in a breath. "So many things make sense now."

Slightly stunned by the news he stood in the company of two police officers, Trent reached for his phone, but Tony held one to his ear, already dialed. His own weapon still raised, Tony fixed his pointed gaze on the gun in Trent's hand.

Trent cast a glance at Alrigo's prone body, tucked the gun away in his back waistband, and dropped down next to Eva. "What can I do?"

"Give me your shirt."

Trent stripped off the T-shirt and handed it over. Eva efficiently folded the material into a square and placed it and Trent's hand over where Ben had been shot.

"Keep pressure on it, like this."

Trent leaned his weight onto his hand. Ben's breath rasped between his lips, but he still sounded better than the man Tony tended while he spoke in rapid Italian on the phone. Didn't look better, with the multi-colored bruises on his face, slightly swollen black eye and split lip, but at least he wasn't coughing up blood like the Italian guy.

Staring down at Ben, he knew Halli was probably sick with

worry. As Eva shifted to check on Alrigo, he dug out his phone and turned it on to see he'd missed four calls. All Simone.

Something wasn't right. If Rachel was fine, why did she keep calling him when she knew what was going on right now?

He hesitated, then dialed his father's cell number, programmed into his phone less than an hour ago. As it rang, he noticed Ben's gaze shift to Eva.

"You're okay?" Ben asked in a low, hoarse voice.

"*Si*. Thanks to you."

Relief flashed in Ben's eyes before they closed and his body relaxed.

Eva clasped Ben's hand, leaning closer. "You should not have done that. I am supposed to protect *you*."

Trent's father still hadn't answered. He checked the cell before glancing over his shoulder at the boat. He had service. Had he programmed the number incorrectly? Why wasn't his dad above deck?

"Ben? *Ben.* Stay with me."

Trent jerked back around at the sharp concern in Eva's voice. Ben had yet to respond and Trent's stomach lurched. Had he failed Halli like he'd feared all along?

Eva leaned closer, a sheen of tears in her eyes. "Benjamin?"

Ben's eyelids fluttered and one corner of his mouth tugged up. "Where would I go?"

She smiled until his eyes closed again and he groaned in pain. Eva's mouth trembled before her lips firmed and she glanced around.

"What the hell happened to our backup?" she demanded.

Trent wondered at the connection the two seemed to have formed during Ben's captivity as Tony spoke over his shoulder from where he still attempted to stem the flow of blood from the other man's wounds.

"They're on the way. Nino relayed the wrong coordinates."

"Warned you not to trust him," Ben whispered as Trent hit 'send' again to try to reach his father and Halli.

"I know." Eva watched Tony for a moment but made no move to help. "How's my partner?"

"Not good." Tony shook his head, helpless frustration evident. "You *stupid* son-of-a-bitch."

Blood from Nino's wounds spread in ever-widening stains on his shirt. Gurgling noises came from between his red-stained lips.

"Drive us to shore if you can't do anything for him," Eva ordered.

Clearly she didn't intend to leave Ben's side again. Unease over his second unanswered call collided with a sudden spurt of anger inside Trent.

"How the hell did we get to *this* with three undercover cops in the mix?"

"We were one shipment away from an arrest when Lorenzo Roselli was shot," Eva said. "Your video would have put Lapaglia away for life, but the only way to make sure it didn't fall into the wrong hands in the system and disappear was to go through with this exchange."

Trent caught Tony's eye when he glanced back. He appeared mostly recovered from the espresso incident. "She didn't know about you," he said to the blond man. "Where do you fit in?"

"I'm with Europol. I was investigating two Lenno officers in the smuggling case when Nino and Eva showed up about a year ago. Nino's activities and a few questionable ties to the mafia required further scrutiny, so they left me in place."

Eva combed the fingers of her free hand through Ben's hair as she asked Tony, "Got any idea why my partner tried to kill me?"

Nino's bloody hand grasped the side rail in an attempt to pull himself up. Trent just barely made out the Italian's words as he tried to speak.

"Sorry…the money…Roselli…"

Trent's brows drew together. What did Lorenzo have to do with the money?

Beside him, Eva drew in a sudden breath. Trent turned to see her staring down at Ben.

"Roselli's not dead," she murmured.

"Not dead," Nino confirmed.

Trent looked back to Nino. A cough spewed red droplets from his mouth, further staining his shirt and arms. Tony leaned back to avoid the spray of blood.

Disbelief rippled through Trent. "Of course he's dead. I saw him get shot—it's on the video. His *body* was found in my pool!"

"Alrigo has connections to get that story out without it being true," Tony reminded. "He wanted to put more pressure on you with *all* the police looking for you, not just the ones on his payroll."

"He was shot three times," Trent insisted, even as Simone's numerous calls slammed into his conscious.

"I saw it, too," Tony said.

"Bullet pr-proof vest." Nino choked and coughed. "Wants...money."

A bullet proof vest? Trent's mind whirled. Lorenzo had showed up to their meeting that morning already wired. They'd discussed the plan and Lorenzo went in, so it was possible he'd worn a vest under his shirt and jacket.

Rachel told Halli Simone looked like she'd seen a ghost.

Simone was sorry... *"should've told you earlier"*...

Lorenzo's not dead.

Amazed relief came and went in a flash. The money didn't make sense. The ransom demand hadn't factored in until *after* Lorenzo had been shot. He couldn't have known Halli would video the shooting, or that Alrigo would hold her family hostage and demand cash for their release.

Unless... A whisper of his earlier suspicions tried to make itself heard through the confusion.

Blindly, Trent replaced his hand on Ben's chest with Eva's. He surged to his feet and moved to shoulder Tony aside.

"How did Lorenzo know about the money before he was shot?" he asked Nino. "Was he working with Lapaglia?"

Were they all?

It took a moment before the man could speak. When he did, his words were punctuated with weak, gurgling coughs and shallow, gasping breaths for air. "Planned to...sell you evidence...your brother's murder...but ...Alrigo shot

Roselli...fucked up the plan...ransom... became a perfect opportun..."

Trent let out a shaky breath. Halli and her family *weren't* part of the plot.

With his next breath, Lorenzo's obvious betrayal hit. A split second later, gut-clenching fear bulldozed all else.

Lorenzo wanted the money. Money that was still on his boat, with Halli, and *no one was answering the phone.*

He grasped Nino's shoulders. "How did he plan to get the money?"

"After...I—"

Nino's face contorted and his body spasmed. The man was dying right in front of him. Trent's fingers clenched, as if he could keep him alive by sheer will.

"Does he know where we are?"

Nino struggled for air, his eyes wide, panicked. Trent gave him a desperate, violent shake.

Tony's hand clamped on Trent's arm. "Take it easy."

He released Nino as the distant sound of sirens reached across the water. Flashing lights approached the shore of Lake Como beyond Isola Comacina.

"We must go," Eva said.

Trent forced himself to pause by Ben as Tony brushed past on his way to the controls. "Halli's on the other boat. I'll get her and—"

"You brought her along?"

Trent bristled at the accusation in Ben's voice. "She refused to stay behind."

"*Halli?*"

"Yes, *Halli*. She's very stubborn. We'll meet you on shore."

He unwound the rope connecting his rental to Lapaglia's boat and tossed it ahead of him. Unrelenting urgency propelled him into the other boat in one leap. He didn't look back as he started the engine and opened up the throttle. Ben was in good hands with Eva, and there was nothing he could do that she wouldn't do anyway.

Halfway to the *Scappare* and closing, his phone rang. He

almost lost the damn thing over the side in his haste to answer. "Halli?"

"Trent—Lorenzo's alive!"

Simone. "He called you this morning, didn't he?"

"Yes. I was so scared. I still am."

Trent wanted to believe the tremor that shook her words, but too much had happened for him to trust anything right now. "What the hell is going on, Simone?"

"I don't know. He said something about finally getting his boat and told me to pack a bag and be ready. I told him I would not go anywhere with him unless he told me what was going on, but he became angry and hung up."

Trent was nearing the cabin cruiser by now. Going against every instinct screaming in his body to thrust the throttle forward, he eased it back for a slow approach. "Does he know Rachel's with you?"

"No. We moved to a neighbor's house for safety."

"Good." Now he trusted her. "Simone, I gotta go, but stay where you are, okay? Don't go home until I call you."

"*Si.*"

He slid the phone back in his pocket and eased alongside the cruiser. All was quiet aboard the *Scappare*. Too quiet. A leaden sensation of dread grew in his chest when neither Halli nor his dad hailed him over the side.

Without regard for the rental, he scrambled aboard his boat. His gaze locked on a smaller metallic blue vessel speeding toward the middle of the lake some twenty yards out at the same time overwhelming gas fumes assaulted his nostrils. Icy slivers of fear froze the blood in his veins. Gut instinct screamed for him to follow the boat but a low groan whipped him around.

His father stumbled up the steps from below deck. Blood trickled down along the side of his nose from a gash on his forehead. He waved wildly when he saw Trent, hollering as he lost his balance and fell to his knees.

Trent's cell rang as he rushed forward. "Dad, where's Halli?"

Greg Tomlin shook his head, surged to his feet and

wrapped his arms around Trent. With a burst of unexpected strength, he drove them toward the side of the *Scappare*. Trent couldn't combat the surprise momentum that propelled them over the railing into the water.

A deafening boom concussed his eardrums as the lake closed over his head. He fought his way to the surface and stared in stunned disbelief at the burning wreckage that seconds earlier had been his boat. Flaming pieces rained down around his head.

Halli!

The magnitude of what'd just happened rocked him to the core. Anguish made it impossible to breathe. *Oh, God...Halli.*

A desperate gasping sound broke through his shock. His father thrashed behind him, struggling to stay afloat. Two powerful strokes brought them together and Trent held his father's head above water with an arm across his chest. He swam for the rental that'd floated far enough away, relatively undamaged from the explosion.

Trent secured his father's grip on the boat and ruthlessly suppressed the crippling emotions coursing through his body. Blame. Guilt. Grief. Grabbing the side, he heaved himself up into the boat. A jagged gouge in the metal railing raked down his bare chest and stomach. Blood welled from the torn flesh as he turned to drag his father aboard, but he felt nothing.

The moment he fell into the boat, his father's rough voice commanded, "Go, go! We have to catch them."

Grief and rage collided inside Trent. "I don't care about the money!"

His father frowned with his usual disapproval. "They've got Halli."

Trent froze. He didn't dare trust the flare of hope that suddenly burned in his chest. "You mean she wasn't...?" He couldn't even say it.

"*No*—they took her with the money."

An instant flashback of the little speed boat left him dizzy. He shook it off and lunged for the driver's seat. Fighting for every second, he started the rental and throttled to full speed the moment they cleared the sinking remains of the *Scappare*.

His father joined him at the windshield and they both searched frantically for the blue speed boat. Trent's heart raced unbearably fast. The roaring wind stung his eyes as he prayed they wouldn't be too late.

Chapter 25

Halli watched the *Scappare* grow smaller and smaller, yet across the bow, she saw Trent's rental boat approach the cruiser. She debated standing to wave her arms, but the gun pointed at her chest was a compelling deterrent. With her heart pounding in her chest, she slid her hand into her pocket and pressed the send button on Greg Tomlin's phone. Then she prayed Trent would figure out what was going on.

Lorenzo Roselli, the man Trent had described as a friend, also noticed Trent's approach and spoke in Italian to the driver. Luca. Halli didn't think it was a coincidence *Luca* was also the name of the *Carabinieri* officer Simone had recommended. She couldn't believe the woman was in on this whole scam, just like Lorenzo. Worry ate her up inside for Rachel at the same time indignation simmered on Trent's behalf.

Luca glanced back with a smug smirk. Halli quickly pulled her hand from her pocket before either of them saw what she was doing, but Lorenzo caught the sudden movement and frowned.

"Where are we going?" she shouted above the wind and whine of the motor.

Please, God, let him hear me.

"Do as you're told and you'll be fine." Lorenzo's fluent English and mildly comforting tone was contradicted by Luca's stone-cold expression.

"Why are you doing this? Trent considered you a friend."

Guilt crossed Lorenzo's face, but it was Luca who answered. "The man has more money than he knows what to do with, while we work and serve…for what? We barely make enough to survive, let alone retire with. Believe me, *carina*, Renzo's friend will not miss a measly million."

It always boiled down to the money, didn't it? God, she hated it. She drew a huge breath, set her jaw, and went over the facts in her mind. Rachel lay injured, in the hands of a conspirator. By all appearances, Ben had been shot, and she had no clue if he was alive or dead. Trent had no clue she was on this boat, and they were drawing farther and farther from sight.

Despair threatened, but she beat it back. Trent might not see her yet, but she trusted him to come after—

A sudden explosion from the *Scappare* eclipsed the brilliance of the setting sun. Trent's cabin cruiser erupted into a ball of fire topped by black smoke. Halli gasped in shock as the sound of the destruction echoed across the water.

Her hand flew to her mouth. *Trent!*

Tears blurred her vision and were instantly whipped away by the wind. The sight of him, even from a distance, had given her strength to not give up. In the blink of an eye, the last visible sure thing that mattered to her in this world was gone.

Lorenzo gaped at the inferno before shouting at Luca in Italian. The man shrugged and laughed. The sadistic sound registered through the hopeless haze Halli had descended into.

Lorenzo spoke again and Luca glanced in her direction. He slowed the boat some, his mouth going tight with obvious anger as he faced forward again. Lorenzo continued to gesture heatedly between the fire and Luca.

A sudden realization pounded through Halli. She was one hundred percent, completely on her own.

Every other emotion was filed away to deal with later as survival mode kicked into gear. She'd been fending for herself for years, but never in such an extreme life and death situation. Before now, the thought would've scared her senseless. It still did, but each passing second solidified her determination that these men would not win. If it was the last thing she did, in any way possible, she'd make them pay for all they'd stolen from everyone.

While Lorenzo was distracted arguing with Luca, Halli lunged for the money. The moment her fingers closed around the handles of the duffle, she pivoted, swinging the bag in a wide arc. Lorenzo raised a hand to deflect the blow and his gun flew from his grasp. Luca's jerk on the steering wheel took them out of the path of an oncoming boat, and Lorenzo toppled over the side with the bag.

Luca erupted in Italian and wrenched the boat around. Halli lost her own footing and slammed up against the motor before sliding down. Pain lanced through her back, stealing her breath. She shook her head to clear a multitude of sparkling stars.

Get up. Get up!

She braced a palm for leverage. Something hard bit into her flesh. Instead of the rough, water-tolerant carpeting of the boat's floor, she encountered the cool steel of Lorenzo's gun.

Halli shot a glance at Luca. She fumbled for the grip as he stretched his arm back toward her. Time distended. She stared into the deadly eye of his pistol, prayed that her family would at least be saved, and finally located the handle of the gun beneath her hand.

A deafening roar filled her ears. Luca's aim waivered as he glanced toward the noise, then did a double take. Halli raised her gun, finger curled around the trigger.

One second of moral hesitation after she aimed resulted in a large body leaping between her and her target.

Shock jerked the gun skyward before she squeezed the trigger. The kick of the gun vibrated violently through her arms, but she hardly noticed as Trent wrestled with Luca for his weapon.

He's alive!

She struggled to her feet. Trent's shoulder hit the steering wheel, making the boat veer sharply to the left. The gun in Halli's hand flew overboard when she was thrown back to the floor.

The boat's throttle remained at half-speed without a driver as the two men fought. Halli pulled herself back up and climbed over Trent and Luca to the controls. She swerved to avoid a police vessel and quickly brought their boat to a stop.

As suddenly as everything had begun four days earlier when Trent threw her into his car, it was all over.

Trent—shirtless—kept Luca subdued until the blond man from the café at the consulate who introduced himself as *Agente* Tony Butelli boarded the boat. Tony handcuffed Luca and transferred him to the police vessel. Lorenzo sat wet and brooding under the watchful eye of another officer, and Greg

Tomlin stood at the helm of Trent's rental boat.

Still completely stunned, with residual adrenalin seeping from her muscles, Halli hadn't looked at Trent yet. At his face. Was afraid if she did she'd fall apart. They were the only two left on their boat. The weight of his hand fell on her shoulder and her entire body trembled. Even her knees wobbled. A soft squeeze of his fingers released the choked sob caught in her throat.

When he turned her around, the first thing she saw was the bloody gash down the length of his bare chest. He pulled her into his arms, his hold so tight she could barely breathe. But she didn't care. He was so warm; she was chilled to the bone. She forgot about the blood and didn't say a word until moments later, when he framed her face with his hands and ran his gaze over her.

"Are you okay?"

Moisture in his eyes deepened the ache in her chest. Tears ran unchecked down her cheeks. "I almost shot you."

"I'm glad you didn't."

"I thought you were dead," she whispered. "The boat blew up."

His eyes told her he'd thought the same about her. Then his lips captured hers in a rough, consuming kiss full of desperation, fear, and relief. Numbed, she sought to absorb as much of his heat as possible. Salt from her tears mixed with the kiss, coating her lips and her tongue.

The enormity of everything began to sink in; how close she'd come to shooting a man, how close she'd come to losing Trent, how close she'd come to her own death.

She broke the kiss, buried her face in his neck, and hung on for dear life. She was probably strangling him, but letting go wasn't quite possible at the moment.

From one of the other boats, someone cleared their throat. "I'm sorry, but we must return."

Trent drew in a breath, his chest expanding against hers. He reached up and gently removed her arms since she couldn't seem to do it herself. After a soft kiss and a shaky grin, he shifted around her to the helm.

"What do you say we go see your brother?"

Unwilling to lose contact, Halli anchored one hand against his back and pressed close as Trent started the boat and Tony joined them on board. She watched the blond man, still a bit dazed to realize he was an undercover agent. "Is Ben...?"

"Eva—Officer Gallo—called a few minutes ago from the *ospedale* in Menaggio," Tony said. "Your brother is in surgery to remove the bullet, but the doctor did not foresee any problems. He should be fine."

Halli's relief was short-lived when another bit of information bobbed to the surface of her mind. "Oh, my God, Trent, Rachel is still with Simone! She—"

"Moved Rachel to a friend's house after Lorenzo called her this morning."

"But ...Luca is Lorenzo's cousin Simone mentioned...isn't she in on it?"

Trent shook his head and explained how Simone got scared after Lorenzo's call that morning, so she and Rachel left the house, and then she tried to call in the afternoon to warn them.

"I can send someone to pick up your sister and meet us at the hospital," Tony offered.

The tears on Halli's face dried in the wind as Trent followed the other boats. By the time they reached land and were transported to the hospital, she'd talked to her sister, arrangements had been set in motion, and Rachel was on her way to Menaggio by police escort.

Halli tried to relax, tried to convince herself it was truly over, but until she saw them both for herself, she couldn't quite believe it. Trent remained by her side; Greg Tomlin in the background. Though she knew she should start to distance herself and prepare for when they went their separate ways, she couldn't help leaning on Trent's strength.

At the hospital, when told Ben's surgery went well and he'd been transferred to recovery, she sagged in Trent's arms with relief. The doctor then took one look at Trent and his father and insisted they all get treated while waiting for her brother to wake up. Greg was ushered into one room, but Trent insisted he and Halli stay together.

The shock of everything that'd happened began to fade. She could breathe again. Rationalize. Take stock of the situation and figure out where to go from here.

The female doctor who gave them their physicals spent twice as much time examining Trent. Halli moved to the window, out of the way. Given the obvious physical injuries he'd endured, the attention didn't strike Halli as strange until she noticed the doctor had three attractive, earnest female assistants to help bandage his chest and check his injured arm. Two other nurses bustled in to stock the already overflowing medical cabinet.

Trent offered appreciation to each one with that famous smile of his, and Halli found herself fighting a wry grin as she crossed her arms over her chest. He requested a shirt of some sort, and the doctor spoke in Italian to one of the nurses. The woman, at least twice Halli's age, nodded, but Halli saw a look of comical regret pass between her and one of the other assistants.

In a brief moment alone, Halli shook her head in mock disapproval at Trent. "You just dashed the fantasies of all the women on this floor."

He twisted around on the edge of the hospital bed, wearing both a frown and smile. "What?"

"Oh, please. Like you didn't notice them all coming in for a peek at you without your shirt? Clearly, word spreads just as fast in Italian."

Surprisingly, a hint of color stained his cheeks. He pushed off the bed and came around to where she'd leaned her butt against the windowsill. Her heartbeat picked up. One corner of his mouth twitched, though the look in his hazel gaze remained serious.

"Does it bother you?"

Truthfully, she was amused *and* jealous. But it was time for that distance she was going to need. She pasted a smile on her face and gave him a careless shrug.

"Why should it? It's not like I have any claim on your body."

A firm bite on her tongue kept the hopeful, pathetic *"...do*

I?" off the end. He might be acting protective and caring since the rescue, but *acting* was the key word. He'd made things pretty clear back on the boat prior to the exchange.

Something akin to disappointment flashed in his eyes. He lifted one hand toward her. "Halli—"

"Ms. Sanders?"

Trent stepped back as if he'd been caught doing something he shouldn't. Halli straightened, giving him one quick glance before focusing on the figures in the doorway. Greg Tomlin waited behind the doctor.

"Yes?"

"Your brother is awake. He is asking for you."

Sensing Trent had been about to say something important, she hesitated. He placed a hand on the small of her back, urging her forward. She ignored her disappointment and followed the doctor.

"Everything went okay?" Halli asked as they walked.

"*Si,*" the doctor assured her.

A nurse hurried up to Trent and offered a blue scrub shirt. He accepted with a quiet, "*Grazie.*"

"Barring no complications," the doctor continued, "he will be discharged the day after tomorrow."

Wow. Trent's hand landed on her shoulder, halting her progress just before they turned a corner. He nodded toward the opposite hall. Walking toward them, pushing a wheel chair, was Simone with Rachel.

Halli gave a soft exclamation and rushed forward to hug her sister. A moment later, she pulled back, wiping her tears with one hand and Rachel's with the other. "You're just in time. We're headed to Ben's room. He's okay."

Rachel sniffed. "I was so afraid I'd never see either of you again."

Too choked up to speak, Halli answered with another brief squeeze before standing. She smiled at Simone and motioned them ahead of her. Once at Ben's room, the doctor told them he'd give them a few minutes, and Simone wheeled Rachel in first. Halli hung back at the door. More tears welled as Rachel grasped their brother's hand and leaned over to press her cheek to his. She wished she could figure out a way to turn off the faucets.

"What are you waiting for?"

She jumped at Trent's deep voice in her ear. Swallowing hard, she managed to blink the tears away and tried to think of an answer that would make sense. All she came up with was a befuddled shrug.

"Your family is safe, Halli." Trent gave her a one armed hug and a reassuring smile. "You can finally go home."

Home.

The word she'd been praying to hear for what seemed like forever, and yet, even in his low, gruff voice, it sounded sad and empty. Not what she wanted at all, if it meant leaving him. But she had no choice.

She took a deep breath and nodded. Squared her shoulders and forced herself to step away from his support.

At the hospital bed next to Rachel, she leaned over to give Ben a careful hug and kiss. Seeing his bruised face up close made her chest ache, but Trent was right, he was safe. Ben looked from her to Rachel as she straightened.

"Some vacation, huh?" His half-smile was tired, but no less cocky than usual.

"Well, I spread my wings, but I lost a whole lot of feathers."

The three of them laughed together. At least one part of her world was right again. She couldn't help but look at Trent where he stood on the other side of the bed with Simone. They'd both played a big part in this reunion.

Ben followed Halli's gaze and smiled toward Trent. "Thank you hardly seems adequate."

Trent's gaze landed on Halli. "No thanks necessary."

God, the look in his eyes made it hard to remember they had no future together. She averted her gaze to Simone, hoping to keep her heart firmly entrenched in reality. Ben hadn't met Simone, so she made the introduction and explained her connection.

A brisk knock on the door drew everyone's attention. Greg Tomlin stepped aside and Halli surveyed the beautiful, petite

Italian woman who entered the room. Waist length curls matched a black T-shirt stretched across her well-endowed chest, serviceable kakis hugged her hips, and to round out the ensemble…a gold badge on one side of her belt, pistol on the other.

The sight of the gun sent an instant surge of alarm through Halli. She drew in a calming breath, reminding herself the bad guys were behind bars and she could trust *la polizia*. It helped that the woman wore an aura of authority as if she'd been born with it, and introduced herself as *Agente* Evalina Gallo.

Ben's tired eyes sparked with clear male interest. He attempted to push himself up a little straighter and Halli smiled to herself. Leave it to her brother to not let a little thing like surgery from a gunshot wound cramp his style. The woman nodded at Trent in a way that made Halli wonder if they knew each other.

Rachel smiled at the newcomer. "I knew you were nice."

The Italian's brows rose in an elegant arch. "Too nice, apparently. You two almost blew my cover."

Ah ha. Sultry-voiced *Agente* Gallo must be the undercover cop *Eva* Tony had mentioned earlier. Ben's reaction made a little more sense, but the last thing she expected was for the police officer to step right up, prop a hip on the bed, and glare at her brother.

"Especially you. More trouble than you are worth, and still kicking."

Ben grinned. "Does me no good to be dead when you change your mind about dinner, does it?"

Ebony curls swept along her back as she shook her head. "Cocky and stubborn."

"When it matters."

Another glance at Trent confirmed he recognized the déjàvu moment. More than anything, Halli wanted to be back in his arms, but she forced her gaze away. Ben slowly reached out to thread his fingers with Evalina's.

"Come on, Eva, one little, innocent dinner won't kill you."

"Innocent? You?"

"You'll be in complete control. Promise."

A secret smile touched the Italian woman's lips. Unspoken communication passed between the two of them. Belying her confident aura, color rose in Evalina's face and Ben's grin widened. Just as Halli began to feel like the rest of them were intruding on something intimate, Evalina blinked and abruptly stood with a haughty shrug. "One dinner."

"Thank you," Ben said softly.

She was all business as she turned from the bed. "My office requires statements from each of you. I can speak with you two here," she indicated Halli and Rachel, "but Mr. Tomlin and Ms. Costa, you will be required to come to the station."

"How's your partner?" Trent asked.

"Dead." The word was delivered short and hard, but the emotion in her dark eyes told him the betrayal hurt her as much as Lorenzo's hurt him.

He glanced at Simone before he asked, "Did you talk to Lorenzo yet?"

Evalina gave a brisk nod. "He was very forthcoming. He got himself into trouble a few years ago with a bad bet and it multiplied from there. Cousin Luca is his bookie, and Nino was married to Luca's sister. Once they found out you and Lorenzo were friends, it did not take much to convince Lorenzo you were a quick fix to his problems."

Trent's jaw flexed. "They were going to sell me proof that Alrigo murdered my brother."

"Yes. Only Alrigo shot Lorenzo before they could get their evidence and execute the plan. Nino 'took care of the body', and Alrigo made it harder for you to hide by having his connections publically implicate you in the 'murder'. With Ben in play, Nino manipulated the situation by suggesting Alrigo demand ransom." Her gaze shifted between Trent and Greg. "You should know, in light of this new evidence, Sean Tomlin's death will be completely reinvestigated."

"Thank you."

Halli felt the relief for Trent that she heard in his words. Alrigo Lapaglia was already dead, but now he'd get public justice for his brother.

The surgeon returned and insisted Ben be left alone to get

some rest. Rachel was escorted to a nearby room to have her leg formally checked, and Evalina suggested it was a good time for Halli to give her statement. Trent squeezed her shoulder on his way out the door after his father. She followed his gaze to Tony, who waited at the doors to take Trent in.

"You okay?" Trent asked.

She automatically stiffened her spine. "Of course."

"Looks like another long night."

To prove she could be as casual as he had been on the boat, she quipped, "And nowhere near as fun as last night."

He didn't laugh as she'd thought he would. He stepped closer and spoke low. "What I said earlier—"

She quickly shook her head and stepped back, holding up a hand. "Please, you don't have to explain. I get it."

His steady scrutiny made her pulse flutter. "Do you?"

"Yes," she insisted. "And I agree with you, let's not make a big deal out of it. I have to go, and they're waiting for you."

Annoyance passed over his features. "Halli, we need to talk."

"Tomorrow." She quickly spun to follow Evalina to an empty room the hospital had provided.

"You never gave me an answer about dinner," he called after her.

Halli felt the eyes of numerous nurses and hospital staff zero in on her as she reached the makeshift interview room. She almost said yes, just to appease him, even though she knew she wouldn't actually follow through. A simple no would be better, but it was too public. In the end, she stepped inside the room and closed the door without answering at all.

Fatigue dragged her feet when the interview concluded and Evalina walked her back to Ben's room. They'd set up a second bed for Rachel and a cot for Halli. Rachel was sound asleep, but Ben opened his eyes and watched them enter.

With a quiet goodnight, Halli went straight to the cot. She dragged the blanket to her chin and wearily fought against thoughts of last night with Trent, only to have the worry of how they'd pay for Ben's surgery and the hospital stay drop into her mind like a grenade. She bit back a groan of dismay.

In the middle of struggling to remember how much she had between her savings and her 401k retirement fund, exhaustion won the battle and her mind shut down.

****

The next day, with her luggage and personal items returned from their rental car, and refreshed after a hot shower, Halli was desperate for fresh air and a cup of caffeine that wasn't tar-black and bitter as plain baking cocoa.

Earlier, she'd managed the detail of rebooking their flights, but when she inquired about a payment plan for all the medical services, the doctor told her not to worry. Easy for him to say. To her frustration, he avoided any further direct answers, stating he had patients to tend.

As if she could argue that. Instead of dwelling on the problem and driving herself crazy as she knew she was prone to do, she escaped. Armed with directions from *Agente* Gallo, or Evalina as she'd insisted, Halli located an almost-perfect cup of coffee a couple blocks from the hospital. She sipped the steaming brew on her way back, thinking nothing would ever compare to the cup of coffee she'd shared with Trent that first morning on his boat.

This past week had been life changing in so many ways. People passed her on the street, smiled and greeted her, and she began to wonder if she looked any different. She felt different on the inside, but did a person *look* different after the crazy week she'd survived?

She thought of the man who'd been beside her every step of the way.

Did a person look different after they fell in love?

In the light of day, she allowed an objective look, so as not to be swayed by delicious, seductive memories in the dark. The Trent she knew, the man she'd fallen head-over-heels for, was so different from the persona he presented to the media. Her heart wanted to believe they'd had a connection, and that he'd felt it, too. That she hadn't misread the concern and caring she'd seen in his eyes.

Her practical side, *Wisconsin* Halli, told her anything she might have imagined between them was nothing more than an illusion. Wishful thinking by a gullible, lonely heart. Just because he said he wanted to talk in that serious tone and asked her to dinner, didn't mean they'd have a happily ever after like in the movies. Shain never stayed with any of his leading ladies.

Yes, Trent had proved to be a genuinely nice guy. But he'd have helped anyone in the same situation. She was no one special.

Early afternoon sunshine warmed her bare arms. She only wished its heat could seep in and melt the chill taking over her heart. A hopeless endeavor, but her steps slowed anyway since she was in no hurry to go back inside.

A crowd had gathered at the visitor's entrance to the hospital, so she bypassed the main doors to see what the low hum of excitement was all about. Her feet rooted to the spot when she saw Trent standing on the steps alongside a podium with a microphone, with *Agente* Tony Butelli and two other men dressed in business suits.

She'd watched enough press conferences on TV to understand the drill, even though one of the suits spoke in Italian and she didn't understand a word. Most likely the world was being advised that international movie star Trent Tomlin had cooperated with police and been cleared of all suspicion in any ongoing cases with the Italian police.

Her gaze focused on Trent like the zoom lens of the paparazzi. Sunlight glinted off his dark hair, reminding her of that morning on the bridge in the Villa Melzi gardens. And yet, the difference was like night and day.

For the first time since she'd met him face to face, the line of his jaw was clean shaven. Despite the distance, the radiance of his smile flashed brighter than the multitude of cameras snapping his picture. It even eclipsed the sun. There stood the man she'd seen countless times in the magazines and on the movie screen, not the man who'd saved her, protected her, made love to her.

She lifted her hand for a sip of coffee, hiding behind her cup as a hard truth registered with the brutality of a bullet straight to her heart. *This* man was way out of her league…and he didn't look any different for having met her.

Against her will, her feet carried her closer. The Italian man in the suit finished speaking and turned the microphone over to Trent. He fielded a dozen shouted questions, diplomatically working his way through each one. Effortless charm had the crowd of reporters eating out of his hand. After thanking the police for reopening his brother's case, he proceeded to make light of the last few terrifying days.

Anxiety rose as Halli waited for him to say her name, but he didn't mention her at all. The omission sparked mixed emotions. Though she didn't relish the idea of the inevitable attention, it hurt he could so easily remove her from the events they'd endured together.

When he jokingly requested recommendations where to order a bigger, better boat, Halli backed away and headed for the hospital's main entrance. The only greater illustration of the vast ocean that separated their lives was the immense waters of the Atlantic, and soon enough, it too would lie between them.

"What can you tell us about the woman who arrived at the hospital with you yesterday?"

Halli's step faltered. She didn't dare turn around. She thought it took him an extraordinary amount of time to answer, until she realized counting the beats of a racing heart was not an accurate measurement of time.

"Nothing, really," he said. "She was a tourist in the wrong place at the wrong time. I barely even know her."

Halli closed her eyes against the breath-stealing stab of pain. *Well, what'd you expect? That he'd declare his undying love in front of the whole world? Get real.* Trent Tomlin didn't fall in love, and if he did, her practical side reminded, it wouldn't be with someone like her.

"Sources say you invited her to dinner," a female voice called out.

"Did your sources tell you her answer?" Trent shot back.

"She didn't give one," the reporter said.

"Guess I'm losing my touch, then, aren't I?"

The crowd laughed, but it was Trent's chuckle that mocked her all the way back to Ben's room.

Chapter 26

Trent curbed his impatience as long as possible before shooting his publicity manager a warning look. He understood the need for the press conference given the news that had been circulating the globe the past few days, but reporters were reporters no matter what country they called home. Like starving bloodhounds, they smelled a story in Halli and hungered for any bit of gossip they could splash across the headlines.

No way. She'd been through enough without them tearing her and her family to shreds. With barely two hours sleep, he'd been on edge thinking about talking to her. His future hinged on her answers to some pretty big questions, but last night he'd sensed a change. A distance between them he worried had already been given too much time to grow.

Jerry's ambush here on the steps was icing on the cake. If it weren't for the international press in front of them, he'd consider strangling the short, media genius right now. Ignore the fact that the guy was doing what Trent paid him lots of money to do, wrap his hands around his skinny little neck, and—

Finally he shouldered Trent away from the microphone, his strong voice and expensive suit lending an air of authority that his diminutive stature otherwise would not have commanded. "Sorry folks, that's all we've got time for. Thank you."

Trent gladly escaped the resulting volley of hastily shouted questions. Inside the hospital, his publicist started toward a secluded corner. "I have two interviews set up for three o'clock, and then—"

"No." Trent kept walking straight ahead.

Jerry changed direction, sputtering and arguing about damage control all the way to the elevator. Trent tuned him out.

On the second floor, he stepped from the elevator to see Halli walking down the hall toward Ben's room. His stomach rolled with nervous anticipation. When he said her name, she turned at the same moment his publicist grabbed his arm. Trent glanced down to see him frowning at Halli.

"Is that her?"

"Don't worry about it."

Jerry tried to hold him back, but didn't bother to lower his voice. "She's not exactly your type. Is there something going on I should know about?"

"No." Annoyance forced the word out louder than Trent intended. Halli spun on her heel and he bit out his next warning in a rough undertone, "It's none of your damn business. Back off."

More sputtering from his manager, but he clenched his jaw to contain a string of emphatic curses and rushed to catch Halli just before she entered Ben and Rachel's room. "Hey."

Good—he didn't sound desperate at all.

She drew up short, hesitated, then turned to face him. "Hey. Good morning. Or should I say afternoon?"

Her smile and expression were completely composed, her tone friendly and carefree. He didn't buy it. Especially when she refused to lift her gaze higher than his chest.

"We need to talk."

"Sorry, Trent, but I've got a ton of things to do before we head back to Wisconsin. Ben's staying a few extra days, but Rachel and I are booked for tomorrow morning."

"You're leaving?" Dumb question; she'd said all along she was heading straight home, and still the news hit with more impact than his boat exploding before his eyes.

"Well, yeah, what else am I going to do?"

"Stay. I can show you around...salvage some of your vacation." He tried a teasing reminder of when they'd met. "You know, that quick spin around the lake? They'll never know you were gone, sugar."

Her laugh was as brittle as her smile. "Thanks for the offer, but I already changed our flights."

"So change 'em back."

She shook her head, fingers knotted together as she stared down at them. "I can't."

Growing dread took the form of anger. "Can't or don't want to?"

Clearly uncomfortable, she just shook her head. A glance to the side brought the realization they were the main attraction there in the hall. *Damn.* This lovely scene would get out just like the doomed dinner invitation.

He took her arm as a flash registered in the corner of his eye. Halli jerked, eyes wide with surprise. This time Trent let the curses flow under his breath and ushered her into her family's room before the reporter who'd made it past security could snap another money-making picture. He slammed the door and yanked the blinds to shut out the world.

"Sorry." Trent's apology was as much for her as for disturbing Ben and Rachel, but when he turned to face Halli, he saw the room was empty save for the two of them. She'd leaned back against the window sill, arms crossed over her chest, chin raised at that angle that told him he was in for an argument.

Shit. Where the hell had this wall of hers come from? Completely invisible; totally impenetrable, but there nonetheless. Good thing he could be just as stubborn. She wasn't immune to the connection they'd shared, and he felt no remorse using it against her now.

He stalked forward, careful to hold back his frustration. Her eyes widened a little, otherwise she remained perfectly still when he braced a hand on either side of her hips.

"Where's the woman who lived life in the moment?" He leaned closer, searching for any crack in her composure, but the move backfired when her fresh scent played havoc with his senses. His next words came out in a gruff whisper. "The one who not only stood by me through danger, but screamed my name as we made love?"

Color flooded her face. "You want Italy Halli," she accused.

"What's wrong with that?"

She shook her head with a husky laugh. "She was a fluke. An accident, like the video and everything else that happened. Once I go back to Wisconsin, I'm just me again. You'd be bored in no time."

Her mouth snapped shut as if she'd said too much. A spark of hope ignited, but she suddenly shoved against his chest. He reluctantly gave her some space and watched her move to the other side of the room. The urge to haul her into his arms was squelched between clenched fists.

"You could never bore me, Halli."

She sighed, then surprised him by turning to meet his gaze directly. "Please don't make more of this than what it was. I mean, it was fun, but none of it was real. You of all people should know that."

His hope flickered in the cold draft left by her words. "Why don't you enlighten me as to exactly what *it* was?"

"Two people in a desperate situation trying to survive."

It was a hell of a lot more than that to him, but her stripped explanation undermined his natural confidence. The lead ball in his stomach grew heavier. He'd never worried about rejection before today, and the utter vulnerability caught him off-guard.

Self-preservation kicked in. He searched in vain for his character. The go-to guy without emotion. He'd gotten the job done; it was time to cut his losses and move on. *Where the hell had that guy gone?*

Somehow, he pulled a cocky half-smile out of the air. "Are we talking about sex again?"

If sadness tinged her smile, he figured it was wishful thinking on his part.

"As you pointed out on the boat, things happen in stressful circumstances, things we both know were never meant to be. There's no blame, no obligation, nothing to worry about."

Such great lines. She'd just handed him a graceful exit from a sticky situation. He didn't want out...but clearly, she did. He finally located his character and headed for the door where she stood.

"So...this is it? You go back to producing television shows and I go back to making movies?" His hand rested on the door handle as he waited for her to look up. When she did, the misery in her eyes made his heart stutter.

Until she said, "I'll always be grateful for what you did for us."

Grateful. If that didn't say it all.

Trent didn't think. Didn't give himself a chance to second-guess the wisdom of grasping her arms, hauling her up on her tiptoes, and crushing her mouth with his. Her gasp of surprise was muffled by his lips. He seized the opportunity to deepen the kiss, desperate to memorize her addicting taste; her intoxicating scent; the heaven of her soft skin.

One last kiss, one last imprint, and he'd leave her to the life she'd planned before fate crossed their paths.

Only...she responded. Pressed her lithe body against his, *damn her*, and opened to the fierce plundering of his tongue. Fire licked through his veins. He might never have let go had the door not opened and slammed into his injured shoulder. Sucking in a pained breath, he set her away from him.

"Whoa—sorry," Ben said, poking his head around the door.

One look at Halli's darkened eyes and glistening lips and Trent knew he had to get out of there before he said something to screw up her neat little wrap job on the past week.

Ben started to back from the room with his IV stand, but Trent gritted his teeth and grabbed hold of the door. "We're done here."

Halli turned away without protest. Ben hesitated, but Trent simply slid his back along the door and into the hall to make his escape.

"Take care, sweetheart."

Chapter 27

Halli no longer wondered. She knew the answer to the question she'd pondered two weeks ago on a sunny sidewalk outside the hospital in Menaggio, Italy.

A person didn't look any different after they'd fallen in love.

Trent hadn't seen her anguish when she lied that none of what they'd shared was real. Ben and Rachel bought her excuse that she was still working through the trauma of the trip. And not a single person at work had commented on how miserable she'd been since her return.

Then again, maybe she deserved her own Oscar.

Since the moment they'd arrived at the hospital until now, she'd been acting. Hours and hours of acting, every single day. Concentrated cheer succeeded in fooling everyone, and subtle makeup hid the evidence of sleepless nights, but she knew the truth as she tossed and turned in the dark.

Denying Trent and attempting to bury her feelings hadn't protected her from further heartache; it'd jump-started the pain.

"Well, if it isn't Halliwell."

Halli cringed, pasted on a smile, and turned from the lobby entrance as her fingers clenched on the strap of her purse. "Hi, Jennae."

Still bitter over a promotion lost to Halli six months ago, the station director's tall, blonde, model-beautiful assistant paused to give her a venomous smirk. "Waiting for a date?"

Usually she didn't let the woman's snide comments hit their mark, but thoughts of Trent left her vulnerable. It took extra effort to lift her chin, keep her smile in place, and tell the truth. "My car's in the shop so my brother's picking me up for dinner."

"Aw, how pathetically sweet." Jennae flipped her stick-straight hair over her shoulder and sashayed away on three inch sandals with a satisfied grin curving her ever-glossed lips.

"How was your little trip to Italy?"

Halli answered with her standard, "Uneventful."

"Just like you planned." The blonde's patronizing chuckle bounced across the carpet before she backed into a conference room.

"Yep," Halli whispered. She shoved the lobby door open to wait outside in the late afternoon heat of August. "Just like I planned."

Definitely an Oscar.

Since she'd returned, not a single one of her co-workers had recognized her in the grainy photos circulating in the tabloids. It never would've crossed their minds that she—boring Wisconsin Halli—could have a sexy, romantic adventure with a movie star like Trent Tomlin.

Some days, even she found it hard to believe. Only in her dreams, held in his arms, did it all seem possible.

You couldn't have paid her to tell anyone *she* was the woman half-hidden behind Trent's shoulder. Jennae would've had a field day with that information. She loved any opportunity to grind on Halli's self-esteem and wouldn't have hesitated to gloat over Trent's absence now.

It was bad enough she tortured herself, staring at pictures and watching Trent's movies while she kicked herself for not trusting the emotion she'd glimpsed in his eyes and accepting his dinner invitation. If she'd taken whatever time he'd offered, she'd have a few more days worth of memories to cling to during her endless nights.

And she might have, if his reply to the question *"Is there something going on I should know about?"* hadn't been such an emphatic, *"No."*

Those last moments together plagued her memory along with everything else. How fleeting the warmth in his eyes that she cautioned herself against reading too much into. How quickly he'd accepted her assertion that the two of them were never meant to be. How swiftly he'd left without looking back.

No fight. Just that last, unexpected, blistering kiss and, *"Take care, sweetheart."*

She checked for Ben's red truck in the mostly empty

parking lot before setting her purse down and dropping onto a nearby bench in defeat. It was stupid to go on like this forever, yet impossible to get Trent out of her mind. No matter what she did, she was left with only one solution.

A solution that made her bury her head in her hands to take a shaky, fortifying breath. After reluctantly toying with the idea for a couple days, now it solidified in her mind and heart.

She had to go see him.

He'd probably flash that charming smile and try to figure out a kind way to tell her she'd been nothing more than stress relief, a passable distraction, and a pain in the ass. Or, he might just flat out tell her to get lost. She drew in another unsteady breath. If he did, she'd salvage the trip by thanking him for paying their medical bills in Italy, hold her chin high, and leave with her dignity intact. *Then* she'd cry in private and try to figure out a way to move on with her life.

But it would be worth the risk. It had to be. Because what she was doing now was not living. Her experiences in Italy proved that truth without question. If there was the slightest chance of being held in his arms again…one more kiss…one more night…

No. She had to be realistic. Wishful thinking would only make it that much harder if he laughed in her face.

The muted rumble of an engine filtered through her conscious. Good. Ben and Rachel's support was just what she needed right now.

She reached for her purse, lifted her head and immediately lost the ability to breathe.

It wasn't the blue Mustang convertible that stole all her oxygen and threw her heart against her ribs; it was the baseball cap wearing, sunglasses cool, scruff-jawed man in the driver's seat.

Trent pulled himself up with a hand on the edge of the windshield and the other braced on the passenger seat headrest. He swung his jeans-clad legs up and over the passenger door and landed on the sidewalk only a few feet away from her bench.

"Hi."

My God, even with just one word, he sounded as good as he looked. Halli rose on wobbly knees, clutching her purse in front of her. Her own *"hi"* stuck in her throat when the sunglasses were tossed back in the driver's seat and she met his gold-flecked, green-hued eyes. Conversely, her "What are you doing here?" came out just fine.

"Showing my confidence who's boss, dammit."

"What?"

"Nothing."

Halli heard the lobby door whoosh behind her and Trent's gaze shifted. He smiled then, looking uncharacteristically nervous, and still better than she'd ever seen him. A second later, Jennae stepped up beside her.

The downward sweep of her gaze and slow upward lift of her lips was pure invitation. "You're not Halliwell's brother."

"Not even close," Trent agreed. His gaze locked on Halli's, one corner of his mouth quirking in that half grin she loved so much. "How about a quick spin around the lake?"

"Ooh, I'd love a ride," Jennae purred.

Possessive jealousy devoured Halli's usual control. Didn't help that Jennae was just the type who usually draped Trent's arm. And he'd smiled at her. Halli turned and lifted her chin, somehow managing to look down her nose at the six inch taller woman.

"*You* are not invited."

Surprise lit Jennae's eyes. A second later she laughed. "Cute claws, Halliwell, but I don't see how it's your call."

"It will always be her call," Trent stated.

Jennae's prowling bravado faltered as her gaze shifted between them. "You two actually know each other?"

"Intimately," Trent replied.

Heat exploded in Halli's cheeks, but she didn't say a word. What the heck was he doing? Jennae's gaze narrowed on Halli a second before her jaw went slack.

"You?" she asked with disdainful disbelief. "*You're* the mystery woman in Italy?"

Realizing Halli hadn't told anyone about them, Trent enjoyed putting the over-confident, insulting blond in her place with a dismissive glance. "If you'll excuse us, this is a private conversation."

He took Halli's arm and gently pulled her with him. At the convertible, he reached past her for the passenger side door. Silky brown hair tickled his lips when he leaned in and whispered in her ear, "I'm not usually a fan of jealousy, but damn, that was hot."

She spun around, knocking his arm away before he could grasp the handle. "She annoys me, that's all."

Trent studied Halli's unreadable expression. For the hundredth time, he beat back his nerves. He'd been an idiot in Italy. Her fears had fed his and convinced him to walk away. But not this time. This time he played for keeps.

He braced his left hand against the side of the car. She backed up, but had nowhere to go as he leaned in and braced his right hand on the other side, trapping her.

"If I hadn't stepped in, Barbie would've lost her eyes to your cute claws."

She stared at his chest and he dipped his chin to try catch her eye and coax a smile. "Admit it. You want me all to yourself."

He got the smile and a laugh.

"I haven't missed your ego one bit."

"And the rest of me?"

When she still wouldn't look him in the eye, he closed the distance between them and removed her purse from her death grip to toss it into the car.

Then he kissed her. Soft and gentle, and full of the love he had yet to share. Her hands rose to his chest. Flattened for a moment, then fisted in his T-shirt. He drew back and waited for her lashes to lift. The longing in her blue eyes sent his heart soaring, but other emotions cast shadows that couldn't be ignored.

"What are you afraid of?" he asked.

She didn't look away this time, though he noted her throat muscles convulsed in a hard, audible swallow. "I'll never be like Jennae, or any of the other women you date."

"Dated. Past tense. And if you were, I wouldn't be here."

Another flicker of hope in her eyes. Before it could flourish, her stubborn little chin tilted and she stated, "I saw the press conference, Trent."

He frowned. *Which one?* Ten seconds into his desperate attempt to recall which event and what he'd said, she filled him in.

"On the steps in front of the hospital," she said softly. Hurt colored her voice as she added, "After everything we'd been through, you said you barely knew me and then joked about where to get a new boat."

Ah. Things were becoming so much clearer. "Obviously, you've never dealt with the press before. If I'd have admitted we had a relationship you wouldn't have had a moment's peace," he countered.

"You told your friend quite emphatically at the hospital nothing was going on between us."

"I told my *publicity manager* there was nothing going on that *he needed know about*. I hadn't talked to you yet, I wasn't going to stand there and tell *him* how I felt."

"Why not? You'd already made it clear how you felt back on the boat."

Her expression mirrored the one she'd worn when he'd inferred their night together meant nothing to him.

"I wanted those words back the instant I said them, Halli."

She didn't appear convinced. He shoved away from the car, hands fisted at his sides as frustration sank teeth into his determination. *She'd* pushed *him* away in Italy, yet now he found himself defending why he'd left.

"The look in your eyes that day…I knew I held your world square on my shoulders and it scared the hell out of me. Living up to expectations has never been my strong suit, and I couldn't stand the thought of letting you down."

"No matter how things turned out, Trent, I wouldn't have blamed you. You'd more than proved yourself."

"Not to myself."

Her hand on his arm urged him to face her again. "And now?" she asked softly.

"I'm working on it."

Their eyes met for a long moment. The air thickened with expectation. Halli knew what she wanted to say, but was still scared to believe in the fairytale staring her in the face. Trent was the one who broke the silence.

"You said what we'd shared wasn't real."

"Can it be after only four days?" she wondered. "You kissed me and then walked away with nothing more than a *take care, sweetheart.*"

"Distancing technique. Remember?" A wry laugh accompanied the swipe of one hand through his hair. "God, you nailed me with that one. Never realized I did that until you threw it in my face."

His parting words took on a whole new meaning. Her heart leapt with joy. Geez! She'd recognized it on the boat, how'd she miss it in the hospital? And all the times she'd gone over the conversation in her head?

Trent took her hands in his. "Since the moment we met, Halli, you were different than anyone I'd ever known."

"Yeah...I annoyed the hell out of you."

"And you didn't like me," he added.

"Only when I thought you'd kidnapped me."

"Still, that was new for me. To add insult to injury, I found myself more and more attracted to you, yet at every turn you gave me the cold shoulder. Women don't usually resist my natural charm, and my confidence didn't handle it very well."

"I suggest your confidence stop confusing ego for charm."

He smiled, but his expression quickly turned serious. "I came to the hospital to see if we had a future together, and you cut me off at the knees with a brush off I'd used myself a time or two. I cut my losses and got the hell out of there."

The blunt statement revealed so much. Halli drew in a shaky breath. "I hurt you."

"Yes."

One step closer and he cradled her hands in his against his chest. He looked into her eyes with such intensity she feared he saw right into her soul. Beneath her hand, his heart beat out an irregular rhythm.

"I know what's in my heart, Halli, and it's very real to me.

The million dollar question is…what's in yours?"

This should be easier. Why was she so darn nervous? "I was going to come see you."

"Why didn't you?"

His frown told her he assumed the worst. She smiled. "Because, I'd only decided about five minutes ago."

His gaze narrowed. "When I pulled up?"

"Seconds before. As usual, your timing is impeccable."

His hold tightened. "Why now?"

"What you really mean is why not two weeks ago in Italy."

"No…what I really mean is, why'd you push me away in Italy?"

"I was scared." Halli stilled. She hadn't meant to say that. She was supposed to have had time to plan this conversation. Rehearse her words so they came out just right instead of raw emotion. But now that she'd started, she took a deep breath and plunged forward. "To be completely honest, I'm still scared."

"Why?"

"Well, my parents for one. I mean, they're in *prison*."

"I couldn't care less about them. *You* are not your parents."

His instant and complete dismissal of that issue left her scrambling.

"Then there's the fact that things like this only happen in the movies."

"And sometimes it happens in real life." His fingers squeezed hers. "Believe me, this is *much* better."

She tried to smile, but the fear choked her next words to a whisper. "But I'm still just me. Wisconsin Halli. Boring Halli. What happens when you get bored?"

"I told you, you could never bore me."

"But our entire time together—"

He reached up to cup her face in his hands. "I didn't fall in love with *'Italy Halli'*. I fell in love with *you*. Strong, beautiful, pain-in-the-ass *you*, with your determination to find your family, your sheer guts for sticking with me through all the craziness, your courage and—"

Halli reached to lay her fingers against his lips. Happy tears welled as she finally released the last of her doubt. It floated into the air and evaporated in the warm rays of the late afternoon sun.

"Say that again."

Trent detained her retreating hand, turned it to press his mouth to her palm. The emotion in his eyes held her equally captive.

"I love you, Halli. Whether you believe it or not, it's true. And if I have to spend the rest of my life proving it to you, I'd like to start today."

She smiled so wide her cheeks hurt. "How about right now?"

Wordlessly, he slid one hand through her hair, tilting her head for his kiss. It was different than any other they'd shared, yet it brought her home in a way she'd never imagined possible. She wound her arms around his neck and kissed him back with all the passion in her heart. Then she leaned her forehead against his.

"I love you, too, Trent."

He blew out a relieved breath and crushed her in his arms at the same time. Her feet left the ground as he spun them in a circle.

"It's about time. I was beginning to think you were just after my body."

She rolled her eyes through a burst of laughter, hugging him tight. He came to a stop, letting her slide down along his body until her toes touched the sidewalk again. Desire sparked along every inch they touched. One glance up and their eyes locked. The fire in his gaze turned the spark into an all out sizzle. His gaze shifted, then returned.

"We seem to have developed an audience," he murmured. "Either you get into my car, or I'm going to have to kidnap you again. But this time, I'm not letting you go."

A one-eighty turned him into a shield between her and a handful of gawking co-workers. She ran her hands down his chest to slide her fingers along the inside waistband of his jeans. His stomach muscles quivered against her knuckles as she raised her eyebrows.

"Is there room for me and your…ego?"

With a low growl, he scooped her up into his arms. "I'll make room. Always and forever."

That promise made, he deposited her in the passenger seat of the convertible. Grinning, Halli watched him hood-slide across the passenger's front corner before he rounded the car and vaulted behind the wheel. The man had flair, that's for damn sure.

The engine roared to life as she handed him the sunglasses she'd dug out from under her butt. "Where are we going?"

"We were supposed to meet Rachel and Ben for dinner, but after that last move, I guarantee you, we're going to be late." He cast her a quick glance, fired by a sexy, wicked gleam. "You okay with *that* change in plans?"

Delicious heat rose in her cheeks and spread through her body. "Are we talking about sex?"

"After the dreams I've endured the past two weeks, damn straight we're talking about sex."

"Mmm." She leaned her head against the seat, smiling as the warmth of his hand enveloped hers. "In that case, I'm *more* than okay with the change in plans."

With the wind whipping through her hair, she enjoyed her ride around Lake Como, Wisconsin with Trent Tomlin, her very own international movie star.

✦The End✦

Lost In Italy

ABOUT THE AUTHOR

I fell in love with books at a young age, so for me the graduation to writing them was natural. An avid reader and fan of movies with a happily ever after, I live in my native Wisconsin with my husband and three children, a couple horses and some barn cats. In my limited free time, I enjoy gardening, canning, and visiting my parents in Northeastern Wisconsin (Up North) at the family cabin on the lake.

~~~

Find me online:

Website and Blog: http://www.StaceyJoyNetzel.com
Facebook: Facebook.com/StaceyJoyNetzel
Twitter: http://twitter.com/StaceyJoyNetzel

Hearing from readers is a very special thing for any writer, so feel free to contact me at any of the above locations. Or subscribe to my newsletter at my blog to keep up with my newest releases. Reviews are always appreciated!

Thank you, and happy reading!
Stacey

Stacey Joy Netzel

TITLES BY STACEY JOY NETZEL

ITALY INTRIGUE SERIES
    Lost In Italy, 2012 Write Touch Readers' Award Winner
    Run to Rome

COLORADO TRUST SERIES
    Trust in the Lawe
    Shattered Trust
    Shadowed Trust

WELCOME TO REDEMPTION
    A Fair to Remember, Book 2
    Grounds For Change, Book 4
    The Heart of the Matter, Book 6
    Hold On To Me, Book 8
    (books 1,3,5,7 written by **Donna Marie Rogers**)

ROMANCING WISCONSIN SERIES
    Mistletoe Mischief*
    Mistletoe Magic*
    Mistletoe Match-up*
 *originally published as MISTLETOE RULES Christmas Anthology (2010 Write Touch Readers' Award Winner)

STAND ALONE ROMANCE TITLES
    More Than a Kiss, contemporary romance
    Chasin' Mason, contemporary western romance
    Ditched Again, high school reunion novella
    Dragonfly Dreams, Christmas novella

PARANORMAL ROMANCE TITLES
    If Tombstones Could Talk, paranormal novella
    Beneath Still Waters, Part One, paranormal novella
    Rising Above, Still Waters Part Two, paranormal novella

FREE READS
    Holding Out For a Hero
    Never Say Never

Stacey Joy Netzel

RUN TO ROME
Italy Intrigue Series - 2

Love him and leave him.

Nine months ago, undercover detective, Ispettore Evalina Gallo, protected her heart the only way she knew how, never expecting to see her savior-turned-one-night-stand again. When he returns to *Italia*—now a person of interest in an investigation of a local organized crime family—her personal connection to the rugged American gets her assigned to the case.

A second chance to make things right.

With his mother's pleas ringing in his ears, Ben Sanders plans to retrieve a stolen bible his father shipped to Italy thirteen years ago, and then get out as fast as he can. But with the arrival of the beautiful detective, he suspects his mother's desire to right past wrongs might not be the whole truth.

Destiny will not be denied.

Now, less than twenty-four hours after entering the country, he's getting shot at—again. In a race from Milan to Rome to find the precious book before anyone else, time is ticking for the one-time lovers. Attraction burns hotter than molten lava, but amid secrets and half-truths, they must learn to trust each other if they have any hope of a future together.

Chapter 1

Present Day

He sucked her lower lip between his teeth for a soft nibble before giving up all pretense of gentleness. Her back made solid contact with the door of his hotel room as it slammed shut. An expected jolt of pain to her head was tempered by the cushion of his large hand as he cradled the back of her head. His mouth opened on hers, his head angling as he pushed his tongue inside with no pause for permission.

A moan of approval vibrated in her throat, and she surrendered to the aggressive possession. It'd been like this from the moment they first touched at the villa. At the beginning, she assumed danger had heightened the combustible sexual energy that pulsed between them. Now she knew it was so much more than that.

Her former Italian lover had nothing on this hot blooded American, and she was helpless to resist. She didn't want to resist. Because even with his left arm confined in a sling, his free hand slid down to caress her body in ways she shouldn't allow without making him pay for dinner first. At the very least.

But whenever he was near, she came alive. The high of getting justice for her murdered father had faded much too fast, and this man counteracted her growing sense of unease. He made her feel again, filled the gnawing hollow chasm expanding within her chest.

His palm flattened on her ribcage and eased upward. Her body was on fire, every cell tingling with elemental awareness. Panting for oxygen, she arched her back, bringing their hips closer while allowing him access up top. He gave a low growl, his palm brushing over the front of her midnight blue, silk dress, and her nipples tightened beneath her black lace bra.

She lifted her leg to rub along the outside of his thigh. The rough denim of his jeans created a sensual abrasion against her sensitive skin. He trailed wet kisses down her neck, his labored breath sending shivers along her spine with each steamy puff.

The shivers raced back up when he grasped her knee to pull her body tighter against his leg.

The exquisite pressure at the juncture of her thighs made her gasp. He chuckled and drew her mouth back to his for another mind-numbing kiss. Keeping her leg high, his hand slid beneath the flared skirt of her dress and skimmed along the underside of her thigh. When he reached the edge of her sheer black stockings and fingered the tiny metal clasps of her garter, his fingers tightened on bare skin above the lace.

"For me?"

"*Sì.*"

"Aw, hell," he groaned. "We're never gonna make it to dinner."

The rough rasp of his voice told her he was equally affected. So did his body. *Va benisimo*. Again, she whispered, "*Sì.*"

She'd dressed with the intent to seduce him beyond control, needing the mind-numbing peace of physical release. The stockings and garters made her feel feminine in a way she'd never dared indulge before him, ensuring she'd get exactly what she wanted tonight.

His hand moved higher, blunt, calloused fingers digging into her flesh as his mouth possessed hers once more. Without warning, he bent at the knees and lifted her, spreading her legs to straddle his hips, supporting her weight with one strong arm. She grabbed for his shoulders to keep her balance.

As if the bulk of the bandages beneath his shirt weren't reminder enough, his breath hissed through his teeth as pain tightened his features.

She quickly shifted her hold to the back of his neck. "Put me down."

"I'm okay."

"You'll hurt yourself more. The doctors will—"

"*Shhh.*" He pressed his lips to the hollow at the base of her neck. His tongue pressed against her wild pulse as he strode across the room with sure strides.

On the way to the bed, his mouth descended to the curve of her breast exposed by her plunging neckline. Anchoring her fingers in his dark blond hair, she pressed closer, lifting herself ever so slightly. He murmured approval, nuzzling aside the silky material of her dress to lave his tongue across her skin.

Her stomach clenched in anticipation of his hot mouth closing over—

"*Gallo!*"

Evalina startled in her chair, the sound of her last name bellowed across the police station jerking her back to reality. Her gaze flew from her spiraling screensaver to the grim expression on her Commissario's face. Mortified to find herself slightly short of breath and tingling in places that should *not* tingle at work, she quickly crossed her arms over her chest and sat up straight.

"Yes, sir?"

"My office. Now."

"Yes, sir."

Evalina did her best to banish the lingering memory of the one man who'd ever truly gotten under her skin. She'd relived that night too many times in the past nine months, damn it. Mind-numbing peace. What a joke. It hadn't worked when she caught her father's killer, and it certainly hadn't worked when she'd slept with the American.

The past was in the past. Allowing it to surface only served to remind her of what she'd never have again. Not that she wanted it, mind you. Involvement, no matter how brief and shallow, only led to heartache.

Shoving to her feet, she checked her navy polo and smoothed her palms over the front of her tan khakis. A few of her fellow officers at the Milan interagency office followed her progress across the room, but knowing their rapt attention had nothing to do with worry, she kept her gaze fixed straight ahead.

She didn't want their concern anyway. No distraction was the key. No family. No friends. Not even a partner these days. Work filled her days—and many of her nights so she could avoid the night version of her earlier daydream. But beyond the job, her life was completely empty.

Conflicting emotions rose up, as they always did with even the briefest thought of the sister who wanted nothing to do with her. They hadn't spoken in almost five years.

Then there was her deceased partner Nino Da Via. Losing a partner in the line of duty was never easy, but him being a dirty cop made it worse. She knew that made no sense. His intent to kill her should've made his death easier to come to terms with, but lately she couldn't shake the feeling of being completely adrift. Lost.

Evalina mentally stuffed Carina and Nino in the Unwelcome file next to her earlier unsettling memory, and stepped into her superior's office.

"If you're looking for the Perini report, I'll have it on your desk before—"

"Close the door," he interrupted without looking up.

Her stomach gave an uneasy flip as she shut the door with a quiet click. Seeing as a closed door had never only taken a moment, she took a seat opposite Commissario Marino and studied his face while he continued to write.

Craggy was the word that came to mind. He'd acquired more lines around the eyes, and the grooves bracketing his tightly pressed, downturned mouth had deepened considerably. With a mental start of surprise, she wondered when he'd started to grey at the temples. For someone whose very life depended on her noticing the slightest detail, how had she missed that?

Dio mio. Evalina fingered the crease she'd ironed into her khaki pants at three a.m. More sleep-depriving thoughts to prey on her mind. The next two weeks were going to be hell.

Commissario Marino set his pen down and lifted his blue gaze. "The Perini report can wait."

"I'd rather finish it before I have to leave."

"Do you have any specific plans for your time off?"

"Just some alone time with me, myself and I."

His jaw tightened. Evalina gave a mental shrug. Her 'time off' was as appealing as a hole in the head, so why bother pretending enthusiasm? Hour upon hour to think about what the hell she was doing with her life made her itchier than a dog with fleas.

And they'd given her no choice in the matter. After she'd screwed up on her last two undercover assignments, she'd been put on probation, then forced to take two weeks of her vacation. It felt more like a suspension, but Marino assured her she would have a job upon her return. Either way, happy Monday.

Staring at her superior, she wondered if she was in danger of burning out, or had she missed her mentor's physical changes because she hadn't been around the office?

That's it, she rationalized with relief. *I haven't been around enough to notice.*

In the silence, Marino heaved a sigh. "As of right now, your vacation is cancelled."

Evalina sat up a little straighter. "It is?"

Her eagerness earned her a sharp glance as her superior extracted a file from atop a tall stack on the right hand side of his desk. "I received a call from Magistrate Baroni about an hour ago. The DAC has requested your help on a case."

The *Direzione Centrale Anticrimine* specifically requested her? *Why?*

She managed to keep the questions to herself, unwilling to jeopardize the opportunity to evade two whole weeks alone with her thoughts.

"At sixteen-o-five p.m. this afternoon, an international courier will land at the Malpensa airport from New York's JFK airport," Commissario Marino continued. "Based on information we've gathered, he'll be meeting with Dante Fedorio of the Fedorio group in Novara."

"I know the name. Why is this a concern?"

"The Fedorio group has been under investigation over the past year for a number of activities—money laundering, transportation of stolen goods, procuring and selling illegal weapons."

The city of Novara was centrally located, a perfect place to set up shop along the commercial traffic routes stretching from Milan to Turin, and from Genoa to Switzerland.

"Mafia?" That would explain the DAC's involvement. Their jurisdiction covered all major and organized crime investigations.

"They have had dealings with the northern families in the past, but essentially run their own organization. We need you to get close to this courier and confirm the true nature of his business before he leaves the country. He's scheduled to depart the following morning, so time is of the essence."

Less than twenty-four hours inside their borders. Considering whom he was meeting with, it was a definite red flag.

Evalina had a quick flash of the morning's newscast. "What about the volcano erupting in Iceland?" she asked. "Any word on when air travel may be affected?"

The Commissario shook his head, lips pressed tight. "Flights won't be cancelled until absolutely necessary. We cannot depend on Mother Nature to do our job."

Her superior's rebuke put her on the defensive. "What's so special about *this* courier?"

"He is the son of a federal prisoner in the United States. Interpol believes—"

"Interpol is involved?" Evalina asked in surprise.

"Yes." Tossing her a brief frown for the interruption, Marino continued, "They believe this courier is reactivating connections within our country in preparation for his father's upcoming release from prison. It's an interagency investigation, and we've been tasked with confirming this man's intentions."

She conveyed her understanding with a brisk nod. Now that she was armed with some details of the assignment, her earlier curiosity refused to be contained. "Why me, sir? Considering how adamant you were about my time off, surely there were other female agents who could do the job?"

"You won't be alone on this assignment." His gaze shifted behind her as he lifted a hand to motion someone into the office.

Evalina swiveled in her seat and received a nasty jolt that would've knocked her from the chair if she wasn't adept at concealing her emotions. The last time she'd seen Europol agent Antonio Butelli was nine months earlier when they closed the case against her father's killer. Butelli looked completely different from his former undercover persona, but even so, the sight of his features shattered the lock on memories she ruthlessly suppressed except when caught unaware by a rogue daydream.

Summoning her undercover face, she met his cool blue gaze. "Antonio."

He inclined his head. "Evalina. Good to see you."

She didn't return the sentiment and noted he'd also reverted to their formal names instead of how they'd known each other while undercover. She preferred the formality. Her mind whirled, wondering why Europol had sent him. Last they'd interacted, he worked internal affairs. In addition to the probation, was she now under investigation, too?

"You and Ispettore Butelli have been handpicked because of your personal history with the courier."

Suspicion and memory collided. Antonio's face remained impassive, but for a millisecond, a flicker of sympathy darkened his eyes. Her stomach dropped as she faced her Commissario's rigid features.

American courier.

Antonio.

Personal history.

Commissario Marino withdrew a photograph from the file in front of him and slid it across the desk. "Not only does it appear the father may be attempting to reestablish the lines of communication with his former associates, but the mother went off-grid less than twenty-four hours after her own release from prison a few days ago."

Evalina didn't need to see the passport photo in front of her to confirm the identity of her target. Suddenly, even a suspension sounded pretty damn good.

Don't miss the rest of the story!

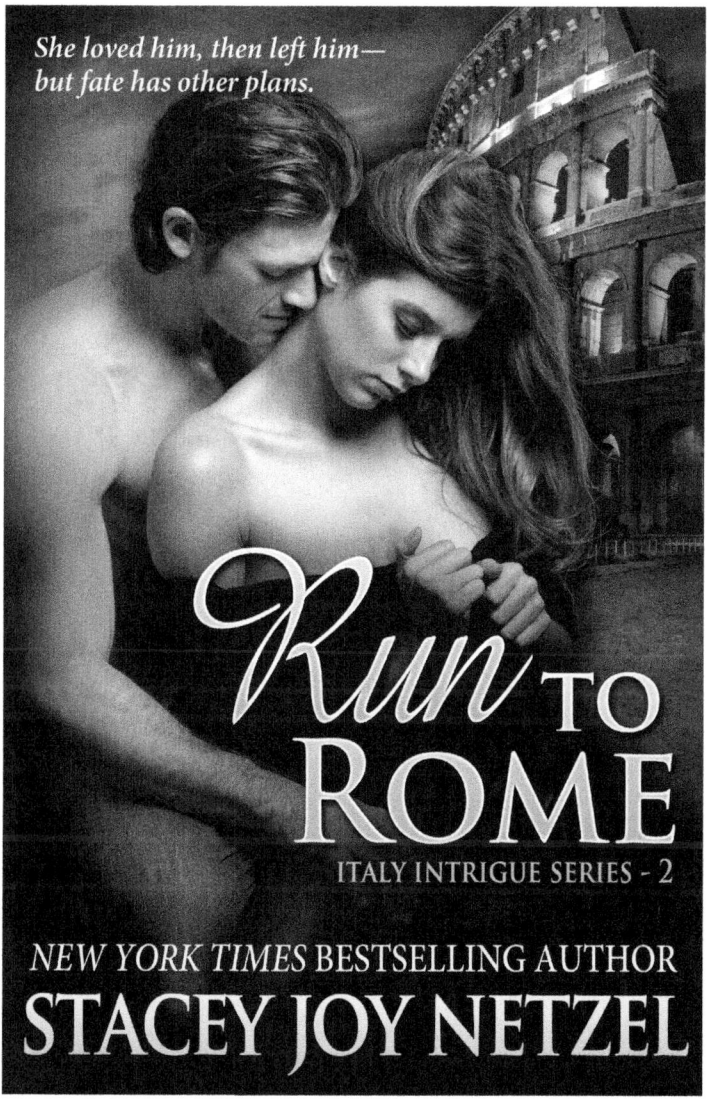

Printed in Great Britain
by Amazon